Other Crooked Lake mysteries by Robert W. Gregg

In the Chill of the Night

A Crooked Lake Mystery

Robert W. Gregg

INFINITY
PUBLISHING

ISBN 978-0-7414-7450-6 Paperback
ISBN 978-0-7414-7451-3 eBook
Library of Congress Control Number: 2012937056

Printed in the United States of America

Published November 2012

INFINITY PUBLISHING

Toll-free (877) BUY BOOK
Local Phone (610) 941-9999
Fax (610) 941-9959
Info@buybooksontheweb.com
www.buybooksontheweb.com

As with my earlier Crooked Lake mysteries, I wish to express my sincere thanks for the contributions of my editor, Lois Gregg; my advisor on forensic pathology issues, Dr. Melissa Brassell; and my advisor on cover art, Brett Steeves.

Once again, I would like to dedicate this book to my inspirational muse, my wife Barbara.

PROLOGUE

The clock on the far wall said it was 9:59. Ginny Smith, the bartender on duty at *The Cedar Post* that evening, knew that the clock was wrong. It had been wrong since daylight savings time had gone into effect, and that was almost two weeks ago. A number of her customers had commented on it, but only rarely did they suggest that it be reset to the right time. Instead, the fact that the clock was an hour behind usually prompted a remark to the effect that the night was still young, that there was still time for another round. In fact, that was what Bill Grandy said to Ginny when she told him it was time to pay up.

"Think I'll have one more for the road. How about you, Gus?"

Ginny didn't give Gus an opportunity to say yes or no.

"You're one of the clever ones, aren't you?" she said to Grandy. She said it with a smile, letting him know that she was onto their game. Nobody ever took offense when Ginny Smith reminded them that it was closing time or that they had probably already had enough or perhaps one too many. Skilled at her job, good natured, and possessed of an excellent memory for names and what everyone's 'usual' was, she was without question the area's favorite bartender and a major reason *The Cedar Post* was such a popular establishment. It didn't hurt that she was also a very attractive woman who was in the habit of dressing in ways that showed off her figure to best advantage.

"But I've got another whole hour," Grandy complained, even if his heart wasn't in it.

"I'm sure you do, and it'll give you plenty of time to get yourself home. Here's your tab."

Bill Grandy fished in his pocket for his wallet and produced a couple of bills.

"You can keep the change," he said with a smile. "But I think you ought to do something about that clock."

Ginny returned the smile and moved down the bar to settle accounts with another late customer.

1

The bar was nearly empty, as it should have been at eleven o'clock on a week night. Ginny counted five men (no women). It had been a relatively quiet evening. With one exception, all of the orders had been for beer or vodka and a mixer. Ginny felt no need to take inventory of her tips. They would be modest, even if several of the men had tossed an extra bill on the counter along with a word of thanks for her service. She was sure that the upcoming weekend would bring bigger crowds, bigger tips. At the moment, she was grateful that cleaning up would not be that difficult.

"Drive carefully." It was what she said every night as she saw her 'night hawks' out to the parking lot. There were only two of them, Bill and Gus Hawkins, left in *The Cedar Post* when a man in a navy blue parka pushed past them into the bar.

Ginny intercepted him.

"Hi, Eddie. I'm sorry, we're closed."

She had no trouble recognizing the man who had come into the bar while she was getting ready to close up for the night. He was Eddie French, someone she saw frequently, less because he did a lot of drinking than because he drove a truck that regularly supplied *The Cedar Post* kitchen with bread and rolls. She didn't remember him ever making a late evening delivery. Perhaps he had come by for a nightcap. If so, he was too late. By about five minutes.

Ginny was debating whether she should make an exception and let him have one after hours drink. But the last of her regulars were still putting on their jackets, so she decided it would be a bad idea.

"Like I said, Eddie, we're through for the night." She looked at the clock, then consulted her wrist watch. "We close at eleven. You know that."

"I don't want a drink," he said. He looked around the room, taking in the two laggards who had stopped to see how Ginny would handle the situation. Then he took a seat at the far end of the bar nearest the door to the kitchen.

"Wait a minute," he said. "I've changed my mind. Let me have some of that stuff in the green bottle."

He pointed at a seldom used bottle of creme de menthe.

"We can't do this, Eddie. I don't set the hours, but we have to close at eleven. Maybe tomorrow. Okay?"

Eddie French started to get up, then sat back down. Slowly. As he resumed his seat, he reached into his coat pocket and produced a gun.

"I want you to open up that cash register, Ginny. And I want you to give me the money that's in there. Just do it, fast like, and then I'll leave."

Ginny had already gone behind the bar and started to wash up the few remaining glasses. She had never expected the delivery man to pull a gun or demand that she hand over the cash in her till.

"Eddie, what do you think you're doing?" she said. She was shocked, but unsure whether to be afraid or angry. "Please, put that gun away. You don't want to do this."

The two men next to the door to the parking lot stopped in their tracks. For a moment everyone froze. The wall clock could actually be heard ticking. It read 10:07.

"I need that money. Please give it to me."

Ginny Smith made a quick decision. It wasn't until later that she thought it through, weighing the alternatives she hadn't considered when she was confronted by Eddie's gun.

"Let me have the gun, Eddie. You'll only regret this. We've known each other for a long time, and this isn't you. So come on, give me the gun."

"But I've got to have the money. I'm in a terrible bind - you know that. It's the kids." The gun remained pointed at the bartender.

"I do know, and I'm really sorry. But this isn't the way to take care of your problem. Besides, your kids are with their mother and I'm sure they're perfectly safe. Come on. Give me the gun."

"I'm way too far behind in my child support," he said, his voice reflecting his distress. "And they're going to evict me from the house. What am I supposed to do?"

"You're supposed to give me the gun." Ginny moved slowly toward him, reaching out across the bar. "Then we can talk about it."

The men by the door, apparently emboldened by Ginny's quiet confidence, hadn't moved.

"I think it's time to go," Ginny said to Grandy and Hawkins. "I need to talk with this gentleman."

They got the message and left, closing the door quietly behind them.

"Now, let's talk. But first, I want the gun."

French laid his gun on the bar and put his head down. He was crying.

Ginny picked up her tip jar and came around to where Eddie was sitting and took a seat on the adjacent bar stool.

"You've been having a hard time. I don't know all the details, but I know it's been bad. I'm sure you'd never have come in like you did tonight if you weren't feeling desperate. I suppose we've all been there one time or another. Do you want to talk about it?"

He raised his head and wiped his nose on the sleeve of his jacket. His eyes were red.

"It was such a stupid thing I did," he said. "But what's the use of talking? I'd rather just go."

Ginny tried to coax him to share his worries with her, but it quickly became apparent that it wasn't going to work.

"This won't be much," she said, "but maybe it'll help a little."

She emptied the tip jar onto the bar and pushed the money over to Eddie.

"I have no idea how much there is, but you can have it." If it was a representative amount for a slow night, forty, maybe fifty dollars.

Eddie stared at it for a moment, gave Ginny a wan smile, and scooped it up and stuffed it into his jacket pocket.

"Are you going to tell?" he asked as he got up from his stool.

"I don't plan to say anything, but those other guys saw what you did. There's a good chance somebody from the sheriff's office will be paying you a visit. I promise to put in a good word for you."

Eddie paused at the door and appeared to offer Ginny a silent 'thank you.'

"Drive carefully," she said.

CHAPTER 1

According to the calendar, spring had arrived almost a week earlier. The weather told another story. The thermometer on the window of the Lakeshore Marina's office said that the temperature on this late March morning was a chilly 37 degrees. Lou Gribbons, the weatherman on the local radio station, had predicted that the day's high might reach the lower 40s, although he doubted it. It was 8:45, and the marina was not officially open. But the manager, Patrick Kelley, had already arrived and turned up the thermostat in the small office. He was sitting at his desk, still in his winter coat, warming himself with the coffee he had picked up at the West Branch diner on his way in to work.

It would be a few more weeks before most of his regular customers started to call about their boats, now parked on trailers in the marina lot, still buttoned up for the winter. While a few of the owners would take care of their boats themselves, most would expect the marina to de-winterize them. It would be a busy season, but the process of readying boats for another Crooked Lake summer was one of Lakeshore's most profitable services.

Kelley had planned to spend the morning checking inventory, making a list of what needed to be ordered if Lakeshore was to be ready for the influx of summer residents. He had a pretty good idea of what he had in stock, but he knew he shouldn't rely on memory. When owners of the boats now parked at the marina arrived back at the lake, they would expect to be putting their Nautiques, their Stingrays, or whatever they used for their summer pleasure into the water right away. Kelley remembered all too well his efforts to placate several customers the previous year, customers who were irritated because Lakeshore didn't have their boats in shape when they got back to the lake. Two of those customers had chosen to take their business elsewhere.

Before turning to his file cabinet and what promised to be a sedentary morning, Kelley decided to stretch his legs. He zipped up his coat and set off for a walk down the marina yard toward a large aluminum shed where his men would soon start working on some of the boats. He had never consciously made it a point to memorize just whose boat was parked where, but in spite of the tarps, which tended to make most of the boats look superficially alike, he found himself checking off owners' names as he walked. That's Collins' Glastron, he said under his breath, and Jernigan's Nautique. And then another Nautique he identified as belonging to Sam Farrington. As he passed a somewhat older Four Winns that belonged to Earl Skinner, he noticed that the tarp was unfastened on one side of the boat. The boat was still covered, but he counted four snaps that were loose.

Lakeshore Marina prided itself on its attention to detail, and Kelley couldn't imagine why the canvas cover on the Skinner boat wasn't securely in place. Had somebody been careless? Obviously, but why would anyone have had a reason to unfasten the tarp? He'd have to talk to his men about it.

He gave the tarp a tug, trying to pull it taut to facilitate fastening the snaps back in place. But it refused to give. Obviously something had to be in the way. More irritated than curious, Kelley raised the tarp to see what the trouble was.

The trouble was a man, curled up on the cushioned bench in the back of the boat.

"Hey, what do you think you're doing here?" He asked the question in a loud and angry voice. "Come on, out. We don't allow this sort of thing at Lakeshore."

Kelley had no idea who the man was, but he knew it wasn't Skinner. He gave the man a vigorous shake. It didn't help to bring him around.

"Damn it," he said to himself. He didn't need this kind of problem. He grabbed the man's thick jacket and tugged hard. There was no response, but an arm flopped off the bench and the man rolled half way over. He wasn't asleep. He was dead.

The one eye Kelley could see was open, staring at him but seeing nothing. A small trickle of dried blood ran down from the corner of his mouth to his chin. The face was cold, colder even than it normally would have been on a chilly March morning.

Patrick Kelley was a no nonsense, sensible person, someone who could be depended on to rise to the occasion. The first thing he did was reflexively to cross himself. Then he looked quickly around the yard, not because he expected to see anyone but because he had to be sure that no one had seen him fussing with the tarp on Skinner's boat. He pulled the tarp down so as to conceal the body. He debated fastening the snaps, but chose to leave them as he had found them. Clemens and MacIntosh would be along momentarily, but they wouldn't be checking on the boats before he had time to get in touch with the sheriff's office. It was important to keep what had happened under wraps until it was in the hands of his good friend Carol Kelleher.

Two minutes later she was on the line.

"Good morning, Patrick," she greeted him in a cheerful voice. "My assistant says you needed to talk with me and that it couldn't wait."

"No, I'm afraid it can't. I've got a real puzzler down here at the marina. I just happened to spot a boat whose tarp wasn't buttoned down, but when I tried to fix it I found a man in the boat. No idea who he is. Should say who he was, because he's dead. That was just about five minutes ago, and the first thing I did was to put this call through."

Carol's cheerful voice gave way to one that was much more sober.

"Any sign of what happened? I mean, I'm sure you don't have people using your boats to sleep in. Especially not in this weather. What does he look like?"

"Like I said, I don't think I've ever seen him. Average looking guy, except he's dead. Some blood on his face. Looks like it came out of his mouth."

"I wouldn't expect you to know how he died, but did you see anything unusual?"

"The whole business is unusual, sheriff. We run a good, shipshape marina. I don't remember anything like this, and I've been here almost twenty years."

"Okay. This guy's probably just some vagrant who thought he'd be getting out of the cold. Probably died of hypothermia. But I don't like it that he was bleeding from the mouth. I'll get somebody down there right away. Just see to it that nobody goes near that boat."

It was not quite 9:20 when Sheriff Kelleher and Officer Barrett pulled up beside the Lakeshore Marina office. Kelley had ben joined by Bert MacIntosh. Bill Clemens had called to say he'd be delayed. Something about a daughter who had missed her bus and needed a ride to school.

"No way to begin the day, is it?" Carol said. "Let's go take a look at this guy, then get him out of here."

A breeze had come up from the north, and a large American flag at the end of the main marina dock was flapping vigorously. MacIntosh had been left to deal with business, and Kelley and the two officers of the law walked quickly down through the boat yard to where the Four Winns was parked.

"It's right here, just as I found it," the manager said. He was about to demonstrate what he had done - or tried to do - but stepped back when Carol waved him aside.

She cautiously raised the tarp and pushed it back so she could see the man in the boat. She wanted a better look at his face, so she gently rotated his head until both eyes were staring at her. There was a problem with the right side of the face, near the ear. More blood. Carol probed the area around the ear with her fingers and quickly found the source of the bleeding. This man had died of a gunshot wound to the side of his head.

"Jim, there's a good chance there's a gun in here. You're a lot taller than I am. See if you can't poke around, see what's under the guy, maybe down on the floor."

Patrick Kelley was looking even more worried than when the sheriff arrived.

Barrett leaned as far over the gunnel as he could and used his long arm to probe for the gun Carol seemed to think might be there. It didn't take long.

"Something here," he grunted. "Feels like one of those snubbies."

The handgun Barrett brought out from the floor of the Four Winns looked small and almost harmless. The sheriff and her colleague knew better. Carol was no firearms expert, but she was sure that this tiny weapon with a barrel no more than three inches long could easily kill a man. Obtaining the necessary information about the model and the owner's registration should not be difficult. Nor was it likely that it would be hard to establish that the bullet in the man's brain had come from this gun. Why had he chosen to commit suicide in a boat at a marina? Getting the answer to that question would be more difficult.

Carol had just started to speculate on how long the man had been dead when MacIntosh joined them.

"Sorry, boss, but there's a call for you. Not quite sure what the problem is, but he's upset about a charge."

"I'll take it. I'm not much good here anyway." Kelley turned to the sheriff. "Can you tell me when the body will be taken away? We've got to clean up Skinner's boat."

"I'll stop by the office in a few minutes," Carol said. There were routines to be followed, and she didn't know just when she'd be able to give Kelley a green light to ready the boat for its owner. As the manager left to take the call from an unhappy customer, MacIntosh peeked into the boat to see what all the commotion was about.

"My God, that's Eddie French!"

"Who'd you say?" Carol asked. She'd heard what MacIntosh had said but had to hear it again.

"That guy French, the one who ran that kid down with his power boat. Ran him down, but got off scot-free. Remember? It was last fall, not long after Labor Day."

Carol did know who Eddie French was, but she hadn't recognized him. It had been Parsons, her main man on the water patrol, who'd handled most of that case. And now she had to deal with the death, apparently a suicide, of a man who not more than four months earlier had been found not guilty of the death of a young boy. Had French chosen to take his life because he was overwhelmed by guilt about the boating accident?

It was then that Carol remembered something that had happened a week earlier. It seems that Eddie French, a troubled young man with a history of problems, had made a futile, silly attempt to stage a hold up at *The Cedar Post*. She couldn't remember who had told her this, but a conversation with Ginny Smith, the bartender on duty that night, had convinced her that the story had been inflated out of all proportion, that no crime had been committed or seriously contemplated. Perhaps she should have pursued the matter further. She would now have to see the area's favorite bartender again.

CHAPTER 2

By noon Eddie French's body had been moved to the morgue in Cumberland, Skinner's boat had been cordoned off with the ubiquitous yellow tape common to crime scenes, and the sheriff had returned to her office. She pulled Officer Parsons off patrol duty on the lake and put him to work gathering information on French. In view of his role investigating the boating accident the previous fall, Parsons seemed to be the logical choice for that assignment. Her own next order of business was going to be a visit to Ginny Smith.

It was sleepy bartender who answered her call.

"Ginny, it's Sheriff Kelleher. You sound as if maybe I woke you up."

"That's okay," was the reply. "I was on duty last night, so I didn't set the alarm. What's up?"

"What's up is that I'd like to talk with you. Okay if I come over to the house?"

"Sure, but can I have fifteen, twenty minutes to make myself presentable? You know where I live?"

Carol promised Ginny that she could have all the time she needed, made a mental note of where the house was, and set off for Southport and an early lunch en route to her appointment.

The sheriff and the bartender had already had one conversation about the hold-up at *The Cedar Post*, and it was doubtful that there was much more to be learned about what had happened that night. But Carol had started to worry that Ginny may have been wrong to treat the episode so lightly. And that she had been wrong not to have had a talk with French herself. At the time she had simply deferred to the owner of *The Cedar Post*, who at Ginny's request had declined to press charges against French. But what if the man had been truly depressed or desperate? Or what if he had subsequently felt humiliated as word of what he had done spread and became a joke? Might those feelings have led to suicide?

When they sat down in the kitchen of the old stucco house on Maple Street, Ginny Smith had gotten dressed and made coffee.

But she looked much more like the fortyish mother of high school boys than she did the sexy bartender beloved by patrons of *The Cedar Post*.

"I hope I haven't screwed up your day's schedule," Ginny said. Her smile suggested that she wasn't really worried about it. "There was a time when I had to be up early, make breakfast for the boys. Thank goodness they're now up and out without my help. How about some coffee?"

Carol was struck by the fact that Ginny hadn't asked what had prompted this visit by the sheriff. She accepted her offer of coffee, and promptly answered the unasked question.

"I'm here about Mr. French," she said. "The delivery man who pulled a gun at *The Cedar Post* recently."

"That's what I figured," Ginny said. "Just a hunch. Why, is he up to something else?"

"No, not exactly. The problem is that he's dead."

"He's dead?" Ginny was obviously more than surprised. She sounded stunned.

"I'm afraid so. It looks like he's committed suicide, and I thought it would be a good idea if we talked a bit more about that night at *The Post*."

"Well, of course, but that's terrible news. Do you know anything about it?"

"Not yet," Carol said, choosing not to say anything about where French had been found. "We just learned about it this morning."

"And you're here because I told you his life was falling to pieces, that that's why he killed himself?"

"Either that, or because he couldn't live with the thought of people having a laugh over what he'd done. When we talked about the incident, I didn't ask if you thought he might be suicidal. But how about it? Did you get the feeling that he might have been?"

"No I didn't, but I guess I didn't take what he did as seriously as I should. He just struck me as a mixed-up kid."

"I didn't know him, but he didn't look like a kid to me. I'd have said he was in his thirties, maybe even forty."

Ginny thought about it.

"I suppose you're right. But he seemed like a kid, you know, someone who has trouble growing up, taking responsibility."

"When we talked before, it was mostly about what he did, what you did, that night in the bar. How well did you know him?"

"Sort of like the people all of us see a lot but aren't our friends. I mean he came by *The Post* regularly, we talked. But nothing personal, more like customers at the bar."

"For how long? Do you know when he took the delivery job?"

"Somewhere around a year ago, I think. I had the impression he'd moved to the area not long before that. I do know that he went through an unpleasant divorce not long after he moved here. That's about the only personal thing we ever talked about."

"So he discussed his family problems?"

"A little," Ginny said. "A couple of times he came in after work and had a few drinks. Funny, he always drank creme de menthe, called it that green stuff. That's when he'd tell me that things weren't going so good at home."

"What seemed to be the trouble between Mr. French and his wife?"

"I really don't know. About all he said was that she didn't try to understand him."

"Do you happen to know if she's still living around here?"

"I think so, but I'm not sure. I'm sorry I'm not more help, sheriff."

Carol was also sorry, but it wasn't Ginny's fault.

"By the way, did Eddie take his gun away with him that night?"

"Yeah, I figured he'd gotten himself back together. I wouldn't have known what to do with the gun anyway. Did I do wrong?"

"Don't worry about it. Look, I've got to be on my way, but maybe you can answer one more question. Did Mr. French ever talk with you about that fatal boating accident last fall?" It wasn't necessary to ask if Ginny remembered the accident; it would have been a major topic of conversation all around the lake.

"I don't recall that he ever brought it up. In fact, he wasn't around much at all back then. I'm sure he felt awful and didn't want to have to hear people talking about the accident. I know I wouldn't have."

"How did you feel about the decision to dismiss the case?"

For the first time Ginny looked as if she'd rather not answer the sheriff's question.

"It was hard. That poor family, losing a son like that. I don't know what I'd have done if it had been one of mine."

Ginny hadn't really answered the sheriff's question.

CHAPTER 3

Carol's decision to give Officer Parsons the assignment of pulling together some information on Eddie French reflected the simple fact that she knew almost nothing about the man and would have to take charge of a pro forma investigation into his suicide. It should not be an onerous task, but in view of his recent divorce it could be an unpleasant one. It wasn't until late the next morning that Parsons felt he had enough hard information about French to lay it before the sheriff.

"There's not a lot, but I don't suppose you'll need much more," he said, handing Carol a thin file of information about French. It contained his birthdate and birthplace, when and where he had graduated from high school, the fact that his parents were deceased, specifics about his marriage and subsequent divorce, his former wife's and sons' address and phone number, and Parsons' own comments on the boating accident story. The names of a number of people who were alleged to have known French were appended. Most of them were from the area, but one was from near Buffalo.

Carol was soon pressing Parsons for more details.

"I'm particularly interested in these contacts. Did you speak with any of them?"

"Just four, and only briefly. But I told them all you'd be in touch, explained why. As you can see, three of the four are from around here. One of them is his boss at the bakery that supplies *The Cedar Post*. Then there's the attorney who represented him during that mess last fall and a neighbor who used to go bowling with him. I get the impression that he didn't have a lot of friends. Maybe earlier in his life, but not now."

"You said you spoke with four people? Who was the fourth?"

"He's likely to be the least important one on my list because he's what you could call ancient history. Here he is." Parsons pointed at the name of George Tiegs on the printed sheet in front of Carol. "Got his name from French's high school in some place

14

called Cheektowaga. That's a name for you, isn't it? Anyway, it's a suburb of Buffalo. I was just verifying French's graduation from there. The person I talked with at the school didn't know French personally, of course - she's much too young. But she seemed eager to help. They had copies of senior yearbooks going back forever, and she started flipping through his yearbook, looking for pictures and stuff. She came across an informal shot of two guys horsing around in the gym. French was one of them, and so was this guy Tiegs."

"So you actually spoke to four people about French." Carol looked at the paper in front of her. "Stearns from the bakery; Longacre, the attorney; Ostrowski, who seems to have been a fellow bowler; and Tiegs, who was a classmate in high school a couple of decades ago. Tell me what you learned from these guys."

"Basically nothing. Like I said, I was just clueing them in to the fact that you'd be calling. We'd agreed I wouldn't be telling anyone what happened to French, so I figured the less said the better."

Carol knew that Parsons had done all, even more, than she expected him to do. After all, she wouldn't be writing the obituary. Eddie French's suicide needed to be handled carefully, respectfully. She didn't want to encourage the local gossip mill, and had already told the men at the marina not to say anything about finding French's body on Skinner's boat. Not yet.

"The only one who seemed curious about my call was Stearns at the bakery," Parsons continued, "but he didn't have time to talk right then, so I don't know whether he knows anything about that attempted hold-up at *The Cedar Post*. The only one I talked with for more than a couple of minutes was Tiegs. Seems he's from a big family that's pretty much lived in the Buffalo area for generations. The young woman at the school knows some of the family and she located his phone number for me. When I asked if he knew Eddie French, he let out one of those big hearty laughs. 'You're talking about old Lefty?' he says. 'I'd forgotten all about that guy. What's he up to these days?' Well, I wasn't about to tell him what he was up to, but I said something about trying to track him down. I think Tiegs was disappointed, but he did tell me that Eddie - he called him Lefty - was the best pitcher the Trojans had back then, and that if I found him I should let his old buddy know where he was."

"That's it?"

"Afraid so. Like I said, Tiegs won't know anything about French after all these years. Maybe some of the people who knew him because of that boating accident will have an idea about his suicide. Perhaps a neighbor, like Ostrowski. I'd assume your best source of information will be the ex-wife."

Carol spent much of the afternoon studying Parsons' summary of what he had learned about French. It told her a lot, but it told her little that was interesting. A pedestrian life, full of small accomplishments and a few big failures, a life that had come to a premature end at the age of 39. But one thing stuck in her mind. It was what the old high school friend had told Parsons: Eddie French had been known, back in the day, back when he was a star pitcher for his high school Trojans, as Lefty French. Did that mean that he pitched with his left hand? If so, there had been a problem under the tarp of Skinner's Four Winns at Lakeshore Marina. The bullet that had killed Eddie French had penetrated his skull just behind his right ear. It would, Carol thought, be very awkward for a left-handed man to have committed suicide by shooting himself in the right side of the head.

CHAPTER 4

Carol sat back in her chair, amazed with the information that Officer Parsons, with an assist from Officer Byrnes, had assembled about Eddie French in only a few hours. They had made good use of the phone, of course, but some of their information had been gleaned from the web. Interesting, she thought, that a bit of electronic snooping could unearth so much about the life of Eddie French, a veritable nobody. Carol found herself wondering just how much of her own life was so easily accessed by people she didn't know, sitting at their computers.

In any event, she now not only knew a lot more about Eddie French than she had the day before, she also knew the names of a number of people who could presumably tell her even more. And she knew how to reach them. There was no one in the office to see it, but she smiled a rueful smile as she gathered up the pages of the file. She had asked Parsons to find out what he could about French, not because she expected to make much use of the information, but simply because she was by nature thorough, a proponent of over-preparing.

And now there might be a reason to have over-prepared. A reason which necessitated a call to Doc Crawford, who'd be doing the autopsy.

She placed the call herself and Crawford, now semi-retired, answered the phone just as she was about to hang up.

"Hi, Doc, it's Carol. I thought maybe you'd decided just to let the phone ring."

"Actually I was repairing a hole in my porch screen. Can you believe that? I'm not one for ignoring my phone, though. Never know when I'm going to be asked to perform an autopsy, usually by somebody named Kelleher. Which reminds me, this French guy doesn't look like much of a problem."

"You've already had him on the table?" Why then, Carol thought, haven't you called me?

"No, not yet. I've got one of those late winter, early spring colds, didn't want to pass it along to French." Crawford chuckled at his own wit. "Truth is, I'm indulging myself. I'm sure you know what happened to the poor guy, just like I do. Pretty obvious suicide. So I didn't think there was any urgency. Don't tell me I'm wrong."

"Probably not, but it is French I called about. I've been assuming, like you, that he committed suicide. Shot himself in the head. Routine case. I hadn't even been particularly interested in what you'd have to report. But something's come up that makes me curious."

"You've always had a fertile imagination, Carol. What is it this time?"

"We've located an old high school classmate of French's, and he claims that back then French was nicknamed Lefty. Which started me thinking about whether he might be left handed. And that raises another -"

"Another question," Crawford interrupted, "and I bet I know what that question is: can I tell you if this guy French really was in fact left handed? Right?"

"Well, yes, I was hoping you could, although I can't imagine how you'd know."

Doc Crawford laughed.

"It's forensic magic. It's nice when you know things that nobody else knows. It gives you a conversational edge, makes it easier to forget about the high cost of malpractice insurance."

"But *your* patients are already dead, so how can they sue?"

"Carol, don't you know that it's often when a doctor's patients are dead that he gets sued?"

"I know, but - oh, you're impossible, do you know that? You'd probably have made a good living as a stand-up comic."

"Sorry, but there are days when I can't help myself. But you want me to be serious, don't you? Okay, there's a very good chance that I'll be able to tell you whether French was a lefty. Like I said, I haven't taken a good look at him yet, and quite honestly I hadn't given a thought to whether he was right- or left-handed. But now I'll make that my first order of business. Because if he is a lefty, I very much doubt that he committed suicide. He'd have to have been a contortionist to put a bullet into his head behind his right ear."

"I'm afraid that's what I've been thinking. I sure hope we don't have another murder on our hands, so promise me that it's going to be suicide."

"I'd love to, but if people called him Lefty I've got a strong hunch that it's going to be murder. It's not a nickname you'd give to a right-hander. By any chance do you know whether French ever played baseball? That he was a pitcher?"

"How'd you know that?"

"Because Lefty is a fairly common nickname for left-handed pitchers. I learned that years ago. My Dad was a great Yankee fan, and I remember he particularly liked a Yankee pitcher named Lefty Gomez. No idea what his real first name was, but Dad explained that everyone called him Lefty because he threw left-handed. If your guy French was a pitcher, it was almost inevitable that he'd be known as Lefty."

"I'll have to add that Yankee pitcher to my inventory of trivia," Carol said. "Chances are I'd learn whether Eddie French was left-handed from somebody else, like his ex-wife. But your report would make it official. So just add that to cause of death and whatever else you think may be relevant."

"I'll stop procrastinating and get back to you tomorrow. And I promise not to make some crack about your epidemic of murders."

"You just did, Doc. Anyway, thanks. Now get back to that patch job on your porch screen."

She'd have to wait another twenty-four hours to be sure, but when she hung up the phone she was nearly certain that she was facing an investigation into the murder of Eddie French. Parsons' file was going to be considerably more helpful than she had anticipated. It contained names of people whose lives had intersected French's. She knew nothing about any of them other than what Parsons had put into his report. In fact, all she really knew about French was the story of the pathetic hold-up at *The Cedar Post* and the fact that he had been exonerated in the death of a young boy in a boating accident.

What had begun to look like a relatively quiet if chilly spring was turning into something quite different. Kevin would be thrilled to hear that he'd be returning to Crooked Lake in another six weeks not just to resume married life but to involve himself in yet another of her cases.

CHAPTER 5

As soon as she was off the phone, Carol got in touch with Deputy Sheriff Sam Bridges and reluctantly told him that Saturday would not be a day off this week. She wanted him to go down to the Lakeshore Marina and do the many things they had not done the previous morning. It hadn't seemed that it mattered when what they were looking at what was so obviously a suicide. But it was no longer obviously a suicide. It was almost certainly a murder, and Earl Skinner's boat required a much more thorough going over. Sam would be checking for prints all over the boat. He would be bringing back cushions, the carpet in the boat bottom, and whatever a close search of the Four Winns uncovered. Patrick Kelley would not be happy to see his customer's power boat taken apart in this fashion, and she could hardly blame him. But if Mr. Skinner arrived back at the lake and came to collect his boat before they had extracted every bit of evidence it might contain, he would simply have to be patient. Hopefully he wouldn't be back for another couple of weeks; hopefully the boat would have yielded up all of its secrets by that time.

Bridges had been instructed to tell Kelley that what he was doing was simply routine. Unfortunately, however, Carol was faced with very much the same problem she had confronted the previous summer in the Hawk's Nest case. In that situation, they had learned early on that what appeared to be a suicide was in fact a murder. She had maintained the pretense that it was suicide for several weeks, and she and Kevin had had one of their rare quarrels when she decided to make public the fact that the woman in the mansion's attic had been murdered. What was she to do this time?

For the moment, perhaps no longer than a day, she wouldn't have to do anything. Few people would know about the discovery of French's body, and there was no proof that he had not committed suicide. But once Doc Crawford confirmed that French was left-handed, a decision would have to be made. Carol was all but certain what that decision would be. She would treat the death of Eddie French as murder by an unknown assailant.

Instead of worrying further about investigative strategy, she once again picked up Parsons' file, found the phone number of Isabel French, and placed the call she had been dreading. It would not be as difficult as it would have been if the woman were still married to Eddie. In light of what Ginny Smith had told her about their acrimonious divorce, Isabel French's reaction might even be one of indifference. But for some reason she couldn't quite explain, Carol hadn't looked forward to telling her that her former husband was dead. After all, Eddie was the father of her children (Parsons' notes said that there were three, all boys). And she had lived with him for - Carol consulted the paper in front of her - eleven years. Wouldn't the ex-wife feel something?

The phone rang eight times, but there was no recording asking that the caller leave a voice message, so Carol chose to let it ring a few more times. Just as she was about to hang up after the eleventh ring, an out of breath voice came on the line.

"Hello, this is Isabel." The woman could be heard struggling to catch her breath.

"Mrs. French? Are you all right?"

"I heard the phone when I pulled into the driveway," she said. "Just give me a minute, please."

Carol waited, wondering why Isabel didn't have a voice messaging service.

"Sorry about that," the ex-wife said after she'd caught her breath. "This is Isabel. Who's calling?"

"This is Sheriff Kelleher." She had considered how best to say what she had to say. As usual, the best alternative was coming straight to the point. "This is the part of my job that I like least, but I'm calling to let you know that your former husband, Edwin, is dead. It looks as if he died night before last. We don't have any further details just yet, but we'll be staying in touch with you."

She hoped that Mrs. French, if she used that name, would not press for more information. Unfortunately, she did.

"He's dead? What happened?"

There was no vocal anguish, no sense that the woman was either shocked or upset. Just a request for details.

"It's too early to tell. We're looking into it."

Carol was waiting for a request for information as to where and how Eddie had met his death.

"I assume you know that Eddie and I are divorced," Mrs. French said, as if to explain the questions she was asking or not asking.

"Yes, I've heard that. But I was sure you'd want to know. I don't know what if any relationship you and Mr. French have now, but I thought you should know about his death."

"Well, of course. I appreciate your call." But then her tone changed. Isabel sounded more anxious. "Eddie was providing support for the kids. Those payments have been terribly important for me. Do you know what will happen now that he's -"

Isabel didn't finish her thought.

"If you're asking about future support payments, I'm afraid I can't tell you. It's a legal matter, and you'll need to be in contact with your attorney. I very much hope that it works out for you."

"So do I, but I'm not optimistic. Eddie owed me a lot of money. He was behind and we're hurting. It's been a real rough winter." She paused and then surprised Carol with a different question.

"Did you know Eddie?"

"No, I don't think I've ever met him."

"Probably just as well. Look, sheriff, this is bad news. He was a bad husband, but we needed him to do right by us. By me and the children. I don't have to take care of arrangements, do I? You know, services, burial, things like that? I'm not sure I'm up to doing that."

"No, I'm sure you have no legal obligation. Like I said, I'll let you know what happened as soon as I know. Is there anything I can do for you in the meanwhile?"

"Not that I can think of. I've got to get off the phone. The kids, you know, all the stuff in the car. I appreciate your call."

"Just one more question, if I may," Carol said. "Was your husband right- or left-handed?"

"I don't understand. What's that got to do with anything?"

"I know it sounds like a silly question, but I'd like to know. Which was he?"

"He was left-handed."

It was what Carol had expected to hear.

"I know you're busy, so I'll let you go now. I'm very sorry to have been the bearer of bad news, I really am."

"It's your job, sheriff. Thanks for calling me."

Isabel French now knew about her former husband's death, but the brief conversation had done nothing to give Carol a better picture of what kind of a man Eddie French had been, much less what might have led to what she was sure was his murder. This had not been the time to ask questions. But she knew that she would have to arrange to have a talk with Isabel. The woman hadn't sounded as if she would spend much if any time grieving, so there was no reason to put off a meeting with her for long. Carol decided that two days would be sufficient. She'd arrange to see her on Sunday.

CHAPTER 6

It was not until she'd had her first cup of coffee on Saturday morning that it came to her. There was somebody else she would have to talk to, and she would have to do it right away. Somebody who wasn't on Parsons' list. Somebody who might know French. Or maybe not. But he and French did have something in common: both had spent time in a Four Winns power boat currently sitting on a trailer in the yard of the Lakeshore Marina. He because he was the boat's owner, French because he had died there of a gunshot wound to the head. Carol could not imagine why she hadn't zeroed in on Earl Skinner sooner.

In all likelihood, Bridges would be inspecting the boat at that very minute. She dialed Sam's cell, betting that Kelley would in fact be standing by his side, nervously watching him doing his thing.

"Is that you Carol?"

"Right. Finding anything?"

"I haven't been at it long. You're not trying to hurry me up, are you?"

"No, of course not. I thought of something I wanted you to ask Kelley about. Should have mentioned it earlier."

"Well, Kelley's right here, making sure I don't do something to hurt the boat. Want to talk with him?"

"Sure."

The manager of Lakeshore Marina took Sam's cell phone.

"Hello, sheriff. I'm really worried about what's going on here at the marina. Officer Bridges is being nice about it, but I'm concerned that my customers will have second thoughts about doing business here."

"I don't think you'll have a problem on that score. People are smart enough to know this isn't your fault. Besides, they'll get a kick out of being able to tell their neighbors about being so close to where it happened."

"What about Skinner? I can't imagine him getting a kick out of it."

"It's Mr. Skinner I'm calling about," Carol said, bringing the conversation around to the reason for her call. "Do you know when he'll be back, when he'll come for his boat? Have you had a heads up from him?"

"He said something about late, maybe mid April awhile back, but I haven't heard anything for a few weeks."

"I need to talk with him," Carol said. "I want to be the one to break the news. Can you give me a number where he can be reached?"

"It's down in the office. Any way you can make him understand this has nothing to do with Lakeshore?"

"What I want to do is find out if he knew French, or should I say if French knew him. I'm not blaming the marina for the fact that French ended up in Skinner's boat. But I would like to know if there was some reason why French chose to curl up in that particular boat. So I'd appreciate it if you'd get me a number where I can reach Mr. Skinner."

"Okay," Kelley said reluctantly. He set off for the office in a hurry, obviously reluctant to miss anything Bridges was doing.

Kelley came back with nothing specific as to Skinner's plans. But he did have a contact phone number, somewhere in South Carolina. Carol and Sam spoke briefly before she rang off, and she reassured Kelley once again that things were going to be all right. She hoped that she was right about that. But her next order of business was to get in touch with the owner of the Four Winns.

Skinner was not at his South Carolina winter home when the sheriff tried his number. But his wife was, and she assured her that he'd be back within the hour. Carol had tip-toed around the reason for the call, preferring to break the news to him herself. For all she knew, Mrs. Skinner was just as able to handle this unexpected news as her husband, but Kelley had talked about Skinner, not the Skinners, so Carol had side-stepped the inevitable questions and said she'd wait for a call back.

It was nearly noon when the owner of the Four Winns returned the call.

"Hello, Mr. Skinner," Carol said, trying to adopt a matter of fact tone."I appreciate you getting back to me so quickly. Are you free for a few minutes?"

She knew that Skinner would be puzzled by the message that he was to call the sheriff of Cumberland County. It was even likely that he would be worried.

"I have lots of time, sheriff, but what is the matter? Your call was just about the last thing I expected today."

"I'm sure it was, and you're just about the last person I expected to be calling. Unfortunately, we have a problem up here on the lake. You store your boat at the Lakeshore Marina, and Mr. Kelley made a startling discovery there Thursday morning. A man had crawled into your boat the night before and when Kelley found him he was dead. It looks as if -"

"There's a dead man in my boat?" It is doubtful that he would have sounded more surprised if she had told him his boat had sprouted wings.

"We've taken him away, but he was there Thursday. Very dead. Kelley would have been in touch with you, of course, but in view of the circumstances it was appropriate that I be the one to give you the news. The man's name is French, Edwin French. Did you know him?"

"Eddie? Eddie French? Are you sure?"

"I'm sure, and I gather that you did indeed know him. I'd like you to tell me how it happens that you and Mr. French knew each other."

Although she had considered the possibility that Skinner would have known French, it had seemed unlikely. Now, suddenly, it looked as if there might be a reason other than random chance for the driver of the bakery truck to choose Skinner's Four Winns to spend his last night on earth. And that in turn increased the likelihood that someone else would know where to find him. And kill him.

"This is simply unbelievable," Skinner said. "I mean, I didn't really know French, and I can't imagine why he used my boat. What happened, he freeze to death?"

"I'll get to that in a minute. But you were going to tell me how it happens that you knew him."

"It's really a non-story, sheriff. Almost a coincidence. You probably know my boat's a Four Winns. Well, French had one, too. One day last fall I was taking my boat down to the marina for winter storage. Had it on the trailer, driving through Yates Center, when I heard this knocking sound. Something had come loose. I pulled over so I could get out and see what was wrong. Turns out I was on the street where French lives. I'd never seen the guy, but he comes over and starts talking about my boat. But what was on his mind, I learned, was that he had a Four Winns himself and wanted to sell it. He seemed to think I could offer him some advice about where he could get a decent price."

Skinner paused, as if to let the sheriff consider whether this made sense to her. It didn't, not yet.

"Well," he continued, "I figured Kelley might be the person for him to talk to because that's where I store my boat and because Kelley always seemed to know a lot about the Four Winns models. Anyway, we chatted for a bit and then I went on my way."

"That's it?"

"Pretty much. He'd just asked me for some advice and I gave it to him."

"And he gave you his name?"

"No, actually, and I don't think I gave him mine. It was just an impersonal five minute conversation."

"How, then, did you know that he was Eddie French?"

"Remember that accident when a kid was killed by a power boat? Happened last fall. Sometime after Labor Day weekend, I believe. There was a piece in the *Gazette* when the judge's verdict on the case came down. There was a picture in the paper of the man who'd driven the boat. It said his name was French, and I recognized him right away as the guy who'd talked with me about selling his Four Winns."

"Did you ever talk with him again?"

"No, just that once. I remember thinking later how strange it was that I'd talked with him about selling the boat that had run down that poor kid - talked with him but never knew he was the one who did it."

"So you didn't know French, only that somebody who'd talked to you about his boat turned out to be French. And he didn't know your name?"

"I'm sure he didn't."

"How about the name of your boat?"

"It's 'Excalibur.'"

"Would French have known that.?"

"He could have seen it, big as daylight on the back of the boat, when we talked that day."

"Which means that he knew you owned a Four Winns, knew its name, knew where you stored it. That might explain why he picked your boat when he was looking for a place to sleep the other night."

"But why would he want to sleep on *anybody's* boat on a cold night?" Skinner asked. It was a good question. "It doesn't make sense."

"I can't answer that, but it might have something to do with a rumor that he'd been evicted from his house. I hope to have the facts on that before the day's over."

"I'm sorry to hear about French," Skinner said, "but I'm not so sure I should be. Just about everybody I know up around the lake was upset that he was acquitted in the death of that kid. Maybe there wasn't enough evidence against him, but somehow it didn't feel right, him getting off like that. And now he dies on my boat. Weird, isn't it?"

Carol had said nothing about how Eddie French had died. But she had made up her mind that this time she wouldn't pretend it had been suicide if the evidence pointed strongly to murder. One way or another, she had to let Earl Skinner know that French had not died of hypothermia. Or, for that matter, of a heart attack.

"There's something else you should know, Mr. Skinner," she said, aware that what she was about to tell him would be even more unsettling than news that French had died on his boat. "Mr. French died of a gunshot wound to the head. We expect that the autopsy will tell us whether he committed suicide or was killed by someone else. We'll let you know when we know."

This time there was no immediate response from South Carolina, just the sound of Skinner drawing a deep breath.

"Why my boat, for God's sake?" he finally said. "Betty and I don't want to be drawn into a mess like this. What are we going to tell people?"

"Mr. Skinner, all that's happened is that you're the victim of a stroke of bad luck. That's what people will be thinking, that's what you should tell them. In the meanwhile, my men are going over the boat looking for any evidence that will help us decide whether we have a suicide or a murder on our hands. I've made it very clear that they're to be extra careful. When do you expect to go back to the lake?"

"We had planned to go up weekend after next. I don't know what Betty will want to do now. We could get away in three or four days."

"If I were you, I'd stick to my plans. No need to rush. It's a lot warmer where you are than it is up here, as I'm sure you've heard. And I can assure you that Mr. Kelley is taking care of your interests. He's a good man, runs a good marina. This could have happened to anyone."

"But it didn't, did it? It happened to me."

As Carol collected her thoughts after her conversation with Skinner, she found herself thinking about the element of chance in what she had just heard. That Skinner just happened to be driving down French's street with his Four Winns in tow. That Skinner just happened to stop to fix a problem with his trailer. That French just happened to be at home and happened to see Skinner and his boat. That French just happened also to own a Four Winns. That Skinner advised French to discuss the sale of his Four Winns with Patrick Kelley at Lakeside Marina, and that Kelley discovered French, dead in a Four Winns, at that same marina. Not dead in just any Four Winns, but in Skinner's. It was all plausible, but Carol, with her aversion to coincidence, couldn't set aside her skepticism. Did it happen the way Skinner had said? Why not? Why would the man have made any of it up? He could not possibly have had anything to do with French's death.

The sheriff shook her head. She knew she had to put a stop to such pointless speculation.

CHAPTER 7

Carol had spent most of the morning on the phone and was beginning to feel antsy. She needed to get out of the cottage, even if the overcast skies held out little promise of a pleasant day. The thermometer on the deck had finally broken fifty, but the trees were not in bud and only a dozen or so daffodils beside the Brock's cottage provided any evidence that spring had arrived. The lake looked cold, as indeed it was; it would be many weeks before she would be taking her first swim of the season.

Still thinking about what Earl Skinner had told her, Carol decided that she would take a drive over to Yates Center and take a look at the house where Parsons' report said that Eddie French had lived. The address was on Woodpecker Lane. She didn't think she had ever been on Woodpecker Lane, but the street name gave its location away. There was a cluster of streets on the north side of town, all of which had been named for birds. While Yates Center had many elegant old homes with large wrap around porches, cupolas, and spacious lawns, such houses were nowhere in evidence on Woodpecker, Chickadee, or the other streets in the 'bird' section of town. Although no railroad ran through Yates Center, these streets were, so to speak, on the other side of the tracks. It was a tract development of architecturally uninspired houses, most of them rentals.

Carol made her way through the commercial section of town, up Mayberry Drive with its attractive mansions, and eventually into the more depressing blocks where Eddie French's house was supposed to be located. Woodpecker Lane was not hard to find; she turned left onto it and began looking for the number. For some reason the house numbers were small, too small to be read from a moving car. Carol pulled over to the curb and got out to take a closer look. The nearest houses were 215 and 217, which meant that French had lived just three places further up the street. She left the car where it was and walked up the block to 223.

The only sign of life on this blustery Saturday morning was a man in front of 221 who looked as if he was putting down grass

30

seed in a small patch of scrubby lawn. Carol exchanged 'good mornings' with him. Not surprisingly, he seemed interested to see a uniformed officer of the law on Woodpecker Lane.

She went up to the door of 223, only to be confronted by a placard which announced that the house was in the possession of the Hutchinson Company.

"I don't think you'll be seeing Mr. French today." It was the guy sewing grass seed next door. "He's gone. Been gone for several days, in fact. They evicted him, that's what they did. It's a shame how they treat us, don't give a damn about our problems, just put us out on the street when we run into some kind of trouble. Eddie, he didn't hurt nobody, but that don't matter. Those Hutchinson people didn't care he was in a bind. All they want to do is squeeze money out of us."

Carol listened patiently to the tirade by Eddie French's neighbor. For all she knew, his critique of his neighbor's landlord was well founded. Perhaps Hutchinson's owned his property as well, and he had had his own problems with them.

"I'm not sure we know each other. I'm Sheriff Kelleher, and you are?"

"Bill Hedrick." He put out his hand. A bit tentatively, Carol thought.

"You know Mr. French pretty well?"

"No, not really. Simon, he knows him a lot better than I do. Is there a problem? Hutchinson's puttin' the screws to him or something?"

"This man Simon, is he another neighbor?" Carol asked, side-stepping the question.

"Sure. He lives in that place up there with the concrete yard. He got tired of trying to grow grass. I should do like he did."

"Do you know Simon's last name?"

"It's Ostrowski. Don't ask me to spell it."

So, Eddie French had recently been evicted from his home on Woodpecker Lane. That might explain the fact that he had chosen to spend the night in a boat at the Lakeshore Marina, although why a boat instead of his own car she couldn't imagine. It did not, of course, explain why he had died - and in all likelihood been killed - on the boat. Perhaps Simon Ostrowski would know more than Hedrick about why French had been evicted and what had been on his mind. He was one of the small handful of Eddie's acquaintances that Parsons had spoken with. Simon the bowling buddy. Carol walked up the street to 227, hoping that Ostrowski was in.

Fortunately, he was. In fact, he hadn't ever gotten dressed for the day. Perhaps he was sick.

"Mr. Ostrowski?" she asked of the man who came to the door. "I hope this isn't an inconvenient time for me to come knocking at your door."

"Yes, I'm Ostrowski, but what is it - you look like the police."

"In fact I am. I happen to be the sheriff, and I'd love to talk with you about your neighbor, Mr. French. If, that is, you're feeling up to it."

"I suppose it's the bathrobe," he said, tightening the sash. "The truth is, I had a late night poker game and slept in this morning. But what's the problem with Eddie? Somebody from your office called about him the other day, but he didn't say why."

"That's what I'd like to talk about. May I come in?"

"Sure. The place isn't very neat, but I suppose you've seen worse."

They went into what looked like the living room, where two card tables covered with empty beer bottles and ash trays occupied the middle of the floor. Through a door on one side of the room Carol could see into a similarly cluttered kitchen. All of the furniture seemed to be either second hand or badly in need of the attentions of an upholstery cleaner. And the room reeked of cigar smoke.

Ostrowski shoved one of the card tables and a folding chair out of the way so they could take seats on a couch which looked as if it might double as a pull out bed.

"You want to talk about Eddie? Maybe you can tell me where he is, 'cause I haven't seen or heard from him in days."

"I'm afraid he's dead." Carol had no intention of elaborating. "We know very little about what happened, which is why I'm here. It seems that you knew him fairly well, so I figured you might be able to help us."

Simon Ostrowski seemed surprised by the sheriff's announcement, but neither looked nor sounded distressed.

"He's really dead? I just thought he'd decided to take a trip, get away from his problems for awhile." It must have occurred to him that he hadn't sounded appropriately saddened by the death of his neighbor, because he quickly added something to effect that he was shocked to hear the news.

"Tell me what you know about Mr. French," Carol said.

"But you haven't told me what happened to Eddie."

"No, and that's because we don't know. You can help us by telling me what you can about him. Let's start with how you knew him. You told my colleague that you bowled with him. That suggests that you and he were fairly close, that you shared time with each other. What did you talk about?"

"Actually, we weren't all that close. He'd only lived here a little more than four months - moved into that furnished rental after he got divorced last fall. I guess I told your man that we bowled together, but I doubt that it was more than five or six times. He wasn't a poker player. And he didn't talk much."

"When he did talk with you, what seemed to be on his mind?"

Ostrowski looked puzzled. He was obviously trying to figure out what lay behind the sheriff's question.

"Nothing in particular," he offered. "The usual things guys talk about. Football, TV shows. He complained a lot about how awful the Bills were. That's probably because he used to live in Buffalo. He seemed to like those reality shows, you know, *American Idol, Dancing with the Stars*. I think he actually watched *Desperate Housewives*. But like I said, he didn't talk much. I guess I'd say he sounded depressed. I thought he'd never really gotten over the divorce."

"Did he ever say why he and his wife divorced? Anything about the settlement?"

"He didn't like to talk about it, but it was pretty obvious that he blamed his wife. Isabel, I think her name is. I don't think she was being unfaithful or anything like that. My impression was that they disagreed about raising the kids and it got nasty. I know that he had very limited visitation rights."

Carol knew that she would have to talk with people who were better informed about Eddie's marriage and divorce than Simon Ostrowski. The ex-wife for starters. And their attorneys.

"It looks like Eddie was evicted from his house. What do you know about it?"

"Yeah, he got the boot just last Tuesday. Mean buggers, those Hutchinson people. The place was a furnished rental, otherwise there'd be all kinds of stuff on the curb. I let Eddie put his personal things in my storage locker out on the Seneca Valley Road. There wasn't much, but he didn't have a place so I told him he could stow it out there temporarily."

"What about his car?"

"He didn't have no car. He used the bakery truck. Least he did last time I saw him."

"No car, no place to live. Sounds like he didn't have much money either."

"That's for sure," Ostrowski said. "He admitted he was behind in his rent. He had an old Ford when he moved in down the street, but it was gone before Christmas. He said he didn't need it, what with the bakery truck, but I think he sold it because he needed the cash."

"Any idea why he was having money problems? Gambling maybe?"

"I don't think he gambled much. Never joined us for poker, that I know. What I think is his wife was bleeding him."

Another thought had occurred to Carol.

"By the way, back to bowling for a minute. Did Eddie bowl with his right or left hand?"

Ostrowski scowled.

"He was a lefty, but what's that got to do with his problems?"

"I'm not sure. Remember, I never knew him. I'm just trying to get a sense of what he was like, that's all."

"Well, I think I've told you about all I know. Like I said, he –" He stopped short. "No, wait. There's something else. Eddie got involved in a boating accident last fall. Some kid was out diving and Eddie ran into him. Never saw the kid. Maybe being the sheriff, you knew about it."

Carol nodded.

"Then you know the boy died," Ostrowski continued. "It happened before he moved in down the street. By the time I got to know him, they'd decided it was an accident. No fault of Eddie's. Anyway, he didn't like to talk about it. I don't blame him. That'd be a tough thing to get off your mind. But what I wanted to tell you is that he did talk about it one day. Not all that long ago, in fact. Seems like he was spooked by a guy who kept calling him about that accident. Eddie asked if I'd ever seen somebody coming around, asking questions about him. He wanted me to tell him if I ever saw this guy."

"Did he tell you what the guy's name was, what he looked like?"

"He didn't mention a name, but he told me a bit about how he looked. Sounded pretty much like an ordinary guy to me, if you know what I mean. Eddie just said not to talk about him to a stranger, but to let him know if somebody'd been asking. Is this important?"

Carol's answer was honest, if hardly straight forward.

"I don't know. Maybe, maybe not." Whether it was important or not, it was quite possible that it would get Ostowski thinking about whether his sometime friend Eddie French's death had something to do with the unnamed caller. Ostrowski hadn't sounded all that swift, but he was surely bright enough to entertain the possibility that Eddie had been killed, perhaps by this stranger.

When Carol left Woodpecker Lane, she now knew four things.

First, Eddie French was undoubtedly left-handed; it wouldn't be necessary to wait for Doc Crawford's verdict.

Second, somebody had been bugging French about the boating accident, and Eddie had been worried enough about it that he had asked a neighbor to let him know if somebody was asking about him.

Third, Eddie had been in financial trouble which was serious enough that he had sold his car and had been evicted from his house for non-payment of rent.

But most intriguing of all, some of Eddie's personal possessions had been entrusted to Simon Ostrowski's care and were now in a storage locker on the Seneca Valley Road. Carol would have to ask one of her men to pay a visit to that storage locker.

CHAPTER 8

Carol would normally have called Kevin Saturday night. It had been their pattern to touch a base at least once a week, and always on Saturday. But he had announced that he had a ticket to a Met production of Verdi's *Otello* on this particular Saturday evening, so she would have to defer their weekend's conversation until Sunday. She had planned to take her mind off the Eddie French case by immersing herself in a novel that had had good reviews, but while she was cleaning up the kitchen after dinner she had another idea. She would listen to Kevin's recording of *Otello*. It was an opera she did not know, although Kevin had told her it was Verdi at his very best. More importantly, she would be vicariously sharing the evening with him. The artists would, of course, be different, and she would be denied the opportunity to see how the opera was staged. But she would be with him in spirit. She knew she would not be with him in reality for at least another six or seven weeks. It had been a depressing thought, but she was in no mood to be depressed. She went into the study and began searching through the rack of CDs for *Otello*.

When she awoke the next morning, Carol was surprised to find that her first thoughts were of the opera she had listened to the previous evening. To her great surprise, she had thoroughly enjoyed it. Kevin had once told her that he found Verdi's treatment of Shakespeare's play even better than that of the bard himself. It had been many years since she had taken a college course in Shakespeare, so she was in no position to agree or disagree with his opinion. But she realized that she had been mesmerized by the opera, from the opening storm and beautiful love duet all the way to the tragic deaths of Desdemona and Otello.

For some reason Carol couldn't explain, she made a sudden decision after breakfast to head down to Southport for the 10 o'clock mass at St. Patrick's. It would be, she realized, the first time she had been to church in more than two months. Was her conscience asserting itself? Or was it simply the need to immerse herself for an hour in the comfort of age old tradition and ritual, an escape from the problems and worries of her job? She doubted that she would be on her way to mass if Kevin were back at the cottage. But he wasn't, and Carol busied herself getting dressed for church. After that, she'd turn her attention to Isabel French.

———

Assured that Isabel was at home and willing to talk with her, Carol set off for the nearby town of Franklin just ahead of one. She had no idea how forthcoming the former wife of the late Eddie French would be. Would his death have brought back to the surface all of the issues that had prompted their breakup? Or would she have remembered the good times and experienced a bit of remorse? Of most interest to Carol was the question of whether Isabel would know of people who might have wished Eddie ill.

The former Mrs. French and her three boys lived in a modest and sparely furnished house on the edge of Franklin. Carol realized that she knew nothing about Isabel's economic circumstances. Probably not good, in view of what she had heard about Eddie's bad record when it came to child support. She didn't even know whether Isabel was employed and, if so, where.

"You don't look like a sheriff," Isabel said as she welcomed Carol into her home.

"I've heard that more than a few times," Carol said, "but I've never figured out just what a sheriff is supposed to look like."

"I guess it's just that I don't know any woman sheriffs. Besides, you don't have a uniform on."

Carol wondered if Isabel French knew any male sheriffs. In any event, she wasn't interested in a discussion of women in law enforcement.

"I just came from church," she said, and changed the subject.

"As I said on the phone, I'm trying to form a picture of your former husband. I've just got a few questions, shouldn't take long. May we sit down?"

"Oh, pardon my manners. Of course. Would you like coffee?"

They went into a living room which said either that Isabel's purse was empty after paying the rent and putting food on the table or that she was indifferent to even basic creature comforts.

"No thanks." Carol took one of the only two chairs in the room and was surprised when Isabel chose to sit, yoga style, on the floor. The woman was tall and thin. Her black hair was worn in a pony tail, her feet were bare, and she seemed to Carol's eye to be almost sexless. She corrected that thought. The word she was searching for was androgynous.

"Are the boys at home?" she asked.

"No. Did you want to talk with them?"

Carol hadn't considered doing so, but she realized that she was curious to see what they looked like.

"No, that's fine. How old are they now?"

"Steven is eight. He's the oldest. Michael is five and Brian is four."

Isabel made no effort to explain just where the boys were at the moment. At a neighbors? Running wild in the streets?

"How are they taking the news of their father's death?"

"Hard to say. Michael and Brian are pretty young. They've barely seen Eddie since the divorce. If I had my way, they wouldn't have seen him at all."

"Why is that?"

"He was abusive. That's why I divorced him. I didn't want him to have anything to do with the boys."

"I don't mean to pry," Carol said, "but abusive is one of those words that means different things to different people. How was Mr. French abusive?"

"It wasn't that he molested them, if that's what you're thinking. There was never anything like that. But he was a hitter. He'd get angry and he'd beat them, specially Steven. I was brought up by an abusive father and I knew what it must have been like for them. We argued about it, I'd try to get him to do something about his temper. He'd promise to change his ways, but he never did. Maybe for a day or two, but then he'd start smacking them around again."

"Did it have anything to do with his drinking?"

"That's why it was so hard to understand. Eddie almost never had a drink."

"Did he actually hurt the boys? I mean was it more than spanking?"

"Oh, yes. He didn't spank, he hit them. He'd haul off and smack them with the flat of his hand. Right in the face most of the time."

"They ever have to go to the emergency room?"

"Steven did. Twice. Once he had a broken finger where he'd tried to ward Eddie off. The other time he had a black eye and a bloody nose."

"Do you remember what it was that set him off?"

Isabel considered the question.

"Most often it didn't seem like anything in particular. Like maybe they didn't do something he'd ask them to do fast enough. Or they left stuff around the house that should have been put away. They're not bad kids, sheriff."

"Did Mr. French treat you like he did the boys?"

This seemed to be a more difficult question for Isabel to answer.

"It wasn't the same," she said after a long pause. "He went after me a time or two before the kids came along, but I stood up for myself, told him if he beat me I'd walk out on him. It must have worked because he never touched me again. Oh sure, he'd holler at me, but mama had always used that old saw about sticks and stones and names never hurting. I guess it stuck with me. No, the divorce was all about how he treated the boys, not me."

"Do you know what kind of a relationship Mr. French had with his employers, his friends? I mean, as far as you know, was his temper ever a problem outside of the house?"

"Eddie never talked much at all about things like that. He didn't bring his jobs home, and he didn't seem to have many friends. We never did anything with other couples. I know he was fired from a couple of jobs, but he wouldn't say why. It might have been because of his temper, things he said or did when he got mad, but he wouldn't talk about it."

Thanks to Parsons' diligence, she had what looked like a complete list of jobs Eddie had held, at least since he had moved to the area. She would need to talk with his employers on those jobs, especially the ones from which he had been fired.

"Do you remember the jobs where he got fired?"

"I think so. There were two I'm sure of. But for all I know he was fired from others and he just never told me about it. The two I know about are Leckonby's and the post office. Leckonby's, they're that outfit that does hauling, maintenance projects, odd jobs. And he delivered for the post office out of Yates Center for awhile."

"So Mr. French didn't really have a steady job while you were married to him."

"No, not steady. And most of them didn't pay too well either. You're probably wondering why I put up with him for as long as I did."

"It's been a tough row, then. Are you working now?"

"I don't have a choice," Isabel said, her tone of voice making it clear that she'd give anything to have that choice. "If it weren't for the young ones, I'd be working full time. But Emily Purdy down at the diner here in Franklin lets me put in as many hours as I can. It wouldn't have been so bad if Eddie had been regular with his payments."

Isabel French had begun to look restless. Perhaps it would be wise to bring this particular interrogation to a close.

"I'm sure you have things you have to do," Carol said. "I appreciate your time today, and I suspect that I'll be back in touch in the near future."

She got up to leave, but Isabel stayed in her yoga position and asked a question of her own.

"You say you'll be back in touch soon, sheriff. I don't think I understand. Can you tell me why you're asking me all these questions?"

Carol had met the woman, sized her up, gotten some potentially useful information. There was no longer any real reason not to let her know what had happened to Eddie. Others knew, and it was inevitable that much of Crooked Lake would know within a matter of days.

"Mrs. French, I haven't been sure how to break this to you, but you have every right to know. Your former husband died of a gun shot wound to the head. It looked very much like suicide. But there's a possibility that somebody else shot him. We aren't sure. That's why I've been asking you questions. I need to know why Mr. French committed suicide - or, more importantly, who might have killed him if it turns out not to be suicide."

Isabel French had sat through this account of how her ex-husband had died without moving a muscle in her face. Now that the sheriff had said what she had to say, Isabel made no comment. She continued to sit silently, cross-legged on the floor, as if in a trance.

Carol was about to add some further word of regret about Eddie French's death when Isabel spoke up.

"You could have told me what happened to Eddie when you first called me. You could have told me before you started asking all of these questions. What are you doing, trying to get me to say something that will make me a suspect in his murder? I don't want to talk any more about Eddie. I know absolutely nothing about his death, and I want you to get out of my house and leave me alone. I have my boys to look after. Eddie could have cared less. You, too. Now go."

Carol said she was sorry that Isabel had misunderstood her, wished her well, and took her leave. She had never given a moment's thought to the possibility that Isabel had killed her ex-husband. By the time she got back to the cottage she had given the matter considerably more thought. Still highly unlikely. But possible? It was, of course, too soon to know.

CHAPTER 9

She had barely walked into the cottage when the phone rang. Kevin? Carol hoped so, but she suppressed the impulse to say something personal and clever.

"Sheriff Kelleher speaking."

"Sorry to disappoint you, Carol, but this is Doc Crawford. Do you have a few minutes?"

"When have I not had a few minutes for you, Doc? Your timing is great - I just got back from Franklin."

"Good. Then why don't you pull up a chair and let me tell you about what happened to Mr. Edwin French."

"I think I know most of it. You're going to tell me he's left-handed, like that Gomez guy. See, I remembered. I hope you're impressed."

"I am impressed, considering you're not into baseball trivia. But I think we both already knew the odds said French was a lefty. No question about it."

"Since we talked, I've heard it from his ex-wife, and she should know. Also from a neighbor who bowled with him. If a guy bowls with his left hand, it's close to certain that he shoots a gun with his left hand, too."

"Glad to hear that you're doing your homework, like me. Anyway, the odds are at least a hundred to one that he didn't shoot himself in the head. Maybe higher. So you're confronted with another murder investigation.

"There's no question about how he died. He was in good shape until that bullet entered his brain. It killed him. Instantly. And I'm sure the ballistics test will confirm that the bullet came from the gun you found on the boat. It's a .22, a Beretta Bobcat, but you probably already knew that. I'll let you see if it was registered to French, but from a forensic point of view it's really a pretty simple case. Oh, and the poor guy had only been dead about six hours."

"You sound relieved, like this time you didn't have to break a sweat. Not like with that woman in the Hawks Nest attic or the Swedish exchange student."

"Come on, Carol," Doc said. "They weren't that big a problem either, except that they'd been dead a lot longer than French. You ever see that guy Ducky on *NCIS*? Now he's a pathologist who really gets the tough cases. Of course he always gets it right, but that's because it's just TV fantasy land."

"Yeah, I watch *NCIS* now and then, and you're my Ducky. At least you haven't failed me yet."

"Well, I'd suggest that we call a halt to these Crooked Lake murders, Carol. Law of averages says that sooner or later you'll come up with one that stumps me."

"I'm hoping that the law of averages gives us a year without a single murder. Not a one. Then maybe I can talk Kevin into finishing our honeymoon."

———

It was late that afternoon that Kevin did call. Carol had gone for a long walk. She had told herself it was to clear her head, take her mind off Eddie French's murder. But it hadn't worked out that way. She had been unable to shake off the puzzle of this undistinguished loner and loser's death. When she arrived back at the cottage, Carol felt more tired and irritable than she had when she set off down Blue Water Point to Meadowbrook Road. She had just hung up her windbreaker when the phone rang.

"Sheriff Kelleher."

"Must we be so formal?" Kevin said, tongue in cheek.

"You have the luxury of being informal. I have to assume it's some criminal ready to confess that he did it. God, it's good to hear from you. Can you believe it's been five days since we talked?"

"Five days, a stupid faculty retreat and then the opera."

Carol didn't want to hear about the retreat. It had quite effectively ruined Kevin's plan to spend his spring recess at the lake. The only time during the term when it should have been possible for them to enjoy some quality time together, and his dean had decided to hold a faculty retreat. Just thinking about it again made her angry. Better talk about something else.

"I don't want to hear about your damned retreat. How did you like the opera?"

"Okay. I've heard better. The tenor was getting over a bad cold and it showed. But even a tenor with a cold can't ruin Verdi."

"You may be surprised to hear that I listened along with you last night. I found your CD of *Otello* and stuck with it all the way through. It's really good, isn't it?"

"What did I tell you? But you tell me, how are you?"

"Fine. Why shouldn't I be?"

"I ask because I had an awful nightmare last night, and it wasn't about what Iago did to Otello and Desdemona. It was about you."

"Me? A nightmare about me? I'm supposed to be in your dreams."

"Well, not this time. You were being stalked!"

"Stalked? That sounds as if somebody had taken a fancy to me."

"This guy wasn't smitten by your looks. Or your uniform. He was bent on killing you."

"I hope you're telling me I made it through the nightmare."

"I think so. You know how those things are. The plot isn't all tied up neatly at the end of the show. Anyway, it was horrible. When I woke up this morning I couldn't get it out of my mind. So I want you to be extra careful, do you hear? You need eyes in the back of your head."

"That's gross," Carol said. "You'd never have married me. I'm all right as I am."

"I hope so, but cops are being killed in the line of duty all the time. Read the paper."

"Kevin, may I remind you that my beat is Crooked Lake. This isn't the NYPD."

"Maybe not, but I'll wager there've been as many crimes up there per capita as there are down here in the city. And I don't mean petty theft."

Carol knew Kevin was talking about murder. She had planned to bring it up, too, but if she did it would only stimulate his nightmare driven anxiety. Kevin forced the issue.

"Enough of nightmares," he said. "What are you up to?"

"I'm not sure I should be telling you this. You'll want to drop everything and come riding to my rescue. But we had a mysterious death over at the Lakeshore Marina the other night. A guy was found dead in one of the boats they store at the marina. He'd shot himself, or so it looked until we realized that it couldn't have been him that did it."

"Are you telling me in your indirect way that you have another murder on your hands?"

"We aren't one hundred percent certain, but I'm afraid it looks that way."

"What are they putting in the water up there?"

Carol ignored this.

"This time we knew right away who the victim is. He's local, or was. Kind of a pathetic character from what I can make out. It just happened Thursday night, so the investigation is just getting started. No early leads."

"Wish I could help, but there's no way I can get away from here. There's talk of merging the music department with fine arts, which would mean loss of our autonomy. You can imagine how that's got everyone all worked up. Meetings, meetings. As if the retreat wasn't enough."

Carol was surprised to hear this. The situation at Madison College must be serious. Otherwise Kevin would be readying excuses to grab an early flight to the lake.

"I can't believe I heard you right. Getting tired of playing detective?"

"No, it's that I'm finally taking seriously your admonition to keep my priorities straight. My dean looked at me a couple of times during the retreat as if he might regret that I've got tenure. Besides, I know you, and I know you'll get your man."

"Or my woman," she said, remembering Isabel French.

"But remember what I said. Watch your back."

"I don't think that will be my problem. What is puzzling me is who would want to kill a sad sack like Eddie French. That's the victim's name."

"Sad sacks can have enemies, Carol, just like the rich and the famous."

CHAPTER 10

It was 2:21 a.m., and it was very dark and very cold on the north side of Southport at the end of Crooked Lake. A breeze was blowing, pushing small waves onto the beach. Otherwise all was still, the night's silence broken only by the occasional car, more than half a mile away on the East Lake Road. There were no street lights in this part of Southport. Indeed, the only street in the immediate area was devoid of houses, its only reason for being there a long abandoned brick building that had once housed municipal vehicles. The moon was full, but for much of the night it had been obscured by cloud cover.

The beach was not deserted, however. From time to time a tiny orange glow could be seen near the base of a large tulip poplar. It was the glow of a cigarette, and the man smoking it was leaning against the tree, motionless except when he brought the cigarette to his lips. He had been there for almost a quarter of an hour, having parked his car on Lake Street and walked down to the poplar and the beach. He hadn't come to the beach in this early morning hour to commune with nature or because he was having a sleepless night. He was there because he had a rendezvous to keep, and the person he was waiting for was late. Not so late as to cause him to give up his vigil, but late enough to make him frustrated. He looked at the illuminated dial of his watch for the third time, shrugged, and fastened the top button on his jacket, the better to ward off the cold night air. Perhaps he should walk around a bit. The exercise would help to warm him up.

Before the man had a chance to act on this impulse, he felt a light tap on his shoulder. In spite of the fact that he had been expecting someone, he was startled. He turned, stepping away from the tree, trying to see who it was that had come up behind him. It was the person he had been waiting for, but his reaction was not one of relief. He had felt anxious ever since he had left his car and walked down to the beach. Now his anxiety spiked, just when logically it should have abated.

There was no one else within several hundred yards or more, and anyone that close would surely be sound asleep. So no one heard what the two talked about. But talk they did, for two, three, almost five minutes. Whispering was not necessary, but they both whispered, as if by agreement that what was said needed to be kept secret. The orange glow of the cigarette went out but the conversation went on. Finally, at 2:34, the late comer took something out of a coat pocket and stepped closer to the man who had waited so patiently. Had there been anybody in the vicinity to observe it, he - or she - might have assumed that something had exchanged hands.

For what seemed like a long time but was in fact only about twenty seconds, the two remained close, almost as if in a tight embrace. And then one of them disengaged from that embrace. The other looked momentarily as if he were going to sit down. But what he did was fold up and sink to the ground, much as a marionette would if its strings were released.

The person who had been late for the meeting with the patient smoker proceeded to walk away down the beach in the general direction of West Lake Road. Not long after his quiet departure, the clouds briefly parted, affording a glimpse of the moon. But there was no one there to see it.

———

At approximately 7:30 that morning, two teenage boys chose to take a somewhat circuitous route to school. They cut down Pratt Street to the waterfront and proceeded to walk along the shoreline, skipping stones from the beach out into the lake. By the time they got to Lake Street, they agreed it was time to get a move on or they'd be late to school. That wouldn't look good on their record, so they headed back into town and the shortest route to Southport High School. They hadn't gone more than twenty yards when, at the base of large tulip poplar, they spotted someone lying on the ground.

"Looks like a homeless man," one of the boys said to the other. "Lousy place to spend the night, if you ask me."

"Suppose we ought to wake him up?" his friend asked.

"It's none of our business. He's probably drunk, and he'll ask for money."

"Yeah, you're right. Why don't we -" He stopped in mid sentence and bent down next to the man on the ground. "This guy's got blood all over his jacket. See?"

His companion took a closer look.

"You're right. I think he's hurt." He studied the man's face, then took a grip on the jacket and tried to pull him into something like a sitting position. It didn't work.

"Know what I think?" his friend said. "I think he's dead."

"I don't want to mess around with him, whether he's dead or asleep. Let's tell Janeway."

The boys hurried up Lake Street and on to the high school building, where their first stop was in an office labeled Richard Janeway, Principal.

It only took ten minutes for word of a possible problem down by the waterfront to reach Pete Blackwell of the Southport police. In less than three more minutes he had arrived at the scene of the middle of the night rendezvous by the poplar tree.

Pete was one of only two members of the small Southport police force, and in his fourteen months on the force he had seen only one other dead body. That man's death had been an accident. The man at the bottom of the poplar tree had not died an accidental death. He had been stabbed in the heart.

"Chief," he said when his call was answered, "we've got a dead man down near the public beach at the foot of Lake Street. He's been stabbed. Looks to me as if he took it right in the heart. Anyway, he bled a lot. I think you should get down here if you can."

Pete listened to what the police chief had to say.

"No, there's no wallet on him. Just a pack of cigarettes and a lighter. Oh, and about a buck and a half in change."

More listening.

"Okay. Anything you want me to do?"

Apparently not, because Pete shut off his cell and took a seat on the ground to wait for the chief and whoever else needed to see the body and arrange for it to be removed from the beach.

It didn't take long for Steve Bellman, the chief of police in Southport, to arrive, announce his tentative belief that the man had been killed only a few hours earlier, and supervise the removal of the victim's body. Southport had been the scene of very few crimes in Steve's short tenure, and none had involved a violent death. This one was likely to be a major challenge. He decided to give Sheriff Kelleher a call and alert her to what had happened. It wasn't that he was reluctant to conduct his own investigation. But the sheriff had had a lot of experience with murders since taking over law enforcement in Cumberland County. She'd appreciate being informed of this one. Or would she?

CHAPTER 11

Carol arrived at her office earlier than usual. Her list of to-do items was long, and she feared that it would be even longer by day's end. Somebody had to talk with Eddie's boss at the bakery. Eddie's belongings, now stored in Simon Ostrowski's locker, had to be gone through. The other people on Parsons' list had to be contacted. There was Parsons himself; she wanted to hear him reconstruct the boating accident for her and pass along his impressions of Eddie French's trial. She'd heard it all before, of course, but that had been back in the fall. Carol would have liked to handle all of these tasks herself. She found it hard to delegate, but she knew she had no choice.

She had started to draw up a list of assignments to give to her officers when the phone rang. Ms. Franks had taken a couple of hours off to help her mother with some problem or other, so Carol answered the phone herself.

"This is Sheriff Kelleher," she said.

"Carol? I didn't expect you to be taking calls yourself. This is Bellman down in Southport."

"Oh, good morning, Steve. Just happened I was closest to the phone. To what do I owe the pleasure?"

"Hardly a pleasure, but something happened last night I thought you should hear about. I didn't hear about it myself until a short time ago. Some guy got stabbed to death down on the town beach early this morning. We got the word because a couple of kids saw the body on their way to school. It's my problem, not yours, but I figured you'd be interested."

"What an awful way to start a week, Steve. I can empathize. Is there something you'd like me to do?"

"Not that I can think of, but I know you've got another murder on your plate. That business involving Eddie French. Heard about it just last Saturday. Anyway, there's no reason to think this has anything to do with your case, none at all. We don't even know who the guy is. But I guess you should know, just on the odd chance the two are related."

50

"I'm not sure whether I should thank you or not. Frankly, I can't imagine that this has anything to do with the French affair, but I'm willing to suspend judgment. Stabbed you say, victim unknown. How old would you say he is?"

She heard the police chief say something to someone else in his office. When he came back on the line he hazarded a guess that the victim was around 40. They discussed the matter for a few minutes, then both excused themselves to attend to the busy day they both faced.

Carol didn't waste any time ruminating on this bit of bad news from Southport. Bellman's murder victim - she'd think of him as X - was his responsibility, not hers. She had her hands full as it was, and there was no reason why she should start worrying about some possible link between the two cases. The Southport stabbing sounded to her like an after bar hours drunken brawl that had gone bad. Nothing like a killing on a power boat, disguised to make it look like a suicide.

Lake traffic was still modest, so the department's patrol boat was only in use intermittently. Which meant that Officer Parsons was not out on the lake that morning. Carol checked the duty board to see where he was, and as it happened he was only about four miles away, answering a call about a minor problem which was unlikely to tie him up for more than another fifteen minutes.

"Bill," she said when she made contact with him, "when you finish what you're doing, I'd appreciate it if you'd come back to the office. I want to pick your brains about that boating accident French was involved in last fall. Okay?"

"Sure. I should be there within the half hour. Just make sure the coffee pot's been refilled. The wind's darn cold out here."

Carol used the time to make a call to Bert Shane, one of the names on Parsons' list. Shane had been identified as the landlord who had rented the Woodpecker Lane house to Eddie French, which meant that he was also the person responsible for evicting French.

"I'm Sheriff Kelleher, and I'm calling about an Edwin French." she said when Shane came on the line. "You represent the Hutchinson Company, right?"

"I do. What's this about French?"

"I believe he rented one of your places on Woodpecker Lane and was evicted from it within the last couple of weeks. Am I correct?"

"Right. I remember because he's the only eviction we've had in quite a few months, maybe a year."

"I need some more precise information than I have, Mr. Shane. Can you tell me just when it was that he rented the house and when he vacated it? And why he was evicted?"

"This is a bit irregular, sheriff. I don't understand what the problem is. Has French filed a complaint against us? We did it all by the book, gave him lots of notice."

"The problem is that Mr. French is dead," Carol said. "We knew nothing about him, where he lived, that he'd been evicted, nothing. Not until he died last week. All I'm doing is filling in the blanks."

"Sorry to hear he's dead, but I don't see how this involves us."

"I have no reason to believe it does. Like I said, I'm just trying to get a picture of a man I'd never even heard of until a few days ago."

"Sounds like there's some mystery about his death."

"That's what we're working on," she said, being deliberately evasive. "So I'd appreciate it if you could help us with a couple of facts. I presume you have a file."

"Give me a minute," Shane said. She could hear the sound of the phone being laid on the desk. Had Shane been annoyed and shown it by slamming the phone down harder than was necessary?

"Okay, here it is," he said after a long minute. "He rented the place from us effective November 19 last fall. The place was furnished - nothing fancy, but what I'd call basic comfortable. The rent was $600 a month. He'd given us a down payment plus the first month. That's it. We sent him reminders, then a warning of what would happen if he didn't pay up. But he never even tried to negotiate a deal to buy himself some time. Weird. Most people, they have money problems they try to get us to modify the contract. We never heard from the guy. We had no choice."

"Did you talk with him?"

"A couple of times," was Shane's answer.

"When was the last time?"

"Back when he signed the papers, when we gave him the keys."

"That would have been in November?"

"Yeah, the day he took occupancy."

"How come you didn't try to see what was the matter when he fell behind in the rent?"

"No need. He knew what was in the contract. We mailed him notices."

"But what if there was some good reason why he didn't meet his monthly payments? What if something had happened to him? Say he'd died during the winter?" Carol asked.

"But he didn't, did he? You just said he passed away only last week."

Carol decided she was glad she didn't have to deal with Bert Shane on a regular basis.

"So you weren't the one who locked him out, took his key back, anything like that?"

"I think it was Judy who went over to the place. It would have been a week ago tomorrow. But he'd already removed his personal stuff. Left the keys on the kitchen table along with a note telling Hutchinson's to go fuck itself."

"I'm going to send one of my men around to your office to get all of the documents in French's file," Carol said. "The contract, copies of the notices you sent to him about non-payment of rent, all of your correspondence with him. In the meanwhile, I appreciate your time."

Carol was careful to return the phone to its cradle gently. No need to sound as angry as she felt. Perhaps Shane would now be worried that he hadn't handled the matter properly. What if he had failed to meet every single one of his legal obligations? What if he had cut corners? Let him stew, she thought.

Officer Parsons was at her door not more than five minutes later.

"Hi, Bill. I see you got yourself some coffee. Think I'll have one, too." She disappeared for a moment and returned with her 'Crooked Lake Is for Lovers' mug.

"No way of knowing whether French's death is related to the boating accident," she said as she settled into her chair. "I can't imagine why it would be, but it's part of French's life history, so I guess I'd better bring myself up to speed on it. Why don't you just tell me all about it. Forget that I was here last fall and ought to know the whole story. Forget that you've already written a lot of it down for me. I'd like to just sit and listen. Maybe you'll say something that'll give me an idea. Okay?"

"Sure, but remember there are people who can give you a better account than I can. The judge for one."

"No, not a better account, Bill, just a different one. I want your impressions of the whole affair, from beginning to end. Make that from beginning to right now."

Parsons proceeded to tell the sheriff what she presumably already knew. On September 23rd Eddie French had driven to the Crooked Lake boat launch site at the state park and launched his old Four Winns for what he described as an escape from his problems. He claimed that he was trying to distance himself from an increasingly difficult home situation and that there was no better way to do that than to motor around the lake. He took his boat down the west lake arm toward the end of the bluff, and then circled back toward West Branch. When French headed north along the west bluff road he approached a group of people who were sunning and enjoying an afternoon drink on a dock on Clappers Point. According to French, some of those on the dock waved at him as he passed. It was then that French's boat struck a boy named Jordan Kingsbury who had been diving for golf balls that his sister was throwing out into the lake from the dock.

According to boating regulations, a boat cannot exceed a speed of five miles per hour when closer than 200 feet to the shore or a dock. It was impossible to know just how fast the Four Winns was going; French insisted that he was obeying the speed limit, whereas the Kingsbury family was sure he was traveling faster. There was no question, however, that the Four Winns was definitely within 200 feet of the dock. Jordan's little sister Susie would not have been able to throw golf balls as far as 200 feet; moreover, the lake was much too deep at that distance for a diver to recover a golf ball unless he was wearing scuba diving equipment. Young Kingsbury wore only a pair of swimming trunks. Boating regulations also stipulate that boats must remain at least 100 feet from where someone is diving. Clearly French was much closer than that to Jordan Kingsbury. However, Kingsbury had not displayed a 'diver down' flag, so there was no way French could have known that somebody was diving near his boat.

"And so," Carol said, "lacking incontrovertible evidence that French was in violation of the boating regs, the judge had no choice but to dismiss the claim that he was responsible for the boy's death."

"Not everyone agreed that Judge Dietrich had no choice," Parsons reminded her. "Joe Kingsbury was convinced that French was guilty of reckless manslaughter."

"I remember," Carol said, shaking her head. "Kingsbury felt betrayed by Dietrich. First he loses his only son, then the man who killed him gets off without so much as a fine."

"I've been on and around the lake since I was a boy. We've had our share of accidents, but nothing quite so sad as that one. If I was Kingsbury, I doubt I'd ever get over it. Losing my son like that. My God, the kid was only thirteen."

"Did you have the impression that the judge was wrong?"

"That's what's so hard. Your heart tells you French has to pay, somehow, for what happened. But there was no proof he was speeding, the boy didn't have a diver's flag - how can you throw the book at French just because he accidentally ran into young Kingsbury? Of course French is dead now, but I'll bet he had nightmares about killing that kid right up until the time he got killed himself."

"We'll never know. What about Kingsbury? It's my impression that he wasn't ready to let Dietrich's decision be the last word."

"He continued to press his case for months," Parsons said. "Kept writing letters to the *Gazette*, even to the Corning and Geneva papers. I'm sure he tried to keep the issue alive wherever he went. Friend of mine who knows him says he couldn't bring himself to talk about anything else. Didn't matter whether he was having dinner with friends, going to a Lions Club meeting in Yates Center, you name it. It was an obsession for him. Word was he wanted to impeach Dietrich."

"Take him off the bench?"

"That's what I hear. Trouble is he didn't have any idea how the system works. It was just a matter of gut feelings, not a well thought out plan to see justice done. It got to the point where it wasn't so much justice as revenge that he wanted."

Parsons' tone of voice said as clearly as words that he was sympathetic both to Joe Kingsbury's feelings and to the judicial dilemma with which Judge Dietrich had been confronted.

"Did you ever hear anything about Kingsbury and French?" Carol asked. "I mean Kingsbury was angry about Dietrich's decision, but how about Eddie French?"

"Well, of course he blamed French for killing his son. Seems French tried to see him, tell him how awful he felt about what had happened. But Kingsbury refused to talk to him. But then when Dietrich made his decision, Kingsbury transferred his hatred to the judge. After all, there was nothing Eddie could have done to make things right, but Dietrich could have if he'd found him guilty and given him jail time. I'm sure Kingsbury has never forgiven French, but my impression is that it was the judge he really hated. Like I said, word is he's still obsessed about it. You ought to talk to him."

"I intend to. And to Dietrich. I think the judge will be frank with me. I should have had this conversation last fall after he rendered his opinion, just never got around to it. No idea what Kingsbury might be willing to say about Eddie French. Probably figures justice has finally been done."

Later, as Carol reflected on what Officer Parsons had told her, she found herself wondering about Joe Kingsbury. She didn't doubt that he hated the judge. But was her colleague right about Kingsbury's feelings toward Eddie French? Might he also have harbored a deep, festering hatred of French, a hatred strong enough that he had finally taken justice into his own hands at the Lakeshore Marina?

CHAPTER 12

Officer Barrett parked in front of storage locker number 28 and surveyed the area. There was no other vehicle in sight, other than the occasional car or truck on the Seneca Valley Road off in the distance. Ostrowski had obviously wanted to come with him, but he had other things he had to do and he'd been reluctant to ask a member of the sheriff's department to come back another day. Barrett was pleased to be alone. He could take his time and not be bothered by the owner of the locker talking to him and offering advice.

The sheriff had told him what she most hoped to find, but had not sounded very optimistic. In any event, his orders were to bring back anything that looked as if it might shed light on the life Eddie French had been living and, more importantly, on the people with whom he had associated.

Whoever had killed French had made no attempt to conceal his victim's identity. To have done so would have been pointless, inasmuch as French was from the area and was widely known, less because he had lots of friends than because of the publicity surrounding the fatal boating accident. The killer had presumably been more interested in creating the impression that Eddie's death was a suicide. This did not mean, however, that the killer had not gone through wallet and pockets, searching for anything that could link him - or her - to Eddie, anything that would have to be removed from the body. What if such a search had found Eddie's key to the storage locker, and the killer had already gone through Eddie's belongings? Or what if Ostrowski was the killer? The sheriff was inclined to dismiss these possibilities. Barrett hoped she was right and that he would find something of interest in the locker.

The door seemed to be slightly warped, but it responded to a hard push and Barrett found himself in a conventionally structured storage room, deeper than it was wide. It was obvious that neither Ostrowski nor French had stored many things there. Eddie's belongings, according to Ostrowski, were to the right, and it was immediately apparent that it wouldn't take long to go through the possessions of the late employee of *Breads to Go*. There were two large cardboard boxes with fitted covers that were filled with clothes. A third somewhat smaller box contained a mismatched set of dishes and cheap silverware. Behind them was a single drawer file cabinet that was nearly empty. Sheets, two blankets, a firm pillow, and a variety of towels had been stuffed into several large green garbage bags. The only appliances were a small pre-flat screen TV, a desk lamp still sporting a 40 watt light bulb, a surprisingly modern clock radio, and a small microwave oven. An old dopp kit sat on top of the file cabinet, and a manila folder had fallen down behind the cabinet, spilling its contents across the floor toward Ostrowski's side of the locker.

It made for a depressing snapshot of Eddie French's life, at least the Woodpecker Lane portion of it. How had Eddie lived those last few days of his life after his eviction from his house? Where had he slept? He had apparently sought out the boat at the Lakeshore Marina for his final night on earth. Or had he? Perhaps his killer had put him on that boat. After all, the bakery truck he had been driving had not been at the marina when they found his body. Where was it? Barrett knew that, in all probability, the sheriff was talking with Buddy Stearns, manager of the bakery, that very morning. Stearns wouldn't be able to answer most of her questions about Eddie. Hopefully, though, he would know something about the whereabouts of the truck.

The most likely sources of information were the file cabinet and the contents of the manila folder. He had been hoping that he'd find a laptop, but there was no sign of one. It might be in the file drawer or buried under the clothes or the bedding, although he doubted it. It was with no sense of enthusiasm that he began a methodical search of Eddie French's belongings.

He gathered up the papers, trying to keep them in the order suggested by their position on the floor. Logically the folder should have been in the file drawer. Perhaps Eddie had taken it out to add something to it. Or withdrawn something from it, and then for some reason failed to return it to its place in the cabinet. Barrett decided to defer examining the papers in the folder until he had checked the contents of the drawer. They were disappointingly few, and there was no laptop among them.

He pulled the door closed behind him and climbed into his patrol car with the manila folder and the three other folders from the file cabinet. The papers in the manila folder - and there were thirteen of them - all seemed to pertain to the bakery. At least all but two had a *Breads to Go* letterhead and appeared to be invoices. The figures meant nothing to him, but they did say something about the establishments the bakery serviced. Two of the other folders were empty and bore no label to tell him for what they had been intended. The third seemed to be about Eddie's personal finances. It contained several bills, a checkbook, and a couple of sheets of what looked like simple arithmetic - columns of figures that had been totaled, others that had been amended or lined out. Unfortunately, Eddie had not been a meticulous record keeper. The log of checks cashed and deposits made was spotty. There were no entries for some of the check numbers and no effort had been made to maintain a day by day balance. The only entry that interested Barrett referred to a $500 deposit, but it was not dated and there was no mention of the source.

Barrett turned his attention to the one piece of paper from the cabinet that had not been in a file folder. It consisted of three names - first names only - and what were obviously phone numbers. Two of those names, Simon and Buddy, rang a bell. Simon was presumably Ostrowski, whose storage locker he was currently visiting. Buddy was probably Buddy Stearns, manager of the bakery where Eddie had worked. It would not be difficult to verify those names by checking the phone numbers. He had no idea whom the third name, JP, referred to. He, too, could probably be identified with the help of the phone number, although it wouldn't be quite as easy as looking up Ostrowski and Stearns in the directory.

It was time to go through the other items in the locker. Barrett took the folders off the seat and put them on the floor of the car. Less conspicuous that way, or so he rationalized this seemingly unnecessary precaution. But he also locked the car and set about the task of rummaging through the cardboard boxes and green garbage bags. It was a job that didn't take much time. As he expected, there was no laptop buried under the blankets or the work shirts. Indeed, he found nothing but clothes, bedding and towels. Not, that is, until he decided on one final search through pockets. All it produced was a small folded scrap of paper. On it was a very brief message: 'Call JP.'

Who was JP? Somebody whose name (or initials) had appeared twice among Eddie's things. Barrett wished there had been a date on the scrap of paper reminding Eddie to call JP. For all he knew, the paper had been in Eddie's jeans' pocket for weeks. But what if he had written the reminder more recently? Shortly before his death? If so, what had he wanted to call JP about? And had he ever made the call?

Barrett didn't know whether he had learned anything important that morning. He doubted it. One thing he did know, however. Carol's first order of business upon hearing his report would be discovering the identity of JP.

CHAPTER 13

"Have you heard about Eddie French?" Carol directed the question to Buddy Stearns, manager of the *Breads to Go* bakery. They were sitting in Stearns' small office in a large cinder block building a little more than two miles below Southport. The pleasant odor of baking bread helped to compensate for the uncomfortable chair and the unusually bad coffee.

"Other than your officer's call saying you wanted to talk to me about him, not much. I haven't seen him in nearly a week. In fact, he hasn't come to work this week."

"You don't know what's happened to him?"

"He's probably got a bug of some kind. It's this damned weather, cold, damp. Helluva poor excuse for spring. He should have paid me the courtesy of a call, though."

Carol studied the man across from her. Average in every sense of the word. Average height, average weight, a head of dirty blond hair and a mustache that could use a trim. Stearns could have been anywhere from 50 to 60. Probably nearer the latter. The limp he displayed when he walked could be the result of an accident, the onset of arthritis, or any one of the many ills flesh is heir to.

"I thought perhaps word had gotten out about Mr. French," she said. "Apparently it hasn't reached the bakery. He's dead, Mr. Stearns. Died last Friday night."

"I'll be damned. Your colleague didn't say anything about him being dead. I figured you wanted to talk to me about that business at *The Cedar Post*. What happened to him?"

"If we'd been having this conversation 48 hours ago, I'd have told you he committed suicide. Now we're not so sure. It looks as if somebody shot him."

"No shit? Somebody shot Eddie? Why in hell would anybody want to go and do that?"

"You think that's pretty unlikely?"

"It makes no sense," Stearns said, shaking his head. "I mean, you'd have to have known Eddie. He always kept to himself, didn't bother anybody."

Then another possibility occurred to him.

"It wasn't some bar brawl, was it? But no, that can't be. It wouldn't have looked like suicide, would it. What do you think happened?"

"That's what we're investigating. It's why I'm here. And why I need to ask you a few questions."

"Why do you need to question me?" Stearns asked.

"It's because, as you just said, Mr. French was something of a loner. So we need to talk to people who did know him. And you seem to be one of those people. He worked for you. From what I hear, you knew him well enough to trust him with one of your bakery's trucks. Let him drive it home at night. And you knew him well enough that you didn't fire him after he pulled a gun on the bartender at *The Cedar Post*. Most employers would regard that as totally unacceptable behavior by an employee. Not to mention illegal."

Stearns' face reflected both wariness and respect for the sheriff. She had obviously done her homework.

"I know it seems odd, but it was because he was the kind of guy he was that I felt comfortable helping him out. And he did need help. He'd gone through a bad divorce. His ex-wife was vindictive - I think that's the word for it. Anyway, she stuck him with big alimony payments, didn't like him near his kids. He was in a real bind, thanks to her. Had to sell his car just to scrape by. The least I could do was let him have the use of the delivery truck. It was no big deal. Otherwise I'd have lost a reliable employee. Eddie needed a break and I gave him one."

Carol considered asking Stearns what his terms were for gas and mileage, but chose to focus instead on *The Cedar Post* episode.

"One break, yes. But you seem to have given Mr. French a second break. How could you forgive an employee who holds up a local restaurant? That's a crime, Mr. Stearns."

"Ginny Smith, she's the bartender at *The Post*, she made it clear that Eddie never intended to use the gun. He was just having some serious problems, felt kind of desperate, didn't know what to do. I know Ginny, you probably do, too. I trust her judgment. Like

I told you, Eddie's ex-wife was really sticking it to him. He was in trouble, and it wasn't his fault."

It was pretty much what Carol had expected. The delivery truck she could understand. The bar holdup was far more troubling, especially for a sheriff sworn to uphold the law.

"By the way, how did you learn about what happened at *The Cedar Post*? I don't suppose Mr. French told you."

"A guy named Bill Grandy told me the next morning. He was there, saw it happen. I called Ginny right away. She confirmed it, but she made it clear that Eddie was just a troubled young man, that he needed help, not kicked out of a job, sent to jail."

"So Ginny Smith was responsible for the fact that nothing was done about the holdup?"

"Well, I guess I did what she thought was right. She was in a better position to know than I was."

"If she had decided to press charges, what would you have done?"

Buddy Stearns looked at his desk as if he might find the answer to the sheriff's question somewhere among the papers there.

"I'd probably have gone along. At least I think I would. Thank goodness, I didn't have to make that decision. Of course he's dead now, so I suppose you could argue that justice was done."

"I'm afraid I can't agree with you there," Carol said. "Mr. French's offense didn't carry the death penalty. In fact, New York State doesn't have a death penalty. Justice will be done when whoever killed Mr. French is convicted."

"You said it might not be suicide. Are you really convinced that somebody killed Eddie?"

Carol had determined that this time she wouldn't keep up the pretense of suicide when she knew it had been murder. It surprised her how easily she could slip back into calculated ambivalence.

"Let's just say that I'd prefer that it had been suicide, tragic as that would be. But we know enough to be virtually certain that somebody shot him. We are treating the case as murder."

"That's terrible, isn't it? Poor guy, all his problems, then on top of it all he gets offed by some weirdo. Life sure can be a crap shoot, can't it?"

Carol thought this was a strange way to put it. Eddie French's killing had hardly been the outcome of what Stearns referred to as a crap shoot. Nor was it likely that the killer was a weirdo. Somebody had tracked Eddie to a power boat at Lakeshore Marina and left him there as an apparent suicide. It had not been the work of a weirdo.

"Did you know that Mr. French had been evicted from his house in Yates Center shortly before his death?"

"He had?" Stearns sounded surprised.

"Not only was he having trouble meeting alimony and child support obligations, he had also fallen behind in his rent. Far enough that his landlord eventually evicted him."

"Good God, poor guy never got a break, did he?"

Yes, Carol thought, you gave him a break. Twice. They just weren't enough.

"I'm sure it helped that he had the use of the delivery truck. He'd really have been up a creek without it."

Carol proceeded to ask a question that had been bothering her: where is the delivery truck? It had not been at the Lakeshore Marina, which raised a further question: how had Eddie gotten to the marina?

"By the way, do you know where the truck is now?"

"No idea," Buddy said. "I thought he still had it. It wasn't parked where he'd been living?"

"I'm afraid not. You're sure Mr. French didn't bring it back here to the bakery?"

"Why would he have done that? Then he wouldn't have had any transportation."

"But you're sure it isn't here?"

"I don't usually pay attention to the vehicles. That's Stew's job. Let me give him a buzz."

Stew, the motor pool man for *Breads to Go*, confirmed what Stearns had said. The truck Eddie French had been using had not been at the bakery since the previous Wednesday when he had last stopped to take on his delivery orders for the day.

"I think you'd better give me the vehicle's identification number, license number, any other info that'll help us find the truck. Given the circumstances, we'll want to give it a thorough going over when we find it. Just leave the search for it to us."

"Sure, whatever you say. By the way, where did you say you found Eddie?"

"I didn't. But it was at the Lakeshore Marina." But she didn't want to elaborate, so she changed the subject. "Mr. French was involved in a very bad accident last fall. Ran over and killed a young boy with his power boat. I'm sure you know about it. Tell me, did you hire him before the accident or after?"

"It was after. Not until November, I think."

Stearns looked uncomfortable.

"But Eddie wasn't responsible," he said. "The judge ruled it was an accident. No way Eddie would have known the kid was diving. He'd been getting a bum rap for what happened, I figured there was no need to turn him down when he applied for a job with the bakery."

So, Carol thought, you gave Eddie another break. That makes three - the job, the use of the delivery truck, the decision not to fire him after the holdup at *The Cedar Post*.

"I'm sure Mr. French was grateful to you for all the support you gave him," Carol, said. She wondered why she kept referring to him as Mr. French, which in turn prompted her next question. "Did your concern for his welfare ever lead to a more personal relationship? I mean, did you do things together socially? Ever go out for a drink at the end of the day?"

"Eddie didn't do much socializing. Marge and me, we have our own circle of friends, and Eddie was caught up in that messy divorce. I think he wanted to be alone. It wouldn't have worked anyway. We had different interests. Know what I mean?"

"Maybe you can help me there. Just what were his interests?"

Stearns obviously hadn't thought much about Eddie's interests.

"I guess I don't really know. It doesn't look like he had much time to develop a hobby."

"One more question, the obvious one. Can you think of anyone who might have killed Mr. French? Anyone who might have been an enemy?"

"No one I can think of. Eddie just wasn't the kind of guy who made enemies. Too low-keyed, if you know what I mean."

Carol knew what he meant, but it didn't mean Eddie hadn't had enemies. His ex-wife was hardly fond of him. Nor was Joe Kingsbury, father of the boy Eddie had killed in the boating accident. For all she knew, there were others. Carol realized that she still knew very little about the man who had turned up dead at Lakeshore Marina on a chilly morning in late March.

CHAPTER 14

She wished she had paid more attention to the boating accident that had claimed the life of the late Jordan Kingsbury. She knew a lot about it, of course. But it hadn't been high on her professional agenda.

There had been good reasons for that, beginning with the fact that she had been down in the city when the accident occurred. Kevin had urged her to take a week of leave that was coming to her, the leave that was to have been their honeymoon until the discovery of Dana Ivers' body in the attic of Hawk's Nest had called her home from Italy. He had been persuasive, and she had taken those leave days and joined him in his city apartment. They had gone museuming, taken in a concert, dined at a couple of posh restaurants. She had even sat in on one of his classes at the college, and come away from the experience convinced that he was really good at what he did, even if she had found some of the academic jargon off-putting. Jordan Kingsbury had been killed in the boating accident the very day she had flown off to the city.

Unlike the Ivers case, there had been no reason to rush back to the lake this time. There was no 'whodunit' to solve. There was no question as to what had happened, who had been killed, who had killed him. It was simply a matter of determining whether Eddie French was responsible, and there was nothing Carol could have done that would have answered that question. So she had let Bridges and Parsons represent the department as the case unfolded.

It had unfolded with a grand jury investigation which returned a true bill, leading to the trial in which French had ultimately been exonerated by Judge Dietrich. The decision to indict could have gone either way, but she had assumed that the terrible loss of a child's life and the testimony of the Kingsbury family members who had been witness to the tragedy were sufficient to meet the relaxed standards of the grand jury process.

Nonetheless, she was regretting that she had not spoken with the Kingsbury family. Or with French, for that matter. Nor had she discussed the case with Judge Dietrich. She had, of course, expressed her condolences to the Kingsburys, and she had placed a courtesy call to the judge. But unlike the all too frequent Crooked Lake murders that had occupied so much of her time since becoming sheriff, she had been essentially uninvolved in the boating accident case.

Now she would have to involve herself. Not for the purpose of reopening the case. The verdict, she was convinced, had been the right one. But she was now interested in learning all she could about the late Eddie French, and inasmuch as the boating accident had been such an important episode in his life over the past year, she would need to talk with people who had been a part of it. What had been their opinion of Eddie? What could they tell her that might help her to understand his death? His murder?

She could have started with Joe Kingsbury. Parsons had been sure that he still blamed Eddie for his son's death, but that much of his anger had been transferred to Judge Dietrich following his finding that Eddie was not guilty of negligence leading to manslaughter. Carol wasn't quite sure why she chose to see Dietrich first. Perhaps it was due to a reluctance to reopen Kingsbury's old, slow-to-heal wound. But it was at 3 pm, not long after her meeting with Buddy Stearns at the bakery, that she was ushered into the judge's office in Cumberland.

"Sheriff Kelleher, it's good to see you. How have you been?"

"Hello, Tom." Carol shook the judge's hand and let him steer her to a chair in a window well looking out over the neatly manicured lawn of the Rest Haven Cemetery. It was a pleasant view, but an unfortunate reminder of the reason she had come to see the judge.

"I gather from your message that you're here to talk about that terrible boating accident. It isn't my favorite topic of conversation, as I'm sure you can appreciate. But I'm glad to discuss the case with you if you wish. Perhaps you can tell me why you're interested. I mean, why now?"

"It's because Eddie French is dead," Carol said. "In all likelihood, he was shot to death just a few days ago."

It was obvious that word of Eddie's death had not reached Judge Dietrich.

"That's terrible. How come I hadn't heard about it?"

"My assistant should have told you when she made the appointment, but it's really my fault. We were treating it as a suicide, but then Doc Crawford confirmed that someone killed him. I'm just getting around to telling people who would be interested just what happened. We haven't issued an official press release yet."

"Just when I think I'm past the point when I'll be shocked by the day's news, something like this happens. You have any leads?"

"Not yet. I'm trying to get a sense of who French was, why someone might have wanted to kill him. It was no accident. Whoever did it went to a lot of trouble, almost had us believing it was a suicide. So I'm naturally interested in the boating accident."

"You think maybe Joe Kingsbury did this?"

"No, but one of the few things I know about French at this point is his involvement in the death of young Kingsbury. I can imagine that the father might have harbored strong feelings against the man who killed his son. Might have, you understand. Anyway, we have to start somewhere, so I thought I should talk to you."

"I see. Have you talked to Kingsbury?"

"I'll be talking with him soon, of course. He'll think I'm zeroing in on him, which isn't true. It's just that I don't know anyone else who might have thought he had a reason to kill French. I was hoping you could help me get a picture of Kingsbury before I see him."

"I may not be a reliable source, Carol," Judge Dietrich said. "Kingsbury was practically beside himself when I handed down my verdict last year. I can understand that he'd be disappointed, even angry that I didn't find French guilty of something. After all, he'd lost a son, and a son he obviously loved very dearly. But he was furious with me, as you may remember. I've got a pretty thick hide, but I don't think I can remember any other case quite like it. He started to harass me, calling me at all hours. First he tried to get me to change my mind. When I made it clear I couldn't do that, it became personal. He attacked me for what I'd done. Or hadn't done. Normally I'd have taken steps to put a stop to it, but I actually felt sorry for him, for his family. So I tolerated it, tried to reason with him. Eventually he stopped bugging me directly and started that impeachment nonsense. He'd become obsessed, really obsessed. Of course nothing came of it and it sort of petered out.

But you can see why I might not be as objective as I should be when it comes to Joe Kingsbury."

"I know how hard it must have been for you, Tom, but I trust your judgment. What I need is your impression of Kingsbury's behavior toward French. What you observed during the trial, whether there was ever any indication that Kingsbury might have felt as vindictive toward French as he did toward you."

Judge Dietrich considered it.

"I guess you could say he looked daggers at French during the trial, but there were no outbursts in court, nothing like that. About what you could expect. Later, French talked to me once, said he'd called Kingsbury, told him he felt guilty, no matter what the verdict was. But apparently Kingsbury didn't want to talk about it, and French never said he'd been threatened. So I told him that Kingsbury was still trying to cope with his loss, that he was having a hard time stopping grieving. I urged him to be patient. Anyway, I never heard from him again, and when Kingsbury stepped up his harassment of me I figured he'd decided to take out his frustration on me instead of French. It sounds like I should have paid more attention, doesn't it? Damn it, I don't like the sound of this."

"Look, I have no reason to think Joe Kingsbury killed French. He'd had many months to come to terms with the fact that his son was dead. Months in which to cool down. Besides, I have a hard time buying the idea of a revenge killing."

"I wouldn't be so sure. If memory serves me correctly, you've had a couple of what I'd call revenge killings right here since you inherited your dad's job. What about the murder that put an end to that Brae Loch opera? Or John Britingham's death?"

Carol started to argue that neither case quite met her definition of revenge, but thought better of it.

"Like I said, I don't want you to think I suspect Kingsbury of killing French. I don't know Kingsbury, and I didn't know French. For all I know, he had a lot of enemies. So let's leave Kingsbury out of this for now. What was your impression of French?"

"He seemed to be a decent chap who'd had one of those awful experiences that you never really get over. He was really broken up about it. I think his attorney had to tell him to stop blaming himself. But I think he chose a bench trial instead of a jury trial because he feared that public sympathy would lie with the Kingsburys. In any event, it wasn't that complicated a case from a legal point of view."

"Did any of French's personal problems come out in the course of the trial?"

"It was suggested that he was so distraught over the breakup of his marriage that he was distracted, wasn't paying attention to whether someone was in the water. But that didn't go anywhere. Too speculative."

"Any discussion of his jobs, the fact that he'd been let go by a couple of employers?"

Dietrich shook his head.

"I wouldn't have allowed that. They'd have been attacking his character, and it would have been irrelevant to the matter at hand. No, the case wasn't about French's life or his persona. It was about what he'd done or hadn't done when he drove past the Kingsbury's dock."

Carol had come to the realization that Judge Dietrich wasn't going to be of much help.

"One last question, Tom. Any advice for me when I talk with Joe Kingsbury?"

"Nothing you wouldn't have thought of yourself. I'd bet it won't take much to get him riled up again. Hard to say how he'll react to news French has been killed, though. It's not likely he'll shed any tears, but he's smart enough to know that you might suspect him. So I wouldn't expect him to tell you how thrilled he is to know French got what was coming to him."

When Carol left the judge's office, her enthusiasm for the meeting with Joe Kingsbury was even less than it had been when she arrived.

CHAPTER 15

Her pursuit of Eddie French's killer was on her mind as she left Judge Dietrich's office, but the third person Carol saw as she headed back to the sheriff's office on State Street was a man she had considered a suspect in another murder case the previous summer. It was Russell Coover, former caretaker of the old Hawk's Nest mansion and leader of a rag tag upstate militia group. She hadn't seen him since they had wrapped up the Ivers case in August, but here he was, walking directly toward her. The smile on his face told her that he had seen her. And that it was going to be difficult to avoid a conversation. She hoped it would be brief.

"My friend the sheriff," Coover said. He had positioned himself on the sidewalk so that she had no choice but to stop.

"Hello, Mr. Coover. I don't believe I've seen you since last summer."

"I'm sure you missed me." His words, his tone of voice, made it clear that he felt he had the upper hand in what he imagined to be a game of one-upmanship.

"Well, that's probably an exaggeration," Carol said. "Too busy, you know."

"Yes, but I know how much you'd hoped that you could collar me for killing that woman in the attic. Ivers, I think her name was."

Carol turned on a reluctant smile.

"My department is always interested in nabbing the guilty, Mr. Coover, and you weren't guilty."

"You're right about that. I had nothing to do with what happened to the poor woman. But there's something you ought to know. Want to guess what I did do?"

Coover was looking very pleased with himself.

"If you want to tell me," Carol said.

"I spent a lot of time with her up in that attic. We didn't talk much, but we fucked like a couple of rabbits. That was a long time ago, wasn't it? What would you say, maybe eight years now?

Sorry I had to lie to you last summer, but I'm sure you understand."

Coover had, of course, vigorously and consistently denied any relationship with Ivers during the sheriff's investigation of her murder. Now he was getting a kick out of telling Carol all about it.

"It didn't matter, did it?" she responded. "Like I told you back then, our task is to solve crimes, not worry about what consenting adults do in their spare time."

"I like that," Coover said. "Our virtuous defenders of public order, always solicitous of the people's rights. Who you messing with now?"

Carol had had enough of Russell Coover.

"I'm sorry to have to cut this conversation short, but I'm really busy this afternoon. Got to get back to the office so I can mess with someone else. You have a good day."

She walked briskly past him in the direction of her office.

"You're welcome to stop by and see me. Any time." He addressed his parting comment to Carol's back. "You'll find me selling cars over at Craddock's Autos, but of course you already know that."

She had enough on her mind without having to dredge up memories of the Ivers case, especially Russell Coover's involvement in it. And he had been right. She would have liked him to have been guilty of that murder. Smug bastard. Bridges would not be surprised when she told him about her encounter with the self-appointed leader of Crooked Lake's edition of the militia movement. She wondered how Kevin would react.

When Carol got back to her desk, she was still irritated by the chance encounter with Coover. But she had to get it out of her mind, and Ms. Franks helped her to do so by reporting that she had a call from Steve Bellman, chief of police in Southport.

"Hi, Steve. What's the word on the guy you found down at the lakeside?"

"That's what I called about, Carol. There's no word. At least I don't have one. We still don't have any idea who he is. That's why I'm asking for your help. Your people cover a lot more territory than mine do, and you're better connected with the surrounding jurisdictions. I figured there's a chance one of your officers might recognize the guy. Odds aren't good, I suppose, but

I wonder if you'd be willing to help us. I hate to ask a favor, but the more people we have on the matter the better."

"No problem, Steve. I'll tell my men to make it a point to stop by, take a look at him. Have you talked to any of our neighbors? Geneva? Elmira?"

"I've made a few inquiries, but it's like I said, you know our neighbors a helluva lot better than I do. 'Course if Donegan was still here -"

He left the thought unfinished. Carol could appreciate Bellman's problem. He'd succeeded long-time Southport chief of police, Joe Donegan, only four months earlier, and she knew he was short staffed.

"We'll be glad to help. In fact, I'll pay you a visit myself first thing in the morning, then make a few calls. Tell me, did this man with no name have a car?"

She hesitated to ask the question. It would suggest that perhaps Bellman didn't know his job. But she needed to know, so she asked.

"There was no car near the beach where the body was found by those high school kids," Steve said. "He could have left it somewhere else, or the guy who killed him could have driven off in it. There's an awful lot of cars on the streets of Southport, Carol."

It won't be easy, Carol thought, but Bellman just might have to spend some time checking the license plates of all those cars on Southport streets. She certainly did not want her officers sidetracked by such an assignment.

Having wished Chief Bellman well, Carol turned her attention back to Eddie French. More specifically, she turned her attention to Officer Barrett's report on what he had found - and not found - in the storage locker on the Seneca Valley Road. It was a disappointing inventory. French had indeed been living on the margin. Moreover, he was either a very careless bookkeeper or had kept more important and more carefully preserved records somewhere else. But where? It was most likely that what Barrett had found was all there was to find, and it was not very helpful. She would have to talk to Buddy Stearns to find out if the $500 deposit noted in the checkbook was likely to be a wage payment from *Breads to Go*. The two references to someone with the initials JP were vaguely interesting, but she was doubtful that they would prove to be important. In any event, learning who JP was would probably be even more difficult than identifying the man who had been killed on the Southport beach.

It took all of two minutes to ascertain that Eddie's weekly paycheck, after deductions, was somewhat less than $500. Not by a lot, but less. Of course he might have deposited two checks totaling $500. Or the deposit might not have included a paycheck. Carol found it interesting that there had been only the one deposit. Perhaps he simply cashed his pay checks. There was a lot more research to do, beginning with a visit to Eddie's bank.

She was straightening up her desk and getting ready to head home when Bridges popped in through the door to the corridor.

"You don't look as if you're enjoying the day." He smiled, as if to say he wasn't serious. But he was right, and not just about the day. The investigation into Eddie French's death was not making much progress.

"Didn't realize it was that obvious," Carol said. "By the way, I ran into your bete noire, Coover, this afternoon. Pleasant chap, isn't he?"

"Not so I'd noticed. What's on his mind?"

"No idea. But he wanted me to know that he'd gotten the best of me in the Ivers investigation. Admitted he'd been sleeping with Dana, in spite of what he told me last summer."

"He didn't share plans for that revolution he's hatching, did he?"

"No, not a word, and I had no intention of encouraging him to talk about it."

"I don't trust him, Carol. Maybe we should make an effort to keep an eye on him. You know, sort of a low key surveillance. Nothing obvious."

"Come on, Sam. We're not the FBI. Or were you volunteering to tail him and tap his phone when you're off duty?"

It was Carol's turn to smile.

CHAPTER 16

Carrie Singletary closed the door behind her, and Kevin was taking stock of the young woman's progress on her thesis when the phone rang.

"Professor Whitman here."

"Hello, Kevin, it's Alice. I was hoping that you had no lunch plans and that we might break bread together at the faculty club."

It was Alice Lassiter, chairman of his department. They had never been close, and he didn't really care for her aggressive, almost peremptory style of leadership. Some of his colleagues believed it could be traced back to the abrupt and unpleasant end of her early and ill-considered marriage to a high school sweetheart. Kevin doubted it. In any event, it didn't matter. And he had no plans for lunch, so he decided to accept Alice's invitation.

"Sounds good to me. You name the time."

"Why don't you meet me there at one. The dean's meeting should be over by then."

Kevin arrived first and took a table for two next to the Madison honorees wall. It was nearly fifteen minutes later that Lassiter pulled out the chair across the table from him and sank into it. The dean's meeting must have been a difficult one, he thought.

"What a waste of time," she said. "Stewart doesn't know when to admit we've exhausted a subject. Any subject. I wish I had the balls to walk out."

She caught the eye of a waiter.

"I'd like a gibson," she said. "Dry."

Alice Lassiter was alleged to have had a gibson for lunch every day of her adult life. Kevin was inclined to believe that her problematic persona was due, not to her failed teenage marriage, but to the daily consumption of gin and vermouth. Or perhaps to the tiny cocktail onions.

"Sorry about the meeting. I have the feeling that our profession might be quite enjoyable if it weren't for all the meetings."

"I'm sure you're right about that," Lassiter agreed. "Thank God my term is coming to an end. I can really use a leave, and I think I have something refreshing lined up for next year."

"Glad to hear it. What's it going to be?"

"I'm optimistic about a small grant that will let me spend the year - well, at least one semester - in Salzburg."

"Sounds good. I hope the grant comes through."

"Stewart has put in a word on my behalf. He's optimistic."

"Who's going to fill your shoes here?"

"I believe you are."

Kevin looked at her as if she'd taken leave of her senses.

"You can't be serious. Everybody knows I'm allergic to administration."

"So I've heard, but Stewart told me he's going to tap you. You know the system. We rotate the chair among the tenured faculty, and you're the only one left who hasn't had a turn."

"But there's no rule that says that's the way it has to be." Kevin was now sounding alarmed. "Francis wouldn't mind doing it again, I'm sure of that."

"Perhaps, but I think the dean has made up his mind. It's just a three year assignment."

The thought of three years as chairman of the Madison College music department immediately produced cognitive dissonance in Kevin's mind. It would mean not only administrative duties, but administrative duties the year around. There would be a small salary bump, of course, but there would be no long summer at the lake, no long weekends over the course of the academic year. What would happen to him and Carol? No, he thought, I must make it clear to the dean that he has to find someone else.

"Why haven't I heard anything about this before?" He looked suspiciously at Alice.

"You know our dean," she said. "He's not only slow to bring a meeting to closure, he's slow to make decisions. I think it was my push regarding the grant that forced him to think about my replacement."

"Well, thanks a lot. No, it's not your fault, but you know that I treasure my summers at the lake, especially now that I'm married to a woman who lives and works up there. I'm already sacrificing a lot of the pleasures of married life. Sticking me with the chairmanship would really be cruel and unusual punishment."

Alice smiled.

"We all make sacrifices, Kevin. You could ask your spouse to join you down here. I remember that you have a nice apartment, and you're a lot closer to the Met and opera. I'd think that would weigh pretty heavily in the balance. Anyway, I'm sure Stewart will be arranging a meeting with you any day now. And I'll be glad to walk you through some of the issues you'll be dealing with."

The waiter arrived with Alice's gibson and took their orders. Kevin was no longer hungry and settled for a bowl of the faculty club's famous southwestern chili.

As soon as he got back to his office, Kevin put through a call to Dean Stewart Coggins' office. There was no time to waste. If he didn't act quickly, he might be confronted with a dreadful fait accompli.

"Hi, it's Kevin Whitman in the music department," he said when the dean's secretary greeted him with a bright, chirpy hello. "I have an urgent need to see the dean. Do you suppose you could squeeze me in for ten or fifteen minutes this afternoon?"

"Unfortunately, Professor Whitman, that won't be possible. He just took off for the airport. It's a conference out in Chicago, and he won't be back until April 3rd."

Damn it, he thought, nearly giving voice to his frustration. And why April 3rd? He couldn't think of any reason why an academic conference needed to last that long.

"Then can you put me on his calendar just as soon as he returns?"

"Let me see." Kevin could hear her flipping the pages of what sounded like a large desk calendar. "I'm afraid he's pretty well tied up until the 6th. How about 10:45 on the 6th?"

Kevin knew that he had a class at that hour, but he couldn't let the matter wait any longer. He'd have his assistant take his class. First things first.

When he got home, he poured a beer and pulled out his cell for a call to Carol. She's not going to be happy about this, he said to himself. And then he caught himself and stopped punching in the cottage number. There was no need to ruin Carol's evening.

Perhaps he'd be able to change the dean's mind. After all, he had a perfectly good case. Even if he couldn't, there'd be enough time for them to bemoan their fate later. Instead of placing the call, Kevin retreated to the kitchen to see what if anything there was for supper. He'd talk to Carol in another couple of hours, after he'd calmed the anxiety that Alice Lassiter had stirred up. Tonight they'd talk about Crooked Lake's latest murder, not whether he might be dragooned into a term as chairman of the music department at Madison College.

CHAPTER 17

When Kevin did make his call to the cottage, he was delighted to find Carol in a mood to talk about Crooked Lake's most recent murder. It would take his mind off the dean's threat to their summer, and it meant that she wasn't worried about him wanting to get involved in her current case. Perhaps the investigation was going well this time; perhaps an arrest was even imminent.

"I assume," Carol said, "that you're busy implementing all those wonderful ideas you and your colleagues cooked up on the retreat, and I really don't want to hear about it. Let me bring you up to date on l'affaire French. That's the name of the guy who got killed last week."

"That's music to my ears. I need the distraction that only murder seems able to provide."

Carol proceeded to walk him through the developments in the French murder investigation since last they had talked. She reported on her conversations with the owner of the Four Winns on which Eddie had been found, the ex-wife, the neighbor and bowling partner, the landlord who had evicted him from his digs on Woodpecker Lane, the manager of the bakery for which he had worked, the judge who had acquitted him of manslaughter in the boating accident. She even mentioned in passing the fact that another man had been killed, this time on the public beach in Southport. But her effort to dismiss the latter as a sad but irrelevant commentary on the 'state of things' around the lake elicited Kevin's first excited interruption of her monologue.

"Wait a minute. Why are you dismissing this man's death?"

"Dismissing it? What do you mean?"

"You sound as if it's unrelated to this man French's death. Do you know that?"

"No, I don't *know* that. But it's a Southport police matter. There's nothing to link it to my case. Anyway, I'm not dismissing it. Chief Bellman even asked if my staff could help try to find out who the guy is. He doesn't have our resources." Carol laughed. "I can't believe I said that. As if we've got men and money to spare."

"What I'm saying is that you're forgetting Kelleher's Law. The law that says 'don't believe in coincidences.' You're always telling me not to trust in what looks like a coincidence. If this weren't a serious conversation, I'd say you're always laying down the law to me, but I'll spare you that one."

"Couldn't resist, could you?" Carol said. "But I really don't see any reason why I should expect there to be a connection between my case and Bellman's."

"But look, two murders on the same lake within - what? - three, or is it four days of each other. This guy French was practically a cipher when you found him, or so you say. Now here's another guy that nobody can even identify. Both men are killed at night, right next to the lake. Maybe they're brothers, escaped cons, aliens. I don't know, but you've taught me not to accept coincidences, and it looks like you're confronted with one."

"If it will make you feel any better about your wife, I'll let you know that I *had* entertained your idea. Not about aliens, but I realized that there might be a connection between the two killings. But it seemed pretty unlikely, and my hands were full. Anyway, I'm going to put one of my men on it, see if I can help find out who this guy is. Or was. And you're welcome to claim credit for reminding me of Kelleher's Law."

"Thank you. If I were up there, I'd busy myself proving that those two guys have something in common, like being killed by the same person."

"And how would you propose to do that? Why don't you help restore some semblance of order at Madison College while I lock up the bad guys up here. Bargain?"

"Of course. Just think about those coincidences. Not to raise another question, but where is that bakery truck you said French was driving when he was killed?"

"I agree, that's a problem. Bigger problem than what happened to that other guy on the Southport beach. The truck should have been at the marina. How else would French have gotten there? Helluva long way to walk. Maybe he got someone to take him there and tuck him in for the night, but I doubt it. Maybe his killer drove the truck away, but then how did the killer get to the marina? Perhaps French and whoever killed him were buddies, drove there together, only to have a quarrel in which his buddy killed him and took the truck home. But where is home?"

"If you knew the answer to that question, you'd nail the killer," Kevin said. "Look, I'm not going to abandon good old Madison and head back to the lake right now. But unless things break your way before the end of spring term, you're going to be welcoming me back with open arms."

"Absolutely, open arms and clean sheets. But if I don't have Eddie French's killer in the dock before your spring semester ends, I'll start looking for another job."

"I think you'll regret that you said that. Kidding aside, though, I hope you get the guy, and I'd like it to happen before my semester ends. Like this week. Or next. Then you can devote all your attention to me."

"And you'll devote all of yours to me. "

When this conversation ended, Kevin was feeling surprisingly upbeat, or at least as upbeat as was possible considering that he wouldn't be seeing Carol for over a month and that he still didn't know whether he could change his dean's mind. Carol, on the other hand, found herself pondering the issues which Kevin had posed.

She agreed with him that they were going to have to find the missing bakery truck, and that if they did she might be much closer to resolving the mystery of Eddie French's death. Why wasn't the truck at or near the marina where Eddie had died? It made no sense. The search for it had been much too desultory when it should have been a matter of the highest urgency. Bridges would have a new assignment in the morning.

When she climbed into bed, Carol tried to relax with that new novel which had just made a splash on the bestseller lists. It didn't work. While she admired the author's prose style, her mind kept wandering to Kevin's argument that two recent murders on the lake, one right after the other, should not be treated as mere coincidence. Skeptical as she was, perhaps she should do more to help Steve Bellman than make a few phone calls and have her men view the body. The more she thought about it, the more she found herself focussing on the unknown victim's vehicle. Like the bakery truck, it should have been somewhere near where the body was found. It still might be, but Bellman had not been able to find it. Of course he hadn't known what he was looking for. A bakery truck with *Breads to Go* prominently spelled out on its panels was one thing; the victim of the Southport beach murder could have been driving anything from a Cadillac to an old Chevy. Or even a Harley-Davidson.

Carol set her book aside, having made a decision to put one of her men wholly at Bellman's disposal. She'd give the assignment to Damoth, young, eager to please, unlikely to be offended by being seconded to the Southport police department.

She still had a hard time falling asleep.

CHAPTER 18

Danielle Emmons had never considered herself a worrier. Had she been familiar with Doris Day's old hit song, "Que Sera, Sera," she would doubtless have claimed that it perfectly reflected her own approach to life. Whatever will be, will be.

But this morning, for some reason, she was uneasy. And it had to do with John. They had a good marriage. Not a perfect one, but who did? He was on the road a lot. In fact, he was on the road that very day. As was his habit, he hadn't said where he was going or exactly how long he'd be gone. There was no need to bore her with talk about his job, or so he had said, and she had gone along. What mattered was that he had been a reliable provider, a thoughtful husband, and a proud father of their two boys. He frequently brought back from his trips a small token of his affection. The last time it had been a boxed set of lavender bath crystals, her personal favorites.

So why was Danielle troubled? John had only been gone since Sunday. It was not uncommon for him to be away for a week, sometimes longer. Why should she be concerned? It wasn't that she feared he was having an affair with some other woman in some other city. There had been a time when that possibility had occurred to her, but she had long since put it out of her mind. Nor did she fear that he had been in an accident. John was an excellent driver. He never drank and she had never known him to speed or tailgate. No, it was something else, something she couldn't quite put her finger on.

Danielle stirred another teaspoon of sugar into her coffee and forced herself to concentrate. The kitchen clock told her it was 8:57. By the time it reached 9:30, she had consumed two more cups of coffee and she thought she knew what it was that was bothering her. But it didn't make sense.

Had John really been acting differently lately or had it been her imagination? Had he really been more distracted, his thoughts somewhere else? Several times she had had to repeat herself before he seemed to understand what had, after all, been some

84

rather banal comment. And had there been something slightly out of character in his manner? Prolonged silence when he would normally be talkative. Or, conversely, moments when he sounded uncharacteristically excited, as if he were on a caffeine high. She remembered the previous Saturday night, when they had gone to the multiplex to see a new film that had had good reviews. She had been mildly disappointed in it, and had asked John what he thought about a point in the plot she didn't understand. He hadn't seemed to have known what she was talking about. Obviously his mind had not been on the film.

What had been on his mind? As she thought about it, Danielle decided that there was something going on in her husband's life that she knew nothing about. Something other than his job. And there was no pretending that it didn't matter, that whatever will be, will be. It wasn't that she had suddenly come to the realization that his penchant for privacy was no longer acceptable. It was that he might have gotten himself into some kind of trouble, and that was deeply troubling to her. For someone unaccustomed to worry, the very thought induced something akin to panic.

She suddenly felt an overwhelming urge to talk with someone, to share this strange new experience of worry. To seek advice. She'd call Lori. Her neighbor down the street would be surprised, but she was an upbeat woman, the original smiley face. More importantly, she was a good listener.

Lori suggested lunch, but Danielle wanted to see her right away if that was possible. It was shortly after ten that they sat down in her neighbor's living room with yet another cup of coffee. It was her fourth of the morning.

"Well, well," Lori said, "what's up with you?"

"I don't know, but I'm not myself. I just need to talk."

"Of course. Be my guest. Something on your mind?"

"I guess so, but I'm not sure what. It's about John."

Oh, oh, Lori thought. She had known John and Danielle Emmons for nearly a decade, and had never seen or heard anything to suggest they were anything but a happily married couple. She decided the prudent thing to do was not to ask questions, to let Danielle say what was bothering her in her own way. Danielle was finding it difficult to say anything.

"Do you ever have a feeling that something's wrong? That something's isn't quite right? Does that make any sense?"

"Maybe," Lori equivocated.

"You know John," Danielle said. "The strong, silent type."

She smiled a wan smile as she gave voice to the familiar cliche. Lori nodded, but said nothing.

"I don't usually worry about him, ask what he's doing, what he's thinking." She looked at Lori as if asking for reassurance that she was right to trust her husband. "But there's something going on."

Lori assumed that her friend, her friend who never worried, had begun to suspect that John was being unfaithful. Danielle was aware of what Lori must be thinking and hastened to assure her that she was wrong.

"It's not that he's seeing someone else. But his mind is on something else. You can tell. We're talking, but he doesn't hear me. Well, usually he does, but there are times when it s almost like he's not there. And it's happening more often. Something's bothering him, and it seems to me that it's important. Important to him, I mean. I'm not sure it has anything to do with me."

What was Lori supposed to say? There was no point in her becoming involved in a guessing game. But Danielle had come to see her because she needed to share her anxiety, and Danielle was a friend. Lori had to say something.

"Maybe you should simply ask John if there's something he needs to talk about."

It was a sensible suggestion, but Danielle did not agree.

"No, I can't do that. John doesn't like to be asked what's on his mind. He'd just tell me I'm imagining things. And if I wouldn't let it go, he'd get angry."

"So what is it you think I can do to help?"

Danielle sighed.

'Nothing, I guess. I just had to share with someone, and I knew you'd be willing to listen." She started to nibble at a well-manicured finger nail, realized what she was doing, and dropped her hand into her lap.

"It may not be a good idea, Danny, but you could look through John's things some day when he's away. See if there's anything that might explain what he's up to."

"I'm not a snoop, Lori. It would just make me feel cheap. Besides, he might catch me at it."

Lori was understandably frustrated.

"Look, chances are this will pass. It's probably nothing important anyway. I'd just give it some time."

She knew it was a weak suggestion, one which wouldn't satisfy her friend. But in the absence of more details, it was the best she could do.

Danielle Emmons was unable to put the issue behind her, and by three o'clock that afternoon she found herself in the room that her husband used as an office, cautiously going through the drawers of his desk and the shelves in his closet. Better to be a snoop and feel cheap than take no steps to satisfy her curiosity - and, yes, her worry - about what was on John's mind.

CHAPTER 19

The owner/manager of Crozier's Auto Shop had a problem. Work on a new Buick and an old Ford had been completed, and he needed to remove them from their bays in order to make room for other vehicles. Unfortunately, there was no place on the lot behind the building to park the Buick and the Ford. It was chock full of other cars and pickups, some waiting their turn in the bays, others waiting for their owners to pay their bills and drive them home, and several belonging to Jim Crozier's mechanics.

The log on the desk in front of Mr. Crozier told him that Frank Dowling would be coming for his Mini Cooper around noon and that Jack Miller had said something about wanting his seventeen year old Dodge ready by five. But there had been nothing from the owner of a *Breads to Go* truck, which took up nearly enough space to park two cars. Why had it not been picked up? All it had needed was an oil change and to have the tires rotated; the job had been completed on Friday, almost a week ago. Jim had trouble remembering who had brought the truck in. Some employee of the bakery who had said to bill *Breads to Go*. He picked up the phone.

"Hello, this is *Breads to Go*. Stearns speaking."

Stearns. Yes, Crozier thought, I remember now. Buddy Stearns.

"Mr. Stearns, this is Jim Crozier over at Crozier's Auto Shop. We've got one of your trucks out back. It's been here for almost a week. We rotated the tires, changed the oil. But we'd appreciate it if one of your people could pick it up. We don't have a lot of space."

"I don't understand. You sure it's our truck? I don't have any recollection of leaving one of our trucks at Crozier's. You're over on the West Lake Road, aren't you? We always take our vehicles to Jardine's up in Yates Center."

Crozier was sure the truck belonged to the bakery. *Breads to Go* was stenciled in large black letters on the side panels. How could Stearns not know where his trucks were?

"Well, your bakery's name's on it, and the guy who brought it in told us what needed doing and said to bill you."

"I'll be damned. Who was the guy?"

"There doesn't seem to be a name on the invoice, just *Breads to Go*."

"The guy who brought it in didn't give you his name?"

"Not that I remember. It didn't seem important. I figured the bakery wanted the work done and would pay the bill."

"Just a minute. Let me talk with Stew."

Buddy Stearns was gone for a long five minutes. Whoever Stew was, he didn't seem to be readily available. Either that or he also was having trouble remembering how their truck had gotten over to Crozier's.

"Mr. Crozier," Stearns said as he came back on the line. "Stew can't account for our truck being over at your place. This is really weird. I'm sorry we've inconvenienced you. Look, I'll send a couple of guys around as soon as one of our drivers gets back."

"When might that be, Mr. Stearns?"

"I can't be sure. Maybe 4:30, close to five."

Crozier was not happy, but the truck would be gone by the end of the day.

It wasn't until later that evening that Jim Crozier recalled something that his wife had said a few days earlier. Something about trouble at the Lakeshore Marina. He hadn't been paying attention. Grace had an ear for rumors; he didn't. But he thought he remembered that the rumor had something to do with somebody being found in one of the boats. He probably should say something to Patrick Kelley, like 'hope all is well at the marina.' After all, Kelley was a neighbor. Their places of business were barely more than half a mile apart.

On the way to work the next morning, Crozier stopped off at the marina and found Kelley down on the main dock.

"Hi, Pat. What's this about trouble at Lakeshore?"

"Trouble?" Kelley asked.

"Just something the wife said. She probably misunderstood some rumor she picked up. Grace is drawn to rumors, and most of them don't amount to anything."

"What did she say?" Kelley sounded concerned.

"Not much. Just that you'd found somebody sleeping in one of your boats, somebody that didn't belong there."

"Damn it," Kelley said, "I thought I'd made it clear to the men that they were to play dumb. But I suppose it's impossible for word not to get out. The sheriff will have been talking to people, and sooner or later everyone around the lake will know what happened."

Patrick Kelley had quickly made the adjustment from frustration to resignation.

"Sorry, Pat, if I've put my foot in it."

"No fault of yours. I should have figured it'd be common knowledge. After all, it happened last Thursday. Or I guess I should say Wednesday night. I'm surprised that more people haven't been asking me about it like you did."

"I'm not here to pry, Pat, but I have no idea what happened."

"What happened is that a guy died on my property last week. Last Wednesday night. We found him under the tarp on one of the boats we'd stored over the winter. The sheriff thinks somebody killed him. It's not good publicity for the marina."

Crozier listened with a look of amazement on his face. Somebody killed - or probably killed - just down the road from his garage.

"Do you know who the guy was?"

"Everybody will know in a day or two, Jim, but I'd appreciate it if you didn't talk about it. Guy's name is Eddie French. He worked over at *Breads to Go*."

Crozier, who didn't like to spread rumors, suddenly regretted that he hadn't asked Grace to tell him more. There had to be a connection between the death of this man and the fact that a bakery truck had sat unclaimed behind his shop for a week.

He promised not to tell people what he had just heard, although he was sure that a lot of other people had heard much the same thing. But he did plan to call the sheriff. After all, it was she, according to Kelley, who assumed that the bakery worker had been killed. He didn't know what had happened the night of this man's death, but he was willing to bet that he knew who had brought the bakery truck to his shop for servicing and who had not come back the next day to pick it up. But why would the manager of *Breads to Go* not have been aware of any of this?

———

Good citizen that he believed himself to be, Jim Crozier made it his first order of business upon arriving at the shop to place a call to the sheriff of Cumberland County. He knew of Carol Kelleher, although he had never met her. If she was of the opinion that somebody named Eddie French, an employee of *Breads to Go*, had ben killed the previous Thursday night at the Lakeshore Marina, she would certainly be interested in the fact that one of the bakery's trucks had been parked at his place of business since that very evening. He was surprised that he had not heard from her before this.

As it happened, the sheriff was not at her desk. The woman on the other end of the line told him that Deputy Sheriff Bridges would be with him in a moment.

"Yes, sir. It's Mr. Crozier, right?"

"Yes, I'm Jim Crozier, run an auto shop on West Lake Road. Funny thing happened to us, and I thought you'd be interested. Last Thursday a guy dropped off a *Breads to Go* bakery truck for an oil change. Wanted the tires rotated, too. He never came back to pick up the truck, so I finally called the bakery. They didn't seem to know anything about it. Then this morning I stopped off at Lakeshore Marina and Pat Kelley tells me that one of the bakery's employees had been found dead on one of his boats. About the same time the truck was left off at my place. It's not for me to say, but it sounds as if the dead man and the truck driver might be the same guy."

Bridges was indeed interested.

"You somewhere near Lakeshore?"

"We're close to half a mile further south. Other side of the road, just a couple of lots from Al Chaney's place. You know, that big old barn of a building that used to be part of an old west lake wine cellar."

Sam knew the area, remembered that there was a small service garage there. More evidence that Crooked Lake didn't have much in the way of commercial zoning regulations.

"Who was it that left the truck off at your garage?"

"I don't know. Never got a name, just instructions to bill the bakery."

"Is the truck still at your place?"

"No, somebody from the bakery came and got it late yesterday."

"You talk with the manager over there?"

"Yeah. Stearns is the name. He seemed puzzled that one of their trucks was at my garage."

Sam tried to hide his disappointment. They would have liked to go through the truck, the truck that Eddie had presumably been using, before it had been reclaimed by the bakery. Too late for that. But at least the problem of the missing truck had been solved.

CHAPTER 20

When Carol walked into the squad room for the morning meeting, the atmosphere was electric. Or so it seemed to the sheriff. Things were beginning to happen, and that always raised the spirits of her officers when they had become caught up in a new case. Carol had been given a heads-up by Bridges on the bakery truck the previous day. Damoth and Barrett, both loathe to bother the boss at home in the absence of an emergency, had chosen to report what they had learned in the morning. But she could tell by the looks on their faces and the buzz in the room that they were pleased with what they would be reporting.

"Is it just my imagination, or is this going to be a good day?" she asked, her voice reflecting the mood around her.

"It all depends," Officer Parsons said, "on how high you've set the bar."

"Thanks, Bill, but I'm in the mood for good news, and it's my guess that there may be some. Sam, why don't you lead off."

Bridges proceeded to tell his colleagues what he had told the sheriff the day before. Everyone was relieved that he wouldn't be expected to be on the lookout for the bakery truck any longer, but they were also quick to realize that one puzzle solved didn't bring them any closer to identifying Eddie French's killer.

"What it looks like," Carol said, "is that Eddie drove the truck to Crozier's, left it there, and walked back to the marina for his rendezvous with death. That makes sense. What doesn't make sense is that he'd do it without letting *Breads to Go* know that they'd be getting the bill. The manager claims he knew nothing about it."

"Do you suppose Eddie just took it for granted that it would be okay?" Officer Byrnes asked.

"Or that Stearns is lying?" It was Barrett who made that suggestion.

"Do you have any reason to think he might be?" Carol asked.

"No, but if I'd been in Eddie's shoes I don't think I'd do something like that without clearing it with the boss."

"Yeah, but maybe they have a policy over there that their drivers take care of their own trucks," Byrnes said.

Carol was interested in this give and take. But whatever the bakery's policy in such matters, it would have been known that Jardine's, not Crozier's, serviced their trucks. Eddie had used Crozier's because of its location near the marina. And Stearns had denied any knowledge of it. She'd have to make it a point to pay Buddy Stearns another visit.

That issue out of the way, Carol turned to Officer Damoth.

"Ken, you look like the cat that swallowed the canary. Let's hear it."

"Well, it's about that other car," he said. He reminded his colleagues that he'd been given the assignment of helping the Southport police find the car belonging to the victim of the knife attack on the town beach.

"Chief Bellman didn't think the guy was from Southport. Said he must have come in from out of town, which meant that his car had to be somewhere around. Anyway, this time of year we don't get a lot of visitors. So I thought the guy was probably from somewhere else in the area, like maybe Corning or Ithaca, maybe even Rochester. But I got lucky. I'll bet you didn't know that I collect license plates?"

"No, I didn't know," Carol said. "Sounds like an interesting hobby."

"It is, and it proved to be a big help. I was on my way down to the police department when I happened to notice a Ford Explorer from Ohio. Ohio plates, nothing fancy like some of the other states. But then I noticed that it didn't have a front plate, just the one in the rear. And Ohio is a two plate state. Well, that seemed strange, so I made a note of the license number and Byrnes and me did some checking and we found that the plate had been stolen some time ago."

Damoth paused, relishing the pleasure of his colleagues' approval of his smarts.

"Any reason to believe the car was driven by the guy who was knifed on the beach?"

Carol's question was deflating.

"No way of knowing," Damoth said, aware that his knowledge of state laws on plates didn't mean he had found the victim's car. "At least not yet. But I talked to the people who live near where the car was parked, and they think it's been there since the weekend. At least a couple of them do. One woman was annoyed because she had a party on Tuesday and some of her friends had to park further down the street. She obviously doesn't like people who leave their cars out front of her house."

"Where's her house?"

"Lake Street, about a block and a half up from the beach."

"What about the car? We ought to be able to figure out whom it's registered to."

"If it's okay with you, we'll check it for the vehicle ID." Byrnes had picked up the story. "Ken had Chief Bellman keep an eye on it, not let someone drive it away."

If its driver was the man who had been killed on the beach on Sunday night, Carol thought, it was unlikely the car was going anywhere. The very fact that the car hadn't been moved in at least four days was perhaps the strongest evidence that it was the victim's car. But Southport could have dozens of cars on its streets that hadn't been moved in days. Even weeks.

"Okay, I'll ask Bellman to get the vehicle ID. He can use the fact the plate was stolen if he's challenged."

Carol was intrigued by Damoth's discovery, but skeptical that they had found the missing car. The squad meeting moved on to other matters.

"Jim, what did you learn at the bank?" The sheriff addressed the question to Officer Barrett.

He had found Eddie French's check book at the storage locker, and it had contained a very limited and careless record of his bank transactions. The Upstate Bank and Trust, when advised that French was dead, reluctantly gave the sheriff permission to look at his account. Apparently he had neither savings accounts nor a security box at the bank, just the checking account, which he had opened upon moving to Yates Center.

"Bank's record is better than French's. No surprise there. But he didn't make much use of the account. Must have done most of his business with cash. Probably kept his money under the mattress. Anyway, if we count just the last six months, he wrote only four checks for more than $50, and he deposited only one that was bigger than that. Funny thing, though, he also made cash deposits twice, once for $500. Here's the statement."

He passed the papers to the sheriff, and then read from his notes.

"Biggest check is to Isabel French, dated December 13th. $450. There's one other to her, dated February 21st, but it's only $185. The other big check was to Justin Longacre. I assume he represented French at that trial for running over the Kingsbury kid. It was for $150. That's strange. I had the impression that he had a court appointed lawyer, didn't cost him anything."

"You're right," Parsons piped up. "Judge got Longacre to take the case gratis."

"The other check was to Walmart. $76.39. Like I said, he deposited cash on a couple of occasions, but the only check he deposited was in the amount of $750, back in December. It was from somebody named Floyd Brinker. Anybody know a Brinker?"

No one seemed to.

"I'm going to want to give that bank statement a careful going over," Carol said. "The checks to Isabel sound like alimony payments. It doesn't look like he was depositing his pay checks, just cashing them. I don't understand the cash deposits. People usually take cash out of a bank, not put it in. And then there's Brinker. Who is he? We'll need to look further back, see what was going on in the account ever since French moved here. Maybe another name will pop up somewhere."

"I don't think so," Barrett said. "It's pretty much the same story ever since he opened the account."

"You're probably right. We'll see. Anyway, let's make Brinker our first order of business. I want to know who he is. Jim, you find him. Got it?"

Barrett nodded.

When the meeting broke up, the energy that had filled the room half an hour earlier had largely vanished.

———

Carol retreated to her office to study the bank statement and make a few phone calls. Th first was to Chief Bellman. She knew she was now unofficially in charge of the investigation of the stabbing death of Mr. X, but the Southport police chief must be treated with the courtesy to which he was entitled.

"Steve," she said when he came on the line, "it's Carol. About your man in the morgue, I think Officer Damoth told you about a car parked on Lake Street that's got a stolen Ohio plate on it. Your guess is as good as mine as to whether the guy who's been driving it is Mr. X. But it looks as if it would be worth our while to get the car's ID, see if there's anything in the glove compartment. It's your case, but I'm willing to tackle the car if you'd like. Just tell me what you'd like me to do."

"It looks like I'm imposing on you, Carol, but you know we've only got two patrolmen down here. Besides, it was your Officer Damoth - nice young man - who found out about the stolen plate. If you can take it from here, I'd be grateful."

When she had first been approached by Bellman, she had only reluctantly agreed to become involved in 'his' murder. Now she was pleased that he was glad to pass the matter to the Cumberland County Sheriff's Department.

"No problem, Steve, I'll keep you posted."

Then Carol put in a call to Buddy Stearns. She had questions for him that she hadn't asked when they had met earlier in the week. It was agreed that they'd meet at two o'clock.

Her other business concerned Joe Kingsbury. The still grieving - still angry? - father she had been putting off talking with. When she finally left the office, it was for a trip down to Southport and the Merchants Real Estate Agency offices. Kingsbury would be waiting for her.

CHAPTER 21

At this stage of the Eddie French case, Carol hadn't the slightest clue as to who might have killed that troubled young man. As she thought about it, she concluded that that was one of the reasons she had been reluctant to interview Joe Kingsbury. She had talked with Buddy Stearns because he had been Eddie's employer. She had talked with Isabel French because she had been Eddie's wife. She had talked with Simon Ostrowski because he had been Eddie's neighbor and bowling partner. She had talked with Earl Skinner because it had been his boat on which Eddie's body had been found. She had talked with Judge Dietrich because he had found Eddie innocent of manslaughter in the death of Jordan Kingsbury. But she would be talking with Joe Kingsbury because it was his son whom Eddie had run down and killed, and because he had been conspicuously angry that Eddie had escaped punishment for the fatal accident. In other words, Joe was the nearest thing to a suspect in her hunt for Eddie's killer.

It was surely too early to be viewing him as a suspect. Yet that is precisely why Kingsbury would assume the sheriff wanted to talk with him, and it would be difficult for her to act otherwise. Nonetheless, she couldn't delay the inevitable session any longer. It was 11:45 when she pulled into the small parking apron next to Kingsbury's real estate office.

It occurred to her, too late, that it might have been better to be out of uniform when she visited him. Oh, well, she thought, this is what sheriffs wear.

Joe Kingsbury had seen her when she got out of her car, and he met her at the front door.

"Good morning, sheriff. Let's go up to my office. We're on the third floor." The building didn't have an elevator, so they took the stairs to a cluster of small offices which appeared to be furnished to look comfortable but not opulent.

"I'm back here, to the right. Mrs. Baker, can you get the sheriff coffee or tea, whatever she wants."

"Thanks," Carol said, "but I'm fine. I won't be needing anything to drink."

"As you wish."

Joe shut the door, pulled a chair up closer to the desk, and urged the sheriff to have a seat. Carol quickly surveyed the wall behind the desk. There was evidence of Kingsbury's certification as a real estate agent as well as a framed diploma from Syracuse University and a fairly large collection of photographs. Presumably the family. Most of them were group photos, but three were of a young, teenage boy, almost certainly Jordan, one standing in a driveway next to a bright red car, one sitting at the desk in his bedroom, and the third poised to dive off the end of a dock. He wore a big smile in all three pictures. Another photo was of the same boy with his father's arm draped across the lad's shoulder. It enjoyed pride of place on Joe's desk, artfully positioned so that it could be seen by both Mr. Kingsbury and whoever was sitting across from him.

Carol knew that she was probably expected to comment on the photo gallery, and she did.

"You have a beautiful family, but these pictures must be a painful reminder of the boy you lost. I'm so very sorry."

"That's all right. It's been hard, but it was months ago and we just have to move on." The way he said it made it clear that Joe had not found it easy to move on.

Carol had come to talk about Eddie French, but decided that perhaps she should keep the conversation on the boy for a bit longer.

"How old would your son be if he were still with us?"

"Almost 14. His birthday's in May."

"A terrible thing, a young man's life cut short like that."

"I know. He hadn't even had his first real date. Didn't get a chance to try out for the high school baseball team. He'd have been good, too."

Kingsbury didn't sound angry. Nostalgic, obviously heart broken.

"I'm sorry I wasn't more involved in the matter back then," Carol said. "Not that I would have been in any position to help, but - well, I just wish it had played out differently."

She was careful not to say that she disagreed with Judge Dietrich's decision.

"You think letting French get away with it was wrong?"

"I didn't know enough about the case - still don't know enough - to be able to answer your question. Let's just say I'm terribly sorry you lost your son."

"Sure, *everyone's* sorry Jordan's gone." For the first time Kingsbury sounded tense. A little angry? "That's cold comfort. My family hoped for some justice. What is it that people are always saying? They want closure. Well, I wanted closure. I wanted to know that the man who did it couldn't just walk away and resume his life as if nothing had happened. It wasn't fair. I still don't sleep well, sheriff."

Kingsbury paused.

"Sure you won't have something to drink? If not coffee, I've got some sherry back here."

"Thank you, no. I've had my quota of coffee already today, and we have a thing about drinking on duty." She tried to smile, but it didn't work.

"Yes, you are on duty, aren't you, and I'm sure you didn't come to see me so we could commiserate about Jordan. So what is it I can do for you?"

Carol was certain that Joe Kingsbury knew about Eddie French's death. He had probably not spent a day since his son's death without thinking about Eddie French, and surely he would have been among the first to hear rumors about what had happened over at the Lakeshore Marina. So what could he do for her?

"There isn't really anything you can do, Mr. Kingsbury. I just wanted to know if you were aware that Mr. French is dead."

"Yes, I know. The way I heard about it, French was murdered. It's likely that lots of people know about it, and I'm sure you aren't making the rounds, talking to all of them. So why are we having this discussion?"

Kingsbury had shifted gears. He was no longer the still grieving father, he was playing defense. He almost certainly assumed that the sheriff was in his office because she thought he might have killed French.

"I'm here because not many people around this area seem to have known Eddie French, and I'm trying to learn what I can about him. In that way it should be easier to understand how he came to be dead. You did know him. I'm sure you wish you'd never met him, but fate had it otherwise. What I want to do is talk with you about Mr. French. You must have learned quite a bit about him as a result of your tragedy and the trial. So you should be able to help me flesh out my very spotty picture of him."

"Are you saying you haven't decided that I killed him?"

"Mr. French was killed just a week ago. At this point I know very little about him, and frankly I haven't even begun to think about who might have killed him. So, please, may we just talk about your opinion of Mr. French. I'm sure you find it hard to forgive him for what happened to your son, but what I'm interested in is how he struck you as you observed him after the accident, during the trial."

"You want me to set aside my fatherly feelings and tell you if he was well-shaved, dressed neatly, was polite, answered questions when asked. Well, of course. But so what."

"No, I don't expect you to pretend to like the man. What I want is for you to tell me what you remember about what he said, what you may have learned about his life, about him as a person, independently of the accident."

"That's a difficult question. I saw him as a guy who'd killed my son because he wasn't paying attention, because he was driving too fast. But I'll try to step back and forget my personal feelings."

Carol said she'd appreciate that, and waited for Kingsbury to calm down.

"He seemed like he was a wimp, to be honest," Joe said. "Said he'd had a tough life, things hadn't gone his way. He was in a hole. It was all a plea for sympathy, and it didn't have a damned thing to do with what had happened that day off our dock. Okay, I'm personalizing things again. Can you blame me? Truth is, he struck me as pathetic. A nobody who had suddenly become a somebody, but not in the way he wanted."

"Did it ever occur to you that he might really be innocent? That what happend was just an awful accident because he didn't know that Jordan was diving?"

Kingsbury's shook his head.

"That's what that damned judge ruled," he said. "As you can see, it doesn't take a lot to get me riled up. But what can I say? Justice wasn't done. I know the system isn't perfect, and I don't think the judge was biased against me. But he was wrong. So will

I ever be able to forgive either French or Judge Dietrich? The answer is no. But let's get one thing straight, I don't go around killing people. My God, I'm a respected member of this community, as was my father and his father before him."

"Let me remind you, Mr. KIngsbury, I'm not accusing you of anything. I have no children, but I believe I can feel your pain. I'd really like to enlist your help in finding out who did kill Eddie French. You could do that by sharing anything you know, or think you know, that might help me."

"How would I know who killed him? Maybe it was a robbery that went bad. Maybe he welched on a loan. For all I know, that unpleasant wife of his got fed up with him and did it. Who knows?"

"You know his wife?"

"No. I just saw her at the trial, and I didn't like the looks of her. I think they deserved each other."

"Are you aware that they divorced after the trial?"

"So I heard,"

"By the way, how did you hear about French's death?"

"Friend of mine told me. Earl Skinner. It was his boat they found French on, but of course you know that. Skinner says it was you that called him with the news. He was really upset that French was using his boat to sleep on, angry with the marina for letting it happen. And he's not looking forward to the publicity when he gets back. I don't blame him."

"How is it you know Skinner?"

"We both belong to the Lions Club."

"Why do you suppose Skinner called you?"

"He knew all about Jordan's death, that French had been responsible. He naturally figured I'd be interested, probably glad to hear that the guy who killed my boy had met his maker."

"Did Skinner ever tell you how it was that he knew French?" Carol asked.

"Some story about both of them owning Four Winns boats."

"French had sold his boat. Did you know that?"

"No. When did he do that?" Joe seemed mildly surprised at this piece of news.

"Quite some time ago, not that long after the trial."

"Do you know who now owns that boat, the one that killed Jordan?"

Carol didn't know, although she was willing to bet that it was a man named Brinker, the man who had written Eddie a $750 check back in December. But there was no point in sharing Brinker's name with Kingsbury. She might be wrong that he had bought the boat, and even if she were right she wasn't about to encourage Kingsbury to start thinking again about the boat that had run over his son.

They talked more about Joe's effort to have Judge Dietrich impeached and the fact that he had never really been able to put the tragedy behind him. But she learned nothing that she hadn't already heard from Parsons and Dietrich. If Kingsbury had had anything to do with Eddie French's death, he had said nothing that would prompt her to begin treating him as a likely suspect. The one thing that stuck in her mind after she left the real estate office, however, was that Joe Kingsbury was a friend of Earl Skinner and had learned of Eddie's death from him.

How strange that the man whose son Eddie had killed and the man on whose boat Eddie had been killed were close friends. Could it be important? Or was it just coincidence? In this case it was probably the latter. But Carol, who was skeptical of coincidences, couldn't shake the thought that the Kingsbury-Skinner relationship would require more of her attention.

CHAPTER 22

Isabel French had finished her shift at Purdy's Diner and on a typical day would have climbed in her car and headed home to relieve her neighbor, who was minding the boys. But today she was not ready to go home, not ready to prepare one more tasteless meal, to argue with Steven about the suitability for an eight year old of some TV show, to collapse into bed for another sleepless night. She'd take a walk, clear her head. She set off down Pelham Drive.

Franklin is a small town, its population fluctuating in the vicinity of 600 people. Isabel had no particular destination, but the direction she had taken quickly led her to the outskirts of town. There was nothing to indicate that she had left town, only more space between houses and finally no houses at all. There were no sidewalks, and she found herself walking along the edge of a field that came down to the road. It was not until she reached a fence that appeared to exist to keep someone's cattle from straying that she thought better of what she was doing. There were no cattle in sight, only a pasture and in the far distance an old barn that looked as if it needed maintenance work.

A stiff breeze had come up, and the chilly weather had started her nose to run. There were no tissues in the pocket of her jacket, so she wiped her nose on her sleeve. Isabel stepped back into the field, walked a dozen paces along the fence, and sat down, her back against it. Why was she doing this? It wasn't just that she didn't look forward to going home, that she wasn't particularly anxious to spend another evening with the boys. They weren't bad kids, but they weren't company. To be honest, she thought to herself, I'm bored. Terribly bored. Eddie is gone, thank goodness. But nothing, no one, has taken his place. She felt trapped in endless days, now actually months, of emptiness. For a brief time it had looked as if Sibyl Cochran might fill the void in her life, but it hadn't worked out. And why should it have? Sibyl was a lively woman, not terribly bright but a chatterbox who made the time pass. And Isabel knew that she and Sibyl were temperamentally a mismatch, and she knew that Sibyl knew it, too.

As she sat and chewed on a stalk of grass, Isabel put Sibyl and the boys out of her mind and acknowledged that her real problem lay elsewhere. It had bothered her since the day the sheriff had come to the house and questioned her about Eddie. And told her that Eddie had died from a gunshot wound, a wound that he hadn't inflicted on himself. Isabel realized that she had not handled her conversation with the sheriff very well. She had answered the sheriff's questions, but she had not really been helpful. Her comments about Eddie's jobs had not been dishonest, but neither had they been very forthcoming. More importantly, her explanation that she had divorced Eddie because he had repeatedly abused the boys, while true, was far from the whole story. The fact is that she had not wanted to talk about Eddie, so she had fobbed the sheriff off with a few answers to her questions that would sound believable and hopefully satisfy her. Moreover, she had ended the tense interview in a way that almost certainly would *not* satisfy the sheriff. For several days she had been dreading a knock on the door, announcing that the sheriff was back to ask more questions.

She should never have married Eddie. She had always liked to be the person in control, going way back to her childhood playground and sandbox. And Eddie had looked to be easy to control. How wrong she had been. He had turned out to have what people called a passive aggressive personality. Instead of the occasional spat followed by a romantic make up, tension between them had simmered under the surface all the time. And it had taken its toll on her. That would have been bad enough if he hadn't also developed a habit of doing reckless things which embarrassed her and the boys. What she had thought of as the final straw had come when he had killed that boy with his power boat. But the real final straw had come only recently, months after the divorce, when he had stupidly held up the bartender at *The Cedar Post*.

Isabel remembered how she had learned of this latest episode. Her neighbor, Janet Bixby, had stopped by and, right in front of the children, had told her what had happened."

"Isn't the Eddie French who pulled the stick up out at *The Cedar Post* last night your ex-husband?"

Of course he was. After all, how many Eddie Frenchs lived in Cumberland County? And it was just the sort of dumb thing Eddie would have done. He wouldn't have meant to use the gun, but it would have been his idea of an appeal for sympathy. She wished that he had been arrested and sentenced to some serious jail time. At least that way he would have been held accountable for his actions. But once again he had gotten away with it, leaving her and her sons to face the gossip.

'I feel so sorry for Mrs. French. There's just no way she can really get away from that dreadful former husband of hers.' Or 'those poor kids, having to cope with stories about their crazy father. I'll bet they'll be teased and bullied unmercifully.'

Well, Eddie had pulled his last stupid stunt. There wouldn't be any more 'Eddie French stories,' not when the inevitable interest in his sudden and violent death had faded away. Perhaps she should pack up and move somewhere far away, somewhere where no one had ever heard of him. She could even arrange to take back her maiden name. As she got to her feet to head home, she wished she had done so a long time ago.

CHAPTER 23

"You have some news about what happened to French?" The manager of *Breads to Go* smiled at the sheriff as he met her at the door of the bakery.

"I'm afraid not, but I thought another chat with you might help." Carol thought his smile looked artificial. They retreated to Buddy Stearns' office and took the same chairs they had occupied on her first visit. She studied the bakery manager. There was something about him that suggested he would be physically weak. Perhaps it was the pallor of his skin, the small, pinched features of his face, or the dusty blond hair and mustache which were so light as to make his eyelids nearly invisible. But what did she know? Appearances can be deceiving.

"I thought I answered all of your questions the other day, sheriff. I'm not sure I can be much help."

"Perhaps not." Carol made a production of fumbling in her jacket pocket for something, finally producing a small notebook. She didn't really need it, having thoroughly familiarized herself with the information she had jotted down in its pages.

"But in my experience it is usually a good idea to retrace my steps, talk with people several times, repeat my questions, try to make sure I understand things."

It was just a bit of boilerplate, but it had gotten Stearns' attention. Was he concerned that he might contradict something he had said to her earlier? Or even that she hadn't quite believed him?

"Well, sure, that sounds like a good way to do what you do. I'm glad to do what I can to help you get to the bottom of this French business."

"Good. And the French business is, of course, his death. The fact that someone killed him. We had been wondering how he got to the Lakeshore Marina where his body was found. The truck which you had been so good as to let him use when he was off duty was nowhere to be found, and you told me it hadn't been brought back to the bakery. But now it is back at the bakery, isn't it?"

"I think so, although one of the other drivers may have it today, making deliveries. I guess I should have reported that we got it back."

"I'm sure you would have, in due course," Carol said, somewhat disingenuously. "But we now know that Eddie French did use your truck to get to the marina, don't we? He left it within walking distance of the marina the night he was killed, down at Crozier's Auto Shop. Why was the truck at Crozier's?"

"I have no idea," Stearns said. "I certainly never told him to leave it there."

"But Eddie apparently assumed that you wouldn't mind. Mr. Crozier tells me that French told him he was to bill *Breads to Go*, as if that were company policy. By the way, what is company policy?"

"Do you mean was Eddie free to get the oil changed when and where he wanted?"

"Something like that."

"Well, no, that's not the way we usually do it. I've got an arrangement with Jardine's in Yates Center."

"Is it up to your drivers when to change oil, take the trucks in for routine maintenance?"

"I think Stew keeps a record so we know when each truck is due for service."

"Why don't we check with Stew and see when Eddie's truck was due for an oil change. And tire rotation."

Buddy Stearns was looking puzzled by the request. And because he was puzzled, he also looked uncomfortable.

"Just give me a minute," he said, and buzzed for Stew.

Five minutes later, the man who presumably kept track of such things made his appearance.

"Hi," Carol stood and shook hands. "What I need to know is when the truck that Eddie French had been using was due for its next oil change. And whether it was ready to have its tires rotated."

"No problem," Stew said, and put what looked like a much thumbed black register on the desk. He opened it and leafed through several pages. "Here it is. French's truck was scheduled for an oil change about May 27th. I don't see anything about tires. Looks like the truck was in the shop to have them look over the brakes, tires, fluids - the works - back in late February."

Stew smiled, obviously pleased that he had been able to give the sheriff the information she had requested.

"Thanks," Carol said, "that should be helpful."

After Stew had gone back to wherever he worked in the bakery complex, Carol said what was surely on Stearns' mind as well as hers.

"It would appear that not only did Eddie French have his truck serviced at Crozier's rather than Jardine's, he also had work done that was quite unnecessary. And I think it's a safe bet that Eddie knew it. So why would he have changed oil and rotated tires last Thursday when there was no need to do so?"

"Beats me," Stearns said, unhelpfully. "Maybe he just didn't know when the truck was due for servicing. After all, it wasn't really his truck."

"No, it wasn't his truck. Most people let somebody use their vehicle, that somebody isn't very likely to feel obligated to do much more than make sure the tank has enough gas to get them home. But Eddie went to a lot of trouble to take care of a borrowed truck that didn't need any special care. He went to the trouble of taking the truck to a garage, telling them what needed doing and whom to bill, and then walking half a mile back to Lakeshore Marina to bed down for the night because he didn't have the truck to sleep in. Doesn't that strike you as odd?"

"You put it that way, I guess it does." Stearns seemed to find Eddie's behavior unfathomable.

Carol had not given any thought to the possibility that Buddy Stearns might be a suspect in French's murder. She still could not imagine what motive he could possibly have for killing French. But there was something wrong here. There was the fact that the bakery manager had given Eddie a job even knowing that he had run over and killed a boy in his power boat. He had allowed Eddie to use a company truck as his personal transportation. And he had declined to fire Eddie after he had staged his hold up of *The Cedar Post*. Now it appeared that Eddie had been sure enough of his boss's support that he had blithely dropped the truck off at an unfamiliar garage and charged the bill to the bakery. It might mean nothing. But then it might mean that there was more to Buddy's relationship with Eddie than met the eye.

"How many drivers do you have, Mr. Stearns?"

The sudden change of subject caught Stearns off guard. "Drivers? I'd have to think."

"Oh, come on, there can't be that many. What is it, five? Eight? I'm thinking of regulars, although you probably have a couple of part timers you can use in a pinch."

"Let's see." Stearns gave the matter some thought and came up with the names of four who had regular routes in the tri-county area, plus an older man who was apparently available on little notice to step in if one of the regulars was sick.

"Why don't you write their names down for me?" Carol said, and handed him a page she ripped out of her pocket notebook. "Oh, and while you're at it, how about their addresses and phone numbers."

Stearns opened a desk drawer and pulled out a notebook of his own that apparently contained this information. Once she had pocketed the list, Carol turned the conversation back to the fact that Eddie's truck had been left at Crozier's.

"It seems obvious to me, Mr. Stearns, that Eddie left his truck - sorry, your truck - at Crozier's Auto Shop because he didn't want it to be seen at the Lakeside Marina. He couldn't very well just leave the truck at the auto shop, so he used the excuse that it needed work. Moreover, he knew that if he left it there, it would be out of sight until he came to get it the next day. Does that sound about right?"

"If you say so."

"No, I don't say so, because I don't *know* if that's why the truck was at the auto shop. My question is simply does that sound like a plausible explanation for what Eddie did?"

"Yeah, I guess so." It was a luke warm answer.

"Okay, but can you think of a reason why Eddie might have been so anxious to keep the truck out of sight?"

"I thought you just said it was because he didn't want anyone to know he was at the marina."

"I think we can agree on that. But why?"

"I'm not very good at these guessing games, sheriff."

"No, probably not." Carol got up from her chair, preparing to leave. "The other day, when I asked you if you could think of anyone who might have killed Eddie, you said no, he was simply not the kind of guy who made enemies. Just now I suggested that Eddie didn't want anyone to know he was at the marina. What if it wasn't just anyone; suppose it was someone in particular he was worried about. Suppose that he *had* made an enemy, and that he feared this enemy might try to find him and kill him."

"But if the truck was hidden, that person couldn't have found him."

"But somebody did find him. Hiding the truck wasn't good enough, was it? I wish you'd think again, think harder, about whether Eddie might actually have had an enemy after all. And who that person might be."

Carol doubted that Buddy Stearns would think very hard about whether Eddie French had enemies, and if he did that he would come up with a name. What really concerned her was Buddy's own relationship with Eddie. What had accounted for his unusual beneficence? He didn't strike her as someone who had been raised on the milk of human kindness.

CHAPTER 24

Officer Parsons looked at the list of names the sheriff had given him. Benny Outland. George Fister. Leonard Sweet. Sean Relihan. Richard Hermanian. The last name was followed by a comment in parenthesis which said he was a substitute driver. Bill knew Sweet, not well, but he'd be able to recognize him. He'd heard of Fister. The others meant nothing to him. They appeared to live all over the area, no two closer than four miles of each other. Carol had charged him with making appointments with each of them and questioning them about French. She'd been interested in whether any of his fellow drivers thought Eddie might have had an enemy. And whether any of them believed that Eddie had been Buddy Stearns' fair haired boy and seemed to resent it.

It was too early for regular lake patrols, and Bill was pleased to have something to do other than cruising the county's highways looking for speeders and helping stranded motorists. Dinner over, he left the kitchen clutter to his wife and started in on the task of lining up appointments with the *Breads to Go* drivers.

Meanwhile, Officer Damoth, who had stayed longer at the office than was his wont, was putting the finishing touches on his report when the sheriff walked in.

"Hi, Ken, didn't expect to see you this late."

"I'm here because I had to see you and I figured you'd be coming through pretty soon. Interesting stuff here," he said, pointing his thumb at the file in front of him.

"The car with Ohio plates?"

"Ohio *plate*, sheriff. It proved to be a bit of luck, that single plate when there should have been two."

Carol felt a surge of adrenalin. The day just might be going to end on a better note than she had expected. She pulled up a chair and sat down next to her young colleague.

"Byrnes said he'd be glad to stay, but I told him it wasn't necessary. Actually, he's the one who talked with the Ohio Bureau of Motor Vehicles. Turns out though that outside of that stolen plate, we're not interested in Ohio. We're looking at a car that's registered and owned by a fellow New Yorker. Want to hear about it?"

"No, I'd rather get home for dinner," Carol said, cuffing her colleague on the shoulder. "Come on, Ken, of course I want to hear it. Now!"

"That's what I figured. Should I start at the beginning?"

"Just bring me up to date and tell me if we know who got knifed Sunday night."

"Okay," Damoth said, clearly thrilled to be able to brief the sheriff on what looked like an important matter for the first time since he had joined the force.

"No problem getting into the car. Unfortunately, it had been cleaned out. No registration, no insurance papers, nothing. Actually there were a couple of maps and a receipt from some store in Brighton, but nothing that said who the owner is."

"But we wouldn't be having this discussion if you don't know who the owner of the car is, right?"

"Yes," Ken said, his face breaking into a big smile. "Thanks to the vehicle identification number, we do know whose car it is. Unless, that is, the car, like the plate, has been stolen. The Ford Explorer is registered to a guy up in Brighton name of John Paul Emmons. I've got his address, phone number. Haven't done a search yet on who he is - you know, personal stuff - because we're not sure whether he's the guy who got himself killed on the beach the other night. So I figured you'd want to take it from here."

Officer Damoth was obviously of the opinion that the owner of the car was going to be Mr. X. Carol was more cautious, although she, too, suspected that they now had the name of Crooked Lake's second murder victim within a week. Chief Bellman would be relieved. At least he should be. On the other hand, she hoped that Mr. X, if he turned out to be John Paul Emmons, would not have been killed by the same man who had killed Eddie French. One murder at a time was enough, although she had a sneaking suspicion that she would be inheriting this one, no matter whether it was related to Eddie's murder or not.

"I will take it from here, and I'll do it right now. I'll call that phone number in Brighton, hope someone's home. Why don't you stick around, unless you've got supper waiting for you."

"Supper can wait," Damoth said, which didn't surprise Carol.

"Let me see that paper," Carol said to her eager colleague. "Okay, it's John Paul Emmons of 430 Windermere Road, area code 585 -"

She stopped abruptly. Seeing the name on the page made it clearer than it had been when she heard the name.

"That would be J. P. Emmons." She had remembered that Barrett had found two references to someone called JP when going through Eddie's meager belongings. "I wonder if he's known as J. P."

"J. P.? Is that important?"

"It may be," Carol replied. "I don't remember if you were in the room when Jim made his report on what he found in French's storage locker, but Eddie seemed to have know someone he thought of as J. P."

"My uncle was a J. P. Justice of the peace over in Fulton County."

"I think we can assume that Eddie wasn't thinking of a justice of the peace, Ken. It's somebody whose first name begins with a J and whose middle name begins with a P. Although I suppose the P could come from the last name."

All of a sudden Carol was much more anxious to put that call through to the Windermere Road address in Brighton. There could be many people who go by J. P. in upstate New York, and French's note to 'call JP' would probably turn out to be irrelevant. But she now had a possible lead in a case which hadn't yet produced many.

The phone on Windermere Road rang four times before a woman with a pleasant voice answered. Carol chose not to introduce herself as the sheriff of Cumberland County. She would probably need to do so, and soon, but it was not her purpose to alarm whomever she was speaking to until she had learned a bit about the Emmonses. The voice had identified herself as Danny.

"Hello, Danny. Are you Mrs. Emmons?"

'Yes, of course. How can I help you?"

"Is Mr. Emmons there?"

"No, he's out of town this week. Can I take a message?"

Carol knew that she couldn't avoid saying who she was any longer.

"Mrs. Emmons, my name is Carol Kelleher. I'm the sheriff of Cumberland County down in the Finger Lakes south of you."

The woman with the pleasant voice interrupted, and her voice now sounded worried. Very worried.

"Is this about John? Has something happened? Is he all right?"

It was obvious that Danny Emmons had been worrying about her husband. The mere mention that an officer of the law was on the phone had produced something akin to panic.

"I don't know," Carol said, even if she was fairly certain that she did know. "But I need to ask you if John was driving a 2005 Ford Explorer when he went off this week?"

"Yes, yes, we have an Explorer. It's blue. Why are you asking me about our car?"

"Do you remember what the license plate number is?"

"I can't remember. I never can remember." Mrs. Emmons sounded as if she were on the verge of hysteria.

"I'm sorry to be asking these questions, but we have found a car that is registered to your husband. It's been parked for quite a few days in the town of Southport. Was your husband going to Southport?"

"Southport?" The woman sounded as if Southport was as alien to her as Baghdad. "He didn't say where he was going."

"When did he leave on this trip?"

"Please tell me he's all right," she said. She was one frightened woman, and unfortunately Carol could not help her.

"Like I said, I don't know how he is. I don't know where he is. Let me ask if your car had Ohio license plates."

"Ohio? Why would it have Ohio license plates? It's registered in New York."

"You should know that the car that is registered to your husband, the car that has been parked in Southport for the better part of a week, has an Ohio plate." No need to make a bad situation worse by telling her that the plate is known to have been stolen.

"That's impossible. Perhaps the car you're talking about isn't ours." Danny Emmons was grasping at straws.

"I'm afraid not. It's your car, of that we're sure. Let me repeat my earlier question. When did your husband leave on this trip, and when did he say he'd be back?"

"He left on Sunday. Sunday, after church. He didn't say when he'd be back. He doesn't talk much about his job."

"I understand. What is Mr. Emmons' job?"

"He travels for a company here. They sell school supplies, and he's sort of like a salesman. Promotion, I guess you could call it. He's all over the state. But he's never mentioned this Southport place you mentioned."

Carol broached the subject that interested her most.

"Does everyone call him John? Or is he also known as J. P.?"

"What are you talking about?" Danny almost shouted the question.

"It may not be important, but I would like to know if his business colleagues, or perhaps his social friends, ever call him J. P."

"You do know what has happened to my husband, don't you?"

"No, I do not, but I was hoping that this conversation might help me to find out."

"I'm sorry, but you can't imagine how hard this is for me. John isn't someone who'd leave his car like you said. He'd do his business, then take off for the next place. But it sounds as if you're saying he's disappeared. Have you seen him? At all?"

It was time to level with this distraught woman.

"Mrs. Emmons, I do know how hard this must be for you. If our roles were reversed, I'm sure I would be feeling anxious. The problem is that something happened to a man in Southport last Sunday night. We have no idea who the man is. He had no identification on him. Unfortunately, he's dead. The only reason I'm calling you is because of the car. It is yours and it has been unclaimed since the weekend. I think you can see why I had to call you. I hope that the man is not your husband."

Instead of wails of anguish, Carol's news was greeted by silence.

"Would it help if I told you what he looks like?" she finally managed.

"Yes, if you feel up to it."

"Well, he's about six feet tall. He works out, so he's in pretty good shape. Oh, and he's forty years old. He's got dark brown hair, although he's got a receding hairline. I like to think he's handsome."

She got to the end of this summary and then broke down. Carol could hear her sobbing and then blowing her nose.

"Mrs. Emmons, I think it would be a very good idea if you could come to Southport and view the body. You might want to drive down with a friend or a relative. If you can't do that, I can send one of my officers up there to bring you down. But we'll never know whether this man is your husband or not unless you make the identification."

"Does what I told you about him sound like that man?"

"It's hard to tell. Your description could fit a lot of people." While this was an honest answer to the question, Carol knew that the chances that Mr. X would turn out to be John Paul Emmons were vey good.

"I should never have allowed John to keep his job to himself so much. He didn't want to bother me with it, but -"

The woman had started to cry again.

Carol tried to find words that would calm her down, but nothing worked. In the end, it was agreed that she would make the trip to Crooked Lake the day after tomorrow and would call ahead to say she was leaving. Carol gave her instructions to the Cumberland office, and made a note to herself to be there to take her to the morgue in Southport.

The one question Carol had been careful not to ask of Mrs. Emmons was if she knew whether her husband was a friend or acquaintance of Eddie French. She would address that issue after Mrs. Emmons had seen the body of Mr. X and, in all probability, identified him as her late husband. And after she had persuaded the grieving widow to answer the one question that had gone unanswered over the phone: did John sometimes go by the initials J. P.?

"What do you think?" Officer Damoth asked. "I only heard your side of the conversation."

"She's a nervous wreck, worried sick that our Mr. X may be her husband. And it looks very much as if he is. We should know by Sunday."

"How about him being a friend of French's?"

"Your guess is as good as mine, so let's not worry about that yet. I think we've made progress today. No reason to get greedy. Let's pack it in."

It was on her drive back to the cottage that Carol remembered something she should have thought about before calling Danielle Emmons. The French file included a short list of phone numbers that Barrett had discovered when he went through Eddie's belongings in the storage locker. One of those numbers belonged to a JP. She should have checked the file to see if it was the same as the one on Damoth's report. Annoyed with herself, she turned the car around and went back to the office.

What she found was that French's phone number for JP was not the Emmons' number. Which meant what? That French's JP could not be John Paul Emmons? But Carol wasn't ready to forget the possibility of a French-Emmons connection. The number on French's short list could be a cell phone number. If so, Emmons could still be the JP they were looking for.

CHAPTER 25

Joe Kingsbury was worried, as well he might be. Why had the sheriff visited his office and questioned him about Eddie French? He hadn't believed her stated reason that she needed his help to better understand just who French was. Nor was it solely because his son had been run over and killed by French's boat. By itself, that should not have planted a suspicion that he might be French's killer. Unfortunately, because it was now too late to undo what he had already done, he had made it clear over a period of many months that he would never forgive French. He'd said it dozens of times to his friends, his professional acquaintances, to anyone who would listen. He'd even said the same thing to the sheriff just the other day. He wished he'd kept his mouth shut, even that he'd expressed some understanding of what French had to have been going through after the accident.

But what worried him most was something he had done in the weeks shortly before Eddie's death, something that might indeed get the sheriff's attention. He had begun a campaign of harassing French. In retrospect it had been a dumb thing to do. But he had found no peace of mind since the accident, and that had been way back in the fall. There had been days when he had sunk into what he supposed was depression. On others he had lost his temper at the slightest provocation, shouting at his wife, his secretary, clerks in stores. Madge had urged him to seek counseling, but he hated the thought of listening as some so-called expert tried to burrow into his mind and coax him back to 'mental health.'

For a time after the trial he had focussed his anger on Dietrich, but he had gradually come to realize that there was nothing he could do to tarnish the judge's reputation, much less destroy his career. That had left French as the only target for his frustration. And gradually Eddie had reemerged in his mind as a monster who had not only killed his boy but whose very existence was tormenting him day and night.

He wasn't exactly sure when he had come to the conclusion that he had to turn the tables. But beginning at the end of February he had begun to call French at his home. At first French had answered the phone, but that had lasted less than a week. Irritated at first, he had actually come to prefer it when the phone went unanswered. It meant that French had figured out who was calling, that he was sitting there alone in his house, his nerves on edge, wondering when it would ever stop. And then he had begun to pay a visit to the Woodpecker Lane residence. He didn't want to see French, or be seen by him, but he wanted him to know that he could never count on a quiet night. So he had taken to knocking, sometimes at the front door, sometimes the back door. Even on a window.

It had become a game. For awhile he believed that he was winning the game. There came a day, however, when he realized that what he was doing was taking its toll on him as well as French. Madge could not understand why he had to go out so often at night. More importantly, it began to look as if French might have come to accept this harassment as a part of his life, something he had learned to tolerate. If so, how could what he was doing ever avenge Jordan's death. And if it didn't, what then?

The last thing Joe wanted to think about was 'what then.' He climbed quietly out of bed, checked the time on his bedside clock (3:18 am), and wandered down the hall and on into the kitchen. He had come for a glass of water, but once there he considered a shot of bourbon. Anything that might take his mind off Eddie French. Anything that might break the seemingly endless chain of troubled thoughts that had kept him awake for hours. The bourbon, of course, had the opposite effect.

What if a neighbor had seen him on one of his visits to Woodpecker Lane? It had been dark, but was it really dark enough so that he could not have been recognized? What if French had told a neighbor about his caller? Of course he had never identified himself, but French would have been virtually certain who was calling him. What if a neighbor had told the sheriff about what he thought he had seen or what he had heard?

He would deny that he had ever stalked French; it was beneath his dignity as an upstanding member of the Crooked Lake community. And it was doubtful that it could be proved that he had done what he might be accused of doing. French would not be available to testify. Everything else would be hearsay, wouldn't it? Yet he felt vulnerable. The sheriff had already questioned him. He was sure that she would be back to question him again. After all, it was her duty to track down Eddie French's killer and bring him to justice. He had no idea whether Eddie had other enemies who could be suspects. What he did know was that everybody knew he was still grieving and that he had shown no inclination to forgive the man who had killed his son. If it became known that somebody had been stalking French, he would immediately be seen as the most likely killer. The sheriff would certainly zero in on him as her prime suspect.

It was after 4 am, and after three shots of bourbon, that Joe went back to bed. Sleep never did come, and at 6:45 he got up and, still groggy, prepared for another day in the real estate business. His mind, however, was not on real estate.

CHAPTER 26

Officer Parsons thought he knew the roads of Cumberland County as well as he did the location of every tool in his work room. Obviously he was wrong. He drove back into Yates Center, inquired at the local CitGo gas station, and finally, a good ten minutes after he'd told George Fister he'd be there, he pulled off the old Massey Road and down an unpaved track to the Fister trailer.

While most people were enjoying the weekend, the *Breads to Go* drivers were busy because their five day work week extended from Tuesday through Saturday, Monday being their day off. On this particular Saturday, however, George Fister had a problem which necessitated an urgent visit to the rare doctor who was willing to see him on a weekend. His problem taken care of, Fister was back home by the time Parsons arrived at noon.

"Hi, I'm Bill Parsons," he said when a young but tired woman came to the door. "You must be Mrs. Fister. I have an appointment to see your husband."

"I know. He's waiting for you."

Mrs. Fister corralled two young kids who tried to slip by her through the open door.

"You know we're not through the workbook yet," she scolded them. "Back to your books. Then lunch."

"We're home schooling them," she said to Parsons as she closed the door, "and some days it's more of a chore than others."

"I can imagine," he agreed. Bill could not understand why any parents would want to tie themselves down with home schooling. He didn't have the time for it, and Myrna was perfectly happy to let the public school down in Southport teach their two young ones to read and learn their times tables.

Mr. Fister made his appearance, and the two men disappeared into a bedroom, which looked like the best place to talk without bothering the day's lesson. The room was small, but it had one comfortable chair. Fister urged Parsons to take it, and proceeded to perch himself on the end of the bed.

"You say you want to talk about Eddie French. That it? Hard to believe he's dead, isn't it?"

"I take it you were surprised to hear he'd been killed?"

"Sure was. We all were. Hell, he was only a few years older than I am."

"I don't plan to take much of your time, Mr. Fister, but you don't look very comfortable. Wouldn't you rather have the chair?"

Fister laughed.

"Truth is, the bed is more comfortable than the chair. Softer, you know. The doc just lanced a boil on my ass, and it's a little tender."

Parsons said something about hoping all would be well in short order, and then got down to the reason for his visit.

"French had been a fellow employee at the bakery for how long?"

"I've been with them for close to two years. Eddie came onboard last fall, so I'd say we've known each other for something like six months."

"How was he to work with?"

"I don't really know. We all have our own routes, didn't see much of each other. Becky and I never saw him socially."

"How about the others? Any of your colleagues friends with Eddie?"

"Not so I'd noticed. Well, maybe Benny. That's Benny Outland. At least he talked more with Eddie than the rest of us did."

"What's been the talk since Eddie's death?"

"You mean what are the guys saying about him getting killed?"

"That's it. Anything about what happened, about who might have done it?"

"Who'd know? Eddie was a loner, didn't talk much. One of the guys joked that it could have been his wife because she'd be mad about his not bein' up to date in his alimony payments."

"So people did know that he was having financial problems?"

"Sure. After all, he'd had to sell his car, use a company truck to get around."

"You knew about that episode over at *The Cedar Post*?"

"Now wasn't that something? He must really have been desperate."

"Any talk about why Mr. Stearns kept him on after that?"

"Sure. Nobody knows, but you're right, there's been talk."

"Oh, and what are the men saying?"

"Well, it depends who you listen to. Benny thinks Stearns felt sorry for him. You know, the divorce, the money problems. I guess I agree with him. Relihan, too. Now Richie - that's the guy who takes a shift when one of us is out, like I was today. He's always going on about what it is between Stearns and Eddie, like maybe he owed Eddie something."

"Does he talk about what he thinks Mr. Stearns might owe Eddie?"

"He's not around much, being a part timer. You'd have to ask him."

I'll be doing that, Parsons said to himself.

"So no one was resentful that Stearns seemed to favor Eddie?"

"I wouldn't say that. Relihan could be kinda pissed. He used to rag some on Eddie, but I don't think he really disliked him. Just thought Eddie should get himself a car, or that the rest of us should have the same privileges he had."

"You heard about Eddie getting his truck serviced down at Crozier's just before he was killed?"

"Yeah. Stew told us."

"You, any of the other guys, ever take it upon yourselves to take a truck in for an oil change, lube, whatever?"

"No need. Stew always knows which truck needs what and he sees to it it's taken care of."

"I know I just asked you this, but aside from somebody joking that maybe Eddie's ex-wife killed him, has anybody mentioned any other name?"

"Not that I've heard."

"Okay." Parsons wanted to pursue the point. "How about you? Who's your candidate?"

"I really haven't thought about it. If I had to pick someone, I suppose it'd be that guy whose son Eddie ran over last fall. But that's not fair, is it?"

Parsons was sure Fister had thought about it. That all of them had. But Fister was right that it wasn't fair to blame it on Kingsbury.

———

When he left the Fister trailer, the day's lessons were over and lunch, which seemed to consist of bologna sandwiches and milk, was being consumed at the kitchen table. Parsons said his good-byes and headed for Franklin, where Benny Outland had said he should be taking his lunch break at Purdy's Diner. As he expected, the *Breads to Go* truck sat at the curb a couple of car lengths down the street. The two men didn't know each other, but the uniform prompted a wave from a booth at the far end of the counter.

Outland was the physical opposite of Fister, who had been short, somewhat overweight, and nearly bald. The man who sat across from Parsons in the booth was well over six feet in height, doubtfully weighed more than 150 pounds, and wore his thick head of hair in a ponytail. He was wearing a Carrie Underwood T-shirt. He shook hands and asked if the officer would care to join him for lunch. Outland had already ordered and been served.

"I think I'll pass, but you go right ahead. Maybe I'll have coffee, though." He motioned to the waitress behind the bar to his left.

"Like I told you, Mr. Outland, the sheriff wants me to talk with Eddie French's fellow drivers, see if we can get a sense of what kind of a guy he was and who might have wanted him dead. I know that you probably didn't see much of him, being out on the road all day in different trucks. But anything you can tell me will be helpful."

"Sure, glad to help," Outland replied with a smile which displayed one conspicuously missing tooth. "Eddie was a quiet guy, but in a way he was interesting. Moreso than the rest of the bakery's crew. Not at all what you'd expect by looking at him or listening to him for a few minutes. When I first met him I thought he was a wimp. You know what I mean? Sort of soft, no real spine. But I guess I'm a talker, and he was new, so I decided to see if there might be more to him than meets the eye."

"And you're telling me that there was."

"I am. Or at least I think so. It's possible it was all an act, but I've got a hunch he was a helluva lot tougher than anybody thought. For all I know, it's what got him killed."

Parsons continued to slowly stir his coffee, but he was suddenly more alert than he had been.

"You think you know why he was killed?"

"No, nothing like that. I don't have any idea why he got killed or who killed him. But Eddie French was into one of those militias you hear about, and I can't see wimps joining up with militias, trying to take on the government."

Eddie French a member of a militia? A colleague of people like Russell Coover? Bill leaned across the table.

"How do you know this?"

"He told me. What's more, he tried to talk me into joining up, too. It didn't happen right away, but he must have figured I was trying to make friends, so he started confiding in me. About his problems with his former wife, about how things were all screwed up, about how people had to stop all this messing around with the little guys."

"Did he ever mention the names of his militia friends?"

"He said they were a tight bunch, didn't like to let every Tom, Dick and Harry know who they were or what they were doing. I got the impression that if I was interested, he'd introduce me. But that kind of stuff isn't my thing. I'm really a live and let live kind of guy. If there are others who feel all pissed off about what the government is up to, it's their business. But I don't pay much attention to politics, and I told Eddie how I felt. He seemed to understand. After awhile, he didn't bring it up anymore."

"Mr. Outland, this is very interesting. In fact, I have the feeling that the sheriff herself will want to talk with you about what you've been telling me. We're looking into every angle that might help get to the bottom of French's murder, and this is a new angle. Let me put another question to you. We know that Eddie was allowed to drive one of the bakery's trucks home. Did that bother you at all?"

"No. Why should it? He didn't have wheels, and he did his job. Never heard any complaints. It seemed like Stearns did right by him."

"How about the other men? Did they all see it like you did?"

"Pretty much. Except for Richie Hermanian. He had this crazy idea that Stearns owed Eddie something and this was how he paid it off."

"Did he ever say what he owed Eddie?"

"No, which is why I didn't pay attention. Richie's a sore head, that's all."

"How did the men react to Eddie sticking up *The Cedar Post?*"

"They were surprised, like I was. But I figured if Ginny Smith didn't want to make a big thing of it, we shouldn't either."

While Officer Parsons was driving on to his final appointment of the day, his mind was on Eddie French, militia man. But somehow the picture of Eddie quietly laying down his tiny pistol and crying on *The Cedar Post* bar didn't quite square with the story that Eddie was ready to take up arms against the government. And trying to recruit a fellow bakery truck driver into that cause.

CHAPTER 27

Jack Felton, the weatherman on the Rochester station, had been promising warmer weather for two days and finally, on Saturday afternoon, it arrived. It was as if spring's thermostat had suddenly been turned up by as much as twelve or more degrees. Bill Parsons, on his way to meet Richie Hermanian, felt the urge to roll down his car window for the first time since the previous October. Carol Kelleher actually took her late lunch out onto the porch of the cottage. The trees on the bluff across the lake were still wearing winter's grey, but the cloud cover which had dominated the area for several weeks had given way to a bright sun. A small Sunfish came into view off the end of the point, a welcome harbinger of change in what had been a disappointing early spring.

Carol had come back to the cottage for lunch only because she'd left her chicken salad sandwich and small yogurt on the kitchen table when she left that morning. Fifteen minutes later she had reason to be grateful that she had been so forgetful.

She had not been expecting a call. In Kevin's absence, she often spent Saturdays at the office, and she could think of no one who would be trying to reach her at this hour.

"Hello, this is Sheriff Kelleher." She reflexively chose the formal greeting.

"Carol! I never expected to find you home."

It was Kevin.

"Well, hello, and why did you call here if you didn't expect to find me?"

"Because I just got some great news and I couldn't wait to let you know. Not even until tonight, so I thought I'd leave a message. Is everything okay? I mean, how do you happen to be at the cottage? I thought you were slaving away, 24/7."

"Forgot my lunch. But what's the news?"

"Are you sitting down?"

"No, but I'll take a seat if you think it would be wise."

"It doesn't really matter. Look, I'm coming back next Thursday. And staying for almost a week. Imagine, five whole days, six nights."

"Fantastic. To what or whom do I owe thanks for this surprise?"

"It's a long story, so maybe you'd better sit down."

"You don't have to tell me now if you'd rather wait until you're here. But I've got at least ten minutes before I have to get back to the office."

"Okay, here goes. I've been afraid my dean was going to stick me with the department chairmanship. It had been rumored. I guess I should say threatened. And it would have really thrown us a big fat curve, because being chairman means a lot more responsibility, not to mention no prolonged summer vacation. I'd have a hard time getting up to the lake except for the occasional weekend and maybe two weeks sometime in July or August."

"And you're going to tell me you aren't going to be punished after all?"

"Right. The dean spared my life and our marriage."

"I take it you haven't wanted to tell me the bad news?"

"I knew it would be a real downer, so I thought I'd try to talk Coggins out of it and not let you know unless I had to."

"I love you, and this just proves what powers of persuasion you have."

"I'm not so sure it's my powers of persuasion, Carol," he said. "What happened is that he had a cardiac emergency, had to rush home from a conference and undergo triple-bypass surgery. I made my 'get well quick' visit to the hospital, hoping I'd find him well enough to beg for a reprieve on the chairmanship. Surprise of surprises, he beat me to it. Said his health crisis was a wake up call, not just for him but for all of us. We got to talking about our families, our need to enjoy this precious life - that's just what he said. He asked about you. I wasn't even sure he'd remember that you were way up there keeping the criminal class at bay. But he did and he asked how we were managing, you on Crooked Lake, me in the city. All I had to do was say it worked because we had our summers and the occasional long weekend. Bless his soul, he told me he was changing his mind about the chairmanship gig. Said he'd give it to Jake Francis, who happens to be a confirmed bachelor. And then came the icing on the cake. Old hard ass suggested I take a few days right now. Never even asked me whether my TA could handle my classes."

"I have the feeling I've heard your last complaint about your dean."

"I think you have. And just possibly I'll work a bit harder to produce that book he thinks I should be writing. Not in the summer, though. That's when we'll be enjoying our precious life."

"Summer and this next week. Think of it as a warm up for the joys of July."

"And August."

"I'd bring you up to date on the latest in the French case, but right now I've got to get back to the office and get to work on it. When should I expect you?"

"I should be able to get a flight Thursday afternoon. I'll call you this evening with the details, and I'm sure you'll be able to drop things and come and get me at the airport."

"I'll be there, whenever you say. I love you and your dean."

———

Carol breezed into her office a little after 1:30, a smile on her face so noticeable that Ms. Franks commented on it.

"You look real happy," she said. "Have you had a break-through in the French case?"

"I can't speak to that yet, but my husband is arriving unexpectedly. That'll put a smile on any girl's face."

There was no smile on Officer Parsons' face when, at four o'clock he finally got away from Richie Hermanian. The utility driver for the bakery had answered all his questions, but had done so in a manner which Parsons had found irritating. If I were Stearns, he thought, I'd sack the man. Yesterday, if possible.

Unlike Fister and Outland, who had been pleasant enough and, in Outland's case, even somewhat helpful, Hermanian not only had a negative personality, he managed to couch all of his opinions in language which was gratuitously offensive. He hadn't liked French. He didn't like Stearns. He had a low opinion of the other employees at *Breads to Go*. Why had he stayed with a business where he obviously had no friends and didn't like the job or the pay? The only reason, Parsons decided, was because he wanted part-time work and wanted to do it without having to spend his time under close supervision or in the company of people he loathed.

He realized that Carol would not be interested in his assessment of Hermanian's misanthropic persona. What mattered to her, and by extension to all of them in their search for Eddie French's killer, was whether he had said anything which might be useful to their investigation. He had hoped to hear something which might explain Stearns' willingness to support French when his behavior made that support counterintuitive. Both Fister and Outland had said that Hermanian seemed to believe that the manager may have owed Eddie something. But Hermanian had not elaborated. Either he had nothing specific in mind or for some reason didn't choose to put it into words. Maybe now that Eddie was dead, common decency counseled against an unsubstantiated charge that there was something not quite right about Eddie's relationship with Stearns. But Hermanian didn't seem like somebody who would be much moved by the counsel of common decency.

They had talked about who might have killed French, but Richie Hermanian had not given him a name. In fact he had pointedly made clear that he wasn't interested in such speculation. Nor had he said anything which indicated that he felt badly about Eddie's death. It had been 'just one of those things' that happen to people who are in the wrong place at the wrong time. Had he meant being in a tarp covered boat in a marina yard on a cold night in March? No, not specifically, just a bad place and a bad time. To hear Hermanian tell it, it could as well have been a supermarket at closing time.

Parsons made his report to the sheriff later that afternoon, and as he had expected she was most interested in Outland's story that Eddie had belonged to a militia. Given the nature of this sparsely populated area between the belt of cities along the thruway and the Pennsylvania border, Eddie's militia was in all likelihood Russell Coover's. They agreed that Eddie was an unlikely militia member, but partly for that reason they knew they should take the report seriously.

When Carol headed back to the cottage, Parsons' typed summation of his conversations with the bakery drivers under her arm, she found herself trying to cope with the cognitive dissonance created by Kevin's homecoming on the one hand and this new revelation about the late Eddie French on the other.

CHAPTER 28

Sabbath or no, both the sheriff and the deputy sheriff would be hard at work on this, the first Sunday in April. Neither of them had a pleasant task to look forward to. Carol had arranged for Danielle Emmons to come to Southport for the purpose of viewing the body of the man who might be her husband. She had no idea how long she would be with Mrs. Emmons. It was doubtful that it would take the woman more than a minute, if that, to decide whether Mr. X was her husband. Carol was almost certain that he was, but that would mean that she would have to set aside her law enforcement hat and become comforter-in-chief for awhile. And then there would be questions, many questions, and coaxing answers from the grieving widow might take quite a bit of time.

Meanwhile, Bridges would be talking to Russell Coover. For some reason she couldn't quite explain to herself, Carol was convinced that that conversation could not be postponed until Monday. She needed to know, and she needed to know it now, whether the alleged leader of the region's shadowy militia group had indeed recruited the late Eddie French and what he could tell her about him. What is more, she was only too glad to let Sam be the one to approach Coover. They both detested him, but Sam was more likely to keep his temper than she was. Or was he?

Danielle had called to confirm that she would be at the Sheriff's Department in Cumberland by eleven o'clock, and that she would be accompanied by her friend, Lori Quentin. Carol had brought along a small box of Danish and had put on the coffee pot. Mrs. Emmons might not be in the mood for a second breakfast, but it seemed a thoughtful thing to do. Carol found it hard to sit still. She alternately stood at the window, looking out at the parking lot, and shuffled papers on her desk. It wasn't until almost 11:15 that a car pulled into the lot. Two women stepped out, one of them a tallish brunette in a light blue seersucker suit, the other a buxom blond dressed in jeans and a white blouse. Carol guessed that the brunette was the anxious wife.

"Hello, I'm Sheriff Kelleher, and you are -"

She paused before extending her hand to the brunette. But she had been right.

"I'm Danny Emmons, and this is my friend Lori. She was good enough to drive me down this morning."

Introductions over, Carol ushered them into the squad room.

"I don't know whether you care for coffee, but the pot is hot and we have both sugar and cream. Also a few Danish, if you're interested."

To her surprise, Mrs. Emmons did express an interest in both coffee and Danish.

"How about you, Mrs. Quentin?"

"Okay, that would be nice."

Carol realized that she should not have been surprised. Danielle Emmons was in no hurry to take a look at the body down in Southport. On the other hand, small talk was hardly the order of the day, and the questions she wanted to ask would have to wait until the body had positively been identified as that of John Paul Emmons.

"I'm sorry that you have to spend a beautiful day like this doing what you're doing," Carol said. "It's nice of you, Mrs. Quentin, to keep Mrs. Emmons company."

"That's what good friends are for."

"I told her I could come by myself," Danny said, "but she insisted. And it did make it easier."

Her attempt to smile as she acknowledged her friend's support failed. Carol had been observing her as she poured the coffee. She was tense, her effort to maintain an appearance of calm palpable. Carol wondered about her age. She looked to be younger than thirty, perhaps no older than her late twenties. Her husband, if Mr. X turned out to be her husband, looked as much as ten years older.

"I've been trying to tell her that this man isn't very likely to be John," Mrs. Quentin said. "I've known him for a few years, and he's - well, he's so solid, so responsible. My theory, like I've been telling Danny, is that somebody stole his car. You know, the Ohio license plate and all that. So John probably rented himself another and went on about his job. Didn't want to worry Danny. That'd be like him."

"It's possible," Carol said, but she was sure it wasn't true. This was no time to try to raise Mrs. Emmons' hopes. And the odds that her husband's car had been stolen, its plate changed, and then been left for a week on a street in Southport were hopelessly long.

"We'll know soon enough," Mrs. Emmons said. "It's good of you to try to give my spirits a boost, Lori, but right now I've just got to be tough."

"You've always been tough, Danny."

"Let's be honest. I've never been tough, Lori. I've let John make all the decisions, let him tell me what I should do, what I shouldn't do. Why didn't I ever make him tell me what he's doing? I mean, I didn't even know he was in Southport. I didn't even know there was a Southport."

"That isn't what I meant," Lori said.

But it was obvious to the sheriff that, whatever Lori meant, Danny had been one of those wives who deferred to their husbands in virtually all matters. Whether he intimidated her or she deferred to him because she was by nature a worshipfully obedient wife, Carol did not know.

"Whatever the case may be, Mrs. Emmons, you're facing a difficult moment. I very much hope that your fears aren't justified, but no one can blame you for having them. I'm sure I would. Maybe we should head on down to Southport. Do you think you're ready?"

"Let me finish my coffee, and then we can go. Is it far?"

"No, it's just at the south end of the lake. It should take us no more than half an hour."

It actually took them twenty-two minutes to get to Chief Bellman's office and the tiny room, capable of holding only one body at a time, that passed for Southport's morgue. It would take a bit longer when tourists invaded the area, but early April was still off-season by Crooked Lake standards.

Bellman, like the sheriff, was accustomed to spending his Sundays out of uniform and out of the office. But on this prospectively important occasion, he was there to greet them. He knew it wasn't nice, but he hoped that the Emmons woman would announce that Mr. X was her husband. That would permit him to release the body, even if it wouldn't tell him who the man's killer was.

The dreaded moment had come, and it took Danielle Emmons only one quick look at the body to realize that her husband was indeed dead.

"It's him," she said, her voice so low that Lori Quentin, now standing back behind the two law officers, couldn't hear her.

Mrs. Emmons turned and flung her arms around the person nearest her. It happened to be Bellman. Carol stepped up and took charge.

"Let's just go outside," she said. "We all need some fresh air."

She guided Danielle back to her friend, leaving Bellman to slide the body back into its place in the locker without an audience.

It was a matter of but a few minutes before they found a bench in the town square. Danny and Lori sat down, but Carol stayed on her feet. It was her intention to let them have a cry and then put them in her car for the trip back to Cumberland. It was only then that she began to think about what difference in might make if Lori Quenton was with them when she started to ask the questions she had to ask Danny. To leave her friend outside or in another room would be cruel to Mrs. Emmons. How it would affect what she said to the sheriff, it was impossible to predict.

Thinking the view might ease Danny's pain, she took the hill to the upper road. A mile or two down the road they passed a pull off where there was a place to sit above a vineyard.

"Why not stop back there?" she said. "I need to ask a few questions, and this might be a good place to do it. Better than that stuffy office."

There were no demurrers, so Carol turned the car around and pulled off at the lookout.

Two benches sat on a ridge with a view which justified the decision to put them there. Danny took her seat, looking resigned to the ordeal that lay ahead. Without asking where she should sit, Lori selected the other bench, leaving Carol to share the seat with Danny.

"I know that you'd rather get in the car and head straight back to Brighton," she said. "I can't pretend that you're eager to answer my questions, but I know you must want to help me discover what happened to your husband and to make sure that whoever killed him is caught. I'll try to be brief, but it's very important that we do this now, even if this is a hard time for you."

"I suppose it's funny," Danny said, "but maybe it isn't as hard as you think. I already knew John was dead. I don't mean I really knew, but I was sure. I was sure the minute you called me."

"What was it about what I told you that made you think he was dead?"

In spite of her words, Danny had a look on her face that reminded the sheriff of war photos of battle weary soldiers, their faces wearing what journalists referred to as a thousand yard stare. She was looking at the lake, far below her, but she didn't appear to be seeing it.

"Nothing in particular," she said after a long pause. "Just the fact that you were on the phone. I don't think I'd ever gotten a call from the police. You know it means bad news."

"You told me John didn't talk about where he was going when he set off on one of his trips. Was there any hint this time that he was worried? Or maybe excited? Anything that was different than usual?"

"I don't know. I didn't think so at the time, but maybe that's because we were in the habit of just saying 'good-bye, see you soon.' You know what I mean?"

"I do, but think about it. Did he seem at all different than usual?"

"You used the word excited. John isn't someone who usually gets excited, but - I don't know, he might have been. Just a little anyway."

"But did he say anything out of the ordinary?"

"Not that I remember."

"He didn't mention Southport?"

"No, he never says where he's going. I'd never heard of Southport anyway. It wouldn't have meant anything to me."

"How about names? Had he talked about somebody in the days before he took off? Not necessarily names, but like he had somebody in mind."

"I'd like to say yes, but I can't. I never knew of anybody he saw in his work." Danny swallowed hard, looked down briefly, than resumed her thousand yard stare.

Carol raised a question that she had hesitated to ask.

"Have you ever had a feeling that just maybe John wasn't doing what you thought he was doing? That he wasn't really a school supplies salesman?"

Danny shifted her gaze to the sheriff.

"Do you suppose that he had some kind of private life I didn't know anything about?" She said it without a hint of animation, much less shock.

"I have no idea. But I wonder if you ever thought about it, wondered if his reluctance to discuss his job might be a cover up for something."

"There was a time when I sometimes wondered if he had another girl in some other town, but I haven't given that any thought in several years."

Perhaps she should have, Carol thought. What if his killer was someone who had reason to suspect that his wife was two-timing him with Emmons? But how would that explain Eddie French's references to JP? *If* John Paul was Eddie's JP.

"Do you recall that on the phone I asked you if your husband ever went by JP instead of John? You didn't answer that question."

"Didn't I? I don't remember. Anyway, he's just been John since I met him. He told me that some people called him JP back in high school, but he didn't like it. He preferred just plain John."

Carol thought about Emmons' given name. It reminded her of the recent pope, John Paul II. But Emmons' parents could not have named their son after the pontiff, who wasn't elevated to that exalted position until 1978. That would have been quite a few years after Emmons was born. She started to put that fugitive thought aside when it occurred to her that she really didn't know exactly when Emmons had been born. Maybe he was younger than he appeared.

"How old was your husband, Mrs. Emmons?"

Danny looked puzzled.

"Does it matter?"

"Probably not, but why don't you tell me."

"He was 40 on his last birthday. That was in January. He was fourteen years older then me. Was that what you wondered about?"

"Good heavens, no." Carol was embarrassed that her question had been misunderstood. "To be honest, I was wondering whether he might have been named for the recent pope."

"Was there a pope named John Paul?" It was such an innocent question that Carol had to suppress a smile.

"Yes, and he died about six years ago."

"Oh. Well, John's family wasn't Catholic, so I'm sure his name didn't have anything to do with the pope."

What's more to the point, Carol said to herself, is that your husband was born about seven years before his namesake became pope. But another thought had come to mind. John Paul Emmons had been called JP back in high school, and he had just recently turned 40. Eddie French was roughly the same age, and he had made two written references to someone named JP. She thought it unlikely that the two men had been in high school together, but Kevin had urged her to think of the two Crooked Lake murders as more than a coincidence.

"You've been very patient, Mrs. Emmons, and I think we're about ready to go back to Cumberland so that you and Mrs. Quentin can head back to Brighton. But I have two final questions. The first has to do with your husband's schooling. Do you know where he went to high school?"

"I couldn't give you the name of the school, but it was somewhere around Buffalo."

"In the city? In one of the suburbs?"

"I'm sorry, but I don't know. I just know he came from over in that part of the state. I didn't meet him until he'd moved to Brighton."

I'll put one of the men on that tomorrow, Carol thought.

"Okay. My last question: Did your husband ever mention someone named Eddie French?"

"No, I'm pretty sure I've never heard that name. Why, do you think he knew this man French?"

It was Carol's turn to say she didn't know. But for the first time since Kevin had reminded her of her aversion to coincidences, she was ready to believe that the two unsolved Crooked Lake murders had indeed been committed by the same person.

CHAPTER 29

Carol took advantage of the fact that it was Sunday and that she was in the office alone to put her feet up on the desk. It had been an interesting if difficult three and a half-hours with Danielle Emmons. One big problem had been solved, but at the expense of turning the French murder case into the French-Emmons murder case. At least that was how it looked to her at the moment, although she was reasonably certain that in just a few days she would know that John Paul Emmons and Eddie French had known each other as students in the oddly named town of Cheektowaga.

All things considered, Danielle Emmons had handled the situation fairly well. The poor woman had not only lost a husband, she was now confronted with the the real possibility that he had been living a double life and that it had cost him his. It was important that her friend and neighbor Lori had been with her and was now driving her back to Brighton. Carol had been concerned about questioning Danielle with Lori present, but it had worked out fine. Lori had not interrupted, and when it came time to go it was clear that it was she, not Danielle, who would be taking charge of the arrangements that had to be made. And there were arrangements to be made, some of them by Carol herself. She should never have let the killing of Mr. X spend the week in limbo, neither Bellman's responsibility nor fully hers. For one thing, an autopsy had never been performed, an oversight that necessitated a call to Doc Crawford that very afternoon. She would make that call as soon as she had contacted Bellman and told him that she was now assuming full control of the investigation into Emmons' death. The police chief would give her no quarrel.

It was following those two calls and while she was organizing her desk that Sam Bridges walked into the office.

"You still here?" he said, sounding surprised.

"As you see," she replied. "I've become a workaholic."

"Well, I hope your day has been pleasanter than mine."

"Let's exchange reports and then I'll let you know."

"Let me grab myself a coke. Anything for you?"

"Sure. Make it two."

She heard two cans fall in the vending machine. Sam set the cokes on the desk and took the seat opposite the sheriff.

"You go first," he said.

Carol walked him through the session with Danielle Emmons, trying to treat it as a breakthrough day, even if it guaranteed more work for the already swamped Cumberland County Sheriff's Department.

"So it came out as you figured?" Sam asked.

"I'm not sure what I thought would happen," Carol said, not willing to say that it was Kevin who had argued that the two murders were somehow related. "Now our task is to find out just what Emmons and French have in common. Tell me about our friend Coover."

"In the first place he claims he never met French, wouldn't know him if he saw him."

"So he's saying French wasn't in his militia?"

"I put it to him right up front: 'it's our understanding that Eddie French was a member of your militia group.' Know what he said?"

"It's your story."

"He got all worked up, asked me where I get all this bullshit about him being in a militia. Gave me the usual line, 'I'm just a law-abiding citizen, minding my own business, blah, blah, blah.'"

"Of course, if he's not in the militia business, how would he know about French." Carol was appropriately sarcastic.

"That's what you'd think. But after he gave me his lecture about what a loyal American he is, patriotic and all that stuff, I asked him if he'd heard about the French murder. He says he heard about it, all right, but it didn't interest him because there was no reason to be concerned about such a wimp."

"He didn't know French, but he calls him a wimp?"

"That he did, and I jumped on him, wanted to know why he thought French was a wimp. He sidestepped the question at first, but when I pressed him on it he started accusing me of harassing him. Harassing. He loves that word. Must have used it half a dozen times. The closest I got to an explanation of why he thinks French was a wimp was a tirade about that episode at *The Cedar Post*."

"That doesn't make sense. I'd have thought he'd defend a guy who pulls out a gun."

"Not this time. What bugged him, or so he said, was that French just gave up the gun. And to a woman at that, which makes him a wimp."

"And I suppose Coover would have a different opinion of Eddie if he'd shot Ginny."

"Could be, although I've got a feeling he'd laugh at that little tiny pistol French was carrying. He goes in for bigger hardware."

"What's your feeling about this? Was Coover lying that he didn't know French? I mean didn't know him personally."

Sam gritted his teeth.

"I think he lies all the time, at least when he's talking to us. But I can't prove it. I told him French had actually tried to recruit people for the militia. I didn't give him Outland's name, but Parsons seems to think Outland's a straight shooter and I'd trust what he says before I'd trust Coover. Do you suppose we ought to start questioning some of the other guys who've been linked to the militia?"

Carol got out of her chair and walked over to the window. It was beginning to get dark.

"I'd like to," she said cautiously, "but all we've got to go on are rumors. These guys don't go around with name tags announcing their membership in a militia. Tell you what, though. Why don't you see what you can do about putting together a list of names, along with whatever information you and the men can come up with that suggests a militia connection. It might come to nothing, but I'd like to take a crack at some of Coover's buddies."

"You don't think Coover could be French's killer, do you?"

Carol shook her head, looking rueful.

"Off hand I can't think of any reason why he might be," she said. "But except for Kingsbury, there's no one else that comes to mind. Maybe Eddie learned something about the militia, what its plans were, and Coover felt he had to shut him up."

"But how would that explain the Emmons guy?"

"It wouldn't, so I guess I can't see Coover as Eddie's killer. Unless French and Emmons were killed by two different people with two different motives. Which brings us right back to where we started. Do you enjoy this business we're in?"

Sam was surprised by the question.

"Sure, otherwise I wouldn't be doing what I'm doing. You getting tired of it?"

Carol shook her head again, smiling this time.

"Not yet. Don't quit on me. If you decided you'd had enough, my would-be detective of a husband would probably argue that he should be your successor. And that would never do. Nepotism, you know. Besides, you're a policeman through and through, and he's just a frustrated academic."

Deputy Sheriff Bridges beamed.

CHAPTER 30

"I found Brinker." It was Officer Barrett who made the first report at Monday's squad meeting.

"You've talked to him?" Carol asked.

"By phone. You want me to go see him?"

"Let's have the facts first. Who is he?"

"It wasn't hard to get his address and phone number. Turns out he lives over near Seneca."

"And you're sure he's the Brinker who bought Eddie French's boat?"

"The same. Talks a lot, answered all my questions. Seemed surprised to be getting a call from the fuzz, though."

"Please, Jim. We aren't the fuzz. You've been watching too many cop shows."

Barrett smiled. Whatever the sheriff's feelings about vernacular euphemisms for officers of law enforcement, he knew she would welcome his report. And she did, even if she was determined to pay a follow-up visit to Mr. Brinker herself.

It seems that he had been in the market for a used power boat when a friend reported he'd seen a Four Winns with a for sale sign on it at the Lakeshore Marina. Brinker had taken the short drive over to Crooked Lake, talked with Pat Kelley, the owner, and gotten French's name and number. Less than 24 hours later he had taken possession of the boat, trailer and all, for practically nothing. Barrett enjoyed sharing Brinker's tale of the transaction.

"The way he tells it," Barrett said, "Kelley had clued him in to the fact that it was the same boat that had run over and killed a boy back in September. Seems Kelley had also informed him that there'd been several other guys who'd been interested in the boat, but they'd lost interest when they learned it was a killer boat. That's what Brinker called it, a killer boat. Guess some people are uncomfortable operating a boat with that kind of history.

"Anyway, it didn't bother Brinker. He says French wanted at least a couple of thousand. And he agrees it was in pretty good shape and worth a lot more than the $750 he gave him. But he had

the impression that French needed cash, needed it bad, so he said
$750 was his final offer. It worked. Tough bargainer, don't you
think?"

The assembled officers agreed that Brinker had indeed been
a hard bargainer. Only Carol entertained some sympathy for the
cash strapped and now deceased Eddie French.

"Did he say anything about French?" she asked. "Like what
his financial problems were?"

"No, just that Eddie had reluctantly accepted his check."

"How about French's accident? Did Brinker talk about that,
give you any idea how he felt about it?"

Officer Barrett was beginning to feel less upbeat about his
report than he had a minute or two earlier. It didn't look like he'd
asked enough questions.

"We didn't go into that, but he was interested in the fact that
French was dead. He'd heard, of course. By now just about
everyone around here has. But he was naturally curious, asked a
bunch of questions. Are we sure French was murdered? Any idea
who did it? I got the feeling he's going to be going around making
sure all his friends and neighbors know that his boat used to
belong to a murder victim."

Carol had no reason to believe that Floyd Brinker had more
to tell her than he had told Barrett. Perhaps, however, she should
talk with Kelley. Was he in the habit of allowing boat owners to
slap a for sale sign on their boats and park than at his marina? Or
was Kelley, like Stearns, willing to give a guy in trouble a break?

After the meeting, she was debating which of several tasks
related to the French case she should pursue first when Ms. Franks
buzzed her to say that someone named Earl Skinner was on the
phone. Carol had almost forgotten the man on whose boat Eddie
French's body had been found.

"Good morning, Mr. Skinner. How are you today?" It was
the best she could come up with on the spur of the moment.

"I'm okay. My boat isn't. Do you know where my boat
cushions are?"

Damn, Carol said under her breath. The cushions should
have been returned to the marina several days ago.

"I'm sorry about that. No excuse, but I guess we've been
pretty busy. We're finished with them. It sounds as if you're back
at the lake."

"We are. I couldn't stand sitting around down in Carolina, knowing about the boat. We got in last night."

"Tell you what. If you're not tied up this morning, I can bring the cushions back. Is that okay?"

"I'd appreciate that."

"Good. Now where are you? At the marina or your cottage?"

Skinner was still at the cottage. He gave the sheriff directions as to how to get there, and they agreed on ten o'clock. Carol would talk briefly with him and then see if she could track down Justin Longacre and discuss Eddie French's trial with his attorney. It was something she should have done sooner.

She had expected Earl Skinner to be slender, but realized as soon as she saw him that that expectation was due solely to his name. He stood about five foot five and looked as if he weighed well over two hundred pounds. He sported a deep tan, evidence, she supposed, that he had spent a fair amount of time on South Carolina's golf courses.

Carol handed him the cushions, which he clasped to his chest like favorite children.

"Come on in. Care for coffee?"

She declined the offer, wondering if he would take the conversational initiative or leave it to her.

"Where do you stand on French's murder?" he asked, taking the initiative as he led her into what appeared to be the music room. At least it had a pair of impressive speakers and one of those tower-like stacks of CDs. She guessed that it might hold upwards of three or four hundred.

Carol doubted that what she had to report would satisfy Skinner's curiosity, but she gave him a brief summary of how things stood, sidestepping the second murder and mentioning no names. Then she raised a question of her own.

"Joe Kingsbury tells me he heard about French's death from you. Are you and Mr. Kingsbury friends?"

"Just good acquaintances, through Lions Club. He's quite a bit younger than I am, you know. My kids, unlike his, are all grown up. And I'm retired."

"But you called him to pass along news of French's death. Did he ever talk with you about the son he lost? About French? The trial?"

"Some. Joe's a private guy, and like I said, we're not really all that close. But we talked some. It was a terrible thing, losing a son like that."

"And French. You told Mr. Kingsbury you knew French?"

"I told him the story of how we met, but I didn't know French so there wasn't much to say. Just that he wanted to sell his boat."

"How did he seem to take the news of French's death?"

Skinner considered the question.

"Hard to say. He probably thought of it as good news, if you know what I mean. But he didn't say so."

"Have you heard that French did sell the boat?"

"No. When did that happen?"

"Back in the fall. Months ago. By the way, did Pat Kelley let people use his marina to sell their boats? I mean was it common to see boats there with for sale signs on them?"

"Why, did French leave his boat at Lakeshore?"

"He did."

"I wonder if Kelley took a cut," Skinner said, sounding thoughtful. "Oh, and to answer your question, I don't remember seeing boats for sale at the marina. Not saying it didn't happen, but if it did, it wasn't common. Now rentals, that was something else, but it was part of Pat's business."

Carol wasn't eager to start speculation about the current owner of Eddie's old boat, but she wanted to see Skinner's reaction to Floyd Brinker's name.

"The guy who bought French's Four Winns, his name is Brinker. Floyd Brinker. Do you know him?"

"Never heard of him." It sounded like an honest answer. And why wouldn't it have been?

When Carol left to meet Justin Longacre, she was firmly of the opinion that Floyd Brinker's and Earl Skinner's relationships with Eddie French had nothing to do with his death. The only connection seemed to be the boat.

She probably should have made an appointment with Longacre, but she gambled that he would be in his office, which was also his house. It sat on a side street near the Southport High School.

Longacre was at home and at work, as Carol had guessed he would be.

"Hello, you're the sheriff, aren't you?" He came to the door himself. Either his secretary was unavailable or he was making do without one.

"I am, and I was wondering if I might have a few minutes of your time."

"Let's see," he said as they stepped into a small office. He examined a desk calendar. He stood between Carol and the desk, so she wasn't able to see what he was looking at. She was willing to bet, however, that Justin Longacre had nothing pressing on his calendar that morning.

"You're in luck. My next appointment isn't due until after lunch. Come on in and sit down."

Carol knew of Longacre, although they had never met. He had been practicing law in the Crooked Lake area for less than two years. She wondered why he had chosen Southport. It didn't seem like a promising location for a young attorney trying to launch a career. She'd done a bit of research, and had discovered that Longacre's was a general practice, that he had run an ad or two announcing his availability for accident and injury cases, and that he had handled a couple of divorce cases. Not French's, however. She thought he looked harassed, but decided it was only her imagination.

"I'm here to talk with you about the French case, the one you handled last fall," she said, getting right to the point of her visit.

Longacre's face broke into a smile, and almost as quickly the smile disappeared. He's pleased to have won that case, Carol thought, but he thinks it's not a good idea to look too pleased in view of his client's recent death.

"Oh, that." He opted for a self-deprecating approach to the subject. "It was just chance that I had that case, you know. French didn't have any money, but he needed counsel. To be perfectly frank, I was pretty new here and I needed business. Figured the case would give me some publicity, whether we won or lost."

"And you did win."

"Funny thing about that. I expected to lose when I agreed to represent French, but it didn't take long before it became apparent that the prosecution's case was pretty thin. The judge was too smart to let sympathy for the Kingsbury kid outweigh the fact that he didn't have a 'diver down' flag anywhere in the area. I guess I was lucky."

"Had you ever been involved in a wrongful death case before?"

"Never. That's why I was lucky. They don't teach you everything in law school."

Don't I know, Carol said to herself. The memory of a couple of her first experiences as an attorney popped into her mind.

"The verdict in the French case didn't seem to go down that well with a lot of people around here. Has that affected your business at all?"

Longacre sighed.

"I wish I knew. People know who I am now. But business isn't appreciably better. Hard to say whether the verdict has anything to do with it. I like to think people are fair, that they know attorneys are just doing their job. You know, innocent until proven guilty. Anyway, nobody's gone out of his way to give me a hard time, not even that poor kid's family."

"You haven't said anything about what happened to French. You do know he's dead, don't you? Murdered in fact."

"Of course. Everyone knows."

"What do you hear? What's the talk about his death?"

Longacre's chair swiveled away from the sheriff, then back again.

"You'd think there'd be a lot of talk, wouldn't you? Well, there hasn't been much. At least not to me. A couple of guys asked me if I didn't think justice had finally been done, but most people probably figure I wouldn't want to talk about it. Funny thing, though. I guess I do think justice has finally been done."

Carol found this a surprising confession.

"I thought you said it was easy to prove French's innocence."

"It was," he agreed. "He was legally innocent. But not morally. Do you understand what I'm saying?"

Carol was well aware that it was not uncommon for lawyers to harbor mixed feelings about the innocence of their clients. Still, she found Longacre's comment interesting.

"So do you have any regrets about the case?" she asked.

"None. I did my job. I guess you could say that God did his."

She strongly disliked this conviction that God intervenes in human affairs to punish those whose deeds he finds offensive. Where is the evidence? After all, evil doers frequently get off scot free. She could not imagine a God who would be so selective, so arbitrary. If Kevin were there, he'd probably say something to the effect that it simply made the case for God a hard sell. In any event, she wasn't about to engage Justin Longacre in a theological argument.

"You took the case pro bono, yet I understand that French paid you something for your services." It was a statement, not a question.

Longacre's face reddened slightly.

"How would you know that?"

"We're investigating Mr. French's death, and that inevitably turns up lots of information that may be irrelevant. Like the check he wrote you back in the fall for $150."

"He said he wanted to thank me for defending him. Naturally I protested, said that wasn't how the system worked. But he insisted. In any event, it was a small check, much less than I usually charge my clients. I think it made him feel better."

"Yes, it probably did. No problem - I just had to ask. One last question, then I'll be going. Did you ever see French after the trial? To talk to?"

"Not that I remember, but - no, there was one time when we ran into each other here in Southport. No big deal, just a chance meeting. Said hello. He thanked me again, but we didn't talk."

"So he didn't ever say he had a need for your services again?"

"No. Why, do you think he might have had some other reason to get himself a lawyer?"

"I was just wondering."

It was 11:40 when Carol left Southport and headed back to Cumberland.

CHAPTER 31

"How about we go to *Harbor View* for dinner?" Marge Stearns greeted her husband as he walked into the house.

"*Harbor View*? You've got to be kidding. They won't open for several weeks."

"Surprise!" she said. "It is open. I called. This change in the weather must have decided them to open early. They started serving dinner last night. So how about it?"

"But they won't be serving waterside. It's still too dark. You won't even be able to see the bluff."

Buddy Stearns knew that his wife enjoyed dining at an outside table close to the water's edge. But it was also obvious that he didn't share her interest in going to *Harbor View* that evening. Unfortunately, Marge had made up her mind.

"Come on. I'm dying for some fish and chips."

"That's not what they call it, Marge. It's fish fry over here."

The Stearns had made a spur-of-the-moment trip to London several years earlier, taking advantage of a special offer she had spotted while browsing the web. Marge had loved it, and had fallen for the customarily denigrated English cuisine. Especially fish and chips.

"I don't care, it's still fish and chips that I want for dinner. So go change. I've already reserved a table."

Buddy knew when he'd lost an argument. Twenty minutes later they were on their way to the poorly named *Harbor View* restaurant. The harbor was nothing more than a dozen interconnected docks which enabled diners to tie up their boats. But they did serve a reasonable fish fry. Or, if one preferred, fish and chips.

There was no need for the reservation. At least not at six o'clock. There were a number of people at the bar, but only three tables were occupied. Buddy had been right about one thing, however. Night was fast falling, and the bluff across the lake, while visible, would soon disappear from view.

Marge was full of small talk. Her husband had other things on his mind, with the result that the dinner table conversation was decidedly one-sided.

"It's not only fish and chips," she said. "Remember those ploughman's lunches we'd get in the pubs?"

Buddy hadn't liked ploughman's lunches. Nothing but cheese, chewy bread, chutney and pickled onions. He hated the onions. Why had his wife become such an Anglophile? He tried to retreat into his troubled thoughts, but Marge was in the process of reminiscing about what had been her only trip abroad.

"Do you suppose we could go back? I'd love to see the Tower of London again. Oh, and Piccadilly Circus. Don't you love those English names? Maybe we could even get out into the countryside. It's supposed to be really quaint."

"You'd have to drive on those awful roundabouts," Buddy said disapprovingly, "and on the wrong side of the road. Anyway, what's wrong with Crooked Lake?"

"I'm not down on our lake, but it's not very exciting. Tell me now, is it? I'd really love to go back to the Tower of London. All those important people they kept there. A lot of them got themselves beheaded. I wonder why they had to do it that way?"

"It's because they hadn't invented the electric chair yet."

"Well, they could have used a firing squad."

"For heaven's sake, Marge. What kind of dinner conversation is this?"

Buddy pushed his chair back from the table and excused himself for a trip to the restroom. It was less that nature had called than that he needed to get away for a few minutes. His thoughts were on matters other than the Tower of London and fish and chips, and Marge was giving him no opportunity to focus on those matters. Not that he would have shared his thoughts with his wife if she were in the mood to listen.

He stayed out of the dining room for as long as he dared. Even so, Marge was quick with the obvious question.

"Are you all right?" She looked worried.

"I'm fine. Just a nasty headache. Do you suppose we could go?"

The main course hadn't been served, and Marge was conflicted.

"Can you wait until they bring us our dinner? We can take it home and I'll warm it tomorrow. Okay?"

Her reluctant husband acquiesced in this compromise, and ten minutes later they paid their bill, left a small tip, and headed home with their dinner in a couple of styrofoam containers.

"What's the matter, dear?" Marge asked as they made their way up the west side of the lake.

"Why do you think there's something the matter?"

"It's not just a headache, is it?"

Buddy Stearns hated conversations like this. He hated this one more than most. But he was determined not to blow his stack.

"It's been a bad few days at the bakery, that's all. We'll get it sorted out. What I need is some time to think. Gotta figure out how I'm going to handle a personnel issue. I'll be okay, but I need to get back to the office. Understand? I'll drop you off. It'll only take me an hour, probably less."

There was no personnel issue that required Stearns' attention. Not at the moment. There had been one, of course, and it involved Eddie French. What he needed to do was to go somewhere where he could be away from his wife and her incessant if good-natured chatter about things that didn't interest him and only made him more frustrated. And worried.

Twenty-five minutes later he was parked on a bar stool at *The Cedar Post*. He had deliberately chosen a stool at the end of the bar farthest from where the waitresses placed their orders. The stool next to him was occupied by a man he'd never seen, a man who was engaged in conversation with a young woman to his left. Ginny Smith, the bartender, was very busy, which left Stearns alone with his scotch.

He had been too kind to French. Helped him out too many times. And the sheriff had noticed. She had commented on how frequently he had done Eddie a favor which defied common sense. Hired him in spite of the fatal death of that Kingsbury boy. Given him the use of a delivery truck, 24/7. Forgiven him that unforgivable episode at this very bar, the one where he had pointed his gun at Ginny Smith and demanded the money in her register. Buddy thought of himself as a thoughtful, generous guy, but he was well aware that what he had done for French strained credulity. The sheriff had not pursued the issue, but it had been clear that she thought it strange.

Perhaps she had forgotten it. He hoped so, but he doubted it. And if she hadn't, what would she make of it? That he really was a prince, someone who was the very model of a good samaritan? In other circumstances, she might have thought so. But these were not other circumstances. One of his employees, the man he had been so kind to, had been murdered. The sheriff's task was to find French's killer, and if she were as intelligent as he assumed she was, she would be interested in things that didn't look quite right. And he doubted that his generous behavior where French was concerned looked quite right. He feared he might have planted a suspicion in her mind, a suspicion which would prompt her to visit him again - and again - and to keep asking questions about French.

"Another scotch?" Ginny asked as she turned her attention to him from the increasingly cozy couple to his left.

"Sure. Might as well." He hoped his response would not encourage the bartender to strike up a conversation. On a quieter night it might have, but Ginny was soon called away to tend to several men who were seeking a refill further down the bar.

Buddy Stearns found himself imagining how he could best answer the sheriff's questions, if indeed, as he feared, there would be more questions. If he tried to make up a story, the sheriff would wonder why he hadn't mentioned it when first she questioned him. And if he did make up a story, it would not only have to sound believable. It would have to stand up to an investigation if the sheriff decided to pursue it.

He considered different story lines as he sipped his scotch. He didn't like any of them. There was simply no way to explain his relationship with Eddie French. Better to stick to the Buddy as good samaritan line. Unfortunately, that always brought him back to the possibility that the sheriff would discover that he had once lived and worked in a town called Cheektowaga. And by now she would certainly know that Eddie French had been born and grew up in that very same town.

CHAPTER 32

On her way back to Cumberland, Carol found herself engaged in a mental inventory of just what her officers were doing on this second Monday of spring. There was a lot to do, and she didn't have enough men to get it done as quickly as she wanted it done. She started with Parsons, and then stopped. Her men. Out of force of habit she thought of them as her men. And all of them *were* men. The only woman under her command was JoAnne Franks, and she ran the office, answered the phone, kept the records, did just about everything except patrol the roads of Cumberland County and pursue law breakers. Otherwise, her colleagues were all men. Bridges, Parsons, Barrett, Byrnes, Grieves, Damoth - she started ticking them off in her mind. Why were they all men?

When she had started what was destined to be an abbreviated career as an attorney, she was one of two women in a firm of ten. At the time she had thought of the five to one ratio as unfair, inasmuch as law schools were already graduating lots of women. When she left Albany to assume her late father's job as sheriff, the ratio had improved, but not by much. Three women out of eleven. She couldn't recall who had been recruited to fill her shoes.

The force she had inherited to maintain law and order around Crooked Lake had all been men, and budgetary constraints had made additional hires virtually impossible. There had been only one, Officer Damoth, and he had now been with them for more than two years. So why was she suddenly bothered by the fact that none of her colleagues were women? She certainly wasn't dissatisfied with any member of her team, much less hoping for a resignation which would give her a chance to bring in a new officer. But for the first time since she had become sheriff she began to worry about the matter. She worried about it all the way back to the office.

The result of all this worrying was that she never finished her inventory of who was doing what with regard to the French case. Bridges was at her door before she had taken off her jacket with a reminder of what he had been up to.

"May I have a minute?" he asked. "I thought you'd like to know where we stand with regard to who's who among Russell Coover's militia."

"Absolutely." Carol remembered that this was one of things she was most anxious to hear about. Surely there must be someone who would be able to confirm Eddie French's alleged flirtation with the area's militia group.

"It's not easy pinning down membership, you understand," Sam said. "I get the impression that as these things go, Coover's bunch isn't particularly well organized. In fact, Coover denies he's even involved in a militia. But you know that. Anyway, I started asking around after our chat yesterday. Nothing official of course, just trying to get a few names. What I have is a short preliminary list - just three guys in fact, and I can't swear my information is accurate. But it gives us a place to start."

"Good. It may come to nothing, but I'm sure that driver for the bakery didn't make it up that French said he was into the militia thing. Maybe French made it up, but I doubt it."

"Here's my list," Sam said as he laid a sheet of paper on the desk. "Any of those names ring a bell?"

Carol read them off: Ralph Ticknor, Joe Hess, Lou Pellerini.

"No, never heard of any of them." The paper she was looking at contained addresses, phone numbers, places of work, and brief notes reflecting Sam's impressions of the reliability of his sources.

"Like I said, these guys may not know what you're talking about if you question them. But I think there's a good chance that Ticknor at least is someone you'll want to see. He's definitely a friend of Coover's. I'll keep on it, and should be able to get you another name or two."

Sam left and Carol reread his report.

Ticknor. She was interested in the fact that he taught phys ed at Yates Center High School. People who are charged with educating our kids shouldn't be fooling around with militias, she thought. But then again, maybe Sam's wrong about Ticknor. She'd approach him with an open mind.

She turned her attention to another matter, the possibility that John Paul Emmons was Eddie French's JP. According to his wife, Emmons had been called JP in high school and didn't much like it. More importantly, he had attended high school in the Buffalo area. Could it have been in Cheektowaga? If so, could it have been the same high school French had attended and where he had earned the nickname Lefty?

Carol got in touch with Officer Parsons.

"Bill, are you where you can swing by the office for a few minutes?"

"Sure, just as soon as I wrap up a small problem in West Branch. What's up?"

"Remember your call to Cheektowaga High School? The one that put you on to that guy Tiegs? Well, I'd like to give you another Cheektowaga assignment. We'll go over it when you get here."

"Sounds like fun." Parsons didn't sound as if he believed it.

The whole idea of a French-Emmons connection might turn out to be much ado about nothing. But it might prove to be the key to an investigation which didn't seem to be going anywhere fast. Parsons could use the phone; indeed he would have to use the phone. But if he could establish that Emmons had indeed been in school with French, a follow-up trip to the Buffalo suburb with the Indian name might be in order. Not only to learn more about the late John Paul Emmons but to flesh out their sketchy picture of French himself.

Fleshing out the picture of Eddie French would also neces-sitate prying more information out of Isabel French about her former husband's life. What about those jobs that hadn't lasted long? What could she tell him about Eddie's habits, other than his penchant for taking out his frustration on his children? Had there been any friends, even casual acquaintances that had made an impression on her? Carol realized that Isabel had told her very little. She also knew that Isabel would not want to talk with her. That had been apparent the last time they had spoken.

Carol was planning what she would say to Isabel, how she could get around the woman's unwillingness to see her again, when Officer Parsons walked in.

"Off to Cheektowaga, is that it?" he said as he pushed open the sheriff's door.

"Maybe. First things first." Carol liked her senior officer, a good natured veteran of years of cruising the county's highways, a man who never let his private life interfere with his duties as a member of the Cumberland County Sheriff's Department. "We know about French's references to JP and we know that Emmons once answered to JP. They're both dead. Let's see whether Emmons is Eddie's JP. You talked with the people over in Cheektowaga. Let's do it again and see if French and Emmons ever crossed paths."

Carol didn't need to spell it out in greater detail. Parsons would know what she wanted, what he would need to do.

"I'll tackle it right away, unless there's something else that's higher priority."

"If something comes up, I'll put one of the other men on it. Just see what you can come up with."

"Aye, aye, sir," he said as he got to his feet.

"By the way, I'm sure you aren't eager to spend a day in Buffalo, especially now that it's off-season for the Bills, but if you find that French and Emmons knew each other back in the day, you may have to go over there and poke around a bit."

"I figured as much. What's your hunch?"

"I don't like to get ahead of the evidence, but I'll bet they were classmates. And if they were, I'll bet their relationship requires our attention. More work for you."

"I'll see what I can do about clearing my calendar."

Carol gave him a big smile as he left the office.

She then turned her attention back to the other things that needed doing on the French case. There was Isabel. And Ticknor. And -

She'd just told Parsons that he needn't worry about a priority higher than Cheektowaga and John Paul Emmons. She'd put someone else on it. Much as Carol had wanted to be the one to talk with Ticknor, it suddenly occurred to her that maybe she should put someone else on that one, too. How about Byrnes?

There was something about all of her men - yes, they were all men - that would make them stand out in a crowd. All, that is, except Byrnes. There was nothing distinctive about his build or his features that would attract attention. Just an average guy. In fact Byrnes liked to refer to himself as an average guy. He also spent less of his time on the road than any of his colleagues, and that was because he was the resident computer expert, the one most attuned to the electronic age. All of this made him least likely to be recognized as a member of the sheriff's department. And it made sense that whoever tried to get Ticknor to talk frankly about the local militia should not be easily identified as a member of the sheriff's department.

Carol went down the hall to what the men called the music room. Byrnes, as she expected, was seated in front of his PC. Whatever was on the screen was changing rapidly as his fingers worked the keyboard.

"What are you up to?" she asked.

"It's that mess involving the Millwoods and the Sheltons. Reminds me of the Hatfields and McCoys, except it's boring."

"I'm going to ask you to give it a rest and tackle something that could be a lot more exciting. Or not. Do you happen to know Ralph Ticknor?"

"I've heard the name. Who is he?"

"Sam thinks he's involved in Russell Coover's militia movement."

"And what should I be doing about this man Ticknor?"

"Nothing if there's a chance he knows you. Or might recognize you. But you remember that one of the bakery drivers told us that Eddie French had gotten involved with the militia. I'd like to know if it's true. Do you suppose you could find a way to talk with Ticknor? Out of uniform, of course. No need to let him know the law is quizzing him."

"We're going cloak and dagger, is that it?" He asked, a big grin on his face. "What's my pitch? I can't just find him, say 'let's have a beer,' and start grilling him about who's who in our local anti-government cabal."

It was the right question, of course.

"Let's back up a bit. First, he teaches over at Yates Center. Phys Ed. You can bone up on him, find out what he looks like, where he hangs out after school. There'll be a way, I'm sure, to just happen to be where he is, someplace where it's natural for a couple of guys to get into a conversation. It should be right down your alley."

"I don't know that I'm qualified to play Sam Spade. But I'll see what I can do. Why not let me do a bit of research, then we can talk about my m.o."

Byrnes and his m.o. Carol shook her head as she walked back to her office to make the call to Isabel French. It could well be a non-starter, she thought, but I believe I just might have made Officer Byrnes' day.

CHAPTER 33

The problem was that she didn't really want to talk to Isabel French. She hesitated, the phone in her hand, and then she put it back in its cradle. Once more she found herself wishing that there was another woman on the force. Somehow this would be a meeting that called for a woman, although she knew she would have a hard time explaining that to her colleagues or even to Kevin. Perhaps particularly to Kevin. Even if there were another female officer to turn to, she would inevitably be young and inexperienced. What made her think that this would-be officer would handle an interrogation with the former wife of Eddie French any better than Barrett? Or Bridges? Especially Bridges.

Carol knew that she would be going over to Franklin herself. The logical and efficient thing to do was to call ahead and ascertain whether Isabel was at home, or if not at home at the diner where she worked. She decided not to do that. She would simply get in the car and drive over, taking a chance that Isabel would be available. What is more, she wouldn't take the shortest route. She would take the hill road over toward Watkins and then follow county road 39. It would be a prettier drive, and it was a pleasant day with a clear blue sky and a breeze that would stir the trees and their early spring buds. It might even lift her spirits and make the encounter with Isabel less difficult. She knew she was procrastinating, perhaps even hoping that Isabel had chosen to take the day off and go up to Rochester or someplace else.

No, she said aloud to herself, I have to see her. Today. She told JoAnne where she was off to and headed for the parking lot.

But Carol had been right about one thing. It was a beautiful drive, and it did improve her attitude. By the time she reached the outskirts of the village of Franklin, she felt ready to talk with Isabel, even to be pleasant to her. The kids were still at school and Isabel was doing nothing more challenging than reading *Redbook*.

Magazine still in hand, the tall, slender woman answered the doorbell. Her face immediately registered her displeasure when she saw who was at the door.

159

Carol managed a smile and what she thought was a cheery hello.

"Hi," she said, "I know I should have called, but I was in the area and I thought I'd see if you were in."

It was, of course, a lie, but Isabel wouldn't know that.

"Is there something wrong?" she asked.

"No, no. May I come in?"

A very reluctant Isabel French stepped aside and motioned the sheriff into a living room that betrayed the fact that the house was inhabited by young children who did not make it a practice to pick up after themselves. Apparently their mother wasn't in the habit of doing so either.

Isabel invited her to sit down, and, as she had done on Carol's previous visit, assumed a yoga position on the floor against a wall. Her feet were bare and she was wearing jeans and a see through blouse. She wasn't wearing a bra. Once again the descriptive word that came to Carol's mind was androgynous.

"How are you doing?"

"I'm doing fine," Isabel answered. "You're not here to see how I'm doing, are you? I've been wondering, why did you go into police work? It can't be a happy way to spend your time."

"I didn't go into police work, Mrs. French. I stumbled into it when my father died. He used to be the sheriff in these parts, and his friends approached me about succeeding him. I was practicing law at the time."

"You didn't have to say yes, did you? But you did, and now you're bothering people like me about a crime we don't know nothing about."

"It's part of the job description, Mrs. French. It's the way we get at the truth. It isn't always pleasant, and, believe me, I don't enjoy what you call bothering people. But I'd have thought you would like to see your ex-husband's killer brought to justice. Am I wrong?"

"No, of course not, but I had nothing to do with it. So why are you here? Again."

"Simply because I have two questions I need to ask, and you're in the best position to answer them."

"So what is it?" Isabel asked.

"Was your husband in a militia?"

It would have been difficult to put a word to the expression on Isabel French's face, but Carol was instantly aware that the woman knew exactly what was on the sheriff's mind.

"Militia? What's a militia?"

It was a feeble attempt to feign ignorance.

"I believe you know what I'm talking about. Was your husband a participant in a local organization that advocated extreme measures, if necessary, to put a stop to government policies it disliked?"

"We never talked about politics," Isabel said.

"Perhaps not, but did your husband ever say anything about belonging to a militia? Did he ever mention that he was going out to a militia meeting? Or a militia practice? Please think hard. You must have known your husband well enough to know what he did with his spare time."

Isabel relaxed out of her yoga posture, stretching her legs in front of her. But her face did not relax. It remained tense, reflecting an inner struggle.

"Is this important?" She was still stalling for time, but Carol was now confident that she would answer the question.

"It is very important. And I need to know what you know. So tell me, was Eddie a member of a militia?"

"I think he might have been. Like I said, we didn't talk much, but he did say something once or twice about having to go to some kind of meeting. He didn't like to be questioned about where he was going or when he'd be back, but I remember him mentioning gun rights. The meetings seemed to be about gun rights."

"Did he ever mention names of the people he was meeting with?"

"Once, when he was angry because I kept asking him where he was off to, he did tell me it was some guy named Hoover. He called him the leader of the militia. And he was really pissed with me, asked me if I was finally satisfied."

"So he did actually tell you he was going to a militia meeting?"

Isabel shook her head in the affirmative.

"Do you remember when this militia business started, how long it lasted?"

"Not long before the divorce. I honestly don't know how long he'd been involved with these people."

"Why is it, Mrs. French, that you haven't wanted to share this information with me?"

The pale woman on the floor across from her blushed. For a long moment she said nothing.

"I suppose I was embarrassed," she finally responded. "I know what a militia is. It's not very patriotic. It would be one more thing the kids would have to live down. God, can you imagine what lies ahead for them? Their dad a child beater, a man who'd killed a boy with his boat, a militia kook - and now a guy who holds up a restaurant? For all I know, nobody knew about the militia business except me. And this guy Hoover. Maybe it wouldn't come out. But I guess it has."

"We aren't sure. Perhaps Eddie was making it up for reasons of his own. Anyway, I'll be talking to the man you call Hoover. Unless it turns out that Eddie's death has something to do with a militia connection, I have no intention of making it public knowledge. We aren't building a case against a militia group, just trying to find who it was that killed your ex-husband."

"You said you had another question?" Isabel may not have wanted to hear it, but she definitely wanted to get this unwelcome meeting over with.

"We talked about Eddie's jobs when I was here last. You told us he had quite a number of them, that he had trouble keeping them. I'd appreciate it if you could give me a complete list of the jobs he held while you were married, plus any others you know about from before the marriage. All of them, including anything you remember about when he started those jobs, when he left, and, if possible, the names of his supervisors."

"But I can't possibly do that. Some of it was a long time ago."

"I understand, and I'm not asking you to do it this minute. But I want you to think about it and put everything you can remember in writing. We need to know who these people are, the people Eddie worked for, the people who may have fired him."

"Do you think one of those people killed him?"

"I have no idea. At the moment I have no reason to think so. But I should talk with them. So please make it a point to give me a list. If you like, I can have one of my men come by your house and pick it up. How about tomorrow, is that possible?"

Isabel was relieved not to have to demonstrate her limited knowledge of Eddie's work resume right then and there. But she knew that a failure to make a good faith effort to assist the sheriff would only raise suspicions about her own motives.

"I'll do my best," she said, "and I'll call you as soon as I can."

"Good," Carol said, hoping that Isabel would set aside the *Redbook* as soon as she left and consult her diary if she kept one or begin wracking her brain if she didn't.

The job list might prove important, but what really interested Carol as she drove back to Cumberland was the knowledge that Eddie French had indeed been involved with the local militia. How deeply and for how long she didn't know. One thing was certain, however. Isabel's Hoover was obviously Russell Coover, and she wasn't going to let him get away with pretending that he didn't know Eddie. Between them, she and Officer Byrnes would get to the bottom of this unexpected development in the case. Whether it would help identify Eddie's killer was another story.

CHAPTER 34

The key to Simon Ostrowski's storage locker was still in her possession. Carol thought it was about time to return it. Not that Ostrowski would be needing the extra key, but it would give her an opportunity to pay him another visit and see if he had remembered anything else about the stranger that had been worrying Eddie French.

Woodpecker Lane looked just as it had the first time: prematurely run down for a relatively recent development, depressing, unwelcoming. Ostrowski had said he'd be home, and there he was, standing on the front stoop as she pulled up to the curb.

"Got news about French for me?" he asked as she came up the walk.

"Not much, but I'm here because maybe you do."

"Me? I don't know nothing I didn't tell you before. Anyway, come on in. Place looks better than it did that day, which ain't saying much."

Carol remembered the post-poker party chaos, and while it was obvious that Ostrowski would never win any good housekeeping awards, finding a seat in the living room was easier than it had been when she first met him. To her surprise, this time he offered to get her something to drink.

"Don't have much in the fridge, but I'm sure there's a beer or two. Or coffee if you prefer. I never cleaned out the morning's pot."

"Thanks, but I'll pass. I came by because I thought you might like your key back. The things Mr. French had put in your place didn't tell us much."

Actually it had told her a few things, such as the presence in Eddie's life of someone called JP and the state of his checking account. But Barrett had inventoried all of Eddie's belongings, and she was convinced that there was nothing else in the locker that might lead them to his killer.

"Didn't figure it would. Eddie didn't go in for what they call creature comforts. Maybe he did once upon a time, but I've got a hunch he was selling stuff to make ends meet at the end."

Carol gave him the key and turned to the real reason for her presence in his living room.

"I've been thinking about one of the things you told me when I was here before. It seems Mr. French had talked to you, told you he was concerned that some stranger was hanging around, asking about him, and he wanted you to keep him posted if you saw this guy. You said he never gave you a name, but that he did give you a description."

"Right, but like I told you, it sounded like just about anybody. You know, pretty normal, not a beanpole or a little runt. Not a kid or an old timer, either. I think he said dark hair, but truth is I didn't pay close attention."

"You mentioned this stranger when you remembered about Mr. French's boating accident. Did he say anything about why the stranger was somehow interested in the accident? Like maybe he was a lawyer? Somebody from the press? Maybe even a member of the family of the boy who was killed?"

"All he said was that someone was bothering him about the accident."

"Did he seem annoyed about what this someone was doing, or was he more worried? Maybe even afraid?"

Ostrowski thought about it.

"You mean did he think this guy was out to hurt him?"

Carol turned the question into one of her own.

"Did he sound as if that might be what he was thinking?"

"Maybe. Jeez, I don't really know. He might have been. I guess I didn't give it much thought. I mean, it wasn't my problem."

"Have you thought about whom it might have been that Mr. French was talking about?"

Simon Ostrowski was obviously feeling guilty that he hadn't taken Eddie French's request for his help more seriously.

"You think I should have?"

"No, Mr. Ostrowski, as you say, it wasn't your problem."

But Carol had been giving some thought to that question, and the name that kept coming to mind was of course Joe Kingsbury.

When she left, dusk was beginning to settle in and lights were coming on in some of the houses on Woodpecker Lane. The only person in sight, however, was a man at number 221. On a whim she walked up the street and said hi.

"You're Mr. Hedrick, right? I think we spoke briefly a week or so ago."

"Sure, I remember. Not often our sheriff comes to visit us. You still on that French case?"

"We are. I'm afraid these things don't get solved overnight."

"Not like on TV, huh?"

How many times have I heard that, Carol thought.

"Anyway, I have a question I'd like to ask you. It's about Mr. French. Did he ever approach you and say something about some stranger who'd been bothering him, maybe hanging around his house?"

"Yeah, now you mention it he did. Didn't say much, just wondered if I'd seen this guy."

Carol was surprised. She should have talked with neighbors other than Ostrowski earlier.

"Did he tell you who it was he had in mind?"

"No name, but I'm pretty sure I know."

"You know?" She couldn't believe what she had just heard.

Bill Hedrick's face wore a broad smile under the Woodpecker Lane streetlight.

"Well, I can't be sure, but I've got a pretty good idea"

"Why don't you tell me bout it."

"I may be wrong, but I'm usually right." He didn't say what he was usually right about. "I think it was that Kingsbury fellow, the one who was in the news last fall. Or at least his kid was."

Carol seized the moment and suggested that they go inside the Hedrick residence.

Unlike Simon Ostrowski's house, the Hedrick place was furnished sparely. It was, perhaps for that reason, much neater. An even better reason appeared at a door down a hall.

"Who is it?" the woman in an apron who was in he process of drying dishes asked.

"Just the sheriff, honey. I'm sure she won't be a minute."

Mrs. Hedrick, if that's who she was, disappeared. Mr. Hedrick turned his attention back to the sheriff.

"Have a seat."

"Yes, I'll do that. Let's talk about how you know Mr. Kingsbury was in your neighborhood. And when. And why you believe he was the stranger Mr. French had spoken of."

"I don't read much, sheriff. Never did. Hated it back in high school. But I do pay attention to the papers. You never know when you'll see something that might be important, like a rise in school taxes or some stupid regulation about burning leaves or using those fancy recycling bins. Anyway, Kingsbury was in the papers a lot back in the fall. Seemed to be quoted just about every week in the *Gazette*. His picture got run two or three times. So I'd know him if I saw him. And I saw him one night just a few weeks ago. I'd just stepped out for a cigarette - Joan, she don't like me to smoke in the house - when I saw a car pull up way down the end of the street. This man got out, walked up this way, looking around like maybe he was trying to read the numbers. He never saw me. Last I saw of him he was going around the side of French's place. Seemed kinda funny, what with him parking so far away and then heading toward the back of the house."

"When exactly did this happen?" Carol asked.

"Can't remember the day, but I'm pretty sure it was close to three weeks ago. It was night time. We'd had supper, were getting ready for bed. It must have been after ten o'clock."

"At that hour it would have been dark. How could you recognize him as Mr. Kingsbury?"

"You sound like one of those defense attorneys on the TV shows. Think I can't see so good, is that it? Look, no offense, sheriff, but I see just as good as I did when I was a young un. It was Kingsbury, or maybe his double."

Hedrick might have seen Kingsbury. From what she knew of Kingsbury's feelings toward French, he might well be the person who was stalking his son's killer. But on a dark night, how could Hedrick be sure it was Kingsbury he had seen? And if it was Kingsbury, how could he not have seen Hedrick, smoking a cigarette on his front stoop, and stepped out of sight sooner?

"Mr. Hedrick," Carol said, "experts will tell you that eye witness testimony is less reliable than we think it is. I'm sure you're confident that you saw Mr. Kingsbury that night, and you may well have. Is it possible, however, that you think you saw Kingsbury because you associated him with French on account of the trial? In other words, is it possible that you thought you saw Kingsbury because you expected to see him?"

Bill Hedrick looked confused.

"I'm not sure I understand. If somebody was hanging around French's house, don't it make sense that it was somebody like Kingsbury? Couldn't have been a thief. Nobody lives on this street that's got anything worth stealing. Like I said, he was a dead ringer for Kingsbury."

"Did you tell Mr. French that you'd seen Mr. Kingsbury that night?"

"I was going to, but I didn't see him for awhile, and then next thing I knew he'd been kicked out of his house. It all happened pretty fast."

Carol reflected on her conversation with Hedrick as she drove back to the cottage. If Kingsbury were ever put on trial for killing French, and Hedrick was called to testify by the prosecution, even a half-way competent defense lawyer should have little trouble discrediting his testimony. That didn't mean that Hedrick hadn't seen Kingsbury. But what if he had? That didn't mean that Kingsbury had killed French. Stalked him, perhaps. Killed him? Carol found it hard to picture this respected real estate agent and member of the Lion's Club as a murderer. On the other hand, she had to confess that she couldn't put herself in the shoes of a grieving father.

CHAPTER 35

Tuesday. Only two more days before Kevin would be getting back to the lake, courtesy of his dean's triple-bypass surgery. Carol had many things to do, but she put them out of her mind for an hour so she could change the bed and neaten up the cottage. No need to go shopping just yet; they'd hit *The Cedar Post* for their Thursday night dinner.

By far the most important news of the day came mid-morning when Officer Parsons walked into her office, a big smile on his face. She was willing to bet that he had discovered that Eddie French and John Paul Emmons had gone to school together in Cheektowaga.

"Struck gold," he said calmly, trying to rein in his excitement. "Our friend French was a year ahead of John Paul Emmons at Cheektowaga High School, making it almost certain that he's Eddie's JP."

"Good work. Any word that they were close while they were there? Or that they kept up a relationship after high school?"

"No. It was too long ago, and the staff at the school were just combing through official records. The names didn't mean anything to them. If we're to learn more about them, it's going to take a trip over there. By the way, I did put through another call to that guy that told me about French going by Lefty back in high school. Tiegs. He was thrilled to hear from me. Thinks maybe he can help us solve our crime. I doubt it. He didn't seem to know Emmons, couldn't recall whether he and French were buddies."

"Okay, we know something. Looks like you'll have to spend some time in Buffalo. Sorry, in Cheektowaga. There have to be people who remember those years. It wasn't all that long ago. I'll bet some of their teachers are still around. What's your situation on the home front? Do you think Myrna will mind you taking off for a couple of days?"

"She'll understand. In fact, her sister's coming down to spend a few days. She'll probably be glad to have me out of the house."

"Let's put our heads together before you set off. I want to make sure we've thought of everything we need to ask people."

"Sure. Tomorrow, say three?"

"Could you make it two?"

"Of course," Parsons agreed.

———

When Officer Byrnes stuck his head in Carol's open door at 4:15, it was immediately apparent that she was due for another positive report. Byrnes tended to be dour, but not this time. His smile was not as broad as Parsons' had been, but the word Carol would have used to describe the look on his face would have been smug: 'I told you I could do it, and I did it.'

"May I assume that you've had a productive chat with Ticknor?" Carol asked.

"Is it that obvious?"

"I'm becoming good at reading faces. Tell me about it."

He took a seat across Carol's desk and launched into his report. It went something like this.

It seems as if Ralph Ticknor was the assistant coach of the Yates Center baseball team, which consisted of only the starting nine and four subs. Why such a small squad needed an assistant coach was not clear. Perhaps they simply had to keep the second member of the school's phys ed staff busy. Carol had asked why Ticknor wasn't doing something more useful, such as coaching the girl's softball team, and Byrnes reported that the principal apparently thought he lacked the sensitivity to deal with the opposite sex, especially the younger members of the opposite sex. The result was that a history teacher who had once played softball herself was drafted for that assignment.

In any event, Ticknor hadn't been particularly busy when Byrnes got to the playing field. Spring's late arrival had delayed the beginning of outdoor practice, and it showed. The Yates Center nine would have to make some quick improvements if it was to compete effectively in its interscholastic league.

Byrnes had taken a seat on a bench along the right field foul line along side three students and a man who might have been the father of one of the players. He had watched for five or six minutes before getting up and walking over to where Ticknor was leaning on a bat and watching the coach rap fungoes to his outfielders.

"Bet you're glad to get outside. Been a nasty spring, hasn't it?"

"Yeah, pretty bad. Your kid playing?"

"No," Byrnes had replied. "I just get an itch for baseball every year when April rolls around."

"Well, I don't think you're going to see much of it from these Warriors," Ticknor had said, using the school's nickname. "You played baseball?"

"A little. How about you?"

"You kidding me? The game's too slow. I'd rather hunt, go fishing."

Byrnes remembered thinking that both hunting and fishing required a lot more sitting and standing around than baseball.

"I oughta hunt more," he'd said. "I've got friends say deer hunting's great around here. Couple of them talk about getting a bear now and then. Can you imagine, bringing down a bear? You ever do that?"

The conversation had gradually segued from hunting to guns more generally, with Byrnes playing the role of someone who was interested but inexperienced, seeking guidance from the worldly Ticknor.

The breakthrough had come when Byrnes mentioned a film he liked. Carol, who knew little about films produced before the 1980s, had never heard of it. *The Most Dangerous Game.* Byrnes explained that it dated back to the beginning of the 30s, shortly after the advent of sound.

"The 30s?" she said, her voice expressing disbelief. "You sound like Kevin."

"I'm sorry," he said. "I don't know anything about your Kevin's taste in films. It just happens that a friend who likes early Hollywood movies invited me over one night to see a film 'I just had to see.' It was pretty primitive, one of those old black and white jobs, but it had a powerful story. The point is that this guy captures people and then sets them free so he can hunt them down. The most dangerous game, get it? It's man."

"Oh," Carol said.

"I figured that Ticknor wouldn't have heard of it, much less seen it. Anyway, I tried to act interested in the idea. Asked him what he thought of it? You know, man as hunter of man."

"Well, that's an opening gambit I'd never have thought of," Carol said.

"Funny, though. Ticknor sounded like it was worth thinking about. And can you believe it, the damned fool asked me if it didn't remind me of what militias are accused of doing. I thought I'd thought about every angle, but I never expected him to say anything like that."

"And?" Carol had been hanging on every word of Byrnes' report.

"I figured I had to be careful, not go rushing into Eddie French's case. So I acted puzzled, like I'd never thought about it that way. But it was like I'd opened a door, and he began to talk about militias. Cocky son of a gun. Never had to push him. He talked about a group he belonged to. No names, but he didn't seem worried about blowing the group's cover."

"How'd you get to Eddie?"

"I just asked. Tried to sound surprised that he'd brought up militias, and said a guy I'd known had told me he'd joined one. I said I hadn't believed him. Of course he asked me who it was, and I said it had been that dumb loser French."

Carol stared at Officer Byrnes with new appreciation of his investigative skills.

"You're brilliant, Tommy, do you know that?"

"Thanks, but I'm not brilliant, Carol. Just patient."

It was the first time he had ever called her Carol.

"What he said about French, well, it puts the lie to our friend Coover. He claimed French did join up, that he had actually come to a couple of meetings. But then Eddie pulled that stunt at *The Cedar Post*. Ticknor thought it was pretty gutsy, but Coover didn't agree. So Eddie got his walking papers before he ever got to participate in one of those shoot-em-up sessions they have."

"And Ticknor never had a clue that you're a cop?"

"If he did, he's a damned good actor. No better disguise than levis, an old wind breaker, and a Yankees cap."

"Was the talk just about French, or did he say anything about what his militia group is up to?"

"Mostly about French. I figured if I asked too many questions he'd be suspicious. I tried to sound as if I thought the militia business might be exciting. You know, sort of like I was thrilled to be talking to a guy who's really into guns. But no, he didn't divulge any secrets. He did say they used that old state forest land on the way to Bari, but it sounded more like fun and games to me."

"Nice work. I'm going to have to have another session with Coover, but I'll keep Ticknor's name out of it. No need to blow my best spy's cover."

All in all it had been a good day. French and Emmons in high school together, French a sometime member of Coover's militia. By themselves these revelations didn't prove anything. But they definitely opened up new possibilities for an investigation that had been floundering.

CHAPTER 36

Carol filled her coffee cup and went out onto the deck. It was a beautiful morning. The clouds were few, and the lake was calm and crystal clear.

"God's in his heaven, all's right with the world."

Now why had that thought come to mind? Robert Browning, if she remembered correctly. But not since she was a little girl had she pictured a white haired grandfatherly figure, somewhere above the clouds, benignly watching over mere mortals down below. She knew, however, why she was in such a good mood. Kevin was coming.

She would be unable to turn the French case over to Bridges and the rest of her men. At least not entirely. But she intended to make the most of Kevin's unexpected visit. They would be romantic. They would enjoy a couple of dinners at *The Cedar Post*. They would rejoice in the fact that Kevin had escaped the threat of administrative duties at the college. And of course they would talk about the latest murder on Crooked Lake. Make that two murders. It would be impossible for Kevin not to ask, and if for some crazy reason he didn't, it would be impossible for her not to tell.

Breakfast over, she went to the bedroom dresser to make sure that her best nightgown was there, clean and neatly folded. It was. She smiled in anticipation, strapped on her gun, and climbed into the patrol car for the drive up to Cumberland.

As she drove she did her best to take her mind off Kevin and focus on the state of her investigation into Eddie French's murder. It wasn't easy, but she started to tick off the tasks that most urgently needed attention.

The nature of French's relationship with Emmons topped the list, but that issue would remain on hold until Parsons returned from Cheektowaga.

Carol next turned her thoughts to what French's former neighbor, Bill Hedrick, had said about spotting Joe Kingsbury on Woodpecker Lane not long before Eddie was evicted.

She was thinking about how she would approach Kingsbury with this information when the car phone rang. It was Officer Byrnes.

"Remember what I told you about my conversation with that coach over in Yates Center? Ticknor's his name." Byrnes sounded excited. "He mentioned something about them using a state forest for practice. And damned if I didn't get a call last night from Billy Gilbert, an old friend who's with the Torrence County sheriff's department. He had no idea we were looking into any militia group, but he thought I'd be interested in something he'd seen - or thought he'd seen - in that state forest over on the county line. You know the place they call The Angle? Well, Billy says he's seen a pickup going in and out of the woods near The Angle, can't imagine what it's doing there. He didn't know whether we'd be interested, what with all we've got on our plate, but he was curious."

Carol was familiar with The Angle. The boundary between Cumberland and Torrence Counties ran in a straight line for most of its distance from east to west. But at one point Cumberland jutted sharply to the north, depriving Torrence of several thousand acres of real estate which were now part of a small state forest.

"You think this might be important?" she asked her colleague.

"No idea. But if Ticknor belongs to the militia, and says they make use of that land, maybe we should take a look, see what they're up to. Because of French, that is."

The Cumberland County Sheriff's Department wouldn't normally have any interest in a local militia unless it violated some law. But what if French's death had something to do with his unproven militia connection? Carol could think of no reason why Coover or any of his men would have been gunning for French. Nonetheless she was curious, and it wouldn't cost her more than a couple of hours to take the trip up to The Angle.

"Tell you what. I'm down on West Lake Road, but I can be back at the office in twenty minutes. Why don't you meet me there, and we can run over to The Angle. Does that work for you?"

"Sure does." Byrnes obviously liked it that he and the sheriff would make the trip together. "See you there."

Carol thought about this particular state forest as she drove. Not more than twenty square miles, a good part of it swampy.

From what she had heard, its trails weren't as well maintained as they were on most state land. She couldn't recall more than a couple of dirt tracks into the woods, one east of Bari, the other near The Angle on the far north side. There was an old shack not far from that entrance, or so she'd been told. It was said to be in disrepair after years of neglect. She had no idea why it was there or whom it had belonged to. But if someone was using the woods at this time of year, long before hunting season, the shack was the only reason she could think of for a pickup to be there.

It was nearly an hour later that Byrnes jerked his patrol car around a clump of vine covered oaks and onto state land. The road, if it could be called that, was in poor condition. It twisted and turned, avoiding trees as it wound its way over bumpy terrain. The shack was not in sight. In fact, the trees managed to shut out much of the mid-morning light, making it hard to see very far into the woods.

"Do you know how far that shack is from the highway?" Carol asked.

"Better part of a a mile. Maybe a little bit more."

"I suggest we leave the car and walk in. It'll save our backs from this wretched washboard track. Besides, if anybody happens to be in there, we don't have to let the car announce us."

"Whatever you say. Gilbert didn't say exactly how many times he'd seen the pickup, but I got the impression it might have been half a dozen."

They worked their way in what must be the direction of the shack. Tire tracks made it clear that someone had been using the dirt road. And recently. They had walked for perhaps seven minutes when Carol spotted the shack.

"What do you suppose that thing is doing here? Do you know it's history?"

"Nothing but rumors, and they're probably wrong," Byrnes said. "It's been here a long time, since before the state claimed the land."

"Doesn't look like we'll be solving your friend Gilbert's problem today. Not, that is, unless the pickup's parked behind the shack. All the same, I think we should split up. I'll stick to the road, you head off that way."

Carol gestured off to the left, where the woods were fairly dense.

"You think it's better to catch him unawares?"

Carol laughed.

"We won't be catching anybody, Tommy," she said. "There's just something about this place that reminds me of those scary stories our parents read to us as kids. Let's pretend we're having an adventure. Call it stalking the pickup. I'll meet you at the shack for a quick look around."

They went their separate ways and within a few minutes their tan and black uniforms blended with the trees, making them all but invisible to each other.

In the stillness of the morning air, a shot rang out, scattering a flock of birds that had settled in the oaks. For a long moment neither the sheriff nor her colleague said anything.

Byrnes cursed under his breath. Damn fool must be shooting squirrels. But then he had another thought: the shot hadn't come from a gun people use to shoot squirrels. What if he's not shooting squirrels? What if he's shooting at us?

"Carol?" he called out.

But the sheriff of Cumberland County didn't answer him.

Byrnes hesitated to call out Carol's name again. Perhaps she was circling around behind the shack to see who's doing the shooting. He instinctively positioned himself behind a tree, then crouched down and slowly began to move toward the shack. He had only gone a few yards before he realized that Carol might not have answered him because she'd been hit.

Two things needed to be done, and there was no way he could both find the shooter and check on the sheriff. He turned his back on the shack and headed towards the dirt road. Increasingly anxious, he began to whisper her name, trying to make his voice loud enough that she could hear him but not so loud as to call attention to himself. There was no reply. He stepped up his pace, stumbling and falling over an exposed tree root in the process. His right hand and wrist hurt like the devil and he was aware that he was bleeding, but Carol might be in much worse shape.

It took only another two minutes to reach the track. There, some distance up ahead, he saw her. She was lying on the side on the road.

"Carol, are you all right?" he said in a hoarse voice as he rushed up the road toward her. It was a reflexive question; obviously she was not all right.

Unlike Sam Bridges, who had seen active duty as a marine, Byrnes had never been under fire. Now he was momentarily out in the open. Anyone in or near the shack would have no trouble spotting him. In all likelihood that person had a weapon in his hands.

He squatted beside the sheriff, his hand on her shoulder.

"Tommy," she said, her breathing labored. She started to turn over, the better to talk to him, but it was immediately apparent that it hurt too much to move. "Have you seen anybody?"

"No. He must be in the shack. He hit you, didn't he?"

"I'm afraid so. It's my gut. See if you can see what it looks like."

Officer Byrnes tried to do what the sheriff had not been able to do by herself, easing her onto her back as gently as he could.

"Don't be embarrassed to poke around. You won't see anything more exciting than my belly button." Her attempt at humor died in her throat.

Officer Byrnes did what he had to do, muttering apologies each time Carol winced or groaned.

"He got you in the abdomen, but I guess you knew that. Off to the right side. It isn't bleeding much. I can't say whether the bullet's still in there or not. Look, we've got to get you to a hospital."

"I know, and I don't think I'm going to be much help."

Officer Byrnes faced a difficult dilemma. He had to get Carol out of the woods and to a hospital. Unfortunately, the patrol car was all the way back near The Angle, which meant a walk of more than half a mile. There was no way Carol could walk that distance; she might not even be able to walk at all. Nor could he carry her. Yet if he went back for the car, she would be there on the roadside for as many as ten long minutes, an easy target for whomever had shot her. Assuming, that is, that he had shot her on purpose. Perhaps he had indeed been shooting squirrels and had had the bad luck to hit the sheriff. But if that were true, where was he? Why hadn't he shown himself?

He instinctively rejected that line of thought. Whoever had brought Carol down hadn't done so by accident. Instead, he was in all probability watching and waiting in the shack or somewhere nearby. If the man with the gun had wanted to take him out as he tried to help Carol, he could easily have done so. But he hadn't. What was his game?

Byrnes considered the possibility that the man with the gun didn't want to kill either of them, that he had only wanted to scare them. That might account for the fact that he had neither fired again nor come out of hiding. Maybe the best thing to do was to call out to him, identify himself, say he needed help.

"We need help," he said. "Why don't I try to get that guy in the shack to give us a hand? I can't believe he meant to shoot you."

"No!" Carol said it emphatically. Her face registered the pain it had cost her. "He's trying to scare us off, and I'm sure he doesn't want us to see him. Unless he's some kind of a nutcase, I have trouble believing he wants to be known as the guy who shot the sheriff." Carol found herself gulping air. And trying to think straight.

"I'm calling 911," Byrnes said.

Carol gave him no argument. Her eyes were closed. Each breath was painful.

Byrnes couldn't get to the car phone, but he had his cell. He knew the West Branch ambulance crew would be on the road within the minute. Then he tried to reach Bridges.

JoAnne Franks proved herself a worthy office manager. Within fifteen seconds she had contacted Bridges and in less than a minute they were in touch with Grieves, the officer nearest to the state land. Byrnes was unsure when help would arrive. He guessed Grieves would be there in twenty minutes, fifteen if they were lucky. Bridges would take a little longer.

He took off his jacket and laid it over the sheriff. She didn't look good. Her face was pale, and it was obvious that she was trying hard not to let on how much she hurt. He wished he knew more about medical emergencies. CPR he could have managed, but nothing in his training had covered bullet wounds to the abdomen. How could it complicate their situation if he tried to reason with the shooter?

"I think I should try to talk with that guy," he said, bending down and speaking into Carol's ear. "The ambulance may not be here for another fifteen, twenty minutes."

"Listen, Tommy," Carol said, and it was clear that she was determined still to be in charge. "We have no idea whom we're dealing with. It won't help me if you get shot, too. I'll be okay, do you understand? But tell Bridges to get more of our men down here. I want to know who's shooting at us and why."

"Yes, sir. They tell me Grieves is already on the way."

"That's good, but it's not good enough. We're no swat team, but I want everybody to be wearing vests. And to play it smart."

The effort to give Byrnes these instructions sapped what was left of Carol's energy. Byrnes had been worried. Now he was scared.

"Come on, Carol. Hang on. They'll be here any minute."

For a moment there was no reply. Then the sheriff managed a weak smile.

"I'm going to be all right. Just don't do something stupid."

CHAPTER 37

The ambulance didn't have its siren on as it turned onto the track into the woods, but they could hear it downshifting gears before they saw it. It was 10:57, almost exactly fifteen minutes after Byrnes had placed the 911 call. The two paramedics were quick and efficient, and with Byrnes' help they slid the sheriff onto a stretcher and lifted her carefully into the ambulance.

"Can we take you back to the road?" one of them asked.

"No, I think I'll stay here until my colleague arrives," Tommy said.

Carol was saying something like "no heroics," but her voice was drowned out by the sound of another vehicle. And it wasn't Officer Grieves. The sound came from the vicinity of the shack and Byrnes and the paramedics caught a brief glimpse of a dark pickup truck as it backed out from behind the building, turned into the woods, and bounced along the track in the general direction of the Bari entrance to the state forest.

Giving chase was out of the question. Byrnes' car was still back toward The Angle, and the ambulance had a more important mission. Finding out who had shot the sheriff was going to be considerably more difficult.

"Best you guys get going," Byrnes said. "Just take it easy on her."

He watched as the ambulance backed all the way down to the county road and took off for Yates Center and the hospital. Then he set off cautiously for the shack, now presumably empty. Presumably. But what if there had been more than one man at the shack? What if one or more men had stayed behind when the pickup took off? The sheriff had been insistent that he not do anything stupid, and he knew that going to investigate the shack would be the height of stupidity if it were still occupied. It was a big if. The odds were against it, but Officer Byrnes had an argument with himself. Prudence won. He sat down behind the largest tree to wait for Grieves and worry about the sheriff.

Fortunately, he did not have long to wait. Officer Grieves joined Officer Byrnes only ten minutes after the ambulance left. Tommy was almost certain that the shack was now empty, but almost certain wasn't good enough. So just as he had settled down to wait for Grieves, the two of them settled down to wait for reinforcements. By 11:45, Deputy Sheriff Bridges and Officer Barrett had joined them, and the four members of the Cumberland County Sheriff's Department were huddled behind Bridges' squad car, putting on protective vests and discussing strategy.

"Are these things any good?" Grieves looked doubtful.

"Kevlar, guaranteed to keep you out of harm's way," said Barrett. "Only if you take a hit in the torso, of course."

This was followed by an awkward silence. They all knew that Carol had taken a hit in the torso and that she hadn't been wearing a vest.

"They'll do the job," Sam said. "Let's go."

In spite of the caution with which the officers eventually surrounded the shack, its 'occupation' turned out to be anti-climactic. No one was in the building, and although the four officers fanned out to search the surrounding woods, it was obvious that no one had stayed behind when the pickup drove away.

The shack, although old, proved to be solidly constructed. The single door was padlocked shut, and both of the small windows were securely fastened. Sam shot the lock off.

Roughly twenty feet long, no more than nine feet wide, and open to the roof, the shack was simply a one room affair, devoid of running water and electricity. In fact, there was nothing to suggest that such modest amenities had ever been contemplated. It had probably been intended as a place to hole up while hunting.

The room would have been completely empty had it not been for the bags of fertilizer stacked along the wall across from the door. There appeared to be two dozen of the bags, each containing 50 pounds of ammonium nitrate fertilizer, all bearing the name of Aegis Crops.

"Well, what have we here," Bridges said, his tone suggesting that he thought he knew the answer to his question.

"This stuff's for farmers," Grieves said. "Can't do any farming in these woods."

"Whoever uses this shack doesn't even have a garden." Barrett thought he was being funny, but Bridges wasn't amused.

"This damned stuff is used to make explosives. Don't you get it? Our friendly neighborhood militia is getting serious."

"You think the guy who shot Carol is militia?" Byrnes, who had urged the trip to the state forest because of what Ticknor had told him, was connecting the dots.

"More likely that than he was shooting squirrels." Bridges was angry, and he had a problem.

"I want to get back to the hospital, and I'm sure Tommy here wants to see Carol. But if we leave it's a good bet that they'll be back to get the fertilizer. We can't let that happen. I want all of it hauled out of here and back to the office, which means that each of us loads a few bags in our trunks. Jim, I want you and Grieves to stick around. No need to play hide and seek with these guys if they come back. If they see you, they'll probably just turn around and get the hell out of here. But they'll be back because they're worried. Make sure you get the license number."

"You really think these are Coover's guys?" Barrett asked.

"I can't think who else it can be. Even if I'm wrong, somebody shot Carol, and we're going to nail the bastard."

It had not been a hard day in any conventional sense, but all of them were emotionally exhausted. Carol had been wounded, and none of them knew how badly. They hadn't exchanged a single word about her condition. It was as if they were all superstitious, fearing that talking about it might bring bad luck and make her prospects more precarious.

CHAPTER 38

"Professor Whitman?"

"Speaking." Kevin could not imagine who could be calling him at this late hour on a week night. Some student who wouldn't be able to turn in a paper at class tomorrow? Probably. They don't usually do it until they rush into class at the eleventh hour with some tale of a family emergency. Or a late night attack of a stomach virus, which probably meant too many beers the night before. He'd heard every excuse known to students and their teachers.

"This is Deputy Sheriff Bridges up at the lake."

"Oh, hello. But please, I'm Kevin, and I think you're Sam." He had seen Bridges on a number of occasions, spoken with him several times, but knew him only as Carol's second-in-command. What could be the purpose of this mid-evening call on a Wednesday evening in April?

"I have some bad news."

It took no more than a split second for Kevin to process this information and realize that something was terribly wrong. Sam Bridges wouldn't be calling him at his apartment in the city unless something bad had happened to Carol.

"Is Carol all right?" It was an appeal rather than a question.

"She's going to be okay," Bridges answered. "She was shot this morning."

"Shot? Somebody shot her?" Kevin could not believe what he had heard.

"Yes, but she'll make it. They operated this afternoon, and the surgeon says she's going to pull through."

Kevin's mind was racing, his imagination in overdrive.

"She's in the hospital? Where? I want to talk to her."

"I know you're worried," Sam said, trying to lower the temperature. "But Dr. Kavanaugh says it all went well. Carol is sleeping, so maybe it's not a good idea to try to call now."

"What am I supposed to do when out of the blue I hear that my wife has been shot? What happened? Where is she?"

"She's in the hospital over in Yates Center. And Kavanaugh's a good surgeon. What she needs now is rest."

"Sam," Kevin said, trying to keep his voice under control, "put yourself in my shoes. I've just learned that my wife has been shot, no idea how badly, and you're telling me to take it easy. I can't do that. Could you? Just tell me what happened."

"It's complicated," he said, realizing that it wasn't a convincing explanation. "She was investigating a problem up-county, in a state forest. That's not important. What matters is that she got hit by some crazy nut, but we got her out and she's going to recover."

"It's not life threatening?" Kevin asked.

"Not according to the doctor. It isn't clear how long she'll be sidelined, but he says the prognosis is very good."

Kevin didn't like to hear about a prognosis. It made it sound as if the odds favored a recovery, when he wanted to hear that she'd be up and about in the morning.

"Give me the number at the hospital. I need to talk to her."

"That's not a good idea. She needs to sleep."

"God damn it, Sam, I'm her husband! It's not up to you to decide whether I can talk with her. Give me the hospital number."

Bridges realized that Kevin was upset by the news, that his anger was not personal. If their roles had been reversed, Sam knew that he, too, would not be satisfied until he had spoken with his wife. Or tried to. He gave Kevin the hospital phone number.

"If you let me know when your plane gets in," he said, "I'll see to it that one of our men is at the airport to pick you up."

"Not necessary. You've got enough on your hands. I'm going to drive. I should be on the road at six, be there early afternoon." Then a final question. "You haven't told me where she got hit."

Sam had not wanted to get into details, and this was the one detail that had given Dr. Kavanaugh pause. But if he didn't answer Kevin's question it would only heighten his anxiety.

"She was lucky. The bullet hit her in the abdomen. It doesn't seem to have damaged any vital organs." Sam wasn't one hundred percent sure of that last bit, but Kavanaugh had been upbeat. Except for his remark that a bullet wound to the gut carried a high risk of infection.

When Bridges rang off, Kevin immediately placed a call to the hospital. It was as Sam had predicted. The nurse on duty on the intensive care floor said that Carol - she referred to her as the sheriff - had taken a sedative and was sleeping. It was obvious that the nurse wasn't going to wake her. Nor was Dr. Kavanaugh available. Kevin tried to persuade the nurse to talk about Carol's condition, but she declined to be drawn into a discussion of the matter, only repeating several times that the patient was sleeping soundly and that the doctor was optimistic. Nurse Ratched, Kevin muttered under his breath as he hung up.

He wasted no time debating what he should do. First he called the airline and cancelled his ticket for the following afternoon. Then he e-mailed Alice Lassiter, his department chair who had tried unsuccessfully to make him her successor in that role. It was a brief message, telling Alice that his wife was suddenly and seriously ill, that he was leaving for the lake earlier than he had planned, and asking her to put up a 'class cancelled' notice for his 9:30 class. No need to mention a shooting. It would only stimulate gossip about this strange relationship between a music professor and a sheriff, a sheriff who lived hundreds of miles away in the boondocks.

Kevin briefly toyed with the idea of setting off for the lake that very night, but common sense prevailed. He was tired and he'd be in no shape to see Carol in the morning. There was no getting his mind off Sam's news. He found himself picturing Carol on an operating table, the doctor probing in her stomach for a bullet. The thought frightened him, made him momentarily nauseated. What happens to our innards if we are shot? His father had hoped that he would be a doctor, but he had hated biology, especially the part that called for him to dissect a frog and a cat. He had quickly abandoned any thoughts of a pre-med major, satisfying his college science requirement by taking historical geology. He'd always liked dinosaurs and rocks, and while the course had been a bit of a bore, he didn't have to dissect anything. Now all he could think about was Carol's gut.

Sleep didn't come easily, and Kevin awoke to a five o'clock alarm no more rested than he had been the night before.

———

It was just ahead of one when Kevin pulled into the hospital parking lot in Yates Center. He had resisted the urge to use his cell to call the hospital at two rest stops along the way. Better to get there as soon as possible, push past the gatekeepers, surprise Carol in her bed. Hopefully the hospital's gift shop would have flowers. He thought he remembered that it did from his brief stay there the summer they were dealing with 'the man who wasn't Beckham,' the summer when that terrible Mel Slavin had run him off the road and down a bank into the lake.

Unfortunately, getting in to see Carol wasn't going to be easy. The nurse gatekeepers were understanding, but they patiently explained that the sheriff had gone back to surgery. Dr. Kavanaugh had decided that he needed to take another look at the wound, and no one seemed to know how long it would be before she would be back in her room.

This was not good. Kevin once more had visions of Carol's gut, and they weren't of the flat tummy he loved. What he imagined was a raw wound, blood, and -

He put the thought out of his mind and tried to wheedle more information out of the nurse who seemed to know most about what was going on. But he quickly learned that hospital protocol didn't allow even a hint of speculation from staff, only boilerplate assurances that Dr. Kavanaugh was a fine doctor, taking good care of the sheriff. Kevin took a seat in the waiting room. He tried to interest himself in an old *Newsweek*, but he couldn't stop worrying about doctor Kavanaugh. Was he any good? If so, what was he doing practicing in this small town in the middle of nowhere? Maybe he valued the beauty of Crooked Lake and the charm of its vineyards and quaint villages more than he did a prestigious appointment at a teaching hospital down in the city. But maybe he was practicing in Yates Center because his skills had atrophied. Or were never all that good in the first place.

These troubling thoughts wouldn't go away. And then Kevin had an idea. He'd get in touch with Doc Crawford. If Carol trusted him implicitly, why shouldn't he? He stepped out into the foyer and punched in 411.

Fortunately, Crawford was in.

"Hi, sorry to bother you, but this is Kevin Whitman. Carol's husband."

"Well, hello there. How are you two doing? Haven't talked to Carol in awhile."

"I need your honest opinion about something."

"Of course. All my opinions are honest."

It occurred to Kevin that Crawford didn't know that Carol had been shot.

"Have you heard what happened to Carol?" he asked.

"Has something happened to her?" Doc Crawford sounded alarmed.

"Yes. She was shot yesterday, and she's in the hospital over here in Yates Center."

"I can't believe this," Crawford said.

"It's true. Bridges called me last night and I drove up from the city this morning. She was shot out in some state woods. The wound's in the abdomen, although neither Bridges nor the nurses here at the hospital are very forthcoming about how bad it is. That's why I called. I thought maybe you could help put my mind at rest."

"This is terrible news. But how can I help you? All I know is what you just told me. I think I better get myself over to the hospital."

"The doctor who operated on her, his name's Kavanaugh. I never heard of him. Is he any good?"

There was a long silence. At least it seemed long to Kevin. He's not sure, he thought. Or maybe he knows that Kavanaugh's just a hack.

"Kevin, listen to me. Kavanaugh's a fine doctor. He's young, but he knows what he's doing. Has a good head on his shoulders. And skilled hands. But I want to talk with him. Did he get the bullet?"

"I don't have a clue. Nobody tells me anything."

"That's what I figured. You're at the hospital, I assume." Kevin acknowledged that he was but that he hadn't seen or talked to Carol because she was in surgery again. "Just stay there. I'll be right over. We'll see what the story is. And try not to worry."

If Doc Crawford had wanted to calm Kevin's nerves, he hadn't succeeded. He sounded every bit as worried as Kevin was. But at least he respected Carol's surgeon. Or claimed that he did.

CHAPTER 39

The clock on the wall of the waiting room in the intensive care wing of the hospital read 2:38. There were five people in the room. A couple whose son had been in an automobile accident sat in a corner, holding hands and trying to ignore a TV set that was tuned to a channel that was running a day long marathon of *NCIS* episodes. One of the other three men in the room wore the uniform of the Cumberland County Sheriff's Department. He was staring straight ahead at the opposite wall, which was devoid of anything other than a pale green coat of paint. Had his eyes not been open, one would have assumed that he was asleep. The other two men wore civilian clothes. The older of the two had taken a pocket calendar out of his jacket and was in the process of writing something in it. He wrote for a moment, then paused, as if to consider what his next entry would be. He tapped the end of his pen against his teeth, then resumed writing. The final person in the room was easily the most agitated, at least outwardly. He kept looking anxiously at the door to the corridor, rolled his shoulders, and couldn't seem to stop biting his lower lip.

It had been an hour and a quarter since Kevin Whitman had arrived and been told that he wouldn't be able to see the sheriff just yet. Doc Crawford, who had expected to be ushered into her room the minute he reached the hospital, had also been told that he, too, would have to wait. Sam Bridges, who had been there for only twenty minutes, had shared what he knew about Carol's injury with her husband and the doctor, but like them had then settled down to wait. The word was that Dr. Kavanaugh would be seeing them just as soon as he could, and that it shouldn't be long. It had already been too long for all three of the men.

The silence in the waiting room was broken from time to time by a phone ringing somewhere in the nerve center of intensive care down the hall. Two people, neither of them Dr. Kavanaugh, had stepped into the waiting room since Bridges' arrival. One was a nurse who was looking for someone who wasn't there, the other a tall, well dressed man who mumbled something and quickly disappeared back into the corridor.

It was at 2:47 that the door opened for a third time and a short stocky man in a doctor's gown and cap walked purposefully into the waiting room. He wore a smile, which hopefully meant that he had good news to impart.

"Hello, I'm Dr. Kavanaugh. And you people must be here because of the sheriff." A look of recognition crossed his face. "Why, Henry, haven't seen you in months."

"Good to see you, Ben," Crawford said. "This is the sheriff's husband, Kevin Whitman, and you probably know Officer Bridges."

Everyone shook hands, except for the couple who had been watching *NCIS*. They knew that their son's doctor's name was Sterling.

It was Kevin who cut to the chase.

"How is Carol?" he asked, impatiently. "Is she going to be okay?"

He thought that Kavanaugh looked awfully young. Too young to be operating on Carol.

"The sheriff is going to be all right," the young doctor began. "She took a shot in the abdomen, but we got the bullet out and cleaned up the damage. She's taken good care of her body, which means she's in good shape to bounce back from a wound like that. No need to go into the specifics, but you can all rest assured that none of her vital organs took a direct hit and that we're monitoring her closely for any post-op problems."

Kavanaugh looked at Crawford, knowing that the pathologist would understand what those post-op problems might be.

"So I can see her?"

"Not just yet, Mr. Whitman. We had to take another look to make sure everything's in order, so she's still under anesthesia. She should come around by 3:15 although I expect she'll still be groggy. If she sounds incoherent, don't worry. It's typical. By morning she'll be sounding like she did when they wheeled her in yesterday. All full of questions. She's probably as worried about you as you are about her. She's a feisty woman, let me tell you."

"When do you expect her to be discharged?" Kevin asked.

"Not sure. I don't want her running around just yet. It could take a week. Plus some down time after she leaves the hospital," he added.

Kevin was flipping calendar pages in his mind. It sounded as if he might well be back in the city before Carol could return to the cottage, much less go back to work.

"That sounds like a long time, Dr. Kavanaugh. Is there something you're not telling us?"

"It's normal, Kevin," Doc Crawford spoke up for his younger colleague. "A gunshot wound like this is quite a shock to the system. She's going to be pretty uncomfortable for awhile, and like the doctor says, they'll want to keep a close watch on how she's healing. You know Carol. Slow down and take it easy aren't in her vocabulary. If I were you, I'd find myself a couple of novels to read and plan on spending a few days by her bedside right here at the hospital."

"Henry's right, Mr. Whitman. She's going to be just fine as long as she doesn't try to do too much too fast."

Bridges jumped into the discussion for the first time.

"I know that's what you'll tell her. Trouble is, she doesn't like to delegate, and she ought to be doing a lot of that for a few weeks. I've already had a squad meeting about this, and the men have their assignments. We'll get the guy who shot her. But what worries me is that she'll push herself, no matter what you say. She'll try to get back on the job when she's not ready. You've got to convince her to let me handle things. You should have more influence than I do."

Bridges had been speaking to Dr. Kavanaugh, but his appeal was directed to Kevin. And Kevin knew that the deputy sheriff had his boss pegged right. She would rebel at the idea of protracted bed rest while others went about the business of law enforcement in the county.

"I'm not sure about my influence, Sam. But I know she's got confidence in you and she's much too smart to ignore her doctor."

Nonetheless, Kevin knew that Carol was going to be increasingly restless and frustrated in the days and weeks ahead. He also knew that he would not be here to help her weather most of this period of enforced inactivity.

Kavanaugh had other patients to attend to, and before leaving reassured everyone once more that the sheriff was coming along nicely. Dr. Sterling finally made an appearance and left with the parents of the boy who'd been in a car accident, presumably to pay him a visit. This led to a conversation about the familiar problem of kids and cars, and to Bridges' observation that they might have spoken too openly in front of the couple about how and where the sheriff had been shot.

"I don't think you need to worry," Crawford said. "I'm sure they're too preoccupied with their own worries to have paid much attention to what we were talking about. Besides, I don't remember anything being said about the shooting, just about Carol's condition. But we're going to be facing a problem of sorts any time now. They're not going to want us fawning over Carol or asking her a lot of questions for very long. It's Kevin who needs the time alone with her, or should I say Carol who needs time with Kevin. So I'd suggest, Sam, that you and I say hello, kiss her forehead, wish her a quick recovery, and be on our way. I can come back when it's convenient, and I'm sure you'll be a regular visitor. Daily updates for the sheriff who doesn't like to delegate?"

The twinkle was back in Doc Crawford's eye.

When the time came, the deputy sheriff and the pathologist paid their respects and, as Crawford had suggested, yielded the bedside chair to Kevin.

It was apparent that Carol had been under a lot of strain. She wasn't in the habit of wearing much makeup, but this afternoon she wore none and her face was pale and reflected pain that medications hadn't entirely brought under control. There was no question of her sitting up in bed to exchange a kiss with Kevin, but she managed a smile and started to apologize for not being able to pick him up at the airport.

It was the perfect opening.

"You sure went to a lot of trouble just to avoid a trip to the airport," Kevin said. Far better to fall back on the easy banter that had defined their close relationship than to start asking questions that said 'I'm worried about you.'

Carol laughed and immediately realized that laughing hurt.

"I love you, but try not to do that again. I'm very delicate right now."

"Actually, your tummy's delicate, but otherwise you're one tough lady. Do they have a civilian equivalent of the purple heart?"

"I don't think so. When did you get here?"

"Not that long ago. Three hours, something like that. And I drove. Sam called me last night, gave me a quick account of what happened."

"You realize that this thing" - she pointed at her stomach - "is going to mean no sex this week, don't you? I'm sorry. Funny, it was the first thing I thought about when I woke up this morning. Or when the nurse on duty woke me up. You'd think they'd let you get as much sleep as possible, but somehow that never makes it into the nursing school curriculum."

"God, but you look good to me. Sam really scared me last night. I mean he said you were going to be fine, but it isn't every day that you get a long distance call saying your wife's been shot. I worried that he was afraid to give me the unvarnished truth. After all, people get shot in combat and in some of the more lawless neighborhoods down in the city, but not up here on the lake."

"Don't I wish. Right now I'm hunting for someone who shot and killed a guy named Eddie French. I did tell you about that, didn't I?"

"You did, but let's save that for tomorrow. Did the doctor say when he expects to have you out of here? I don't much like the ambience, especially those green walls."

Carol didn't like the question because she didn't like the answer.

"He's being deliberately vague. 'Four days, maybe five, maybe a week. We'll take it one day at a time.' I guess the wound wasn't as bad as it could have been, but it was bad enough. Apparently it's going to take awhile."

Evidence that it might take awhile presented itself moments later. There was no hiding the sudden look of acute discomfort on Carol's face. It didn't last, but it had been there.

"It hurts?"

"It comes and goes. So does the feeling that I'm terribly tired. You came in and I suddenly felt wide awake. But it doesn't last."

At that moment a nurse popped in.

"I'm afraid we're going to have to shoo visitors away. I know you're her husband. Dr. Crawford told me. It's nice to meet you, and I know you'll be coming back. But there's things we have to do with her, hospital things. And she's very tired. Let's say two more minutes, okay?"

The nurse popped back out, pulling the curtain shut behind her.

"She's right. Isn't it crazy? I haven't done a thing all day, yet I'm tired. On a scale of one to ten, it's an eight or nine. I think they call it dog tired."

"Then get some sleep. I promise to camp out here tomorrow."

"I'd suggest you come close to noon. The morning is mostly hospital routines, you wouldn't see much of me. Maybe you should talk to Sam and find out when he plans to come by. I'd rather talk with you, but I'm still the sheriff, so he has to keep me posted on what's going on."

"I think he's worried that you aren't willing to let him run things while you're laid up."

"He knows how to run things. But it's his priorities. He's hell bent on bringing in the guy that shot me. And I'm sure he's got the men believing that until they do, everything else is on hold. I want to know who did it, too, but we're in the middle of a murder investigation. We can't suddenly ignore that case while we chase after someone because he shot me. I appreciate Sam's loyalty, but I want him to pay attention to Kingsbury, and to Stearns, and all those people involved in the French case."

"Those are just names to me."

"I know. I'll bring you up to date tomorrow. But right now I really am running out of steam."

Right on cue, the nurse reappeared.

"Time's up."

"Just one more kiss and I'm gone."

When he walked out into the hospital parking lot, Kevin felt a huge sense of relief. She hurts and she's tired, he thought, but she's still the same old Carol and she's going to make it. He was scheduled to return to the city on Wednesday, but there was going to be a change of plans. He'd call the college and explain that his wife needed him far more than his students did. He'd do it first thing in the morning. On second thought, he'd place the call that very afternoon. Just as soon as he got back to the cottage.

CHAPTER 40

The Sheriff's Department hadn't experienced anything like it since Bill Kelleher had his fatal coronary over six years earlier. Now Big Bill's daughter and successor as sheriff was lying in the hospital, victim of a gunshot wound, and the office was once more in turmoil. It wasn't that Deputy Sheriff Sam Bridges was over his head, his fellow officers suddenly leaderless. Nonetheless, everyone was uneasy. The men had reacted in their different ways to the fact of Carol's injury, but they seemed to share a sense that everything had changed. No one now on the force had ever been wounded in the line of duty. Indeed, no one on the force had ever been shot at. It was as if their badge had somehow protected them against the worst that the area's malefactors could do.

Sam had reminded them at the squad meeting the morning after Carol had been shot that Carol herself had been briefly held hostage by the 'scarecrow' murderer at the Random Harvest Winery. But that crisis had ended well, and the perpetrators of Crooked Lake's recent spate of murders had been brought to justice with nary a scratch on the members of their small company. Sheriff's Department 7, murderers 0.

Of course there was no evidence that Carol had been shot by someone who was in any way involved in the death of Eddie French. It could have been an unfortunate accident, the shooter simply a nervous kid who couldn't shoot straight. Or who had panicked. But none of Carol's officers believed that to be the case.

It was early on Friday morning, less than 48 hours after Carol had been shot, and the officers were once again en route to the Cumberland office and the daily squad meeting. By this time they had all been informed of Carol's condition and they knew that the prognosis for her recovery was good, even if it might take some time. Nonetheless, most of them were having a hard time dealing with what had happened and the way it had affected them.

———

Had his colleagues asked him, Tommy Byrnes would have said that he was doing fine. But he wasn't. He had accompanied Bridges to the hospital on Wednesday, but Carol had been in surgery and he had been unable to see her or talk to her. What he had wanted to tell her was how sorry he was that she had been the one who was shot. Why her and not him? He had been unable to get it out of his mind that he had somehow failed her during their casual investigation of the report that something unusual was going on in the state forest. He couldn't think of anything he might have done, other than let the sheriff take to the woods while he stayed on the open dirt track as they approached the shack. But that made sense only in hindsight. Who would have expected that the shack harbored someone with a gun?

Then there was the matter of his inability to help Carol once she had been hit. He had felt helpless, capable only of calling for help and covering her with his jacket. His badge, his uniform, his police training - none of it had made a difference. Any casual bystander could have done just as well. Tommy had spent the better part of two days wondering if he was really cut out for the job he held. He was most at home when he was back at the office, trying to uphold his reputation as the squad's computer whiz. But the sheriff's department didn't have the luxury of an officer who spent all of his time at a desk in what they jokingly called the music room. He had to be out on the road, and he had just demonstrated that maybe he didn't belong there.

As he neared the turnoff to headquarters, he realized that he dreaded attending the squad meeting. Nobody would say anything, but what would they be thinking? Here comes Tommy, poor guy. Didn't really know how to handle things, did he? Carol's lucky she's going to pull through. No thanks to Tommy. He knew this wasn't fair. None of them had ever criticized him, said anything which might be interpreted as lack of confidence in his abilities or his judgment. Not Bill or Jim, not the younger guys. Not even Sam. But he couldn't talk himself into a better frame of mind.

He parked at the far end of the lot, took a deep breath, and set off for one more of hundreds of morning briefings.

———

Bill Parsons backed out of his drive and headed for Cumberland and the umpteenth morning squad briefing since he had joined the force more than twenty years ago. This was a briefing he hadn't expected to be attending. It had been his plan, or rather his assignment, to be in a suburb of Buffalo called Cheektowaga, searching for information which would prove - or disprove - that Eddie French and John Paul Emmons had been friends during their high school days. But Carol's misfortune had put an end, at least temporarily, to that trip. He had checked in for the meeting he was to have had with the sheriff before setting off for Cheektowaga, but of course she wasn't in her office. Instead she was in surgery at the Yates Center hospital, and calling to cancel her meeting with him had been the furthest thing from her mind.

JoAnne knew only that the sheriff had been shot and that Sam and several of his fellow officers were either at the scene of the shooting or at the hospital. Parsons had shaken off the shock that came with news of what had happened, and decided to wait for what he was sure would be Sam's instructions.

It soon became apparent that he would not be going to Cheektowaga the next day, and probably not for quite a few days. Bridges was back at the office by late afternoon, and the word had soon been passed down that finding Carol's shooter was going to be the first order of business. Yesterday's briefing had been largely devoted to reporting on her medical prognosis, the discovery of ammonium nitrate fertilizer in the shack, and strategy for dealing with the implications of that discovery and its likely connection with Carol's shooting.

Bill was familiar with such quick changes in plans. They had occurred from time to time over the years when the sheriff's department had been confronted with some new and unexpected crisis. Nonetheless, he was having trouble digesting the fact that he was not going to be pursuing the French-Emmons relationship. Bridges might well be right to put everything else temporarily on the shelf. The sheriff's recovery was bound to be uppermost in everyone's mind, and the discovery of the fertilizer could well signal a more urgent problem than the hunt for French's killer. It might even point them in a different direction as they pursued the French case.

Still, he had the feeling that it was a mistake not to be following up on what he had learned about French and Emmons both being in school together. Hopefully it wouldn't be long before they had found out enough about what had been going on over at The Angle that he could take that trip to Cheektowaga. In the meanwhile, he was hoping that Sam would have an upbeat report on Carol's condition and that he would give him a green light to go and visit her.

———

It still troubled Officer Barrett, nearly two days after the events at The Angle, that they had been unable to find out who had shot the sheriff and why hundreds of pounds of fertilizer which could be used in making explosives had been stored in an old shack there. He had been certain that somebody would come back to the shack later in the day of the sheriff's shooting. He had been excited to be charged with posting watch at the shack. Grieves had been doubtful that the shooter would return. But Jim had agreed with the deputy sheriff: either the shooter or one of his colleagues in the militia movement would reappear, and soon. And why not? The militia would be anxious about their fertilizer; if nothing else, curiosity would draw them back to The Angle.

But it had been a boring and uneventful afternoon. They had neither seen nor heard anyone. Nor had Officers Damoth and Hinkle, their relief that evening. At yesterday's morning squad meeting there had been a heated discussion about it. Grieves was convinced that nobody would be coming back. Whoever had been there would know that the fertilizer had been carted away, that a new storage site would have to be found. Moreover, he could be certain that the shooting of the sheriff had stirred up a hornet's nest and that coming back to The Angle would be like walking into a trap.

Not everyone had agreed with Bridges that they were even dealing with a militia group. Sam conceded that they lacked proof, but insisted that it was highly likely and that they would have to proceed on that assumption. Jim had supported Sam and had been the strongest advocate for a continued presence in the vicinity of the shack. Thus it was that Sam had put him in charge of what would be called the Militia Watch.

Officer Barrett entered the briefing room on Friday morning, ready to undertake his new responsibilities and determined this time not to let the people who had shot Carol and planned to blow up an as yet unidentified target get away. Jim liked his job, even on routine days. He liked the prospect of taking on the shadowy militia even better.

———

Sam Bridges was worried. Although the sheriff was out of the woods, both literally and figuratively, she would almost certainly not be back in harness for at least another couple of weeks, very probably longer. While she would insist on helping to shape decisions from her hospital bed, as a practical matter he would be the de facto acting sheriff. It would simply be impossible for her to deal minute by minute, even hour by hour, with developments on the law enforcement front. She would hate to be in that situation. She would hate it even more in another day or two when she was no longer heavily medicated and sleeping much of the day away. But it couldn't be helped.

What worried Sam was that he was going to have to demonstrate over the days ahead that he was up to the task that had befallen him. He had never doubted his ability to discharge his role as the department's second-in-command. But he had never sought the responsibility of being county sheriff. When Carol's father had died, some of the officers assumed he might put his hat in the ring to succeed him. But he didn't want the job. He knew his own limitations. No, that wasn't the way to put it. He knew his own ambitions, and they were shaped by what gave him satisfaction. He liked the informal camaraderie with his fellow officers. He liked the fact that for the most part he wouldn't have to take the job home with him at night. He liked the fact that he didn't have to run for office or fight budget battles or bear the brunt of public criticism for mistakes made, be they real or only imagined.

At the moment he was faced with a major problem. Everyone in the area would by now know that the sheriff had been shot and seriously wounded. The shock of this news would soon wear off and people would begin to demand to know who had shot her and why it was taking so long to apprehend her attacker. And he would be the one who would have to provide the answers. Carol herself would want him not to treat her situation as the first order of business. 'I'll be all right,' she'd say. 'Don't worry about me. That's Kevin's job, and Dr. Kavanaugh's. You stay focussed on the French case.'

But he couldn't do that. Instead, he'd have to move heaven and earth to find whoever had shot Carol. And who had put the fertilizer in the forest shack and for what purpose. To do this he would have to ignore Carol's argument about his priorities. He'd have to find a way to smoke out Russell Coover, because he was convinced that Coover was behind what had happened and what had been found at The Angle this week. Proving it, however, would be a very tall order.

He'd taken important preliminary steps the day before. This morning he would begin the process of tightening the screws. Sam parked his car in the space reserved for the sheriff. His face was grim as he climbed the stairs to the squad room and the morning briefing.

CHAPTER 41

In view of the hospital's morning routines and Carol's need to have an early talk with Bridges, Kevin had not set his alarm. The long drive and the emotional distress caused by the news from the lake had taken their toll, so it was not surprising that Kevin had sacked out early and not awakened until after nine on Friday morning. Thursday evening had not been the one they had planned. There had been no dinner at *The Cedar Post*. There had been no fire in the fireplace, no romantic fireworks. Much as he loved the cottage, it didn't do much for his mood without Carol. She had anticipated his arrival, of course, so there was plenty of food in the fridge. But he hadn't been hungry, and he didn't like to drink alone.

Once up, he moved quickly to make coffee, toast a couple of English muffins, and shower and dress for what he hoped would be a much better day than yesterday had been. No need to head for the hospital until close to noon, so he thought he'd take advantage of the decent weather to jog the length of the point and back to see who among its denizens were in residence. He needed the exercise, and it would give him something to do other than moping about the cottage and clock watching. As it happened, however, Kevin did not go jogging on this mild April morning.

Instead, he spotted something in his study which caught his attention. It was a small stack of CDs on his desk. Carol must have been listening to some of the operas in his collection. Pleased and interested in what had been her choices, he crossed over to the desk. On the top of the stack was what he regarded as a so-so recording of *Carmen*. He was about to see what was beneath it when he noticed something else. It was a yellow pad, one of his ever present stock of yellow pads, but it was covered with Carol's handwriting. Kevin believed in respecting the privacy of others, even his wife, but he couldn't miss the heading she'd scrawled across the top of the pad: French Case. He hadn't been aware that she was bringing her work home, but here was evidence that she'd been doing just that.

Kevin knew very little about the French case, although he had assumed that Carol would be telling him all about it while he was at the lake. It was obvious from their brief conversation at the hospital that she feared Bridges would shift it to a back burner while he pursued her shooter. It suddenly seemed like a good idea to take a look at her notes on the yellow pad.

He pulled out his desk chair and picked up the pad. Under the prominent heading, which she had underlined several times, was a series of names. Arrows ran from one name to another, sometimes to two or even three names. In a couple of instances an arrow had been crossed out. The result was a page full of confusion. It was obvious that Carol had been brainstorming, trying to establish relationships among the people on her list. The name that seemed to be a part of every nexus of arrows was Eddie French. That at least made sense, inasmuch as he was the person whose murder had triggered this brainstorming exercise. There was nothing to indicate when she had made her list of names and connected them with arrows, although he guessed it had been fairly recently. He wondered if she had done it while listening to *Carmen*. Or maybe - he looked for the title of the next opera in the stack - *Lucia di Lammermoor*.

There were eleven names on Carol's list - twelve if he added one that had subsequently been crossed off. They would presumably be people who had surfaced during her investigation of the French case. Kevin pictured her sitting at the desk, leaning back in the chair, searching her brain for reasons why they might have killed French or how they might help her find the person who did while the music of Bizet or Donizetti provided background accompaniment.

The eleven names were not arranged in alphabetical order, and he had no idea whether the order in which they were listed (other than French himself) reflected Carol's suspicions about their culpability in the crime. The list looked like this.

Eddie French
Isabel French
Earl Skinner
Joe Kingsbury
Simon Ostrowski
Bill Hedrick

Buddy Stearns
Benny Outland
Russell Coover
Ralph Ticknor
John Paul Emmons

The name which had been crossed out was Floyd Brinker. The only name he knew for reasons other than that Carol had mentioned it when discussing the case with him was Russell Coover. It would have been hard not to remember Coover. He had been a suspect in the death of Dana Ivers in the Hawk's Nest case the previous year, and although Kevin didn't know him personally he knew enough about him to know that he was a particularly loathsome specimen of humanity.

He refilled his coffee cup and returned to the study, thinking about what he might learn about Carol's current case if he spent some time studying the maze of arrows on the yellow pad. He proceeded to spend most of the next half hour doing just that. Unfortunately, he learned almost nothing that he didn't already know, which was very little. He wished she had made some notes about the people whose names were on the list, something that would provide a clue as to why they were there. But of course Carol wouldn't have needed to do that. After all, these eleven people had been on her mind for days, even weeks in some cases. He found himself recalling the *dramatis personae* of some of the other murder cases that had roiled Crooked Lake in recent years. It hadn't taken long before he'd felt they were almost like old acquaintances. In all likelihood, he would feel much the same way about the eleven on Carol's list by the time he returned to the city. If, that is, her recovery from the shooting went as smoothly as Dr. Kavanaugh predicted.

Kevin hadn't really thought about Carol's condition this morning. She would have to spend a few days in the hospital, but she was going to make a complete recovery. Kavanaugh had said so, and seeing her and talking with her had effectively dispelled his anxiety and made an optimist of him. But how could he be sure? Suppose there were complications? These suddenly worrisome thoughts brought him quickly back to earth. His contemplation of Carol's names and arrows had awakened the detective in him, when he should be paying attention to the more immediate problem - getting her back on her feet.

He made a snap decision. He was going to go back to the hospital. Not closer to noon, when she would have had a briefing from Bridges, when the doctor would have made his morning rounds, when the nurses would have finished with whatever it is that hospital routines demanded of them. He'd go now. He might still have to wait awhile, but maybe he could see her sooner than she had expected. He belonged at her side, not marking time at the cottage, trying to involve himself in the murder case de jour. There would be time for that later.

CHAPTER 42

To Kevin's surprise, Carol had been moved from the ER to a room on another floor. Good news, he thought. The curtain had been pulled back along its track, so that he could see her the minute he stepped out of the elevator. She was sitting up in bed. More good news. The nurse on duty gave him a warm smile and told him the coast was clear.

It was all he could do not to wrap his arms around her. They settled for an awkward kiss.

"Do I look a little better than yesterday?" she asked.

"You always look great, but I'm delighted to see you sitting up. How do you feel?"

"Better, or they wouldn't have moved me up here. And you can't fool me. I don't look great. I should know because I saw myself in the bathroom mirror this morning."

"Mirrors have been known to lie. No kidding, though, what's the word from Kavanaugh?"

"I think he's encouraged. No sign of infection. I'm on a liquid diet for another day or two, then it's soft toast, that sort of thing. But I really am better. It still hurts, but compared with Wednesday, I'm ready for a triathlon."

Kevin pulled the room's only chair over to the bedside and sat down.

"What does he say about coming home?"

"He's still cautious, but I pushed him and he finally says it might be Monday, even Sunday."

"You can tell Kavanaugh that I'll be there to take care of you. In fact, I plan on staying through next week. So you've got yourself a live-in cook and butler."

It was Carol who eventually shifted the conversation to matters of crimes and misdemeanors.

"I don't know when they'll be coming to change my bandage or take me somewhere for a test. They never tell patients these things. So let me talk shop for a few minutes while we have a chance. Okay?"

"Absolutely, just so you don't tire yourself out."

"I'm good for another half hour or so. I wanted to tell you about Sam. He was here around 9:30, and we had - I was going to say an argument, but that isn't fair. More like a disagreement. It's like I told you yesterday, he's hell bent on finding the guy who shot me. He's convinced the shooting has to do with Russell Coover's militia. And he isn't making much headway. Coover seems to have disappeared, and a couple of the men we think belong to the militia claim they don't know what we're talking about. Which, of course, just makes Sam more determined to keep everyone on a militia watch. He even pulled Bill Parsons off a trip I wanted him to take. I may be sidelined for a few days, but I'm still the sheriff, so I told Sam he had to let Parsons go to Buffalo."

"Buffalo? What's that got to do with this guy French's murder?"

"Sorry, I forget that you aren't up to speed. Remember our conversation about the second murder, the one down in Southport that happened just a few days after French was killed?"

"Sure, and I remember telling you I'd bet it was no coincidence. Probably the same killer. You think I'm right?"

"We don't know, but we do know that both French and the other victim - name's Emmons - went to school in a place called Cheektowaga at about the same time."

"Cheektowaga? You aren't making this up, are you?"

"Come on, why would I do that? Cheektowaga is a suburb of Buffalo, and I'd arranged for Parsons to go over there and see what he could dig up about our two murder victims. We can talk more about this another time, but there's a real possibility their deaths could be related."

"Like I told you." Kevin couldn't resist saying it.

"Anyway, you can see why I want Parsons chasing down their relationship, not posting watch over in the state forest or trying to find Coover."

"You don't sound as if you think our friend Coover has anything to do with French's death. Or this other guy's."

"I didn't say that. I think Coover knew French and is denying it. We have no idea whether he'd ever heard of Emmons, much less knew him."

Carol paused and took a deep breath. And flashed Kevin what passed for a smile.

"You're hurting again, aren't you?" he asked.

"Not too bad. Like I said last night, it comes and goes. But don't think I'm ready to dismiss you. I've got something I'd like you to do for the good of the cause."

"I hope you're talking about the French case, not that you want me to get you a bed pan or something."

"I am ambulatory, you know," Carol said. "No, what I want you to do is get into your car and take a drive up north of here to a place called Brighton, which isn't far from Rochester. I'd go myself, but Dr. Kavanaugh would not be pleased. So I've all but committed you to taking a trip to Brighton tomorrow. You'll be my alter ago. I didn't tell the other party that you're my husband. That wouldn't sound quite right. Not very professional. But I don't want to take somebody else off Sam's 'Get Coover' team. Besides, you can handle it better than any of my officers, and I know you're itching to put on your detective's hat."

"I'm flattered, but I thought I'd come back to the lake because I needed to take care of you."

"Actually, you'd already made plans to come back to the lake before you knew I'd had an accident. And I don't need taking care of. Well, maybe a little. But I do need your help, and you're going to get bored just sitting by the side of my bed. So it's off to Brighton."

"Do you want to tell me what this is all about?"

"Of course. But it'll take a few minutes."

"Should I take notes?" Kevin asked, half facetiously.

"Not necessary. Just pay attention. I got a phone call this morning, or rather a call came in for me at the office. It was from a woman named Danielle Emmons, the widow of our second murder victim, who happens to live over in Brighton. She wanted to speak with me, and said it might be important. After some hesitation about bothering me in my bed of pain, JoAnne put her in touch with the hospital. Danielle proceeded to tell me that she'd made a discovery she thought I might like to know about. Sorry, I think I'm rambling."

"You're doing fine, considering that you're probably all doped up."

"Is it that obvious? Anyway, what she told me is why I want you to go to see her. But first, you need to know something about Danielle Emmons."

"I'm sure that will help."

"The only time I met her was when she came over to identify the body that turned out to be her husband. But it was pretty clear to me that their's was a strange kind of marriage. I think she loved her husband, but he didn't tell her much about what he was doing or where he was doing it. And she was reluctant - maybe even afraid - to ask him. His job kept him on the road a lot, but when he left he never told her where he was going or when he'd be back. I think she occasionally entertained the thought that there might be another woman, or women, in his life, but she seems to have convinced herself that it wasn't so. It wasn't just his present life which she didn't know much about. Her knowledge of his life before they met was also limited. In short, John Paul Emmons was an unusually private person, and Danielle Emmons chose not to test their marital contract by demanding that he be more forthcoming. Do you get the picture?"

"I do. I've known a couple like that, and I can't for the life of me imagine how they make it work."

"Let's fast forward to the present. Danielle knows that her husband is dead, so there was no reason not to probe into the life she knew so little about. As she poked around, one thing she discovered is a locked file cabinet in his closet. She claims she didn't even know the cabinet was locked, which tells a lot about how willing she was to live with his paranoia about privacy. To make a long story short, she got someone to come in and open the file cabinet for her. It's what she found there that I want you to take a look at. It wasn't all that clear from our conversation that we're going to learn anything that will answer the question of just who Emmons was, or what his relationship, if any, was with French. Not to mention why he was killed or who might have killed him.

"But his wife is now, rather belatedly, very interested in filling in those blanks. And she is ready, even anxious, to help us catch her husband's killer. There was a time when I was afraid that she would prefer not to know, that she would be afraid of what she'd learn about her husband's shadow life. But she has a close friend who, I'm guessing, persuaded her to face the past, no matter how painful it might turn out to be."

Kevin had listened attentively to this recital of Danielle Emmons' relationship with her husband. He didn't like the idea of leaving Carol, but she wanted him to do this, and he was beginning to feel again the familiar sense of excitement that seemed to come with Carol's investigations of murder on Crooked Lake. It'd only take a day. He'd do it.

"Okay, I'm to hit the road tomorrow. Who am I supposed to be?"

"I wish you could just be yourself, my charming husband. But how about you're a private investigator who works as a consultant with the Cumberland County Sheriff's Department? I've asked you to follow through on the issue of who might have wanted to kill John Paul Emmons. Can you cope with a flimsy cover like that?"

"Why not? You have to remember that my years in the classroom have given me lots of experience in pretending that I know what I don't know. It's the secret to professorial one-upmanship."

"That's awful," Carol said in mock horror. "But seriously, do you think you can do this? I think Mrs. Emmons is ready to cooperate."

"Did she say what was in the file cabinet?"

"Photos, mostly. Old ones. Some of them seem to have names on the back. She thinks they're from John Paul's time in high school, but she can't be sure."

"It sounds as if there might be a connection between my trip to Brighton and Officer Parsons' trip to - what is it? - Cheekasomething."

"Cheektowaga, and yes, there could well be a connection, which is why I want you to get up there right away."

They talked for another fifteen minutes, with time out for a nurse to take some blood, before Carol admitted that she'd like to have a nap. They agreed he'd come back around four o'clock, at which time Carol promised a more thorough report on the French case. She'd already fallen asleep when he pulled the curtain closed, said good-bye to the duty nurse, and headed back to the cottage.

CHAPTER 43

As Officer Parsons tooled down the thruway toward Buffalo, he was conscious of the fact that the traffic around him slowed perceptibly. It was a familiar phenomenon, drivers reacting to the presence of a patrol car. The fact that his car lacked the colors and logo of state police cars didn't seem to matter. For all other drivers knew, a Cumberland County Sheriff's Department car might be able to pull them over for speeding anywhere. Parsons had no such intention. He was interested in getting to the Cheektowaga high school where Eddie French and John Paul Emmons had been students just as quickly as he could while staying within the posted speed limits.

Sam had told him of the sheriff's instructions just before ten, and he had hit the road fifteen minutes later. He would have preferred to make an earlier start, but he calculated that he would still reach the school in plenty of time to speak to several people and make a few appointments for the following day. The thruway was busy but not congested until he neared the Buffalo Niagara International Airport. Although he had studied the map and was watching the signs for the left turn which would take him to the high school, he missed it. As it turned out, correcting for his mistake was not a problem. Not nearly as much of a problem as navigating the school's tight security system. It was nothing like the open, accessible schools in the villages around Crooked Lake. Bill wondered whether this was an unusually rough neighborhood. He hoped that it hadn't had a Columbine-like incident.

Once in the principal's office, people were friendly. He made it clear at once that he had no complaint about the school or any of its personnel, but that he was seeking information about former students, young men who had matriculated there as much as a quarter of a century ago.

"I hope that none of our graduates have done something to harm our reputation." It was the principal, a young woman who had introduced herself as Candace Hargrove.

"Not in the way I think you mean," Parsons said. "Let me explain why I'm here. I represent the sheriff's department in Cumberland County. It's east of here, over in the Finger Lakes. Within the last two weeks we have had two suspicious deaths. Neither one died of natural causes; in fact, one was shot to death and the other was stabbed to death."

The principal and her administrative assistant were obviously shocked.

"We are, of course, investigating their deaths, and it has become apparent that we will need to know more about the two victims. About their backgrounds, inasmuch as that may have something to do with what happened to them."

"You don't think they were killed because they went to our school, do you?" The principal's voice made it clear that she thought the very idea was preposterous.

"At the moment we don't know what to think. I'm sure it wasn't because they were students at Cheektowaga High. But they were killed within a week of each other, and the only thing they have in common, as far as we know, is that they were both students here at about the same time. Naturally this makes it important that we talk with people who may have known them back then."

"When did you say it was that they went to school here?"

"I believe one of them graduated in 1988 and the other a year later."

"Excuse me," the principal's administrative assistant spoke up. "Can you tell us the names of these students?"

"One was Edwin French, the other was John Paul Emmons."

"French. Yes, I remember. Someone called the school about French recently. Caroline told me about it. Caroline, she works in the front office. She didn't mention someone named Emmons."

"I was the one who called, and Caroline, if that's her name, was very helpful. But she wouldn't have mentioned Emmons because he was still alive when I called. In fact, we had never heard of Emmons, much less that he had graduated from Cheektowaga."

"And now you need our help," the principal said, sizing up the situation. "There's been a rather large turnover of faculty since these two men matriculated here. This is only my fourth year, and

I don't suppose there are more than six or seven people left who might have known those boys. Peggy, why don't you look in the teachers' file drawer and see who was here back in the 80s."

While Peggy, the administrative assistant, tackled that assignment, Ms. Hargrove invited Officer Parsons to join her at a round table in the corner of the office under a large floor to ceiling window. It was apparently where she held informal meetings with visitors, for she asked Parsons if he'd care for coffee and soon produced two cups if it, along with sugar and cream, from a coffee maker on a sideboard.

"I'm afraid it's Friday and the school day will be ending in about twenty minutes," the principal said. "Except for baseball practice and play rehearsals and - you know, there are always a thousand extra-curricular activities. So it may not be easy to see the teachers you're interested in."

"I understand. But I can see them tomorrow if need be, or even come back another time."

Ms. Hargrove stirred her coffee and smiled.

"I do hope that nothing comes of this. Nothing about Cheektowaga High, I mean. Of course we always hate to lose our alums, especially at such an early age and in such an awful way."

Peggy interrupted, setting a file folder on the table.

"This is the summary profile of the faculty. I just gave it a quick look-see, and there are a few old-timers."

The principal opened the file and ran a finger down a column on each of several pages.

"Yes, like I said, it looks like there are ten. No, wait, Briscoe retired last year. Why is he still here? Let's make that nine." The principal had actually guessed there would be six or seven faculty who might remember French or Emmons, but nine wasn't far off.

Bill listened while the principal rattled off names and what they taught, while Peggy dutifully made notes for him.

"It would help if I had some idea of what kind of courses French and Emmons took while they were here," he said.

"That will be more difficult, but I'll see what we can do."

"What about coaches? I know French played baseball. In fact I believe he was one of your better players."

"You may be in luck on that one. Jake Ralston's been here longer than anyone but Ellen George. He would definitely have been on the staff back when French was playing. I don't really know just what he was coaching then, but he's the baseball coach now. You could probably catch him on the practice field in another half hour or so."

When Bill said thanks and good-bye to the principal and set off for the practice field, he had a list of nine 'old-timers,' some of them not all that old, who had made their careers at Cheektowaga High. He thought that two were doubtful because of the subjects they taught, but then he had no idea what either French or Emmons was interested in while in high school.

The baseball field was across the street and down the block. Although school wouldn't be out for nearly another ten minutes, there were seven members of the team, already in uniform, on the field. Presumably they didn't have a class during the last period of the day. Or perhaps they gave their sport priority over their academic responsibilities.

There was nobody on the field who looked as if he might be Coach Ralston, so Parsons took a seat on a bench where he could see coaches and players as they arrived. Most of the team had assembled and was engaged in calisthenics before an older man sporting horned rim glasses and wearing a green and white windbreaker stepped smartly onto the field.

"Okay, twice around the field. Come on, Richey, not the infield. All the way to the fence."

The coach could not help but notice the man in the police officer's uniform. He walked over to the bench.

"You follow the team?" he said, extending his hand. "We play Garfield tomorrow, over on their field."

"You must be Mr. Ralston," Parsons said.

"That's me, but I don't recognize the uniform. You aren't local."

"That's right. I came all the way over from Crooked Lake to check out your Trojans." He gave the coach a broad smile, and proceeded to tell him why he was there.

"You're investigating a crime? I sure hope it doesn't involve any of our kids."

"Nobody on the current team, but I'd like to talk with you about someone who played for Cheektowaga twenty some years ago. Do you think you can spare me a few minutes?"

"Sure. Let me speak to Robbins. Be right back."

213

Coach Ralston caught the eye of a younger man who must have been an assistant coach. They talked briefly, the man named Robbins nodded, and Ralston rejoined Parsons by the bench.

"So what's this about a former player?"

"The trouble is that he's dead. He was killed a couple of weeks ago over our way. If we're going to find who killed him, it looks like we'll have to learn a bit more about him. We know what he was doing since he moved to our neck of the woods, but almost nothing about his life before that. He graduated from the school here in 1988 and he played for the baseball team, and that's about it."

"What's this guy's name?"

"French. Eddie French. We hear that he went by Lefty when he was in high school."

"Well, I'll be damned," Ralston said. "Somebody killed Lefty?"

"Somebody did, and there's no reason to believe his being a Cheektowaga grad has anything to do with it." Bill chose to defer mentioning Emmons for the moment. "But it might help if you could tell us what you know about him."

"What I know is he's one of the best pitchers the Trojans ever had, certainly since I came aboard, and that was in '82. It was his arm that took us to the regional finals two years in row."

"We'd heard he was good, but I'm more interested in what he was like. What about his personality? Did he get into trouble a lot? Have many friends? Do much besides baseball?"

"You know, that's interesting," Ralston said, looking thoughtful. "I was relatively new here, not much more than a kid myself. Probably wouldn't remember much of anything about Lefty if he'd just been an average player. But you tend to remember the really good ones. And it was funny about him, like he was two different people. When he had his uniform on, he was all baseball. Focussed, worked his ass off. But the way I recall, when he wasn't playing or practicing he'd sort of disappear into his shell. Quiet, a loner, no friends that I remember. A real introvert. You'd have thought he'd have eaten up all the kudos he got. Not French. After a game he'd be the first guy to take his shower, change clothes, leave the locker room."

"You say he didn't seem to have many friends. Let me try a couple of names on you. George Tiegs? John Paul Emmons?"

"Tiegs doesn't ring a bell. I'm not sure about the other one. He might have been on the baseball team. But I didn't say French didn't have friends. It's just that I never saw him palling around with anybody. I think the guys on the team were puzzled, but he was so important to the team that they didn't want to rag on him. Who are these guys you mentioned?"

"Two other Cheektowaga grads. Tiegs is the one who remembered French as Lefty. Emmons is one of the reasons I'm here. Like French, he got himself killed over on Crooked Lake. Less than a week after French. You can see why we decided it might be useful to talk with you people at the school. It isn't often that two alums from the same high school, graduated a year apart, get killed within days of each other twenty-two years later."

"That is strange, isn't it? What were they doing over where you come from?"

"French was working there. For a bakery. Emmons, we're not sure. He lived in Brighton - that's up near Rochester. We have no idea why he was on Crooked Lake the night he was killed. Another question. As far as you know, did French have a girl friend? Do much dating?"

"I don't know. You always see the girls hanging around at practice, after games, waiting for some guy. My memory may fail me on this, but I don't remember anybody waiting for Lefty. I can't say he didn't have a girl friend, but I sort of doubt it."

"What kind of student was he?"

"There was never a question about his eligibility, so he must have kept his grades up. You'd have to talk to some of his classroom teachers."

"Anyone in particular who might be able to help me get a better picture of him?"

"Not too many teachers here who were on the faculty back then. Maybe Janet Newsom, she taught English. Just about everybody who went through high school here would have had her at least once. Or Sarah Underwood. She's popular, has a reputation for liking the boys. Not in a bad way, you understand, although there are those who say she's not above playing favorites. There was a fellow who taught phys ed in one of the middle schools. Name's Kemp. I remember him because he called me when French entered high school here, told me he was going to be one of the great ones. I appreciated the heads up."

"What's the name of his middle school?"

"Parkland, but I don't think he's there anymore. In fact, I'm pretty sure he isn't. But they could put you onto where he is now."

It was time for both men to move on, Ralston to get his team ready for the Garfield game the next day, Parsons to track down several teachers and get himself a motel room for the night.

CHAPTER 44

The sheriff had three more visitors on Friday. While she had expected to see Sam and Kevin again, she was both surprised and delighted when Officer Byrnes dropped in at 4:35.

"I've only got a minute or two, but I had to see for myself that you really are making progress," he said. He had not seen Carol since the ambulance took her away from The Angle on Wednesday. She was in surgery when he and Sam made it to the hospital that afternoon, and, like the rest of the force, he had been working overtime on the militia connection ever since.

"You're my hero, Tommy. Your company kept me sane the other day. I'm sorry we ran into a buzz saw out there in the woods."

"I don't feel much like a hero. I honestly didn't know just what to do when you got shot."

"You did everything you could have. It's just as well you didn't try to do more. I understand Sam's got you all watching that damned shack and tracking down the militia boys."

"Right, and so far no luck. You heard about the fertilizer, didn't you?"

"Oh, yes. I think Sam was reluctant to tell me, afraid the shock to my system would be too great. As you can see, it wasn't. I take it that the fertilizer hasn't been tied to Coover's group yet? Or the shooting. I'm sure Sam would have told me."

"Not unless something happened this afternoon. We can't find Coover and Ticknor's pretending he doesn't know anything about a militia. A couple of other guys Sam thinks are in cahoots with Coover are also playing dumb."

"So, as far as we know, the fertilizer could belong to the state. They need it to feed a lot of bushes they're going to plant around the shack. And the guy who shot me was just some kid who mistook me for a squirrel."

"You're in pretty good humor for someone who took a bullet in the gut," Byrnes said, smiling.

"I'm trying hard to keep things in perspective, Tommy."

"Look, I've got to get back and check in. Maybe one of the guys found Coover. But I'm glad I stopped by. You're looking good, really you are. Just don't hurry back until you're ready."

"You sound like Sam, do you know that? My mind tells me I'm ready to come back, but my body isn't quite there yet. Besides, the doctor has me tied to this bed. Thanks for stopping by."

"I had to see you," Tommy said as he backed out of Carol's room. For some reason, those five words gave Carol a lump in her throat.

———

Sam arrived at almost the same time that dinner did. Inasmuch as dinner was again all liquid, if jello can be counted as liquid, Carol preferred to be seeing Sam. He tried to put on a happy face, but it was immediately apparent that the local militia was still proving to be elusive.

"Looks like another bad day," Carol said. "No Coover?"

"No Coover. It's pretty clear that he's made himself scarce to avoid having to answer our questions."

"I thought he had a job selling cars."

"He does, but they tell me he's taken some time for personal reasons. He didn't tell them what those personal reasons are or how long he'd need to deal with them. We even got in touch with his ex-wife, and she doesn't know where he is. She also made it very clear that she doesn't care. His house is locked up, the car gone. And you know he doesn't have any close neighbors. We've checked the pubs and coffee shops he's said to frequent. Nobody's seen him recently. That's not quite true. Our friend Ginny Smith says he stopped by there Tuesday evening, had a couple of beers by himself, left early. She didn't talk to him other than 'hello, what are you having.'"

Sam sighed.

"Looks like we'll have to concentrate on Ticknor," Carol said.

"But it's like I told you yesterday, he claims to know nothing about the state forest, much less any militia."

"Who's talked to him?"

"Grieves. Says he can't understand why the police are bugging him."

"Put Byrnes on him."

"I wanted to, but I figured Ticknor would be sure to recognize Tommy as the guy he talked to at the high school baseball practice."

"That probably made sense when Grieves tried to get him to talk, but it looks like those guys know by now that we know what they're up to. So what can it matter that Ticknor realizes we were onto them even before that ruckus in the woods. Let him recognize Tommy. He'll have a tough time denying what he told him."

"If you say so," Sam sad.

"I do, and it makes sense. After all, Tommy's the guy who knows exactly what Ticknor said. Harder to argue with Tommy than it would be with any of our other men."

Sam wasn't sure this was a good strategy, but he'd do as the sheriff ordered.

"What about the fertilizer? Any lead on that?"

"Better news there. It was sold in at least three different stores. The nearest one is up in Marcellus, suburb of Syracuse. What's more, it looks like the purchases were made by several different people. So they went to some trouble to fool the state's Department of Agriculture and Markets. There are records, have to be according to the law, but the names we've got don't belong to anyone in the county. With one exception, that is, a guy who lives in a retirement home in Corning. Name's Thurston, and he must be in his 80s. It's obvious that Coover's men are guilty of more than shooting at you. They're stealing people's identity and illegally buying that bomb-making stuff."

"Assuming that it's Coover and his group who're guilty. We have no proof."

"But it is Coover, isn't it? I mean, there can't be two militias stirring up trouble around Crooked Lake."

"Probably not. We're not sure there's even one. But we're damned well going to find out. One way or another, I'm still very doubtful that Coover had anything to do with French's murder."

"Yeah. I'm betting on Kingsbury. At last we know he had a good reason. Or what he thought was a good reason."

Sam left Carol thinking about motives for murder and the unpleasant and now missing Russell Coover while she forced herself to drink her dinner.

———

Her tray had been removed and she had started to read a copy of *Time* when Kevin stepped out of the elevator and came down the hall, his hands behind his back.

"I was hoping you would jump out of bed and meet me half way," he said as he leaned over to kiss her.

"I'm conserving my energy. Am I about to get a present?"

"You are, and no flowers. I thought about it, but flowers always remind me of hospitals and being sick, so I thought I'd do something more upbeat. Voila!"

He brought his hands out from behind his back and placed a rose colored box, fastened with a red ribbon, on the blanket.

"Am I supposed to guess?"

"By all means. Just try to imagine what might be on my mind."

Carol looked hard at the box, then at Kevin.

"It's something to wear, isn't it?"

"That's easy. The shape of the box gives it away. You still haven't told me what's in the box."

"I'm embarrassed to guess. What if I'm wrong?"

"I was going to say I wouldn't hold it against you, but actually I'd love to hold it against you."

Without another word, Carol proceeded to open the box, fold back the tissue paper, and lift out a lovely silk nightgown. Never, she thought, had black looked so lovely.

"It's beautiful, and I'd put it on right here and now, except this isn't the time or place."

"Agreed. I thought it might encourage you to hurry up and get well so maybe we could have ourselves a special evening before I have to go back to my students."

Carol's smile disappeared momentarily.

"I'd love that, but you know I'm in no position to make promises. When do you think you have to leave?"

"Not for at least another week. I've been busy on the phone. Two of my colleagues have agreed to take all but one of my classes. One of them is Alice Lassiter, my hard-nosed chairman, if you can believe it. I'm confident I can cover the other class, too."

"That's fantastic. I may not be up to a black nightie night next week, but I'm sure I'll be back at the cottage. Who knows, I may even do some cooking."

"No way. That's my job. Let's not rule out you modeling the nightgown, either."

"Come on, give me a kiss."

They settled down for what turned out to be nearly two hours of animated conversation, some of it about the French case but most of it simply companionable talk between two people in love. Once again, it fell to a night nurse to break it up and send Kevin on his way back to the cottage on Blue Water Point.

CHAPTER 45

Officer Parsons managed to see two members of the Cheektowaga faculty on the principal's list that afternoon. He spoke to several others on the phone that evening and made an appointment to see one of them at her home on Saturday. But he was destined not to see the phys ed teacher who had recommended Eddie French to Coach Ralston, inasmuch as he had left Parkland Middle School many years ago and the principal at Parkland had no idea where he might be at the present time.

Of the members of the faculty he spoke with while he was in Cheektowaga, two proved to be of no help at all. One did not remember French and doubted that he had ever been in any of her classes. Another recalled that French had been quite a baseball player, but he was sure he'd not been in his trig or calculus classes. 'It's the college-bound kids who take my courses, not the jocks,' he had said. 'They typically look for gut courses, and I don't teach gut courses.'

He had been able to catch Sarah Underwood after school as she was cleaning up her desk and stuffing what looked like a pile of homework papers into her briefcase.

"May I help you?" she had said as he wrapped on the glass of the open door.

"I hope so. You are Ms. Underwood?"

"I am. Is there some problem?" The uniform seemed to send a signal to that effect.

"No, no. Well, not right now. My name's Parsons, and I represent the sheriff's department in Cumberland County. I wonder if I could talk with you for a few minutes about a student who attended school here awhile back."

"Of course, although I'll need to know whom we're talking about."

"Edwin French. He went by Eddie, and I understand he was often called Lefty."

"Goodness, that was a long time ago. I believe Eddie graduated around 1990, maybe earlier."

222

"Yes, I think it was 1988. You knew him?"

"I did, but not well. It may depend on what you want to ask me."

"I'd like to hear how you knew him, what your impression of him was. In other words, just about anything that will help us to get a better picture of the man."

"I must say, this sounds very mysterious. Has he done something awful?"

"It isn't what he's done, but what's been done to him. He was killed recently. Murdered. Nobody over our way seems to know much about him, which makes it hard to go about catching his killer. Do you see my problem?"

"Well, if nobody knows much about him now, he hasn't changed very much. He was a big hero athletically when he was here. I suppose you know that much about him. Ask anybody about Eddie French and they'd say he was that great pitcher for the Trojans. Ask anybody to elaborate and they'd be stumped."

"How did you know him?"

"I didn't. I tried to get to know him. He took one class with me, world history. He was actually a marginal student, and I figured I might be able to help him. So I asked him to come by after class and talk. I thought if I could get him interested in things like the Roman Empire, maybe he'd make more of an effort. Anyway, I urged him to come around after school. I even invited him over to my house once or twice. But he wouldn't do it. Always some excuse - baseball practice, had some chores at home, wasn't feeling well. It was always something. I finally gave up. So when you ask did I know Eddie French, I'd have to say no."

"Do you remember anybody he seemed close to?"

"Not that I remember. Like I said, I only saw him in class just that one semester. If he had friends, it must have been outside of school."

Ms. Underwood had shaken her head, her expression sad.

"What a shame. And to come to an end like this."

His Saturday appointment was with the English teacher, Janet Newsom. Her directions to her home were precise and it took him less than fifteen minutes to get there from the motel. The house was the only one on the street that had resisted efforts to be modernized, add wings, and, in two cases, be turned into mansions. It looked as if it had been built in the 20s, with a large front porch complete with swing, whereas its neighbors turned their backs to the street in favor of decks in the rear of the house.

A tall, slender man with gray hair and his arm in a sling opened the door.

""Hello, I'm Officer Bill Parsons, and I think I have an appointment with Mrs. - or is it Ms. - Newsom."

"It's Mrs. Newsom. She's my wife. You must be the policeman who called her yesterday. Don't think we've had the law at our door since kids staged that rampage last Halloween. Come on in. I'll tell her you're here."

Parsons was escorted into a large parlor with a decor which reinforced Parsons' first impression of the house. He was offered coffee, which he accepted. The English teacher made her appearance before her husband produced the coffee, hobbling with some difficulty and the help of a cane.

"Mr. Parsons, I believe," she said as she took a seat in a chair across from him. "This is an unusual occasion, as you must know. You expect me to help you explain the death of a student of mine whom I last saw almost a quarter of a century ago. It isn't often I'm called on to do something like this."

It isn't often? Parsons found himself wondering whether there had been other, albeit rare, occasions when Mrs. Newsom had been questioned about the fate of one of her students.

"I'm sorry to have to ask you to reflect on Mr. French. But it appears that you may actually have known him."

"Of course I knew him. He took three courses with me, par for the course in those days. Two years of high school English and a special tutorial in his last semester. You remember students like French."

"A special tutorial? What does that mean?"

"He didn't have quite enough credits to graduate on time, and we had an arrangement that students like him could take a makeup course for that one last credit hour. It was no big deal. He had to write a couple of papers for me, prove he could create coherent paragraphs. He got his credit and graduated with his class."

"I can appreciate it that you might remember someone who'd taken three courses with you, but over twenty years ago? There must have been something about Mr. French that makes him memorable."

"Of course you're right, and it has nothing to do with his baseball accomplishments. I hate baseball. I hate football and basketball, soccer, too. It's all some of the kids do. There's the varsity season, then there's club teams the rest of the year. They never have time to read a book, or much interest in reading period. I try to get them interested in Mark Twain, or Jane Austen or Hemingway, even Conan Doyle, for heaven's sake. It's always 'no time, got to practice, game tomorrow.' They don't want to stretch their minds."

Bill thought that this was a bit too harsh. He was very pleased that his boys were active in sports.

"So Mr. French wasn't a reader. What else can you tell me about him? Don't be concerned about how it might have to do with his death. I'm just gathering impressions - information about his habits, his friends, what he was like."

"Well, he was a loner. Definitely a loner. He didn't seem to hang out with a group like most of the kids do. Always sat in the back of the room. Of course a lot of them do that. Sit in the back, I mean. I'm pretty sure there's a correlation between where people sit and their grades. But Edwin was different. With him it was as if he was trying to sit as far away from his classmates as he could."

"Did he participate in class discussion?"

Mrs. Newsom smiled and shook her head.

"I can't recall that he ever said anything in class. Like I said, he was a loner. I always had a funny feeling about him, though. I'm not sure it's my business to say this, because I don't know whether it's true. But I remember wondering whether he'd been molested as a boy."

Parsons was surprised, and said so.

"Do you mind my asking why such a thought occurred to you?"

"It wasn't just that he sat alone, kept to himself. He didn't like to be touched. I'm one of those teachers who believe in a pat on the back for a job well done. Sometimes it's not just a figure of speech. I'll never forget a day when Edwin had actually turned in a pretty decent paper. I gave him a pat on the back. Literally. His response was unforgettable. He practically jumped out of his skin. Told me never to touch him again. I was embarrassed, for me and for him. Needless to say, I never touched him again."

"But why would that make you think he'd been molested?"

"It probably wouldn't have, except for the fact that I had a brother-in-law whose nephew *had* been molested. The family knew that for a fact. Anyway, that young man behaved just like Edwin, refusing to let anyone touch him. They'd seen a therapist, and she attributed his aversion to being touched to his personal experience. I probably shouldn't have said anything. After all, I'm just an English teacher, not a psychiatrist. It could have been just a coincidence, Edwin and my brother-in-law's story."

Yes, probably so, Parsons thought. But it was interesting nonetheless, although he had no idea how, if true, it had anything to do with Eddie French's death. Janet Newsom had little more to contribute, other than expressing the hope that they would catch whomever had killed her former student.

He had one more stop to make before heading back to Crooked Lake. The phys ed teacher who had given Cheektowaga coach Jake Ralston a rave report on Eddie French was no longer at Parkland Middle School. But Parsons had called the school and persuaded the principal to see him on Saturday.

William Boland, the fortyish principal of Parkland, made it a point to assure Parsons that he wasn't at all inconvenienced by the officer's request for a meeting.

"I'm always here on weekends," he said. "Couldn't run this ship on a forty hour week."

"I don't propose to take much of your time," Bill assured him, "but I'm up here, out of my own territory, trying to gather information about this man Edwin French. He graduated from Cheektowaga High in 1988, and seems to have spent his middle school years here at Parkland before moving on to the high school. Like I told you on the phone, their baseball coach, Jake Ralston, says that one of the people who may have known French best taught phys ed here at Parkland. Kemp's the name he mentioned. I know he's no longer at Parkland, but I'm hoping you can tell me where he went when he left here."

"When you called, I had no idea who Kemp is. I've only been here for a few years, and I'd never heard of him. But I figured I could ask around and there'd be somebody who'd remember him. Seems his name is Douglas Kemp, and that he was here from 1982 to 1991, which was well before my time. I quickly discovered that people were reluctant to talk about him. He apparently left under a cloud."

"1991. That's twenty years ago. Does anybody know where he is?"

"Nobody I've had a chance to talk to. In fact, nobody knows where he went when he left Parkland. He quit during the spring break in 1991. Told the principal he was having some personal problems and couldn't finish out the year. The story is that they tried to get him to take a leave of absence, but he chose just to quit. I guess he left without saying anything to anyone. At least the people I talked with, people who had known him fairly well, tell me he never got in touch, never explained what his problems were, never told them what he was doing."

"You say he left under a cloud. What's that about?"

"I don't really know. My sources - that's a funny way to talk about your colleagues, isn't it? - they would rather not say. Apparently Kemp was popular, got along well with the faculty and with the kids, especially those that were into sports. But there were rumors, and his Parkland colleagues didn't like the idea of bringing them up again after all these years. In fact, and I have to admit this is awkward, they didn't want me to give you their names. You should know that the people I'm referring to are veteran teachers, solid citizens. They seemed truly uncomfortable talking about Kemp."

Bill debated whether he should insist on having the names of the principal's 'sources.' He decided against it. If the sheriff thought otherwise, she could bring pressure on Boland. But he couldn't think of a reason why it could be important. Kemp had known Eddie French, but he'd spoken highly of him and there didn't seem to be any reason to think that he'd quit a middle school job because of French, who'd already graduated from high school three years earlier.

Officer Parsons drove back to the lake with mixed feelings about what he'd accomplished in Cheektowaga. French remained a stick figure, very much the loner he had been more recently on Crooked Lake. He had been a marginal student, hadn't liked to be touched, and had made his local reputation entirely on his ability as the star southpaw on the high school baseball team. The only intriguing piece of information had come from his former English teacher, and it wasn't really information, only a suspicion on her part: that Eddie French had been molested at some point in his youth, and that the experience had significantly affected his persona.

CHAPTER 46

Kevin felt strange. Here he was, two days after arriving back on Crooked Lake to spend time with his wife, and he was driving away from her, away from the lake, in the direction of a city he'd never visited. At least Carol was coming along about as well as Dr. Kavanaugh expected her to. That was the report that morning when he had stopped at the hospital to see how she was doing and to say good-bye. She had had some discomfort during the night, but the doctor had told her it was nothing to worry about and, good trooper that she was, she had assured Kevin that she was doing fine. She had had her first taste of semi-solid food since Wednesday morning, had taken a walk twice around the floor she was on, and had been kidding with the nurse when he had arrived at nine o'clock.

It was now 9:40 and he was on the outskirts of Canandaigua. Carol had paved the way for his visit as a consulting detective for the Cumberland County Sheriff's Department. He was to take a close look at what Danielle Emmons had found in the file cabinet, ask the questions suggested by what he saw, push the widow to think harder when she drew a blank, and bring the cache of material in the cabinet back with him.

The closer he got to Brighton, the more he found himself ready to accept the day away from Carol and embrace this assignment. He still didn't have a very good picture of the French case and who might be a suspect in his murder and why. But Carol had done a good job of profiling Mrs. Emmons. He hoped that what they learned from the contents of her husband's file cabinet would not add to the pain she must be feeling over his murder. Somehow, however, he expected that it would.

When he was ushered into her home, he found that she had company, presumably the close friend of whom Carol had spoken.

"Mr. Whitman, this is Lori Quentin. You won't mind if she stays, will you?"

"No, of course not." Kevin was surprised that Carol had let him keep his own name. It was, he realized, one of the advantages of women keeping their maiden names when they married.

"This is very difficult for me, as the sheriff will have told you. I'm not sure whether I really want to know about John Paul's other life."

"Yes, you do, Danny," her friend said. "You'll never have closure if you don't."

"I know, and this is why Mr. Whitman is here. But I can't pretend it's easy."

"I understand," Kevin said. "But you don't really know that your husband had another life. It's possible that his death, tragic as it is, didn't have anything to do with a so-called other life."

"You're kind to say that, but I'm sure you're wrong. Anyway, we are going to go through that file, and you're going to ask me questions and I'll try to to tell you what it means, as best I can. Don't expect me to know much. But before we do that, won't you have some coffee?"

Danny may have been playing the role of a polite hostess. Or she might have been postponing the inevitable. Kevin would have a cup of coffee, even if he wasn't really interested in one.

"Now," he said, setting his cup down on the coffee table, "what do you have to show me?"

"It's right over here." She went over to a bookcase and removed a small sheaf of material and brought it back to the couch.

"This is all?" Kevin was surprised. He had expected a much more substantial pile of memorabilia.

"Actually, there's a lot more. But they're nothing but John Paul's stamp collection. I guess he was an active collector when he was younger, but I've never seen him doing things with his stamps since we were married. He probably thought he would, but he just never had the time. But aside from the stamps, that's it. Please, don't think I would withhold some of John Paul's things."

"Of course not. I suppose I was hoping for more because it might have given us a better sense of your husband's life. But maybe there's something here which will be helpful."

Danny turned to the photographs first. She set them in front of Kevin and sat back down beside him on the couch. Lori had apparently been shown the pictures earlier. She kept her seat across from the couch near a door to what looked like the dining room.

There were four photos sized 8 x 10 or larger, plus three small wallet sized pictures, all head shots.

"The small ones are all of John Paul. They're old. This one was taken when he graduated from high school." She handed Kevin a shot of Emmons in a cap and gown. "I'd seen it before. In fact I have a larger framed version of it in our bedroom. I'd never seen the others, but he was obviously younger. My best guess is that this one was taken when he was in middle school, probably when he was 12 or 13. He looks a lot like he did later, except you can see he's wearing braces."

Kevin studied the second of the three shots. There was a definite resemblance to the young man in graduation garb, although to Kevin's eye they also looked as if they could be brothers. The third photo was darker and not as well composed. It was a candid shot, not a posed picture taken for a yearbook or some more formal occasion.

"What do you make of this one?" he asked Mrs. Emmons.

"I think it's John Paul, although I can't swear to it. He never showed me a family photo album, so I don't really have anything to compare it with. But it looks quite a bit like the one of John Paul in middle school. Too bad it's so dark."

"You've never seen other photos of your husband? Other than these here on the table, I mean."

"Only the one in the bedroom. It's sort of like his not talking about things. He never shared his early life with me."

Kevin looked hard at the three photos. But there wasn't much there, just a young boy, nothing particularly revealing about his face. Empty was the word that came to mind.

"Now these larger photos, they must have meant more to your husband. They've all been carefully mounted. It looks like they might have been framed at one time, though I can't be sure. Can you tell me about any of them?"

"Not much. This one is of his family."

She held up one of a man and a woman and what were probably their three children, two girls and one boy. It was a posed picture, taken by a local photographer, one Gustave Emmerich of Cheektowaga according to the printed matter on the back. The boy looked to be around 8 or 9; one of the girls was older, the other younger. It was a handsome family, and the boy did indeed look a lot like the middle school boy in the small photo.

"I presume you've met John Paul's family."

"Once," she said. "At our wedding. So I'm sure this is his family. But I never met them until that day, and I've never seen them since."

Strange, Kevin thought. He could imagine a situation where a daughter didn't like her in-laws, or vice-versa. But never even to have seen each other before or after the wedding. That is surely unusual.

"Are his parents still alive?"

"I think so, but we never talked about them." Danielle Emmons was obviously embarrassed.

"And the sisters?"

"His younger sister, Lucy, she's made contact a few times. I think John Paul was fond of her, but he wasn't anxious to make her a part of our lives. I suspect he thought it would open a door to the rest of the family, and he didn't want to go there. I've seen her twice, I think, once when she was in high school and then again about three years ago when she just happened by. She lives somewhere down in Westchester and was up this way for some reason. I don't remember what it was, but I know she hadn't come in order to see us. Anyway, John Paul was on the road so it was just me."

"Do you have the addresses of your husband's parents and sisters?"

"Only Lucy's. Her married name is Crane."

"Okay," Kevin said, setting down the family picture. "What about these others?"

There were three others. One was a group picture of what looked like a little league baseball team. Another was of two boys, one of them Emmons, leaning on each other, smiling and looking slightly goofy. And the third showed an older man standing by a pickup truck in an open field.

"I'd never seen any of them before," Danielle answered. "John Paul is one of the two boys in that picture over there. And that's him in the team picture. See, in the back row, second from the left. Doesn't he look like he does in the middle school picture?"

He did, which made it likely that John Paul had played some baseball when he was in middle school. And that he had had a good friend back then. Eddie French? Kevin realized that he'd never seen a picture of French.

"Did your husband ever talk about playing baseball? Or mention any of his high school friends?"

"No. Like I've been saying, for some reason he treated his past life before he met me like a closed book. He never talked about it, and I'm afraid I was reluctant to ask him. The few times I ever said anything about something he'd done, he'd simply say it wasn't important or he didn't want to talk about it. I wish I'd stood up to him."

"Don't feel guilty, Danny." It was Lori. "It wouldn't have gotten you anywhere."

"Now what about this other picture, the one of the man by the truck. I suppose you don't know who he is either."

"No, I don't, but I've been studying these pictures and it seem to me that he looks like the man in the team picture. Do you think he could be the coach?"

Kevin set the pictures side by side. There was a definite resemblance between the men. He wasn't prepared to swear that they were the same person, but he wouldn't be surprised if they were.

"He could be. But why would your husband mount the picture of a young baseball team's coach? Did he ever mention a coach he knew back in middle school?"

"It's like everything else. He just didn't talk about people he'd known."

"I never knew your husband, but I find it interesting that he chose to blow up candid shots of a friend and a coach he presumably knew in middle school and mount those enlarged pictures. He probably mounted them to protect them, possibly to frame them and hang them on a wall. Why, we don't know. I'll be reporting all of this to Sheriff Kelleher, and I'm sure she'll follow up by trying to identify both the coach and the friend. They must have meant something to your husband. Whether it has anything to do with his death is another story. After all, the photos were taken many years ago. But this isn't my department. I'll put the pictures and my report in the sheriff's hands, and I'm sure she'll be in touch with you."

"I appreciate that. I also found a letter and this memo in the file. None of them make sense to me. It's the letter that's most interesting. "

Danny handed Kevin a brief, hand written letter. There was no envelope, and it had no date or mailing address on it.

Dear JP, remember me?

You may be interested to learn that Kemp is alive and living on Crooked Lake, same as me. That's down south of you toward the Pennsylvania border. It's been a long time since we talked about this, and I have no idea whether you've changed your mind. But now may be the time.

No need to add a phone number or an address. You can check in the local directory. I hope to hear from you, or better to see you.

Same old Lefty.

"You have no idea who this Lefty person is?" Kevin asked.

"No idea at all. Don't you think the letter sounds mysterious?"

"Yes, it does." Kevin knew, of course, who Lefty almost certainly was. "The letter may not tell us what Lefty is talking about, but it may explain why your husband was in Southport when he was killed. He must have decided he needed to talk with Lefty."

"Which means that Lefty, whoever he is, killed him. He lured him down to that lake and stabbed him. Is that it?"

Carol and Kevin had made no contingency plan for such a question. But he could think of no good reason not to tell the truth.

"No, I think that's not only unlikely, I think it's impossible. The sheriff believes she knows who Lefty is, and he died days before your husband did."

"Then what's the meaning of this letter?"

"That is something the sheriff will have to determine. And I suspect she'll make it her first order of business when I give her my report of this meeting with you."

Carol's first order of business would actually be getting well and out of the hospital. But Lefty's letter wouldn't be far behind. The brief memo in the file cabinet virtually guaranteed it. It contained the following information:

E. F.
223 Woodpecker Lane, Yates Center
315-513-4447

CHAPTER 47

It wasn't only Officer Parsons and Kevin who made headway on their assignments on this Saturday in April. Deputy Sheriff Bridges, frustrated for several days in his efforts to find Russell Coover, finally ran his man to ground on Saturday afternoon, barely half an hour before he'd decided to call it a day. And Officer Byrnes, now in uniform, dropped by the baseball field to catch a few innings of a game between the Yates Center Warriors and the Franklin Tigers.

The game was not going well for the locals, which didn't surprise Tommy in view of what he had seen at practice on Tuesday. But the score was less important than the fact that Ralph Ticknor would be there in his capacity as assistant coach. The crowd was sparse, so Tommy was able to slide into a seat behind the Warriors' dugout. Ticknor noticed him along about the fourth inning, but appeared not to recognize him. A couple of batters later, however, he turned around from his seat on the bench and stared at Byrnes. The officer's resemblance to the man with whom he had discussed hunting and militias several days earlier had clearly dawned on him. He turned his attention back to the game, but Byrnes was now confident that they would be having an interesting discussion as soon as the game ended.

There seemed to be some rule that if one team held a lead of ten or more runs at the end of the sixth inning, the game would be considered ended. Franklin's lead at that point was 13 to 2. Game over. The home team wasted no time in collecting its gear and heading for the gym and the showers. Officer Byrnes wasted no time in jumping over the rail and saying hello to Coach Ticknor before he could collect a bag of bats and follow the team back to the school.

"Mr. Ticknor, it's a pleasure to see you again," he said, putting out his hand.

The assistant coach felt obligated to shake hands. Too many people nearby, too many people watching.

"I'd hoped that you were wrong about the Warriors," Byrnes said. "But I guess you were right. With a bit more defensive skill, it might have been close, but -"

He had no intention of rubbing it in, so he left unsaid any reference of the Warriors' lack of offensive punch.

"You're the man who came to our practice last week, aren't you? The one who told me about that old movie."

"I am, and I wanted to come back and see a game. Sorry I didn't bring your team any luck."

"It's not luck they need," Ticknor said. "Talent's more like it."

If the assistant coach thought that he could finesse the purpose of this encounter, he was mistaken.

"I know that you have to get back to the gym, console the boys, and get on home for what remains of the weekend. But I have a question or two, and it makes sense that we should talk now. Let's sit here in the dugout for a few minutes."

"I'd love to talk, but I have school responsibilities."

"I'm sure you do, but I think my agenda is more important than yours. Here," Byrnes said, motioning to a seat at the end of the bench, "have a seat."

Ralph Ticknor, well aware that he was on the defensive, took a seat on the dugout bench. He looked distinctly uncomfortable.

"Mr. Ticknor, or Coach Ticknor if you prefer, there seems to be some discrepancy between what you told me when last we met and what you told a colleague of mine. You talked quite a bit about a militia and the use it made of the state forest up on the county line. Yet you told my fellow officer that you didn't know anything about a militia and that you'd never been in those woods. I think you've been hunting there, but what's more important, I think you've been there for other reasons, you and your local militia group. Perhaps you can explain this to me."

"It was a dirty trick you played on me, officer. Seems to me what us guys were doing was perfectly legal. And then all this shit comes down. I don't get it."

"What you need to get is that we went to the forest on a tip, our sheriff gets shot by somebody hiding in that shack there, and when we enter the shack we find a lot of stuff that's used to make explosives. How do you explain that?"

"I don't know nothing about the sheriff being shot. Or about explosives. It's true I've been there with a militia, but we're just a bunch of guys who have some fun playing hide and seek in those woods. I've seen the shack, but I've never been in it."

"You lied to Officer Grieves. Why should I believe you now?"

"But it's the honest truth."

"Perhaps I should talk with Mr. Coover, tell him what you told me the other day. I'm guessing he doesn't know that you've been helping the sheriff's department."

The expression on Ralph Ticknor's face told Tommy that the man was trapped between what used to be called a rock and a hard place. Whom did Ticknor fear more, the sheriff or Russell Coover?

"I haven't done nothing wrong," he said, mangling the king's English again. "Why do you want to do this to me?"

"I'm not doing anything to you. I'm only asking you to tell me what you know about what's been going on in the state forest. About shooting our sheriff. About all that ammonium nitrate fertilizer."

"Can we talk about this later, after I get back to the gym and have a word with our boys?"

"No, we'll talk now, unless you'd like me to talk to Coover."

Ticknor looked like he could use a cigarette.

"Okay, look, they've been stocking up on fertilizer, putting it in that shack. It's not my idea. All I did was haul a few sacks of it in."

Officer Byrnes interrupted him.

"Whose name did you use when you bought those sacks?"

Once again, Ticknor's face betrayed the fact that he knew he was trapped.

"I don't remember."

"But you didn't use your own name. And I'll bet it wasn't Coover's."

"No, of course not. He told us we'd get in trouble."

"You didn't use your own name, but you're still in trouble, aren't you?"

"I don't know what you're thinking, officer, but I'm a law abiding citizen. I've never harmed another living soul. That business about the sheriff being shot, I didn't have nothing to do with it. I don't even know who did. Anybody could use those woods, take a shot at something. It was probably an accident."

"We'll see. Fortunately for you and your militia buddies, the sheriff is going to recover. So let's talk about fertilizer. No, let's talk about explosives. I'm sure you know that that fertilizer you guys had out at the shack is used to make explosives. Of course you also need fuel oil, but that's no problem. Or were you planning on becoming farmers?"

"I already told you, I've never been in that shack. I bought some fertilizer because I was asked to, and I don't have no idea what it's for. It's just fertilizer as far as I'm concerned."

"You should ask more questions of your leader when he tells you to do things like buy fertilizer with a fake name. Let me spell it out for you. You either know what your militia is up to, or you're blindly following orders that are going to get you into a lot of trouble. What I'd do if I were in your shoes is forget about the militia, forget about Coover, and find the time to get over to the Cumberland County Sheriff's Department and tell us everything - and I mean everything - you know about what's going on."

Ticknor didn't respond.

"Okay," Tommy said. "I'll tell the sheriff exactly what was said here. And I'd give you until noon on Monday to come around and give us a statement. Now why don't you go back and tell your boys how badly you feel about how they got creamed today."

Officer Byrnes left without another word, leaving the assistant coach sitting on the dugout bench, thinking about his options.

———

Sam Bridges had been searching for Russell Coover for the better part of three days. The man had simply disappeared. And then, to Sam's great surprise, there he was, right in front of him, stopped at an intersection in West Branch, waiting for the light to turn green. Sam was idling behind the pickup, ready to make a left turn in the direction of Cumberland. He had always been interested in bumper stickers, and found himself reading two of them that adorned the back of the pickup. TAKE AMERICA BACK. ARMED AND ANGRY. It was just as the light was changing that he remembered where he had seen them before. They, and the blue pickup, belonged to Russell Coover.

Coover shot across the intersection, heading north at a speed considerably faster than the one that was posted for this rural road. Sam flicked off his turn signal and followed the pickup. It was immediately apparent that if he was to speak to Coover, he, too, would have to exceed the speed limit. In fact, the pickup was rapidly losing the patrol car. Sam hated high speed chases. But it was imperative that he interrogate Coover, and Coover obviously didn't want to be interrogated.

The road bent sharply about two miles north of West Branch, and the pickup disappeared from view around the bend. Sam worried that Coover would try to shake him by turning off onto one of the many farm roads in this part of the county. But when he came to the bend in the road he again spotted the pickup. Time to activate the dome light, let Coover know that he was in fact being chased.

The patrol car was faster than the pickup. Sam was slowly gaining ground, and after almost three miles he was less than two hundred yards behind his quarry. Coover suddenly made a sharp right onto Tolliver Road. What's he doing, Sam asked himself? It was a gravel road, bearing the name of a farmer who had owned a large patch of land in the area back in the early 20th century. The trouble was that it didn't go anywhere. It just meandered for a few miles and then dead-ended next to an old, decrepit and deserted trailer.

Sam's first thought was that Coover didn't know that the road led nowhere. But how could he have assumed that he'd shake the patrol car on a poorly maintained gravel road? He then had a second thought. Perhaps Coover did know that the road wound its way through unplowed fields and scrub brush and down into a hollow where it abruptly ended. Maybe that was the point of his detour. Could he be luring Sam into a trap?

He turned onto Tolliver Road but he slowed down. There was no need to hurry; he couldn't lose Coover now. And it was better to approach the pickup cautiously. Would this unpleasant champion of the militia movement actually try to kill the deputy sheriff? The very thought seemed absurd. But what if he had already tried to kill the sheriff? What if he believed that he and his followers were really engaged in some kind of war against the government and the rules and policies they hated?

Sam felt for his gun. It was where it should be, in its holster. He could still see the pickup, now perhaps four hundred yards ahead of him. The two vehicles maintained roughly that distance between them for another mile before the pickup disappeared down into the hollow. Sam slowed down to a 15 mile an hour crawl. When he reached the little hillock above the hollow and started down toward the trailer, he spotted the pickup. Coover had parked it facing up the hill and was now standing beside it, watching as the patrol car approached.

As he rolled to a stop a car length from Coover, Sam could see that he had no gun in his hands. If he had contemplated a confrontation with the deputy sheriff, he had thought better of it. Sam stepped confidently out of the patrol car.

"So it's my old high school buddy Russell," he said, smiling at the putative militia leader.

"High school buddy, my ass. What the hell do you think you're doing?"

"I'm about to write you a speeding ticket," Sam replied.

"What did you expect me to do?" Coover was angry. "I'm driving through West Branch, minding my own business, when you start chasing me. What's a guy expected to do when suddenly, with no cause, the police come after you like gangbusters?"

"I like to think that an officer of the law is our citizens' best friend. All I wanted to do was have a nice little chat with you. But you chose to take off at something like 80 miles per hour. And that makes it hard to chat. So instead of a friendly conversation, I'm ticketing you."

Coover made a point of spitting on the ground between them.

"What you're doing is hassling one of your citizens."

"If you say so. Matter of fact, I think we'll still have that chat. You've been real scarce since Wednesday, and you know what happened Wednesday. The sheriff got shot. Quite a bit of ammonium nitrate fertilizer was discovered in the state forest. These are what I'd call interesting developments, and I'd be interested in your reaction to them."

"I don't have any reaction to them. I was sorry to hear about the sheriff, and I don't know anything about any damn fertilizer."

"I think you can do better than that, Russell," Sam said. "This all happened where you and your boys play your weekend games. It wasn't just an accident that our people were out in that forest land."

"What do you mean?"

"The sheriff and my colleague Tommy Byrnes were there because we'd had a tip about your militia using it."

"A tip? From who?" Coover looked concerned. He hadn't even offered his usual denial of being involved in a militia.

"A little bird told us. We didn't know about the fertilizer, but we'd been told that the militia made use of those woods. And that one of the members of the militia was the late Eddie French. That's what I wanted to chat with you about."

"Who told you this?"

"Like I said, a little bird. And it looks like our tipster knew what he was talking about. You're in trouble, Russell. You're very lucky that the sheriff is going to recover from her wound. But we aren't about to ignore the fact that she was shot at and hit. Or that there were hundreds of pounds of a fertilizer that's used in making explosives hidden away in that old shack. I say were, because the fertilizer is now in our safekeeping. Which should be reassuring."

"You're way off base, Sam. You don't know what you're talking about. If you're determined to give me a ticket, then go ahead and write the damned thing. But I want out of here. The very sight of you makes me sick."

Coover was trying to sound wronged. And tough. But he had obviously been shaken by what Sam had told him. If he suspected that the sheriff had been poking around in the forest because she'd been tipped off by somebody, it was apparent that he didn't know who had done the tipping. The local militia was about to be rocked by some serious friction.

As he drove away from the hollow, Sam pondered the significance of the fact that Coover had not reacted to the mention of Eddie French's name. Did that mean that he was dropping the pretense that he didn't know French? Or was it simply that Sam's news had made him anxious, and that in his anxiety he had temporarily forgotten that he had denied knowing French?

CHAPTER 48

It was nearly two in the afternoon on Sunday, and the sheriff of Cumberland County, dressed in other than a hospital nightgown for the first time since her surgery on Wednesday, was being helped into a wheelchair for the first stage of her trip home. She was very glad to be going home, but mildly irritated that Dr. Kavanaugh, Nurse Hopkins, and a bruiser of a hospital orderly were so insistently fussing over her.

"Really, I can do this myself," she said as the orderly tried to tuck a blanket around her legs. "And I don't see why you insist I have to use this wheelchair. I can walk, you know."

"Of course you can," the nurse said, helpfully. "But you've had quite a shock to your system, and we don't want any accidents getting you to the car."

"It's hospital policy," said Dr. Kavanaugh. "We'll turn you over to your husband once you're downstairs. You must consider yourself fortunate that I'm letting you go today."

"You're all worried that I'll do something stupid, aren't you?" Carol managed a smile.

"You can stop worrying," Kevin said. "She's in good hands."

"The best," Carol agreed. "Anyway, you've given me a list of what I must not do, and it's a mile long."

She waved the discharge papers that she'd been given.

"Remember that I'll be by your cottage at ten tomorrow," Kavanaugh said. "Just don't go spreading the word that I'm making house calls. I only do it for V.I.P.s."

Fifteen minutes later they were on West Lake Road, Kevin at the wheel, Carol beside him.

"Try to slow down when you see a rough patch of road," she told him. There had been some road work outside of West Branch, and the bumps had been painful.

When they got to the cottage, Carol climbed gingerly out of the car, leaving her earlier bravado behind.

"This may not be quite as easy as I thought it would be," she said, making no objection to the arm that Kevin wrapped around her as they went up the step onto the back porch.

"The doctor always knows best," he said as he helped her to a seat on the living room couch. "Just tell me when it's time to lie down. And let me see that list of do's and don'ts they gave you."

"Are you afraid I'll ignore my orders?"

"No, I just want to see if there's any restriction on you having a glass of wine with me to celebrate homecoming."

He scanned the page, looking for what he feared would be a warning about consuming alcohol. Unfortunately, there it was, line seven, instructions that the patient should forego alcoholic beverages as long as she was taking some impossible-to-pronounce medication.

"Damn. How long are you supposed to be on that prescription Kavanaugh gave you?"

"I don't know. It's all in that unintelligible medical shorthand. You're going to have to take it down to the pharmacy in Southport and get it filled."

"Maybe you can talk Kavanaugh into ordering a pill that needs to be taken with wine."

"I'll do that. In the meanwhile, you'd better go ahead and fill the prescription. I'm fine, or I will be if I can lie down until you get back."

"You'll be okay?" Kevin sounded worried.

"I'm already okay. Just walk me back to the bedroom."

Carol was asleep when Kevin returned with her meds. He pulled a light blanket over her and went down to the beach.

It wasn't as warm as it had been since he'd returned to the lake, but the temperature hadn't dipped back into the 40s where it had been stuck for most of March and the beginning of April. He wished he knew just how long it would be before Carol would feel like herself, before she would be up to a dinner at *The Cedar Post*, before she would be ready for a canoe ride, before she could model the black nightgown for him. He dreaded the thought that he would probably have to return to the city before some of these things were possible.

There had been too little time to do more than give Carol a quick summary of what he had learned in Brighton. They had talked enough that he knew things were beginning to move on the

French case, that Sam and Officers Parsons and Byrnes had presented her with interesting reports that he wanted to hear more about. There was even the fact that somebody named Hedrick had come forward seeking a reward for passing along crucial information that might solve the puzzle of Eddie French's death. Maybe he and Carol wouldn't be able to do everything that he was so anxious to do before he went back to his students at Madison College, but they would certainly be able to talk at some length about the murder du jour. If she felt up to it, they'd begin tonight.

A light dinner behind them, they made themselves comfortable on the couch. Carol, for the first time Kevin could remember, asked if she might have a cup of tea.

"Hot tea's a sick person's drink." He was being flippant.

"Actually, it's favored over coffee in many places. And right now I don't feel like coffee."

"You may feel like tea, but I'm not sure we have any in the house. "

Kevin got up to search the cupboards. He found a tin of Earl Grey, left over from last summer's ice tea season."

"I hope you won't mind if I don't join you," he said as he started boiling water.

"Have whatever you like. What's your take on what you found at the Emmons place?"

"It's like you said. He was hiding his past. And the stuff he'd hid in the file cabinet doesn't shed much light on it. I still don't know much about this man French, but it's pretty obvious that Emmons knew him and that they had some kind of a relationship, although I'm damned if I know what it was all about. When you told me somebody'd been stabbed in the park right after French was shot, I said it wasn't just a coincidence. And I was right, wasn't I?"

"Do you want me to say that you're always right?"

"No, just most of the time. Anyway, nothing in the cabinet tells us why they were killed. Got any ideas?"

"It's the letter that's important. There's the reference to Kemp, and we know from Parsons' report that a phys ed teacher that French and Emmons had in Cheektowaga was named Kemp. Which suggests that the coach in the baseball team photo may be - probably was - Kemp, who according to French's letter, is now alive and well on Crooked Lake. But that doesn't tell us what

French meant in the letter when he says it's been a long time since they talked about this. About what? Or when he says he has no idea whether Emmons has changed his mind. Changed his mind about what? About this, presumably, whatever this is."

"I'm inclined to agree that the Kemp French refers to was the Cheektowaga coach. But so what? You've told me a lot about the French case, and you've never mentioned the name Kemp. Do you know of any Kemps living in this area?"

"No, but that would be a good job for you to tackle. How about you make me a list of Kemps in Cumberland County?"

Kevin sighed.

"If memory serves me right, I wasted a lot of time a few years ago trying to identify all the people around here with names like Beckham. And it turned out that the guy you were looking for wasn't Beckham after all."

"This is what happens in my business," Carol said. "You chase down a lot of leads, and most of them take you to a dead end. So you think the coach is a dead end. Right?"

"On the contrary, I'm intrigued by the fact that this coach appears in two of Emmons' photos, one with his team and the other by himself. The team shot I can understand. Lots of kids and their parents save pictures of school teams. What puzzles me is that Emmons has a picture of the coach all by himself. That suggests that maybe he had a special relationship with Emmons."

"One he wanted to hide away in a locked file cabinet? It makes no sense."

"How about Parsons' report?"

"It tends to confirm that back in high school French was much like he was here, a quiet loner," Carol said. "Funny, isn't it. A star baseball player, which we assume goes with an outgoing personality, yet he's a recluse. Didn't even like to be touched. That's weird."

"But one of his teachers thought it might have had something to do with his being molested. That's worth thinking about."

"But is it? Just because she had a distant relative who'd been molested and also didn't like to be touched?

"You're probably right," Kevin said. "But just look at the recent stories in the press about kids who've been molested by their coaches. I don't know whether any of those kids were averse to being touched, but they sure were molested and by a coach. And here we seem to have a missing coach and a guy who might have been molested according to one of his former teachers. Maybe that missing coach molested French."

"I'll grant you it's possible. Anything's possible. But it doesn't make sense to me. What possible connection can there be between French being molested back when he was in school and French getting killed almost a quarter of a century later? Anyhow, we don't have a clue where that coach is, or even whether he's still alive."

Their conversation shifted to the militia and the fertilizer in the shack. They rehashed what Byrnes and Bridges had told Carol about their confrontations with Ticknor and Coover. Hopefully, they'd know by noon the next day how Ticknor would respond to the threat to let Coover know what he'd told Byrnes. They also agreed that while French's death might possibly be Coover's doing, they could see no reason to connect him to what had happened to John Paul Emmons.

It was not close to her usual bedtime, but by nine o'clock Carol admitted that she was tired and ready for the sack.

"Then get thee to bed," Kevin said. As he said it, it occurred to him that they hadn't discussed sleeping arrangements. "How do you feel about sharing the bed? I don't want to throw a monkey wrench into your recovery."

"I couldn't possibly sleep with a monkey wrench, but you're another story. Let's try it, and if it proves to be a problem I'll politely ask you to move into the study."

"You're sure?"

"I'm sure. I've got to start getting used to you, you know."

Carol got up and made her way slowly toward the bedroom, only to turn around and raise another issue just before she got to the door.

"Wait a minute. We never talked about this guy Hedrick. Remember? French's ex-neighbor who's decided he should get a reward for helping us nab Joe Kingsbury."

"Kingsbury? Do I know about him?"

"I've mentioned him, the father of the kid Eddie ran over and killed with his boat last fall. Hedrick's convinced he saw Kingsbury sneaking around French's place, and all of a sudden that's as good as proof Kingsbury killed French."

"Can't this wait until morning?"

"It will have to, but I want you to know that I have another mission for you."

"Another mission?" Kevin asked, looking puzzled.

"Right. We'll talk about it over breakfast. But I'm going to want you to pay Mr. Hedrick a visit. Wearing your hat as my private investigator, of course, just like you did with Danny Emmons. We never offered a reward for information on French's death, but if Hedrick thinks he's entitled to one he may know more than he's told us. So you're going to grill him, see what it is he really knows about Kingsbury."

"Sounds like fun, although you'll have to bring me up to speed on this Kingsbury person."

"After I get a good night's sleep. Come here and give me a kiss."

Kevin was happy to oblige.

CHAPTER 49

When Kevin awoke on Monday morning he was aware that Carol was not across the bed from him. It took but a quick second for him to remember that she should be. He raised himself on an elbow and called out.

"Carol? Are you all right?"

There was no answer. Alarmed, he disentangled himself from the sheet and got out of bed. The bedside alarm clock said it was 7:50. Now fully awake, he went out into the hall. There was no smell of coffee perking.

"What are you doing?" Carol said, closing the bathroom door behind her.

"That's what I've been wondering. I woke up, found you gone."

"People do need to use the bathroom, you know. Should I have left you a note?"

"Sorry. I just expected to see you, and when I didn't I thought - well, I guess I didn't think. I just started to worry."

"As you can see, I'm fine. You didn't punch me in your sleep or do anything else you need to apologize for. But I'm still going to crawl back under the covers and let you make breakfast. You can even serve me in bed. I figure I might as well take full advantage of my status as a convalescing wife."

"You really did sleep okay? The wound's not acting up?"

"Let's just say I'm aware of it, but it didn't keep me awake. Why don't you get cracking in the kitchen. I'll have coffee, toast and a soft-boiled egg. Remember Dr. Kavanaugh is stopping by at ten, and you're going to start looking for people named Kemp. And make an appointment to see Mr. Hedrick."

"Give me a minute to find my bathrobe."

By a quarter to nine they had finished breakfast and Carol had briefed Kevin on Joe Kingsbury's status as a suspect in the death of Eddie French. She had also filled him in on what Bill Hedrick had seen, or claimed to have seen, on Woodpecker Lane.

Carol decided that she wanted Kavanaugh to think she was just about ready to go back to work.

"I'm going to shower and get dressed," she told Kevin. "I'm tired of the doctor seeing me in a night gown, having a bad hair day. You could make the bed and clean up the kitchen. We have to make a good impression or he'll want me back in the hospital."

"And that we can't have. Don't forget to press him on when you can start enjoying a glass of wine."

By noon Dr. Kavanaugh had come and gone and expressed his pleasure at Carol's progress. Kevin had identified eight people named Kemp who lived in the area covered by their telephone directory, but none of them had the same first name as the former Parkland Middle School coach. Which meant what? That the Kemp referred to in French's letter to Emmons had moved away since the letter had been written? That Kemp had an unlisted phone, or relied on a cell phone instead of a landline? That the Kemp French was talking about was someone other than the ex-Parkland coach? That seemed unlikely, but it couldn't be ruled out.

Frustrated by this assignment, Kevin turned his attention to making an appointment with Bill Hedrick.

"Hello, this is Joan."

"Mrs. Hedrick?"

"Yes, that's me. What can I do for you?"

"Is your husband at home by any chance?|"

"He's at work. Can I take a message?"

Kevin had no idea what Hedrick's wife knew about her husband's conviction that he was deserving of a reward for fingering Kingsbury as French's killer. Which made leaving a message problematic.

"When do you expect him home?"

"He usually comes home for a quick lunch, but he's running late today. Maybe he decided to - wait a minute, I think he's driving up right now."

Two minutes later, Kevin was talking to Hedrick.

"Mr. Hedrick, I'm John Ensign. I understand that you've spoken with the Cumberland County Sheriff's Department about someone named Kingsbury. I consult with the department on their cases from time to time, and they've asked me to talk with you about Mr. Kingsbury. They need more information. Is there some time when I could come by your house? Sometime soon if possible."

Kevin and Carol had agreed that using his own name might be unwise in this case. Hedrick wouldn't be familiar with Kevin Whitman, but he might have seen and remembered the brief notice in the *Gazette* about the sheriff's marriage to someone with that name.

"Of course," Hedrick said, sounding excited. He shouldn't have been. Kevin knew that Carol had no intention of giving him a reward. "How about after supper tonight? Say eight o'clock?"

"At your home?"

"Yes, that'll be fine. Do you know where Woodpecker Lane is? It's in that section -"

Kevin interrupted.

"I know where you live, Mr. Hedrick. The sheriff explained it to me. I'll be at your home at eight."

Carol had mixed feelings about Kevin's news that he'd be spending the evening on Woodpecker Lane rather than the cottage. But she was anxious to see whether Hedrick would be able to make a stronger case against Joe Kingsbury.

Kevin spent much of the afternoon stocking the larder and preparing something for dinner, while Carol borrowed the study for what turned out to be a two hour work session with Bridges. Sam was conspicuously uneasy with this ad hoc arrangement, which Carol found amusing. When Sam left, she poked her head in the kitchen door.

"Sam's funny, don't you think? I think he feels as if he's intruding on our personal life. Or at least our personal space."

"I didn't notice. Too busy with my casserole."

"He's a good man, and a private one. I think he worries about us, or at least he did before we got married. Couldn't imagine our long distance relationship."

"It took me awhile to get used to it, too."

They endured another wine-free cocktail hour and agreed that Kevin's casserole was okay but not one of his better culinary efforts. It was shortly after 7:30 when he took off for Woodpecker Lane.

———

Kevin wasn't sure what to expect when he and Bill Hedrick sat down in the neat but spartan living room up the street from Eddie French's former home. He suspected that Hedrick was trying to con the sheriff's office, but he knew he had to keep an open mind.

"The sheriff tells me that you saw Mr. Kingsbury up this way awhile ago, snooping around French's place. This may be important information. But I'm sure you can appreciate that the department has to proceed cautiously. They can't bring some kind of action against someone and have it turn out that he was just trying to locate an address after dark. Mr. Kingsbury's a respected member of the Crooked Lake community. It would be embarrassing if the sheriff's office charged an innocent man with something he didn't do, wouldn't it? And it could be bad for you, too. You could be vulnerable to a civil suit, one that could wipe you out."

There, Kevin thought, he's on notice that this is no time for mere speculation, much less for a ploy to make some money.

Hedrick had listened attentively as 'Mr. Ensign' made his little speech about the perils of false accusation.

"Oh, I understand this is a serious business. But like I told the sheriff, I saw what I saw. Him creeping around, peering in the windows. I can't prove he killed Eddie. I'd have to have seen it with my own eyes, which I couldn't have. But what I did see looks like a pretty big clue, and I know how important clues are if you're going to get the guy who did it."

"Why don't you describe the man you saw. What was he wearing? How tall was he? Things like that."

Bill Hedrick proceeded to describe the man in considerable detail, right down to the color of the jacket he was wearing. Kevin remained skeptical. As Carol had recounted Hedrick's story, Kingsbury or whoever it was had been some distance away from the streetlight.

"If you don't mind, Mr. Hedrick, I'd like to step outside for a minute."

Kevin got up and went to the front door. A puzzled Bill Hedrick followed.

"Now, what I'd like you to do," Kevin said as they went out onto the stoop, "is go down to French's old house and stand as close as you can to where he was when you saw him. I'm going to stay here in the doorway. Is this about where you were standing that night?"

"Sure. Just far enough outside so my smoke wouldn't bother Joan."

"Good. Now go ahead on down to French's."

"Is this about right?" Hedrick called out from a distance of about sixty feet.

"If that's where he was when you saw him."

The days were gradually getting longer, but it was still much closer to the equinox than the solstice. It was already dark outside, and no light shone through the windows of the house from which Eddie French had been evicted. In all likelihood, the landlord hadn't found a new tenant yet. Kevin could see Hedrick, but he was a shadowy figure, unrecognizable at that distance, in that light.

"Okay, you can come back now."

"What was that about?" Hedrick asked.

Kevin was surprised that he needed to ask.

"I wanted to know how easy it would be to see somebody poking around French's house."

"What do you think?" The man who hoped his identification of Kingsbury would earn him a reward looked anxious. Kevin was not about to give him a direct answer.

"Hard to say. I could see you, of course, but I want to think about it. Let's go back inside."

Kevin had two more questions he wanted to ask.

"Was Mr. French at home that night you say you saw Kingsbury?"

"I'm not sure."

"But were his lights on?"

Hedrick didn't like to say so, but he again admitted that he couldn't remember.

"When did this happen? What was the night when you say you saw Kingsbury skulking around the French place?"

"Like I told the sheriff, it was about three weeks ago."

"I'd like you to be more specific. What was the date?"

"It doesn't matter, does it?" Hedrick was definitely unhappy with the way the discussion was going.

"It may matter a lot. Your story would be much more convincing if we had a date and we could prove that Mr.

Kingsbury was not at home that night." Or, Kevin thought, your story would collapse if we had a date and could prove that Kingsbury *was* at home that night with his family as witnesses.

"I wish I could help you," Hedrick said, looking worried that his quest for a reward might be disappearing before his eyes. "I'll try to think back, and I'll let you know if I come up with a date."

I doubt that you will, Kevin said to himself. Without a specific date, we can't prove that you made all of this up.

When, back at the cottage, Kevin made his report to Carol, he made it clear that he believed she had been right: Hedrick had jumped to the conclusion that the man he had seen was Kingsbury because he'd followed the coverage of French's trial and was aware of Kingsbury's feelings toward the man who had killed his son.

"I can't believe he could have identified Kingsbury, a man he only knew from newspaper photos, in such poor light. I suppose it could have been possible if French's house had been lit up like a Christmas tree, but I doubt it. And Hedrick can't even remember whether lights were on in the house."

Which didn't mean that the man Hedrick had seen was not Kingsbury. But it did mean that his testimony was for all practical purposes worthless.

CHAPTER 50

It had been a bad night. Not that her wound had begun to bleed again, or even hurt. It was actually healing faster than Dr. Kavanaugh had expected. But Carol had had a restless night, and the problem was her mind, not her body. She had tried all of the tricks she knew to get back to sleep, including that old standby, counting from one to one hundred backwards. None of them worked.

The problem was easily diagnosed. There was a murder to solve, a murderer to apprehend, and she was out of the loop, confined to her home where all she could do was fret about the progress of an investigation in which she was only marginally involved. Everyone had joked about it when she was in the hospital. Poor Carol, they had all said, inactivity will drive her crazy. Dr. Kavanaugh had read her the riot act about a premature return to work. So had Bridges. So had her own husband. But it *was* driving her crazy. And keeping her awake at night.

She had finally given up at 6:30. She moved quietly so as not to disturb Kevin, claimed her bathrobe from the chair in front of the TV set, and went out onto the deck. She wanted her coffee, but more than coffee she wanted a breath of fresh air. The sun wasn't up yet, but the eastern sky above the bluff across the lake gave early evidence that it was going to be a pleasant day. Carol pulled her robe tighter around her and stepped down the steps and out toward the lake. It wasn't until she was on the grass that she remembered that she hadn't put her slippers on. No matter. The grass felt good beneath her feet. In another month or two she would be making this short trip from the cottage to the water on an almost daily basis in order to take a swim.

That thought reminded her of how terribly lucky she was. The bullet that had taken her down in the state forest could just as easily have killed her. Or caused so much damage that she would now be in intensive care, fighting for her life, not contemplating the pleasure of swimming in Crooked Lake. But it hadn't, and it wasn't because she had been hit by a marksman who wanted only to warn her. Of that she was certain. Had the bullet struck her just a bit higher, or even a few inches further to the left, she might not have made it to the hospital. Carol knew that she should be offering a prayer of gratitude, not feeling frustrated that she was confined to the cottage.

She waded out into the shallow water, knowing it would be cold. It was even colder than she had expected it to be. To her surprise, however, she liked it. She gathered her robe up and walked a bit further into the lake, enjoying the sensation. Her head wasn't telling her to relax. Perhaps her feet would.

When Carol returned to the cottage, she felt somewhat better than she had when she reluctantly crawled out of bed. She had also decided that once Kevin was up and about she would enlist his help in a serious brainstorming session. She had shared some of her thoughts about the French case with him, but they hadn't really tackled the case in anything like a systematic manner. There was still much he didn't know about what had happened or who all of the principal players were. If she was destined to be sidelined for awhile, she would need his help as her alter ego, and that would not be possible unless she laid out what she knew and where that knowledge was leading her. Besides, working together to solve the murders which had rocked Crooked Lake in previous years had become a surprising stimulant in their relationship. Murder as an aphrodisiac. Carol smiled to herself as she made her way to the kitchen to start the coffee pot.

"I smell coffee." Kevin yawned as he said it. His hair badly needed a comb or a brush.

"Look at yourself in the mirror," Carol said. "It looks like you have a bird's nest on your head."

"I'm sure you've seen worse. When did you get up? I hope your wound isn't misbehaving."

"It'll be okay. I just couldn't sleep, and the reason has everything to do with Eddie French. So after breakfast the two of us are going to sit down and talk about it. No road trip for you today. You're going to listen while I tell you what I know about the case. And then you're going to put the little grey cells to work and tell me who killed Eddie."

"The little grey cells. I like that. You're casting me as Poirot. I doubt that I deserve the compliment, but I'm game to try."

"I'm not going to offer any of my own opinions. I want to hear what you think, not what you think I want to hear."

"Just the facts, ma'am."

"What kind of a line is that?"

"I'm channeling Jack Webb from the old *Dragnet* TV show. It's from the '50s and '60s, well before your time."

"How about before your time, too? You're showing off again."

'I wouldn't dream of it. But I agree, it's time to bring me up to date. Give me a minute to do something with my hair, then breakfast. And if you'll let me shower first, then we'll talk about murder."

"Good. I think I'm up to waffles, so hurry up."

Forty minutes later, both now looking presentable, Carol and Kevin settled into chairs in the study and began to dissect the problem of Eddie French's murder.

As agreed, Carol spelled out in as much detail as she could everything that had happened since Eddie French's body had been discovered on the Four Winns at the Lakeshore Marina. She talked about Eddie and his ex-wife, Isabel. She talked about Buddy Stearns, French's employer; Joe Kingsbury, whose son Eddie had run down and killed on the lake; and at least a dozen secondary players, from Earl Skinner to Ralph Ticknor. And then there was Russell Cover, and, of course, John Paul Emmons. Kevin tried to keep track of this growing roster of 'people who mattered.'

"Surely some of these people can't be suspects in French's murder," Kevin said.

"Of course not. Unless you convince me otherwise."

"So, if I read you correctly, you're only suspicious of Kingsbury, Stearns, French's ex-wife, and maybe Coover."

"I wouldn't put it that way. I find it hard to picture any of them killing French. And even supposing they did, why kill Emmons, too?"

"Assuming French's killer murdered Emmons. We don't know that, although I think it's highly likely. But let me tell you how it looks to somebody who'd never even heard of some of these characters until this morning. Okay?"

"That's the point of this little exercise. And I promise not to roll my eyes if I disagree." And so began two hours in which

Kevin weighed in on the mystery of who had killed Eddie French and John Paul Emmons, and why.

"You haven't zeroed in on anyone," Carol said when Kevin suggested it was time to take a break. She sounded disappointed.

"No, and for the same reason you haven't. There's too much you don't know, too many unanswered questions. There just isn't a logical suspect."

"Don't I know. I was hoping you'd have a gotcha moment. You'd think of something I'd missed."

"Let's take a look at those unanswered questions." Kevin picked up his yellow pad, now full of his scribbled notes. "This is what I've got, no particular order.

"Why is Isabel French so reluctant to be forthright with you? Something must be holding her back. She hasn't even produced that list of Eddie's former employers that she promised you. Why should that be a problem? And what else is she holding back? She certainly can't be invoking spousal privilege now that Eddie's dead.

"Question number two. Was Joe Kingsbury hanging around French's house on Woodpecker Lane just shortly before Eddie was killed? Whether Hedrick really saw Kingsbury or not, we know that Eddie thought someone was bugging him, and given his history with that family it's very possible that it was Kingsbury he had in mind. But if it was Kingsbury, why was he doing it? It was months after the accident. Had something happened in the interim that suddenly set him off?

"Then there's the question about Buddy Stearns' behavior. Why was he so solicitous of French's welfare? Why did he extend favors to Eddie which were, to say the least, counter-intuitive? Maybe Stearns is just a real sweetheart, although the way you describe him he doesn't sound like one. If that's not the explanation, what is?

"And what about our friend Coover? I know that he's still pretending he knows nothing about this militia business. That explains why he claims not to know French, in spite of the fact that Eddie joined the militia. But why did Eddie leave the militia? And what was Coover's role in what happened?"

Carol interrupted.

"You're convinced that what happened to me and the stock-piling of fertilizer has nothing to do with the French case?"

"No, I'm not convinced. But if there's a connection to the French case, I don't see what it can be. Anyway, back to my unanswered questions. And having just been up to Brighton and talked with Mrs. Emmons, I have a few. Ready?"

"That's what I'm here for."

"The big question concerns the Cheektowaga coach named Kemp. It's really a two part question. Where is he? And more important, who is he? I mean who is he that French and Emmons would have had an interest in him long after their middle school days?

"Then there's a question that's important only if the man in that picture Emmons kept hidden is in fact Kemp. Assuming it is, why would Emmons have kept it, and gone to the trouble of keeping it locked in a file?"

"Sounds as if those two questions are actually the same question."

"I guess you're right. Which brings me to my final questions. Was Eddie French actually molested at some point back in his school days, as his former teacher has suggested? That leads to the obvious follow-up question: if he was molested, who was the molester? Kemp? And, inevitably, to the question of whether Emmons was also molested."

Kevin settled back on the couch, as if to say that the ball was now in Carol's court.

"I'm disappointed," she said in mock seriousness. "And to think I thought you'd be supplying an answer or two to some of those questions."

"Well, I'm new to the case. But now I know what you do, and we know what has to be done. You've got to tighten the screws on Isabel French, Joe Kingsbury, Buddy Stearns, and Russell Coover. And if Coover continues to act dumb, squeeze his friend Ticknor. From what you've told me, all of them know more than they're telling you. No point in pressing Mrs. Emmons harder. I doubt she knows whether her husband wore jockeys or boxers. But one of your boys has to push the Cheektowaga school harder about Kemp. I'll bet you can unearth someone who's got a pretty good idea why he walked out of his job in the middle of the semester."

"We're on the same page, but then I figured we would be. Trouble is, I'd like to be tightening those screws myself."

"Is there anybody you'd like me to tackle?"

"It wouldn't work with the locals. Besides, my B-men can handle them."

"Your B-men?"

"I hadn't thought of it until just now, but I was thinking of Bridges, Barrett, and Byrnes. I wish I had another woman on the force, though. Isabel is going to be a tough nut to crack."

"How would it be if I went over to Cheektowaga before I have to head back to the city?"

"That's been Parsons' assignment, and he could be offended if I benched him in favor of the boss's husband."

"So I stay here and cook and make sure you don't do anything rash. Is that it?"

"It is, and you can begin by seeing what's for lunch right now."

After lunch, Carol confessed that the morning's brainstorming session had been tiring and that she'd like a nap.

"It's like Kavanaugh said, isn't it? You may be feeling a lot better, but it's going to take time."

"A nap is a far cry from spending the day in bed, Kevin. Just watch me. I'll be up and running by Thursday at the latest."

Tired or not, Carol didn't fall asleep quickly. She had a problem. Something was bothering her, something she believed was important. But it had vanished as quickly as it had come to mind, and she couldn't for the life of her recall what it was. This failure of short term memory frustrated her. Together with the sounds of Kevin cleaning up the kitchen, it kept her awake for a good ten minutes, when, overwhelmed by fatigue, she finally dozed off.

CHAPTER 51

One of Kevin's favorite authors had long been Tony Hillerman. Kevin had never visited the American southwest, the red rock country of the Four Corners area. But it came to life in his mind whenever he revisited one of Hillerman's novels. He was reminded of that part of the country when he stepped out onto the deck on Wednesday morning. Not that Crooked Lake looked remotely like the Navajo reservation where Hillerman set his novels. But what brought it to mind was the black sky that seemed to be rolling up the lake from the south. To the north and east the sky was still blue and nearly cloudless. Not so from the direction of the Pennsylvania border. It was not a solid black, like a curtain; instead it reminded him of a huge mound of discarded black tires, piled high and slowly but inexorably falling down upon each other. Rain was coming, almost certainly what Hillerman's Navajos called 'male rain,' a heavy, perhaps violent downpour that would soak the ground and drive people inside. Gentle or 'female' rain rarely came from such a dark and ominous sky. In fact, it had been many months since Kevin had experienced anything like what he was sure was coming. He was reminded of the summer when just such a storm had picked up his canoe and smashed it against a neighboring tree.

Carol should see this, he thought. And before all hell lets loose.

"Breakfast can wait," he called out as he hurried back into the cottage. "Come out here and take a look at the storm that's about to hit us."

She turned off the burner under the frying pan and joined him on the deck.

"I don't remember any talk about rain," she said.

"You fell asleep before the 11 o'clock weather report. But this looks like more than they were talking about. It's beautiful, isn't it?"

"I like blue skies better, but I'll concede that it's impressive. Good thing we're not planning a picnic."

"When is Bridges coming over?"

"9:30. Not just Bridges. I told him to bring Byrnes and Barrett, too. You may have to find somewhere to hide out for half an hour."

"I'm not allowed to sit in?"

"Do you want to?"

"I'd love to. And I wouldn't say a word, just sit there looking wise."

Carol thought about it.

"It might not be a bad idea," she said. "Give you a chance to form an opinion of my boys. Have you met them, other than Bridges?"

"I'm not sure."

"Okay, you're in. You can serve coffee. Just don't take notes. It'll make 'em nervous, wondering what we're up to."

Kevin wondered what the neighbors were thinking as three patrol cars pulled in behind the cottage on Blue Water Point. Fortunately, most of his neighbors were summer residents, not yet back at the lake for the summer. But the Snyders were there, and so were the Brocks, although their precocious grandchildren were still in school down on Long Island. Just as well. They had already been front row spectators for two murders on Crooked Lake. Kevin was mildly surprised that their parents were still willing to let them visit their grandparents, considering what they had witnessed at the lake in recent summers.

It had started to rain as the officers trooped into the cottage, which elicited apologies for wet shoes. Bridges started to remove his, but Carol would have none of it.

"This is just a cottage," she said as she steered them into the living room. "Has everyone met my husband? This is Kevin."

It was an awkward moment. Kevin suspected that the B-boys were wondering what Carol had told him about them. He tried to break the ice.

"I've got coffee duty this morning. Any takers?"

Bridges had the good sense to speak up and say he'd love some, with cream and sugar. Byrnes and Barrett followed the deputy sheriff's lead, and within a matter of minutes they had all taken seats, crowded together in the small living room, while Kevin went about the task of filling mugs in the kitchen.

Carol answered the expected questions about how she was coming along, and quickly steered the discussion to the business at hand.

"I'm the one who's been talking with French's wife, his boss at the bakery, Buddy Stearns, and the father of the boy he ran over in his boat last fall. That's Joe Kingsbury. But inasmuch as I'm officially still recovering from surgery and under house arrest, courtesy of Dr. Kavanaugh, I'm going to have to ask you to take over and talk with the three of them. And to get started today. It's not that anyone of the three is a prime suspect in French's murder. We don't have a prime suspect. I'm not even sure we have a suspect, prime or otherwise. But what bothers me about Isabel French and Kingsbury and Stearns is that they aren't leveling with us."

Carol went on to explain what she meant in each of their cases.

"I'm no fan of that good cop, bad cop stuff, but I think it's time to take off the gloves. When I last talked with them, I didn't really push hard when they became evasive. But it's been awhile, so maybe they think we've lost interest in them. What I want you to do is pay them a visit, unannounced. Make it clear that it's time to tell the truth. We know Kingsbury was sneaking around French's house because we've got a witness. I'm no longer buying Stearns' good samaritan routine. And we know that Isabel knows more about Eddie's past life than she's letting on, and I'm fed up with her lack of cooperation. So we lean on them. Call it the bad cop routine if you like, but make them sweat."

"What's the time frame?" Barrett asked.

"Today, unless one of them is sick in bed or vacationing in the Caribbean. I'd like to be able to interrupt Stearns and Kingsbury in their offices, insist that it's important. Now, not tomorrow. I wouldn't mind if we got to Isabel while she's at work at that diner over in Franklin. Just don't let them put you off."

"You think one of them did it, don't you?" It was Bridges.

"No, actually, I don't. But I've got a strong feeling we're not going to find out who did until we break down their walls of denial. Okay? Sam, I want you to see Stearns. Jim, you take Kingsbury. Which leaves Mrs. French for you, Tommy. Any problems with that?"

It was apparent that her officers didn't want to argue with their boss, not at least while she was still recovering from a gunshot wound, not when she was so obviously in a mood to get tough. There were some last minute questions, but by a quarter to eleven the three men had all walked out into a pouring rain and driven off to put the screws to Buddy Stearns, Joe Kingsbury, and Isabel French.

"Very impressive," Kevin said, when he and Carol once more had the cottage to themselves. "Is that the way all of your staff meetings go?"

"Of course. They know who's boss. But no, that's not quite right. I didn't want to give Sam an opportunity to start in on the importance of breaking up Coover's militia. He still thinks we should make that priority number one. That and catching the guy who shot me."

"I'm surprised you don't agree with him."

"I do agree that we have a militia problem. But Sam hasn't been able to get Coover to change his tune, and I still hope Ticknor will decide to come over to our side. Anyway, I'll worry about that tomorrow."

"By the way, what about those assignments? I mean, how'd you decide who gets to do what?"

"Hunches. Kingsbury's situation is the easiest. We can claim to have a witness to his presence on Woodpecker Lane, even if we're dubious about Hedrick's identification. So I put Barrett on him. He's the least experienced of the three, but he's like a terrier when he gets his teeth into something. It makes sense to put Bridges on Stearns. He'd be the most likely to see through a phony story, and I still think there's something phony about Stearns' story. Which left Byrnes for Isabel. I gave her to him mostly because he's still feeling guilty about my getting shot, and I suspect he'd think asking him to interrogate a woman would be just about the ultimate compliment."

Kevin looked doubtful.

"Only a woman could come up with a reason like that," he said, making no effort to control a wry smile.

"We'll see. My hunch is that Byrnes is the most likely to learn something useful."

"By the way," Kevin said, changing the subject, "that dark sky's really opened up."

"I know. I almost feel guilty sending the guys out in weather like this."

"They'll cope. And you get to stay inside, warm and dry."

"I don't want to stay inside, Kevin. I'm tired of this."

"When is Kavanaugh coming by?"

"Not until three. Can you believe, one whole week and a day since my big event, and I'm still on convalescent leave. What's there to do with the rest of the day? Stare out the window at the rain, or look at the new *National Geographic* and all those pictures of people from Outer Mongolia and Uganda. That's no substitute for -"

"What's the matter?" Kevin asked. Carol had stopped in mid-sentence and seemed to be staring off into space. She had remembered that 'important something' which had eluded her the night before.

"Where is the stuff in that file you brought back from Brighton?" She suddenly looked excited.

"Back in your office, I suppose. You had Sam take them, and I assume that's where they went. Why?"

"You're going to get in the car and go up to Cumberland. I'll call JoAnne and have her get the pictures. I want you to bring back the one of the little league team and the one of the coach. And while you're gone, I'm going to call that middle school, Parkland."

"What's this all about?" Kevin was pleased to see Carol come out of her funk, but he had no idea what had caused the turn about.

"I'll tell you when you get back. I'm going to call JoAnne." She went into the study.

Five minutes later Kevin had made the dash through the rain to his car and set off, windshield wipers running at top speed, for the Cumberland County Sheriff's Department.

CHAPTER 52

Kevin was back from his trip to Cumberland, had taken off his wet shoes and jacket, and was waiting for Carol to tell him why she was so excited.

"There they are," he said, handing her the photographs from John Paul Emmons' file. "Enough of the suspense. What's up?"

"I'm not going to tell you. Not until you take a good hard look at the photos and tell me what you see there."

"I've already looked at them. Twice. Once with Emmons' wife, and once with you when I got back from Brighton. They're old pictures of Emmons' school days back in Cheektowaga. What I've seen is his little league team and the coach. The coach we assume is Kemp. What am I supposed to be looking for now? A squirrel running across the grass?"

"Just look. Does what you see give you any ideas?"

Kevin stared at the pictures, long and hard as he'd been asked to do.

"Damn it," Carol said suddenly. "I completely forgot that you haven't seen any of my not-quite-suspects, other than Coover, assuming he qualifies. The point of all this is that I think I know who the coach is."

"You're sure it's Kemp"

"No. I'm pretty sure it isn't Kemp."

"Forgive me, but I'm confused."

"Understandably. I think the coach is someone I know. The coach in these pictures looks very much like somebody right here on Crooked Lake, somebody with whom Eddie French had a relationship. And somebody I've spoken to on several occasions. You've never met him, but we were talking about him just yesterday. And one of my officers will be interrogating him today if all goes well. Want to guess who?"

"Well, it has to be Kingsbury or Stearns. I doubt that the coach is Isabel French in disguise. But don't you think it's unlikely that either Kingsbury or Stearns coached baseball in Cheektowaga?"

"Perhaps, but I think one of them did, and I think his name is Buddy Stearns," Carol said. Kevin hadn't seen her this animated since he'd returned to the lake.

"Stearns, the bakery manager?"

"Right. I want you to meet him, see if you don't agree with me."

"But these photos are from a long time ago. Emmons would have been no more than twelve, and you said he was about 40 when he was killed. That's close to three decades. People change a lot over that many years."

"Emmons would have changed a lot. So would French. But that's a matter of pre-adolescents growing up, becoming adults. If I'm right, Stearns could have been in his late twenties, probably his thirties. He was already an adult. Those intervening decades wouldn't have changed him nearly as much as it would a twelve year old."

"You sound pretty sure of this."

"I'm not sure. When I first saw the photos, it didn't occur to me. But then something began to bother me, and I realized that it was the resemblance between the coach and Stearns. I've got to figure a way for you to see Stearns. Up close. Maybe even talk to him."

"You want me to go out to the bakery and buy a loaf of bread?"

"That's a thought." Carol considered it and decided that they did indeed need bread.

"On second thought, it's a pretty lame idea," Kevin said. "Maybe they don't sell it at the bakery. I've always bought bread at a grocery store. And what if Stearns isn't there, or is busy cleaning the ovens or something."

"I've got another idea." Carol reached for her cell and dialed Sam. He picked up immediately.

"It's Carol. Sounds like you haven't seen Stearns yet." Apparently there'd been a slight hitch in his morning's plans, and he was just about to set off for the bakery when her call came through.

"Let's make this quick. I've just had an idea. A *big* idea. I think there's a real possibility that Buddy Stearns was a coach in Cheektowaga many years ago. I think -"

Kevin was watching Carol, wondering where this conversation was going. It was obvious that Bridges had interrupted. He must be more than a little surprised by what he had just heard, Kevin thought.

"Just bear with me. I know we've been thinking about someone named Kemp, but we've got these two photos of the coach, one with his team and one all by himself. They were taken back when Emmons and French were in middle school. And the coach looks a helluva lot like Stearns. Wouldn't it be something if I'm right? This is what I want you to do. Turn around and come back to the cottage. I want you to pick up Kevin and the photos. He and I've been talking about this, but he's never seen Stearns. I want him to meet Stearns, get a good look at him. And I want you to get a good look at the coach in the picture. And don't worry, Kevin isn't going along to do anything but size the guy up. He's under orders from me to say nothing except hello and good bye. Okay?"

Carol listened for another minute, repeated herself that it was still Sam's interrogation, and put her cell down on the coffee table.

"That was quick," Kevin said. "You're asking me to ride shotgun."

"I'm asking you to commit to memory everything about this man in the photo," she said, "and when you get back I want you to tell me whether he's Stearns."

"I'd bet Bridges isn't pleased to have me along."

"He's been worried that I listen to you more than I do to him for several years now, but he knows better than anyone that he's my deputy, not you. He'll be just fine."

Fifteen minutes later, Sam joined them. This time he was definitely too wet for the living room, so the three of them sat at the kitchen table while Carol talked tactics.

"I don't want you to say anything about my suspicion that he used to live and work in Cheektowaga. You're trying to get him to tell you why he was so damned considerate of French. Don't hesitate to let him know that you don't believe he did it out of the kindness of his heart. You're welcome to go so far as to ask if he'd ever known French before he took him on at the bakery. But I don't want to tip our hand until we have proof that he's the coach in the photos."

When the men ventured out into the driving rain once more, Carol closed the back door and headed straight to the study. She'd planned to call Parsons and schedule another trip for him to Cheektowaga. Instead, she leafed through the pocket calendar and the phone numbers she'd entered there since the discovery of Eddie French's body. The one she was looking for was the Parkland Middle School. It was time to find out more about a man named Kemp. With luck, she'd be put on to someone who remembered him. If not, she'd try to be patient until Parsons returned from his next trip to the Buffalo area.

CHAPTER 53

"I'm afraid he's got a client with him, officer," Kingsbury's secretary said. She was looking disapprovingly at Barrett. He had always thought umbrellas a bit too effeminate, particularly for an officer of the law, with the result that he was dripping wet.

"That's okay. I'll wait."

"Is it important? He's has another appointment in fifteen minutes."

"It's important. I'm sure he'll want to talk with me."

The secretary pursed her lips.

"There's a restroom just down the corridor in case you'd like to brush the water off your jacket. Just punch in 47. It's been a terrible storm, hasn't it?"

"Thanks, but I'll be fine." He found a copy of *Sports Illustrated* in the rack and settled into a chair against the far wall.

He pretended to read, but he was paying attention to the secretary as she did what he expected her to do, call Kingsbury to let him know that an officer from the sheriff's department was here to see him. She had turned away from him and spoken quietly, but he wasn't fooled.

It was only five minutes later that the door to the inner sanctum opened. A middle aged woman came out, Kingsbury right behind her, helping her with her raincoat. Barrett was willing to bet that the real estate agent had decided to cut the meeting short.

"It's Officer Barrett, I understand. Glad to meet you. I hear that the sheriff is in the hospital. How is she?"

Word of what had happened had spread quickly and widely following the shooting. Kingsbury would have heard the news. Discussing the sheriff's condition would be his way to break the ice this morning.

"Fortunately, her wound wasn't as serious as it might have been. She's out of the hospital, and should be back on the job any day now."

"That's good," Kingsbury said, sounding relieved. They retreated into his office. "I didn't think I'd live to see the day that something terrible like this would happen. Have you apprehended whoever shot her?"

"Not yet, but we'll get him. Anyway, I'm here today because the sheriff wants me to ask you some questions."

"Questions? I believe I've answered her questions."

"I'm sure you think you have, but she's not satisfied. I think it's best if I get right to the point. Not long before Eddie French was killed, it appears that you started to call him on the phone and visit his house. Why did you do that?"

"Where on earth did you hear that?" Kingsbury sounded indignant.

"He talked about it with his neighbors."

"This is nonsense. I never phoned him. I never went to his house. Either French made it up or these neighbors of his are lying to you."

"Now why would they do that?"

"All right, so what if they didn't lie. Which would mean that French must have become paranoid and began to imagine things. It wouldn't surprise me."

"Can you think of any reason why French would have thought that you might be stalking him?"

Kingsbury hesitated. He thinks he sees a trap, Barrett said to himself.

"Maybe he thought that you blamed him for your son's death and were thinking of taking the law into your own hands. Were you?" Barrett asked.

"For heaven's sake, no!" Kingsbury almost shouted the words. "Are you accusing me of killing French?"

"Of course not. I'm just trying to understand why you decided to stalk French."

"I didn't stalk French," Kinsgbury said, with emphasis on each word.

"Okay. Stalk may be too strong a word. But you were seen at his house, and you weren't ringing the doorbell. I'm not sure what the right word is; let's just say you were sneaking around the house, peeking in windows, things like that. By the way, you do know where French lived, don't you?"

Silence.

"You do have his address? I should say his former address?"

"I'm not sure," he said, somewhat tentatively. "I think he moved sometime after the trial."

"It's on Woodpecker Lane, up in Yates Center. Look, Mr. Kingsbury, I'm not trying to put you on the spot." It was a lie, and Kingsbury would know it was a lie. "But you were seen one night on Woodpecker Lane, hanging around French's home. The neighbor who saw you is certain it was you. He's willing to testify to it in court if necessary. So why don't you simply admit that you were there and tell me why?"

"Who's this neighbor who claims he saw me?"

Barrett smiled.

"Let's just say it's one of the people French talked to, asking them to keep an eye open, let him know if you came around."

Another silence. And then a question.

"How could anyone identify somebody in the dark?"

He may be right, Barrett thought, but right now he's grasping at straws.

"It's never as dark as you might think, especially when there's a streetlight nearby. That's not a problem. So why did you choose to spend time on Woodpecker Lane?"

"All right, I did go up there to see French." Kingsbury looked uncomfortable. He sounded uncomfortable. But he had decided to change his tune. "I was curious about what he was doing, whether he had feelings of remorse about what had happened. But he wasn't home."

"When was it that you tried to see him?"

"I really can't remember. Maybe a couple of weeks before his death. I just did it on the spur of the moment. No reason to put it on my calendar."

"I appreciate your candor, Mr. Kingsbury. The sheriff will, too." Officer Barrett did not think Kingsbury had been candid, and he would say so to Carol.

On this way back to the cottage, Barrett was feeling good about himself. He had been given a different assignment, a difficult one that the sheriff would have liked to tackle herself. And he'd done well.

Carol was indeed pleased with Barrett's report. But she was already of the opinion that Kingsbury would admit to 'sneaking around on Woodpecker Lane' when told that a neighbor had sighted him. Unfortunately for Officer Barrett, she did not manage to disguise that fact, which he found somewhat deflating.

"You did great," she said, realizing that he might be feeling under appreciated. "He could just as easily have assumed you were bluffing."

Somewhat mollified, he set off to police the roads of Cumberland County.

———

It was mid-afternoon when Ms. Franks made her third call of the day to the cottage. Unlike the others, this one was more than mildly interesting.

"That Emmons woman up in Brighton called for you," she said. "I wasn't sure whether to bother you or not."

"You aren't bothering me, JoAnne. I may be letting my wound heal, but I am on the job, even if I'm not at the office. Did she say what she wanted?"

"Not really. Something about her husband's money. I told her I'd see if you could call her back."

"And so I shall."

Carol searched through her pocket notebook and found the Emmons' phone number.

"Mrs. Emmons?"

"No, this is her neighbor, Lori Quenton. You remember, we met when we came down to - you know, you wanted Danny -"

"Yes, indeed, Mrs. Quenton." The woman was apparently not comfortable talking about identifying John Paul Emmons' body. "I understand that Mrs. Emmons wanted me to call her."

"Yes, and she's right here."

Carol heard what sounded like thumping sounds and then the familiar voice came on the phone.

"Sheriff? What is this about you having an accident?"

Apparently Franks had been discreet; an accident sounded much better than gunned down in a forest.

"Yes, but I'm coming along just fine. You called about a money issue, is that right?"

"John Paul's money actually. Someone called from a local bank. Not the bank where we had our checking and savings accounts, but one I didn't know about. The person who called had obviously heard about John Paul's death. It was in the papers. Anyway, he called to tell me that my husband had a small account there. It was just in his name, and he figured I ought to know about it. I'm not sure how these kind of things get sorted out legally, but that's not what really worries me. I've been thinking about how John Paul had his secrets, and now here's another one. There is only $1000 in the account - apparently two $500 cash deposits. I know John Paul always had his paychecks automatically deposited in our joint account at the Lake Ontario Bank, so I can't imagine what this other account was for or where the money came from. The man at Brighton Savings Bank didn't seem to want to say too much. I guess I'm calling to see if you think this may be important."

"I can't say, but I'm very glad you called. It could be important. You said the bank is Brighton Savings. Do you know which branch and the name of the man who called you?"

There followed a moment of silence, and then a rustling of paper.

"The man who called is Dennis Kimmel. I don't know how he spells that. But the number he gave me is 585-729-1110."

"Thank you. I think it's unlikely that this account will turn out to be related in any way to what happened to your husband. He probably simply forgot to mention it to you. But we're following up on any leads we have, so I appreciate it that you called. I'll see if I can find out anything further, and I promise to stay in touch."

"Yes, please do that."

Danielle Emmons sounded worried. Carol had said she doubted that Danny's husband's small private account had anything to do with his murder, but in fact she suspected that there might be a connection. Where could those $500 deposits have come from? And why would John Paul have chosen to sequester them in an account his wife knew nothing about? Was it simply because he was by nature secretive? Or in this case was there a more immediately compelling reason for doing so?

CHAPTER 54

Kevin had tried to keep a conversation going as he and Deputy Sheriff Bridges drove to the *Breads to Go* bakery. It hadn't been easy. Sam was pleasant but obviously uncomfortable to have the boss's husband in the passenger seat. Kevin had deliberately avoided mentioning the French case, opting for the male bonding of sports talk.

When they arrived at the bakery, however, it was Stearns who was uncomfortable, not Bridges. Sam made it clear that he was there only because the sheriff was temporarily incapacitated; he explained Kevin's presence with an attempt at humor which Stearns didn't seem to find amusing.

"Mr. Whitman here just came along for the ride. I think the sheriff wanted to get him out of the house for awhile."

Perhaps she does, Kevin thought, although he knew that the real reason he was there was to get a good look at Stearns and hopefully decide whether the bakery manager had also been a middle school coach in Cheektowaga many years earlier.

It was Sam's interrogation, and Kevin wanted to blend into the wallpaper. Unfortunately, the office was small, so small that Kevin was surprised that there was even a chair for him. He and Bridges sat side by side across the desk from Stearns, close enough that he was able not only to study the manager's face but to notice that he had bad teeth, that he needed to get rid of nose hair, and that his mustache didn't quite conceal the fact that he had an old scar at one corner of his mouth.

Kevin tried to concentrate on matching Stearns' face with the face in the photo he had studied so carefully back at the cottage. But he was also paying close attention to the questions Bridges was asking and the way in which Stearns reacted to them. The interrogation was going very much as Carol's had.

"Why were you so helpful to French?'" Sam asked.

"It just seemed like he was a young man in trouble who needed a hand up."

"But why so many times?" Sam persisted. "Didn't it seem that he was taking advantage of you?"

"No, I thought he was grateful."

"I'd have thought the other drivers would have resented it." Stearns parried Sam's suggestion.

"I think they understood."

Finally, Sam's frustration showed.

"I don't believe you, Mr. Stearns. I'm sure Mr. French was grateful, but I don't believe you were so kind to him just because you're a helluva nice guy. Come on, let's have it. Why did you do it? What was your relationship with Eddie French?"

Kevin had been studying Buddy Stearns' face throughout this back and forth dialogue. The man had been patient. There had been no hint of anger. But the patience suddenly vanished, the anger flared.

"Goddam it, I'm sick of this. I've told you what I told the sheriff. And I'm getting tired of repeating myself. Eddie French was in trouble. He was also a good worker. I helped him. I'd think you people would respect me for my willingness to help a guy in trouble. But no, you're determined to find some ulterior motive. Well, there isn't one."

"No need to get bent out of shape, Mr. Stearns." Sam said. "Anyway, you're sticking to your story. That's what I'll tell the sheriff. If something occurs to you, you know where to reach us. I think Mr. Whitman and I will be on our way."

Sam stood up, nodded toward Stearns, and made his exit, Kevin right behind him.

"So, what did you think of that?" the deputy sheriff asked as they pulled out of the bakery's parking lot.

"Hard to say. If he's lying, I don't think you'll get him to admit it unless it turns out he once coached French and Emmons back in Cheektowaga."

"Do you think he did?" Sam looked doubtful.

"He looks a little like the guy in the photo. But the picture is twenty five, thirty years old, he's wearing a baseball cap, doesn't look like he has a mustache. I'd want to see the photo blown up. Anyway, I'll bet that one day you're going to want to show it to Stearns, see how he reacts."

"Yeah, probably."

Neither of them said much during the rest of the trip back to the cottage. Bridges was obviously frustrated by his inability to coax more information from Stearns, and Kevin was reluctant to talk about it. It would only compound Sam's frustration.

When they arrived at the cottage, another car was parked next to Kevin's Toyota. Dr. Kavanaugh was making another of his rare house calls.

"Hello, we're back," Kevin said. "Are you decent?"

"Give me two more minutes," the doctor said, his voice coming from somewhere down the hall.

"No, I'm not decent, but he's almost finished. Any luck?"

"Pay attention to the doctor. We'll tell you about it when you're ready."

It was closer to five minutes than two when Carol and Dr. Kavanaugh joined Kevin and Sam in the kitchen, where they were reheating the coffee pot.

"Your wife is making good progress," Kavanaugh said. "Vital signs all good. Now we're getting to the difficult part. She's feeling pretty much like herself, so she's raring to go. But you're going to have to pull back on the reins for another week, make sure she doesn't do something stupid."

"I'm not in the habit of doing stupid things," Carol said in her own defense.

"Glad to hear it, but be extra careful just the same. I'll see you on Friday."

The doctor pulled the door shut behind him, and Carol promptly demanded a report on the visit to Buddy Stearns.

"You go first," Sam said to Kevin. "I haven't got much to say."

"Sam was tough," Kevin said, "but Stearns is sticking to his story."

"I figured he would," Carol said, "but what I'm most interested in is whether you think he's the coach."

Kevin and Sam looked at each other for a moment.

"We don't know," Kevin said, aware that Sam wanted him to be the one to address this question.

"Well of course you can't know for sure, but what do you think?" Carol sounded impatient.

"If I *had* to guess, I'd say that Stearns and Kemp are the same man. But that doesn't make sense, does it? Can you get this photo enlarged?"

Kevin put the informal shot of the coach on the kitchen table.

"What are you looking for?"

"A scar." Kevin did not elaborate.

"Want to tell me what you're talking about?"

"Stearns has a scar near the corner of his mouth. It's pretty well hidden by his mustache. The coach in the picture doesn't have a mustache, and it's impossible to tell if he has a scar. But if we could enlarge the figure, we might be able to see one."

Carol shook her head.

"But maybe Stearns didn't have a scar back when he was coaching in Cheektowaga. *If* he was coaching in Cheektowaga."

"I know. But what if he did? A scar right there at the left hand corner of his mouth. Then I'd tell you Stearns is Kemp. No scar, then forget it."

"Okay, I'll see what we can do. Now let me tell you what I've been doing. And it's not stupid. It has to do with Kemp. Let's have another cup of coffee."

Kevin filled their cups.

"I couldn't believe that there was no one at the Parkland Middle School in Cheektowaga who knew what had happened to Kemp when he upped and left in the middle of a semester. So I called the principal, told him it was a matter of urgency, and that I wanted him to talk with his veteran faculty members and put any of them in touch with me who had been at all close to Kemp. I expected I might have to wait a few days, but somebody named Gus Sturdivant called me back just before Doc Kavanaugh arrived."

"I hope he had more to say than Stearns did," Sam said.

"Yes and no. He had no idea where Kemp is. He didn't even know where he'd gone to when he left Parkland. But he did know Kemp, not well, but well enough to have something to say about him that I found interesting. Parsons had reported that Kemp apparently left Parkland under a cloud, so I pressed Sturdivant on the matter. It seems that a couple of girls in the school had accused Kemp - his name is Douglas Kemp - of fooling around with them about a year before he quit."

"Fooling around?" Sam asked.

"Sturdivant chose his words carefully, but it was clear that Kemp was alleged to have touched the girls inappropriately. Put his hand on their knees, maybe put his hand under their skirts. It was quite a scandal, but then the girls changed their story, said they'd made it all up. According to Sturdivant, it was a nasty couple of months. Kemp threatened to sue, so the school board decided to conduct an investigation into the whole mess. In the end the girls were expelled and the board publicly apologized to Kemp. Then about six months later he abruptly tendered his resignation and just disappeared."

"Interesting, but how does it explain French's death?" Sam asked. "Or that other guy's?"

"Wait a minute," Kevin said. "Before we go there, what about those two girls? Did Sturdivant tell you their names?"

"He couldn't remember," Carol said. "Probably not important. They would probably have married, changed their names, moved away. It was a long time ago."

"Of course, but what if you could track them down? They'd remember Kemp. They might be able to help you decide whether Stearns is Kemp."

"That would be a long shot, don't you think? Even if we could find them, I can't imagine they'd want to revisit a bad mistake they'd made back in middle school."

"Probably not, but you can be pretty persuasive. It's worth a try."

Carol thought about it.

"Parsons talked with one of Eddie's old English teachers, a woman named Newsom," she said, changing the subject. Or maybe not. "She's the one who speculated that Eddie might have been molested at some time in his life. Remember? It was all about his aversion to being touched. Now here we are, talking about a couple of girls claiming that Kemp touched them inappropriately."

"Yes, but it was just a prank," Kevin said. "They weren't molested, and there's no evidence that French was molested."

"But what if their first accusation was true and the retraction was false? Maybe they got cold feet and decided to back off."

"I have trouble picturing the girls doing that. Why would they let themselves get expelled if they'd told the truth?"

Then another thought occurred to Carol.

"We're talking about two cases of possible molestation, French's and the girls'. I've always assumed that people who do that are either attracted to young girls or young boys, not both. Besides, the only reason we're even talking about French is because of what that teacher said, and she may just have an overactive imagination."

"I don't know about some teacher's imagination, but we're not experts on pedophilia or whatever you want to call it. Maybe guys with that kind of problem switch off, young boys one week, young girls another."

"That's really crude, Kevin," Carol said.

Sam had been watching this verbal ping-ponging between Carol and Kevin with great interest. So this is how it works, he thought, a robust form of pillow talk. Ironically, he didn't find it threatening. In fact, he realized that he respected Kevin's input.

"Sam, why don't you get back on the trail of the guy who put a bullet in my gut," Carol said. "I'm going to get back in touch with Parkland Middle School, see if I can get some information on those two girls."

"What about me?" Kevin asked after Sam had departed.

"Listen to an opera, give some thought to dinner. Think kind, lovely thoughts. No, wait a minute. I've got a better idea. Why don't you start thinking about how we might be able to prove that Kemp and Stearns are the same person. Start with the scar, but that won't be enough. If Stearns is Kemp, he'd have to have changed his name, and that requires a few legal steps. Think about it."

CHAPTER 55

While Carol was busying herself on the phone to Cheek-towaga and Kevin was learning the intricacies of New York's policies for legally changing one's name, Tommy Byrnes was talking to Isabel French in nearby Franklin. She was surprised that the sheriff's department had felt it necessary to pay her another visit. But she seemed relieved that the representative of the department was not the sheriff herself.

"I hope you don't think I'm being rude," Isabel said. "Or disrespectful. But I didn't like the sheriff. She was determined to pry into my private life. I've known women like that."

Byrnes inferred that Isabel French was not the prying kind.

"I'm sorry it felt that way, Mrs. French. In my experience, all police officers probably do their share of prying, if that's what you'd call it. I guess it's our job. We have a problem, and the only way to solve it is to ask lots of questions. I'm sure it isn't pleasant for you, or for anyone for that matter. I can appreciate that you haven't wanted to talk about your life with Mr. French. The way I hear it, it was painful. But we have the responsibility of finding out who killed your former husband. That's why we keep asking questions. I hope you understand."

He had tried to sound sympathetic, reasonable. But he did have questions to ask, and he would be prying.

"It doesn't sound so bad when you say it," Isabel said.

"Thank you. I'd like to ask about where you and your husband lived and worked before you moved to our area. I believe you were going to provide us with a list of his former jobs and things like that."

"I think I was, but I just haven't gotten around to doing it."

"But we're stymied at the moment. It might help if we had that information."

"I'll try," she said, and made an effort to look as if she were trying hard to remember. "We met in a place called Herkimer. It was sort of nowhere. For a time we lived near Syracuse in a suburb called Fayetteville. The last place before the lake here was

Brighton, up near Rochester. I can't imagine that that's much help."

"It may be," Byrnes said. Brighton, that's where John Paul Emmons had lived. This was potentially critical information. He decided to focus on Brighton for the moment and get back to Eddie's jobs later.

"Brighton. I've been there. Did you like it?"

"No. I hated it."

Her vehemence surprised him.

"I'm surprised. What about it didn't you care for?"

"Oh, nothing in particular. We just didn't fit in." Isabel French had decided that she'd overstated her negative feelings about Brighton. Tommy doubted that she had.

"It was the people there, is that it?"

"You might say so."

"That's too bad. My parents moved to a town in South Carolina when I was little, and they never felt welcome. So I think I know how you felt."

He hoped that this small fabrication would make her more receptive to his next question.

"Like I said, I've been in Brighton. Even know a few people there. Did you and your husband know a couple named Emmons?"

It was a shot in the dark, a roundabout way of raising a question he had planned to ask at some point anyway. The expression on Isabel's face told him that he had struck a nerve. Naturally pale and devoid of makeup, she now looked as if she had seen a ghost.

"Emmons. No, I don't think so." Too late, Byrnes said to himself.

"It was a terrible thing. About that man who was found dead in Southport recently, down in the park at the foot of the lake. Have you heard about it?"

"There was some talk about it down at the diner."

"Well, that man, we've discovered, was John Paul Emmons."

Isabel's eyes widened. For a brief second, Byrnes thought she might faint.

"I'm sorry. I didn't mean to shock you. But you really did know Mr. and Mrs. Emmons, didn't you?"

Isabel made an effort to pull herself together.

"You knew that Eddie was a friend of Emmons, didn't you?" she said, her voice barely audible. It was an accusation.

"No, Mrs. French, I didn't. But it seemed strange that both your husband and Mr. Emmons were killed right here on the lake within a few days of each other. Two men of the same age, two men who had graduated from the same high school in western New York. It raised a question in my mind, and I thought it might be a good idea to ask you that question. Would you like to tell me about your relationship with the Emmonses?"

Isabel looked at her watch. The boys wouldn't be home for another hour and a half.

"There's not much to tell," she said. "I never met them. But Eddie had known him in school, and he called him a lot when we lived in Brighton. I think they even got together from time to time. That's how it all began."

"I'm afraid I don't understand. What was it that began?"

"My divorce."

Isabel got up from her chair and took a seat on the floor next to the wall, just as she had when talking with the sheriff. Tommy thought it strange but said nothing.

She extracted a handkerchief from her jeans' pocket and blew her nose.

"Do you want to hear this?"

"I'm not sure what it is you want to tell me," he said, "but if you think it will help us get to the bottom of your husband's death, I'd appreciate it if you'd tell me about it."

"It was because I overheard Eddie on the phone one time. I know he was talking to John Paul. He'd say, 'now listen up, JP' - that's what he called John Paul, JP. Anyway, what they were talking about was something that had happened a long time ago, back in school in that place over by Buffalo. At first I didn't understand, but I finally caught on. They'd been molested, sexually molested, by somebody named Kemp. I couldn't believe it. I remember wanting to cry, to take a bath, to go see my mother. But I couldn't. She was dead. "

Byrnes didn't dare to break the spell by interrupting.

"What I did was tell Eddie I'd heard him on the phone. He was awful. He screamed at me, told me it was none of my business, and then just walked out of the house, slamming the door. That night I knew I had to leave him. Guys who have that done to them when they're kids, they become the same way. They do it to other kids. I knew I couldn't let Eddie near our boys."

"It must have been a nightmare," Tommy said. "But you didn't get a divorce until you moved to the lake."

"I wanted to, oh, God, I wanted to. But Eddie wouldn't hear of it, and I guess I didn't have the courage. But then he ran down that boy out on the lake, and, well, that was the last straw."

"Did you and your husband ever talk about this man Kemp?"

"No, he wouldn't talk about it. He just said I was mistaken, and then he'd turn it around and call me a liar."

"You're pretty sure you weren't mistaken?"

"Absolutely. You can't hear something like that and then think maybe you misunderstood what they were talking about. Eddie was too specific, like he was trying to make Mr. Emmons remember what had happened. It was disgusting."

Before he left, Byrnes had made notes of Eddie's employers. It was obvious why Isabel had not been more forthcoming with the sheriff about her life with Eddie. She had wanted to avoid talking about Brighton and what she thought of as the most horrible of all the things she held against him. But today she had finally unburdened herself of this nightmare.

It was with mixed feelings that Tommy drove back to the cottage to report to the sheriff. He was pleased with himself, pleased that he had induced this troubled woman to talk about something which she found abhorrent. But it also bothered him that he had caused Isabel French so much pain by doing what she had found so offensive, prying into her memory of one of the lowest points in her life.

CHAPTER 56

The members of the Cumberland County Sheriff's Department had taken to joking about it among themselves, calling the cottage the Blue Water Point Annex. Carol would have appreciated the joke, but her men weren't sure how she would react, so they didn't call it that in her presence. Or in Kevin's. But as a matter of fact, the cottage *had* become a second headquarters simply because Carol was confined there, courtesy of Dr. Kavanaugh. Initially the officers called to make arrangements to see her rather than walk in unannounced. As the days went by, however, it had become occasional and then common practice to stop by without an appointment, knock on the back door, and go on in as soon as Carol gave a 'coast is clear' signal. She had actually encouraged such informality, even if it meant that once in awhile one or more of her men caught her in her bathrobe.

But it was almost ten days since she had been shot, and Kavanaugh had at last given her permission to have a glass of wine - one a day, max - and told her that she would be allowed to go back to the office on Monday - only for half a day at first. She and Kevin toasted the good news with that first glass of Chardonnay on Friday evening.

"We really do have things to celebrate," Carol said, "and not just the condition of my gut."

"Not so fast. You're better, but we haven't wrapped up the French case yet. "

But, as Carol said, they had learned a lot. Russell Coover was still denying that he'd known French, and Buddy Stearns had yet to volunteer a convincing explanation for his generosity to him. But Joe Kingsbury had acknowledged being on Woodpecker Lane shortly before Eddie's death. Isabel French had admitted to knowing a lot more about her husband's past than she had previously let on. And they had learned quite a bit about an accused child molester named Douglas Kemp, who seemed to have known both Eddie French and John Paul Emmons.

Moreover, Kevin was inclined to believe that Buddy Stearns was really Kemp, although they weren't yet in a position to prove it. He had been encouraged by what he had learned about the process of legally changing one's name. Apparently it was not all that complicated.

It was Carol's phone conversation with Naomi Cormac, however, that had produced some of the most interesting news of a busy day. It had taken a number of calls and Carol's determination not to accept 'no' for an answer. She had finally learned the names of the two girls who had made allegations of sexual misconduct by Douglas Kemp. One of them was Naomi Falkirk, and by a stroke of luck Carol had discovered that Miss Falkirk had become Mrs. Cormac and had moved from Cheektowaga to another Buffalo suburb.

After that, the only problem was persuading Mrs. Cormac to revisit the unpleasantness of that year at Parkland when the allegation against Kemp had been made and withdrawn, followed by her expulsion from school.

"I felt like a tabloid gossip columnist," Carol said. They had had this discussion earlier that afternoon, but like a persistent itch, she couldn't leave it alone. "This is the downside of police work, trying to get people to talk about things they want to forget. Things they thought they'd successfully put behind them. I actually felt dirty. Have you ever had that experience?"

"Probably not in the way you mean," Kevin said. "But I was never in police work. I'd think most people would rise to the occasion if they thought it might help solve a crime."

"I don't agree. Sure, there are always going to be publicity seekers, but most people don't want someone digging into their private lives. Anyway, Mrs. Cormac couldn't believe that I knew the story. At first she seemed to think I was going to reopen the case against her after all these years. That's one of the problems people have when somebody introduces herself as a sheriff."

"But you're not just any sheriff, Carol. You won her confidence because you could put yourself in her shoes."

"Maybe. Truth is, what did the trick was that she knew Kemp really was a molester."

Naomi Cormac, reluctantly but convincingly, had told the sheriff what had happened at Parkland. She had acknowledged that the original accusation against Kemp was true, and that she and the other girl had withdrawn the charge only because people at the school turned against them - faculty and students alike. It seems that Kemp was popular and that nobody believed the girls.

Carol had asked Cormac whether Kemp was rumored to have molested boys. Naomi couldn't recall such a rumor.

"I think I would have heard," she had said. "Sandy and I were cheerleaders, and we hung around a lot with the guys on the teams. Someone would have said something. Why, do you think Coach Kemp would have been doing it with boys?"

"We have reason to think he did," Carol had said. "Did you know Eddie French?"

"Eddie? My God, do you suppose Coach Kemp was fooling around with Eddie?"

"I take it you knew Eddie."

"Of course. He was a great pitcher. Well, not so much in middle school, but he was fantastic in high school. I went to almost all his games. But Eddie and Coach Kemp?"

No, Carol had insisted, that wasn't what she was saying. Eddie had been killed, and she was trying to recreate his past, the better to understand why he had been killed and who might have killed him. She had been struck by Naomi Cormac's reaction to the news that Eddie was dead and that the sheriff's call was really about him.

"Somebody killed Eddie? That's terrible. It was an accident, wasn't it?"

"No, he was murdered."

"Murdered?" Naomi had found the news unbelievable. "But why? He was such a sweet boy. Quiet, even lonely, if you know what I mean. He never bothered anybody. Except when batters on the other side couldn't get a hit, and I can't imagine a baseball player killing a pitcher who'd struck him out."

Neither Carol nor Kevin could imagine it either. They talked about it for the better part of an hour that evening. In fact they were still discussing the news from the Buffalo area when Sam Bridges interrupted their conversation to report that the sheriff's real office in Cumberland had a visitor. A visitor whose black and blue and bleeding face had taken a terrible beating.

CHAPTER 57

It began at 7:35 when the only person in the sheriff's office was Sam Bridges. The evening had been quiet, and Sam was playing solitaire at the big table in the squad room. He had just had a brief conversation with Officer Damoth, who was over on the East Lake Rroad, checking on a report that there had been some disturbance at the Roadside Tavern. Happily, the seriousness of the problem had been overstated. When Damoth arrived, he found the alleged troublemakers enjoying a friendly beer and exchanging 'war' stories going back to their high school days.

Sam had no sooner said good night to Damoth when somebody began pounding on the door.

"Hold your horses," he called out as he made his way to the door at the top of the stairs. "I'm coming."

He flicked on the hall light. At first he saw no one, but then somebody appeared from off to the right and out of sight. Even in the weak glow from the ceiling light in the hall it was apparent that the man was hurt.

'What's the trouble?" Sam asked as he opened the door. His visitor lurched sideways, then caught himself against the door frame and stumbled into the office.

"Here, here," Sam said, sizing up the man's condition. "There's a chair right over there. Give me your arm."

The man shook off the offer of help.

"I need to talk to the sheriff," he said, collapsing into the chair.

"The sheriff's not here. I'm Deputy Sheriff Bridges. What's happened to you?"

Sam bent over the stranger in the chair, examining his face, which he thought looked like the face of a boxer who was about to crash to the canvas after a brutal beating in the ring.

"You look like you've been in a fight. Why don't you just sit still and I'll get some water and clean the blood off your face."

"I don't want you messing with my face," he said. "I need to talk to the sheriff."

"Like I said, she's not here. You're going to be all right. Just talk to me. Who are you?"

"I'm Ralph Ticknor, and I need help."

Deputy Sheriff Bridges looked more carefully at the man in front of him. He knew who Ticknor was. By this time everyone on the force knew about Ticknor and about how Byrnes had gotten him to talk about Russell Coover's militia group. Sam had never met the man, but he realized that this was an important moment. What had happened to him? Why had he come to the enemy's lair?

"Mr. Ticknor," he said, carefully measuring his words, "I know you're going to tell me what's happened, but your face really does need some attention. We've got a medicine chest in the back room, and I think there's something there that will help. Just give me a minute."

Sam started for the back room, then paused. He didn't want Ticknor to have second thoughts and bolt for the door when his back was turned.

"You stay there. I'll be right back and then we can talk."

Ticknor nodded.

"I'll be okay."

Five minutes later Sam had wiped off Ticknor's face and applied an ointment where the skin had been broken. That it stung was obvious. There was no way to arrest the discoloration of the bruises around his eyes.

"That's better, but not by much," Sam said.

"Do you have a mirror so I can take a look?"

Sam walked him back to the bathroom.

"That son of a bitch Coover tried to kill me," Ticknor said as he examined his ruined face. "Well, maybe not, but he was brutal. I think I'm pretty strong, but he's something else."

"How did you happen to get into a fight with Coover?" Sam asked.

"It wasn't a fight. He just started pounding on me."

"Why did he do that?"

They walked back to the squad room and Ticknor took a seat without waiting for Sam to urge him to sit down.

"I've never been in a police station," he said. "Didn't think it'd look like this."

"What did you think it would look like?" Sam asked, choosing to let Ticknor talk about the beating when he was ready.

"I don't know. This doesn't look much different from the faculty lounge over at the high school. You wouldn't by chance have any coffee, would you?"

"We usually do, but I'd have to start from scratch right now. How about a coke," Sam said, gesturing toward the soft drink machine.

"Sure, that'd be fine."

Sam brought out cokes for both of them.

"Now you were going to tell me what happened between you and Coover."

"Yeah, I guess so. I thought we were friends."

Ticknor leaned back in his chair and took a deep breath.

"Mind if I ask for a cigarette? I don't have any on me."

"Sorry." Would the man ever get around to telling his story? "I quit a few years ago. Besides, the sheriff has a thing about smoking inside."

"I figured as much. Look, I can't believe I'm here. One of your men suggested it'd be a good idea for me to come in, but I couldn't see any percentage in it. Until tonight that is."

"Okay, your loyalty was to Coover. Guys don't like to rat on a friend. But Coover beats you to a pulp, and that's not something friends do. Why'd he do it?"

"I thought maybe that officer of yours had told Russ I'd talked to him about the militia. Turns out it was my own stupidity. I should have kept my mouth shut, but I didn't. I told one of the other guys about my conversation with your colleague, and he passed the word on to Coover. Anyway, I got this call today. Russell said to come on over, he had an idea he wanted to share with some of us. When I got there he lit right into me, didn't even give me a chance to explain myself. He called me every name in the book. Traitor, that was the worst. Told me I'd better start watching my back. I don't like to say it, but I'm scared. Russ can get crazy sometimes."

"I know Coover," Sam said. "Known him since high school. He's a hot head, and he takes this militia shit seriously. He's a dangerous man, and it's smart of you to talk with us. Because one of these days he's going to pull some stunt that's going to get him and his whole damn militia gang into deep trouble. Like with that fertilizer. You do know about that, don't you?"

"Do you think he really intended to blow something up?"

"I think he'd like to draw attention to himself, to his cause. I certainly can't see him collecting ammonium nitrate fertilizer unless he's been contemplating using it. What do you know about that fertilizer we found in the shack?"

"Like I said to your officer, nobody ever told me what it was for. I just hauled some of it over to the shack."

"What about the day the sheriff was shot? Were you in the shack that day?"

The look that came over Ralph Ticknor's battered face answered Sam's question before he could speak.

"Yeah, I was there."

He hadn't answered the question Sam was asking without actually asking it. He didn't have to. Sam now knew who had shot the sheriff. He wanted to land a punch or two of his own on the face across the table. But he didn't.

'Why did you come here tonight, Mr. Ticknor?"

"Where should I go? I figured you people might be able to help me."

"Now just why should we do that?"

Ticknor had broken out in a sweat. The room was a cool 67 degrees fahrenheit.

"Because he's going to fix it so what happened out there at The Angle is all my fault."

"How's he going to do that?"

"When I got to his house, he asked to see my gun. I didn't know what was on his mind, so I handed over the pistol. It was then he started hitting me. With my own gun! He finally stopped, and then he said they'd nail *me* for shooting the sheriff. He had the gun that did it, and he said you'd have the bullet, so a match would be a piece of cake. And he laughed at me."

"I see," Sam said, thinking that Ticknor had it about right. "So how am I supposed to help you?"

"Don't you see, he's tying to frame me?"

"But you did shoot the sheriff."

"All I did was what Russ had told us to do. Keep everyone away from the shack. I didn't try to hit her. I didn't even know it was the sheriff. Why would I want to hit her?"

"You tell me."

"But I didn't, honest to God. I'm no good with a hand gun. All I was trying to do was scare her, get her to go away. But Russ is going to blame me for what happened out there. And he'll get away with it. He'll deny everything, it'll be all my fault. Can't you see why I had to come over tonight?"

Sam was thinking fast, thinking about this totally unexpected visit by one of Coover's militia men. It could be as Ticknor had said. Or it could simply be a preemptive effort to save his own ass. Sam hated Coover. But he had also been nursing a hatred of the man who had shot Carol, and here that man was, sitting across the table from him, admitting what he'd done.

"Are you asking me to lock you up for the night?"

Ticknor looked around, as if to make sure there was no one else in the room to hear him.

"Could you do that?" It was an appeal. Ticknor really was scared.

"We aren't in the business of using our lockup to protect people from their enemies," Sam said, his voice tinged with sarcasm. "But inasmuch as you've committed a crime and confessed to it, I think I could book you and find you a cell for the night."

From Ralph Ticknor's perspective, this was both good news and bad news.

"Doesn't it help me that I came in, told you the truth tonight?"

"Tell you what," Sam said. "You need to call your lawyer. I'm supposed to advise you not to talk without advice of counsel. You understand? Do you have a lawyer?"

"I don't know any lawyers. I just want you to keep Coover away from me."

"I can't just stick you in a cell until we do some paperwork." Sam knew the drill, but he was uneasy. He was on unfamiliar ground. "Give me a minute. I need to make a call."

That call was to the cottage on Blue Water Point, where Carol and Kevin were talking about things that had happened miles away in suburban Buffalo a generation earlier. It took but eleven words from Sam to shock Carol back to the present.

"I'm sitting across the table from the man who shot you."

CHAPTER 58

The early spring weather had been erratic. The first few days were unseasonably cold, only to be followed by a stretch of unseasonably warm weather. Then the rain had come, three miserable days of it. But when Carol awoke on Sunday morning, the sky was clear and the thermometer on the deck promised a pleasant April day. She suddenly knew what she was going to do, what she had to do.

She hadn't slept well. In part it was the result of the excitement generated by the news that Ralph Ticknor had turned himself in, opting to cooperate with the sheriff's department rather than the militia. But it also had something to do with her disappointment that it had been Ticknor rather than Russell Coover who had shot her. Never mind. She was going to break out of her cocoon today.

She peeled the blanket and sheet off her husband.

"Come on, Kevin. We've got things to do."

Kevin grunted and tried to pull the covers back over him.

"It won't work," she said. "Get up. Now!"

"What's going on?" he asked, looking and sounding confused.

Carol leaned down and kissed him.

"Do I have your attention?"

"We didn't set the alarm, did we?" He struggled to sit up in the bed.

"That was last night. It's almost eight o'clock. Sunday morning. Do you hear me? I need a ride."

That got his attention.

"A ride? We're not going anywhere."

"Yes we are, and I don't want to hear anything about Kavanaugh's orders. I'm not setting off for Florida. All I need is a chance to get out of here and enjoy a nice day. And you're going to be my driver."

There followed a few minutes of half-hearted protests, a pancake breakfast, and the ritual of showering and dressing. By shortly after nine they were ready for Carol's big adventure.

"So where is it that you plan to go?" Kevin asked.

"Out! I've got a bad case of cabin fever, and need to get out of here. We're going to go out to the end of the bluff, enjoy the spring buds, the early daffodils, whatever's in bloom. But we're going to get there by way of Cumberland. First stop, the sheriff's department."

"You have to see this Ticknor person, is that it?"

"If you were in my shoes, wouldn't you want to see the guy who shot you?"

"What do you think you're going to do when you see him?"

"How about showing him my scar?" she said facetiously. "I'm not sure, to be honest. But I want to hear what he has to say for himself. What he has to say about Coover."

"Bridges told you all that last night."

"I want to hear it for myself. Frankly, we've got a bit of a problem. We can't just keep him in the lock-up while we figure out what to do about Coover."

"It sounds as if you're not sure you want to charge Ticknor for the shooting."

"Funny, isn't it? I'm withholding judgment until I see him, get more information about what Coover is up to. What do you say we get going?"

"Okay. But let's not overdo it. Remember, Kavanaugh said you weren't to go back to work until Monday and he also said just a half-day to begin with."

"How could I forget? You've already reminded me three times this morning."

The road to Cumberland was largely devoid of traffic on this Sunday morning, and they made the trip in good time in spite of the fact that Kevin drove cautiously in an effort to spare Carol the potholes. Bridges had long since gone home, turning the night watch over to Officer Barrett. Not surprisingly, he was surprised when the sheriff walked in the door.

"It's you!" It wasn't a particularly felicitous greeting.

"Yes, Jim, it's me, I hope I don't look like an unwelcome ghost."

"But I thought you wouldn't be back until next week."

"It is next week, Jim, as of midnight. I hope you have things under control here."

"Oh, sure. Everything's fine. I'm just minding the store until Grieves comes on."

"Good," Carol said. "Mr. Whitman and I don't plan on being here long. We'll leave just as soon as I have a few words with your prisoner. Why don't you bring him up."

"You want to talk with Ticknor?"

"Yes, I do." Carol walked over to her colleague and put her hands on his shoulders. "Jim, I'm really all right. I caught a bullet in my stomach, not my head. I know what I'm doing. All I'm going to do is ask Mr. Ticknor a few questions."

"Of course," he said and disappeared in the direction of the cells.

"Are your men always this skittish?" Kevin asked.

"They're worried about me. And you're here. Jim doesn't know what to make of that. Maybe you should sit over here in the corner."

"The silent chauffeur, is that it?"

"Whatever. But I'll ask the questions."

Ralph Ticknor entered the room, sans handcuffs but with Barrett in close attendance.

"Mr. Ticknor, please have a seat.," Carol said. "No, not there. The one across from me, if you please. That's good. Now I'd like you to tell me just why you're here."

The phys ed teacher cum militia member had never met the sheriff, and it was obvious that he wasn't happy to be meeting her under these circumstances.

"I guess I'm here because you wanted me to come and talk with you."

"Yes, I did want to talk with you. I'm sure Officer Byrnes made that clear over a week ago. But you don't seem to have made an effort to see me until last night. Why are we having this conversation now?"

Ticknor pointed as his face, which didn't look much better than it had the previous evening when Bridges had tried to clean it up.

"See this? It's what Russell Coover did to me yesterday."

"You're here because Mr. Coover beat you up. You want us to press charges against him?"

Ticknor wasn't quite sure how to answer this question.

"I don't know about pressing charges. That might just make him madder at me."

"Well, of course. I'd be surprised if he didn't get mad. Officer Bridges tells me you're afraid of Mr. Coover. Why don't you tell me what happened between the two of you."

"Like I told Officer Bridges, he seems to think I've betrayed him."

"How did you betray him?"

"I guess I talked to people about that militia organization of his, said things he didn't like me saying. For him, it's a big secret."

"And why is it a secret? I know he's the leader of a militia. A lot of people know it. What is he up to that he thinks should remain a secret?"

"It's just that he's paranoid. I thought it was just a lot of talk about how bad the government is, how we've got to stick up for our rights, our guns. Nothing wrong with that. But for him it's real serious stuff."

"You aren't answering my question, Mr. Ticknor. Does it have something to do with the fertilizer we found over by The Angle?"

"I suppose so." The discussion was moving quickly to the shooting of the sheriff.

"Did Mr. Coover ever explain to the other members of this militia of his what he planned to use the fertilizer for?"

"Not in so many words, but we knew it could be used for explosives."

"And you went along with some plan to make explosives, even if you didn't know how they'd be used."

"Sort of, I guess."

Carol leaned across the table.

"According to what Officer Bridges tells me, you didn't just 'sort of' go along. You were protecting those bags of fertilizer. In fact, you went so far as to shoot at officers of the law when they came near the shed where the fertilizer was stored. And Mr. Coover blames you for the fact that those officers of the law were nosing around the shed. You were indiscreet. You told us that the militia was using the state forest land. To top it off, you were responsible for my officers seizing all that fertilizer. You also made the mistake of shooting me, so now the militia's in real trouble. No more fun and games. Your pal Coover's ass is in a sling. Small wonder he's mad at you."

"I'm so sorry I hit you, sheriff," Ticknor said. "I didn't mean to, honest. I'm no good with a handgun."

"I'd say you were pretty good with a handgun. You could have fired into the air. That would have gotten our attention. Maybe you didn't intend to kill anybody, but I think you intended to hit me."

"But I didn't know you were the sheriff. I may not be all that smart, but I'm not stupid."

"No, I'm sure you're not," Carol said, trying to keep her voice under control. "But you could see that I was in uniform, that whoever you'd taken a shot at was an officer of the law. It isn't a good idea to start shooting people who work for the sheriff's department, whether they're the sheriff or one of her men, like Officer Barrett here."

She paused and took a sudden deep breath. Kevin was afraid that she had experienced a pain where she had been wounded.

"Back to Mr. Coover," she continued. "Officer Bridges tells me you wanted to stay here in our lockup because you feared that Mr. Coover would come after you again. Do you really believe that?"

"You don't really know him, sheriff. He's a mean son of a bitch - sorry about my language, but it's true. If he's killed once, he could do it again."

Carol leaned across the table again, her face reflecting her reaction to what she had just heard.

"Coover has killed once? What are you talking about?"

"That French guy. He rubbed Russ the wrong way, and now he's dead. I don't want to end up like that."

"Wait a minute," Carol said. "I don't want you to end up like French, but where did you get the idea that Mr. Coover killed him?"

"Didn't he?"

"What makes you think he did?" Carol repeated her question.

"The guys were talking about French's death, and Russ, he said something about him deserving what he got. He was still angry that French had bad-mouthed him, told tales on the militia."

This led inevitably to a discussion of what French had said, to whom, and when. It soon became clear that Ticknor's knowledge of these things was mostly second-hand, that the tensions between Coover and French had not actually been on display in a group meeting. It also became clear that Ticknor had no evidence that Coover had killed Eddie, although Carol chose not to pursue the matter. Let him believe it, she thought. He'll be more help to us the more he fears Coover.

The fact that Ticknor had volunteered the information that he had shot and wounded her gave Carol added leverage in building a case against Russell Coover. When she and Kevin left for their ride over to the bluff, she was confident that the local militia was on its last legs, whatever Coover's role had been in the death of Eddie French. In the meanwhile, Ralph Ticknor would remain 'a guest' of the Cumberland County Sheriff's Department. And he would have the services of legal counsel as soon as she could make a few strategic phone calls.

CHAPTER 59

"What did you think of that?" Kevin asked as they headed back toward the lake.

"Not now. I want to talk about it just as much as you do, but in case you hadn't noticed, spring is in the air. I've been staring at walls for eleven days, or is it twelve. The hospital, the cottage. Let me enjoy this weather for awhile. Then we'll find a place to park and talk."

"Good idea," Kevin agreed, and they drove the next half hour in silence.

Carol was right. It was a beautiful day. The view of the lake from the bluff down toward Southport was spectacular, as always. The trees were just beginning to put out leaves and the birds had taken notice. They parked on a turn-off and sat quietly for a few minutes. Kevin reached across and took Carol's hand, giving it a light squeeze.

"Why is a place like this always having to cope with crimes?" Carol didn't expect an answer. "You'd think people would thank their lucky stars they live here and live and let live."

"Most of them do," Kevin said. He sounded wistful.

"I know, and I have to deal with the ones who don't. You asked what I thought of Ticknor. You were there, why don't you tell me. And by the way, thanks for leaving the questioning to me."

"I'm not sure what I'd have done if Barrett hadn't been there," he said, half seriously. "But Ticknor shot you, not me. So I want to know what you think."

"I think it has nothing to do with Eddie French's murder. And that means it doesn't have anything to do with what happened to Emmons either. Coover and his boys are the scum of the earth as far as I'm concerned, but Coover didn't kill French. Do you agree?"

"I suspect you're right, but what makes you so sure?" Kevin asked.

"You were there. It makes no sense. Coover has his own agenda. Let's call it his belief that he's living in a society that's out to emasculate him. Is that the way to put it? Anyway, I can't see him getting bent that far out of shape by somebody like French. Not when there are more likely candidates to be French's killer."

"In effect, you're saying the only reason Ticknor thinks Coover may have killed French is because Coover just gave him what was probably the beating of his life. I agree, the killer you're after isn't Coover."

Carol smiled.

"If not Coover, who?"

"I think it's going to boil down to one of two men, Kingsbury or Stearns," Kevin said. "But I'm a latecomer to the investigation, so I'd rather hear your opinion."

"Let's roll the windows down. If we're going to talk about my suspects, I'll need some fresh air."

"There. Is that better?"

"Much." She took a deep breath and then turned her attention to the question of who had killed Eddie French. "There was a time when I thought Eddie's ex-wife might have killed him. She thought the divorce would have gotten rid of him, but it didn't. The way she saw it, the life he'd lived, the things he'd done, they were like a dark cloud that she just couldn't get away from. She worried about her boys, fearful, I think, that they'd never get out from under that cloud. But the more I thought about it, the harder it became to imagine her as someone who'd resort to violence to solve her problem. After all, one of her big issues with Eddie was that he could get violent when he was disciplining the kids. I can't exactly explain why I feel this way, and I may be dead wrong. But I doubt it."

"A woman's intuition?"

"No, Kevin, a perceptive person's intuition."

"Okay. So if it wasn't Russell Coover and it wasn't Isabel French, all that's left are Kingsbury and Stearns. Unless there's somebody you haven't mentioned."

"As of now, that's it. It's a short list, and I'll be surprised if it turns out that our murderer is someone we haven't even identified."

"So who's your candidate?"

"In a way, neither of them makes a lot of sense. Take Joe Kingsbury. He sure had a motive, and he doesn't deny that he feels justice wasn't done in his son's death. Moreover, he admits to spending time around French's house on Woodpecker Lane not long before Eddie was killed. But if he felt the need to avenge his son's killing, why wait until spring? Isn't it more likely that he would cool off as the months passed? More importantly, there's no evidence he even knew Emmons, so if he did kill French we're left with two unrelated crimes just when it's beginning to look as if French and Emmons had a common enemy."

Kevin was listening carefully and shaking his head in agreement.

"But Stearns doesn't make much sense either," Carol continued. "Let's assume he used to be Kemp, coached at Parkland Middle School, and molested the two boys. We don't know any of those things for certain, but I won't be surprised if it turns out that they're true. But it would have happened years ago, much further back in time than the Kingsbury boy's death. I suppose that as they grew older, Eddie and John Paul could have come to an adult appreciation of what Kemp had done to them as kids. So they might have developed a visceral hatred of Kemp. But assuming that they found him, now calling himself Stearns, why isn't it Stearns that gets killed? Do you see the problem?"

"Yes," Kevin said, "but maybe that's because we're asking the wrong question. I've been trying to put myself in Eddie's killer's shoes. Why might I want to kill French? And Emmons, too, because I still believe that the same guy killed both of them. What if the two men who got killed threatened to reveal what Stearns - or Kemp, if you like - had done to them? That could ruin a man's reputation, especially up here in this cozy little neck of the woods where everybody knows everybody else. If Stearns really did molest these guys back when they were in middle school, I can believe that he'd do almost anything to keep the story from getting out."

"Of course," Carol chimed in. "And one of the things he might do is go out of his way to be nice to Eddie. He'd give him a job in spite of bad references, ignore the boating accident, let him have the use of a bakery truck 24/7, wink at the hold up at *The Cedar Post,* all to keep him quiet about their past relationship."

"Right, but what if he decides that being nice isn't enough. So he kills him. That's a pretty dramatic step, don't you think? What could persuade him to switch from giving Eddie all kinds of breaks to killing him?"

Kevin's mind was racing, his random thoughts escalating into what he hoped would be a coherent argument.

"How about blackmail? Stearns not only takes him on, gives him all those perks, but he pays him to keep his mouth shut. And Stearns begins to realize that there isn't any end in sight, that Eddie could keep right on bleeding him. He's desperate. He becomes a murderer."

Carol considered Kevin's theory.

"It makes a certain kind of perverse sense, but we can't prove any of it. French and Emmons are both dead. If Eddie's former wife knows anything about him blackmailing Stearns, she hasn't mentioned it. Which isn't surprising. I can't imagine Eddie telling her where his irregular alimony payments were coming from. And Emmons seems not to have shared much of anything with his wife. All we've got is that he had a separate account. How can we prove the money in that account came from Stearns? Maybe it was from poker winnings, and he was trying not to let Danny know he was gambling with their money."

"You sound like you don't buy the idea that these guys were blackmailing Stearns."

"No, I'm simply putting myself in the shoes of a good defense attorney."

"Which only means that you're going to have to keep on digging," Kevin argued. "We both know that. But I'll bet you Eddie and his friend hatched a plan to get the guy who took advantage of them back in junior high and then got themselves killed for their efforts."

"Boy, are you ever jumping the gun. We don't know that Stearns was once a coach named Kemp. I need to see a court record proving it. We don't know that Kemp actually molested either French or Emmons. All we have to go on is Isabel French's story that she overheard a conversation between her husband and Emmons. But what did she hear? Only one end of that conversation, so she could be mistaken. Other than that it's just a suspicion by one of Eddie's old teachers, and she didn't even say who might have been the predator. And while I'm throwing cold water on your idea, why be so sure that they conspired to blackmail anybody? What do we know about their post-high school relationship? Almost nothing, and most of that from the unreliable Isabel. I'd like to believe that you're onto something important, but it's a house of cards, ready to collapse at the slightest breeze."

"You're the lawyer. All I do is read whodunits. So of course you're right. We have to get more information out of those teachers who knew Kemp back in Cheektowaga. We need to squeeze Isabel for everything she can remember about what Eddie was up to and where. Not just what she's comfortable talking about. I mean everything. And we'll have to check the records in every jurisdiction where Stearns might have lived if we're going to prove he used to go by Kemp. No, it won't be easy, but I'm convinced I'm right, that this is a case in which blackmail proved to be a very bad idea."

"I know what I have to do, and I'll do it. You might even be able to help. But there's something we're overlooking. Remember Eddie's effort to hide the truck the night he was killed? It doesn't look like it worked, does it? If you're right about Stearns, he managed to find him down at the marina, snuggled up in Skinner's Four Winns, even if the truck was out of sight at Crozier's. That would be like looking for a needle in a haystack."

"I don't think Stearns had any problem finding French that night. In fact, I don't think Stearns was the guy Eddie was worried about. It was Kingsbury he was hiding from. Kingsbury had been sneaking around his house, and Eddie knew it. He figured being evicted gave him a chance to lose the grieving, angry father. But why would he want to fool Stearns? On the contrary, he'd have arranged for Stearns to meet him and make a blackmail payment. To do that, he'd have told him where he'd be. Neat, isn't it? He'd be taking some more of Stearns' money, and at the same time he'd be encouraging Stearns to feel even sorrier for him. Poor Eddie, now out in the cold, trying to stay warm under somebody's boat tarp."

"You can't prove any of this, can you?"

"Maybe not, but don't you think it adds up?"

"I'm not ready to tell the *Gazette* just yet that I've got a great story for their next edition. But I am ready to pursue our leads in Cheektowaga and Brighton more vigorously. And you can make yourself useful by seeing if you can come up with hard evidence that Buddy Stearns is really Douglas Kemp."

"One of these days Dean Coggins is going to remember that he hasn't seen me in the halls of Madison College in quite awhile. Give me one more week. I want your latest murderer apprehended before I resume my academic career."

"You aren't running a risk of getting fired, are you?"

"If they were really missing me down there, I'd have heard from my dean by now."

"Maybe that means you haven't been missed. Doesn't that worry you?"

"I've got tenure, you may recall. And it was my dean who told me to get up here and take care of you, which I've been doing. You're my witness."

They agreed that tomorrow they would launch a major effort to tie down all the loose ends, of which there were too many. Little did they know that Monday would bring developments that would make that major effort unnecessary.

CHAPTER 60

Carol got a big round of applause and a few unexpected hugs when she walked into the squad room for her first meeting in almost two weeks. She had, of course, met with her officers a couple of times at the cottage, but she thought of Monday morning as her real return to work. She thought it appropriate to let Sam lead off with an update of what had happened and not happened since the last briefing, with special attention to the fact that Ralph Ticknor was now in the lockup at the sheriff's department. Everyone was anxious to hear what Carol intended to do about Ticknor and hopeful that Coover had finally gone too far. She wasn't sure yet what she would do about her shooter; she was, however, confident, that Coover had indeed gone too far.

Mindful that she was under orders to put in only a half day, Carol retreated to her office to tackle the paperwork that Sam and JoAnne had thoughtfully left in her in basket. She had reduced the pile by about a third when JoAnne buzzed to say that she had a call from a Mrs. Cormac.

There were several people she had half-expected to hear from, plus a few others she had planned to call. Naomi Cormac was not among them.

"Mrs. Cormac? This is a surprise. I wasn't expecting to hear from you."

"No, I don't suppose so. But I have an important question I need to ask you. When we talked before, you told me that Eddie French had been murdered. It wasn't until later, when I called Sandy, that it struck me as strange that you were asking me about my being molested back in school and also telling me about Eddie's murder. Sandy asked me -"

"Excuse me, but who is Sandy?"

"Oh, I thought I mentioned her. Sandy Gardner. She's a friend, an old friend. She's the one who, along with me, brought the charge against Coach Kemp. In fact, it was her idea. I wish I'd listened to her back then."

"I'm not following you. I thought you said that both of you accused Kemp."

"We did. But Sandy didn't want to say we'd made it up. She was all for sticking with our story, but I guess I got cold feet. In the end, she went along with me. Anyway, I'm calling because Sandy asked me to. She wants to know if the man who did those things to us is the same man who killed Eddie French. Okay, it's not just Sandy. I want to know, too."

Carol didn't like where this conversation was going.

"Look, Mrs. Cormac, I really don't know if the coach is the man who killed Mr. French."

"But you think he is, don't you? The more Sandy and I talked about it, the more it seemed like you wouldn't have called me if you hadn't thought that Eddie's killer used to be a coach at Parkland. Am I right?"

Of course Naomi Cormac was exactly right.

"We had considered that possibility, but like I said, we don't know."

"You haven't found Eddie's killer, is that it?"

"Let's just say that the case isn't closed."

There was a long pause on the other end of the line. Was the Gardner woman there with Mrs. Cormac?

"This is what we think," Naomi said. "Sandy and me, that is. We don't know much about murders, but it sounds like you're suspicious of somebody but can't prove he did it. And you think this guy might be our old coach. So here's why I called. We want to see him. We want to know if he's the man who got away with doing those things to us. And killing somebody who was a high school hero."

This was going to be difficult. The investigation was at a point where the intervention of outsiders could very well complicate things. Carol liked to be in charge. Why let these two women she'd never met and about whom she knew practically nothing drop into Southport and confront Buddy Stearns?

"I can appreciate your interest in the matter. You probably haven't given a thought to Coach Kemp for years, and now I've opened old wounds. I'm sorry. We can keep you appraised of how things are going, but my investigation should be handled by professionals."

"I don't think you understand, sheriff. Sandy and I knew the coach very well. How can you forget someone who has done what he did? I know he's older, but I'll know if he's the one who did it. So will Sandy. We don't want to interfere. All we want to do is meet with the man you think might be Kemp. It won't take but five minutes, and we'll let you know if he is."

Carol knew she shouldn't let this woman come anywhere near Buddy Stearns. But for some reason she couldn't quite bring herself to say so. Against her better judgment, she proposed a compromise.

"If you were to do this, Mrs. Cormac, I would have to insist on a few things. Are you willing to do it my way?"

Naomi had no choice, inasmuch as she had no idea who it was she and Sandy would be meeting with. Kemp? She hoped so.

"We will have to agree on a day and a time, and I will need you to meet me in my office before you see this man. I want to make it very clear how you approach him, and one of my men will come with you. He won't go with you into this man's place of business, but he'll be nearby in case anything goes wrong."

"What could possibly go wrong?"

"Probably nothing, but I'll be responsible for your safety. Is there some day when you'd like to come down here?"

"Yes, today."

What have I gotten myself in for, Carol thought?

"That may not be possible, Ms. Cormac. I don't know whether the person you'll be seeing is in town and will be at work. Tell you what. Give me your number and I'll call you back just as soon as I've done some checking. By the way, how far are you from Crooked Lake?"

"Sandy's already at my house, and Map Quest says it should take us a little more than two hours, certainly no more than three."

It took JoAnne five minutes to learn that Buddy Stearns was indeed in town and would be at the bakery until five o'clock. A brief call back to the Cormac address confirmed that the two women would be at the sheriff's Cumberland office by one. And so began a series of events which would bring the French murder case to a swift and unexpected end.

———

Carol tried to imagine Cormac and Gardner as cheerleaders. Now presumably forty years old, give or take a year, they were still reasonably attractive and looked as if they had taken care of themselves since leaving school. Each claimed to be in a happy marriage, and each announced that she had three lovely children. What did they hope to find? The man who had molested them back in middle school or a complete stranger?

One way or another, the women were obviously anxious to get on to their rendezvous. Carol spelled out the ground rules for this unusual meeting. Their alleged reason for stopping in at *Breads to Go* was that one of them had had her first job in a bakery and thought it would be fun to turn back the clock for a few minutes. The manager's name was Stearns, and they were not to accuse him of anything or ask him if he once taught at Parkland Middle School in Cheektowaga. They were not to mention Eddie French. They were only to observe the man while making small talk, and when they left they were to let the sheriff know whether they believed that Stearns had been their molester. And if the answer was yes, she wanted them to be absolutely certain. She frankly doubted that they would be certain, not after so many years.

Officer Byrnes would lead the way down to the lake and through Southport to the bakery. He would park close by but out of sight, and the two women would meet him there when they had finished.

Byrnes estimated that he'd be waiting for ten minutes, fifteen at the outside. Unlike the sheriff, who obviously didn't like to be doing this, Tommy thought it was a good idea. Or that it would be if the women could positively identify Stearns as the former Parkland coach.

Ten minutes passed. Then fifteen. It was nearly half an hour before Naomi Cormac's Honda nosed into the space to the left of Byrnes' vehicle.

"How did it go?" Tommy asked as he rolled down his window. He thought it better to put it that way than to ask straight out whether they had made a positive identification.

"It was terrible," Sandy said. "Let's head back. We need to see the sheriff."

He was mildly disappointed not to get a heads up on the meeting, but he knew the sheriff would let him stay to hear whatever it was that had been so terrible.

The four of them took seats in the squad room. Sandy Gardner didn't wait for the sheriff to ask questions.

"It's him, Coach Kemp. The miserable bastard. Stearns my foot. When did he stop answering to Kemp? A snake can shed its skin, but it's still a snake."

Naomi Cormac was shaking her head in agreement.

"You really can be sure?" Carol asked. "Remember, I can't settle for probably. Why don't you tell me what it was that told you he was Kemp?"

"A lot of things, but in the end he said so himself."

Whatever Carol had expected, this wasn't it.

"He actually told you?"

"That's right. I put it to him straight. 'You used to coach at Parkland Middle School over by Buffalo, and your name is Kemp.' You should have seen him. He was almost foaming at the mouth."

"Instead of denying it," Naomi said. "he just said 'so what.'"

"Wait a minute." Carol was visibly upset. "I thought I'd told you that you weren't to challenge him, just study him, see if he looked like, talked like, the man you'd known."

"I know," Sandy said. "But if you'd been us and you'd just learned that you were talking to a grown man who'd pawed you and tried to have sex when you were just twelve years old, you'd have done just what we did."

"We knew who he was before we ever accused him," Naomi said. "It didn't take a minute to figure him out."

"How was that?" Carol asked, her mind already starting to pose the troubling question of what next.

"Same size, same features, the usual stuff. He even sounds pretty much like he did. But he's got some injuries that give him away. There's a big scar above his lip. Something happened to him back in Cheektowaga, and we remember that he grew a mustache to cover it. He's still got that scar, and his mustache doesn't really cover it, not up close."

"I knew he was Kemp the minute I saw his hands," Sandy interrupted. "His right hand. It was on his desk, and you couldn't help but see those two fingers where the joint was bent almost at a right angle. He probably hurt them playing ball when he was a kid. But I can still see those fingers walking up my thigh, heading for my crotch. It was a long time ago, but when I saw his hand it seemed like yesterday."

"Did you mention Eddie French?" Carol asked, worried that these two angry women might have done just that. They had.

"I know what you wanted us to do and say, but we were furious. We were reliving an awful time in our life, and here was this man who hadn't just taken advantage of us. He'd killed a classmate who was really special. It would have been impossible not to throw that in his face."

If damage had been done, it was now too late to rectify it.

"How did Stearns react when you brought up Eddie's name?"

"I thought he looked afraid. Not like when we first mentioned Parkland. But he sort of got it together and told us to get the hell out of his office."

"Officer Byrnes here says you were with Stearns for almost half an hour. What kept the conversation going for so long?"

"I guess we just kept piling on. You know, getting it out of our system. Isn't that right?"

"That's just what it was," Naomi said. "We were mad and he was mad. I don't think he could believe that two kids he'd messed with were actually sitting there, telling him off."

Carol could picture the scene.

"Do you think anyone else heard you?"

"I don't have any idea. We were sure loud enough, all three of us. But no one came into his office while we were there."

Carol arranged for Naomi and Sandy to make depositions before letting them leave. She would like to have been able to hear what else they had to say on the drive home, but had the feeling that she had a fairly clear picture of what had transpired at *Breads to Go* that afternoon.

The important next question was how now to approach Buddy Stearns. It was imperative that she see him quickly, but she was reluctant to let it appear that she had set him up. With that in mind, she deferred calling him until evening when she and Kevin had finished supper.

"Hello, Mrs. Stearns? This is Sheriff Kelleher. I haven't been in touch with your husband since before I had my accident, and I'd like to see him at his convenience. Is he there by any chance?"

"Oh, sheriff." The voice that came on the line was unsteady. The woman sounded as if she were crying. "What am I going to do?"

"Have I called at a bad time?"

"I don't think I can talk now. They just called from the trooper's station. I can't stay on the phone."

"The trooper's station? Has something happened to your husband?"

"It was over near Seneca Falls. They tell me Buddy's car was in a bad accident. I told him not to go, but he wouldn't stay and talk. Now he's dead."

CHAPTER 61

Unfortunately, the phone call early on Monday morning was from Alice Lassiter, the chairman of Kevin's department at Madison College.

"Kevin?" she said in a cheery voice that immediately told him bad news was coming. "I hoped I would catch you before you took off to do whatever you're doing up there. We have a problem. Jake Francis, who's been taking most of your classes in your absence, had a fall yesterday and fractured his hip. Pure bad luck. He'll be out of commission for a spell, and he won't be able to meet his own classes, much less yours. So I'm afraid I've got to ask you to get back down here post haste."

And then, as if remembering why Kevin was at the lake instead of his city apartment, she asked about Carol.

"What's the good word about your wife? I hope she's on her feet again."

Kevin groaned, softly he hoped.

"Carol is better, doing pretty well considering what she's been through. But I'm sorry to hear about Jake. How long does he expect to be out?"

"His doctor is vague. Probably the rest of the term. It's not like he broke his arm. Anyway, you're needed at dear old Madison, like tomorrow. It sounds as if Carol is able to take care of herself."

The way Lassiter said it made it sound as if she thought Carol was fine and Kevin was just taking a protracted holiday.

Kevin knew that he was in no position to complain. Jake had been teaching his classes; now it looked as if he'd have to reciprocate. And Carol really was able to take care of herself. But the timing was simply terrible. Buddy Stearns' death in a car accident the night before meant that the French case had reached a crisis point. He desperately wanted to be on hand as Carol dealt with this bizarre turn of events. It was only the day after he had argued, persuasively he thought, that it was Stearns who had killed

311

French. And Emmons, too. Yet he was aware of how hard it could still be to prove it. With Stearns dead, it might well be impossible.

Carol's conversation with Mrs. Stearns had been brief, but it had taken her the better part of an hour and a half to make contact with the state police station, talk with the trooper who had been at the scene of the accident, explain her interest in Stearns, and arrange for two of her men to get over to Seneca Falls.

Anxious as she was to take the trip herself, she knew that she had already exceeded Dr. Kavanaugh's half day limit by several hours. She knew that she wasn't one hundred percent, perhaps not even close. So it was Bridges and Parsons who set off for Seneca Falls on Sunday evening.Their report when they got back to the cottage at eleven p.m. made it clear that Stearns had gone off the road and into a stand of trees where the secondary road curved, and that the proximate cause of the crash was that Stearns was drunk.

"Way over the legal limit," Sam had said.

At Carol's insistence, her men had searched the car, or what was left of it, for any evidence that Stearns had left anything that could explain what he was doing. Perhaps a suicide note. They couldn't find one. But they made an extremely important discovery in the car's trunk, under the mat beside the spare: two New York State license plates and a plastic bag containing documents belonging to the car of John Paul Emmons and to Mr. Emmons himself.

"Son of a bitch," had been Sam's reaction. "He took them from Emmons car and substituted that damned Ohio plate."

Under normal circumstances, the four of them sitting in the cottage living room and discussing the accident would have been expressing their sadness that another life had been snuffed out on the highway due to drunken driving. But these weren't normal circumstances. Stearns had been a suspect in the murder of two men, and the plates and documents that lay before them on the coffee table pointed directly at the accident victim as the man who almost certainly had killed Emmons.

It was not until later, when Carol and Kevin tumbled into bed after a much longer day than either of them had planned, that the sheriff rolled over onto her side and gave voice to her doubts.

"We think this just about wraps up the case, don't we? Well, we're wrong. Now we'll never have a chance to interrogate Mr. Stearns-Kemp one more time. We've got a lot of work to do."

———

It was work that Kevin would be uninvolved in. By Tuesday he was back in the classroom, playing catch-up. By Tuesday, the forces of the Cumberland County Sheriff's Department were busily engaged in trying to tie down the many loose ends of the case against Stearns.

No question, it now looked as if Stearns and Kemp were the same person. It looked very much as if Kemp had molested French and Emmons when they had been in middle school. It looked as if French had found Kemp, now Stearns, and had concocted a plan with Emmons to blackmail him. It looked as if Stearns had put an end to the blackmail plot by killing the blackmailers. But evidence that these things were true was still short of fool proof.

"But Stearns is dead now. Does it matter?" It was Officer Parsons who asked the question.

Carol insisted it did.

"I'm sure that Stearns is our murderer. But we may not be able to prove it. And what if we can't prove it because it isn't true. That would mean that somebody else killed French and Emmons. What if we call it a day, say the case is solved, and there's still somebody out there who really did it? Kingsbury? Can we be absolutely sure it's not him? I don't want to be responsible for letting a killer walk free because we'd pinned the crime on a man who happened to be conveniently dead."

"What happens now? Can you try a dead man for murder?" Sam asked.

"It wasn't my legal speciality, Sam," Carol said, "and I don't want to speculate. But I'm no longer interested in putting Stearns on trial. I just want to be so sure he killed French that we won't be missing the real killer."

For another two weeks Carol and her crew scoured upstate New York, questioning and requestioning anybody who might have had more knowledge of Kemp or Stearns, French or Emmons. The result was invariably the occasional hint of a suspicion, a memory of something that hadn't seemed quite right, an ephemeral thought that just wouldn't come into focus. The hope that Stearns' bank records might lead to proof that Emmons' secret account and French's strange cash deposits were the result of blackmail payments was quickly dashed. Inquiries in Southport came to naught. So did they in Brighton, in Cheektowaga, and in every other city and village that had seemed momentarily promising.

By the end of April, Carol had to confess that either Buddy Stearns had murdered French and Emmons or that she had a cold case on her hands. She was in a bad mood when she called Kevin on the last Friday of the month.

"Hi, down there. I really wish you were here."

"And I wish I were there. The good news is that classes and exams end in about ten days, so I'll be back at the cottage before you know it."

They had talked almost every evening since Kevin had left the lake earlier in April, so he was up to date on how things stood on the French case. Good but not great.

"I've thrown in the towel on the case. That may not be the way to put it, but there doesn't appear to be anything more I can do to make it certain that Stearns did it."

"Stearns did do it, do you hear me?" Kevin said. "We both know that. Of course he'll never stand trial or spend time behind bars. But at least we know he won't molest anyone else or kill anyone else. I'm still convinced he committed suicide by running his car off the road. He heard those women and realized that it was starting all over again. He'd killed two people and still hadn't escaped his past."

"You know I don't share your confidence that it was suicide. It was the booze that killed him. By the way, I finally called Mrs. Cormac and told her what had happened. Probably should have done it sooner, but I'd been waiting for more hard evidence against him and it never came. Funny, Cormac didn't sound elated as I'd assumed she would. She thinks she and her friend were responsible for his death. She wasn't sorry, but it really brought her up short to think she killed somebody. You know what I mean."

"In a way, she's right. Do you sometimes wonder where you'd be now on the case if she hadn't insisted on meeting with Stearns?"

"I do, and I have mixed feelings. What still puzzles me is that Stearns or Kemp molested both guys and girls. All those pedophile cases that have plagued my church only involved boys. I'd always figured that priests and others who have this kind of impulse are just interested in boys. That it's a homosexual thing."

"But it isn't. Remember that colleague of mine who gave me some help in the Father Rafferty case? He's the one who's been studying pedophilia in the church. I was curious, too, so I sought him out after I got back to the college. One of things he set me straight on is that this man Stearns was technically a hebephile, meaning he was interested in kids in early puberty, not little children. But to your point, while most hebephiles are attracted to kids of one gender only, there are those who are, I guess you'd say, bisexual. And that's Stearns. He molested French and Emmons, and he also molested Cormac and Gardner. And probably others we don't know about."

"Ugh." Carol made a noise which sounded as if she were gagging. "What an awful research field. I'm glad you're interested in Verdi and Puccini and those other opera composers You don't suppose any of them were hebephiles, do you?"

"No idea. And if they are, I promise not to make it the subject of my next paper. What matters is the music."

"My next problem is deciding what I'm going to say to Isabel French and Danny Emmons. Isabel is sure to know. It was in all the area papers. I'm not sure about Danny. It wouldn't surprise me if Isabel has suspected Stearns of Eddie's death, but then what do I know. The woman is really opaque. In Danny's case I doubt that she's made the connection. Either way, they'll be tricky conversations."

"If I were you, I'd tell them you're convinced their husband's killer is dead. They'll understand that you can't bring Stearns to trial. I doubt that you'll help either of them find closure. Isabel will still be worried about the alimony she won't be getting. Danny's going to keep on regretting the dialogue of the deaf that was her marriage to John Paul. But I'd tell them anyway."

"That's what I plan on doing. Now how about I give you an update on our friend Coover."

"The bad news with the good, I suppose. I'm still surprised you let Ticknor off the hook."

Carol had earlier told him about what she'd decided to do with the man who had shot and wounded her. It was obvious that she was not going to charge him, and that she was prepared to live with criticism of that decision. The Crooked Lake community would be surprised, to put it mildly, and Sam Bridges clearly thought she was making a big mistake. But she had decided that he was really a weak willed pawn of Coover's, not a dedicated foe of the local establishment. Moreover, his knowledge of what the militia was up to could be instrumental in putting a stop to Russell Coover's fantasies. She had located an attorney who could represent Ticknor's interests, and the three of them had worked out a way to expedite his transition back to a more normal life involving probation and community service. Unfortunately, a normal life would not include a return to the faculty of Yates Center High School. He had known that it would be unlikely; the principal made it clear that it was going to be impossible. Carol reported that he and his wife were considering moving to the Watertown area where his sister and her family lived.

"And Coover?" Kevin asked. "Still standing his ground?"

"This is where it really gets interesting. We'd been so busy with Stearns that we were slow to bring the state's Department of Agriculture and Marketing into the fertilizer case. They don't really have a lot of muscle, but they're working on it. Anyway, my real interest wasn't to see that Coover got slapped with a fine for breaking a state law. I wanted to put an end to all this militia nonsense. You ready for this?"

"It sounds as if something big has happened."

"If he was behind bars, I'd call that big," Carol said. "But it's almost as good. He's gone. Packed up practically overnight and skipped town. With no forwarding address. It happened day before yesterday. I didn't even know about it until this morning."

"I take it he's not just taking a vacation."

"It doesn't look that way. He seems to have rented a U-Haul, loaded his guns and his favorite toys and flags, and hit the road. As far as we know, he told no one - not Craddock Autos where he was working, none of the guys we think he'd roped into the militia. By now he could be as far away as Maine or as close as Elmira. I hope he's burned his bridges and doesn't become some other sheriff's problem."

The conversation gradually turned to matters more personal. Not surprisingly, they enjoyed it more.

"Twelve days at the most," Kevin said. "As soon as I've graded all my finals I'll be back at the cottage. We've got some catching up to do, in case you've forgotten."

"How could I possibly forget?"

"I can't believe that I was there for over two weeks and we never -"

Carol interrupted.

"I'd rather not talk about what we didn't do. How about what we're going to do? There's a certain black silk nightie that I'm saving for the occasion. And in the course of the evening, I'll let you see how my scar is coming along."

Made in the USA
Middletown, DE
11 June 2015